the postcard

the postcard

zoë folbigg

HEAD of ZEUS

An Aria Book

First published in the UK in 2019 by Aria,
an imprint of Head of Zeus Ltd

9 7 5 3 1 2 4 6 8

A catalogue record for this book is available from
the British Library.

ISBN (PBO): 9781788549875
ISBN (E): 9781789542134

Typeset by Divaddict Publishing Solutions Ltd.

Printed and bound in Great Britain by
CPI Group (UK) Ltd, Croydon CR0 4YY

Head of Zeus Ltd
First Floor East
5–8 Hardwick Street
London EC1R 4RG

WWW.HEADOFZEUS.COM

To everyone who believes in love at first sight...

I

There's a man in my room, I know there is.

A pale and weary woman reclines onto a chaise
longue, with a deliberate sigh and a fake yawn. As her
jaw stretches, the pretend yawn morphs at the corners of
her mouth into something real and she inhales the sweet
and humid air that's smothering her, that's pushing her
into the cradle. She's exhausted. In a town where people
flock from all over the world for tranquillity and spiritual
nourishment, her body feels battered and the noise in the
woman's head hurts. Her temples are sore. Her limbs are
thinner than they should be, thinner than they ever have
been, and she's tired from walking, walking, walking,
with one eye on lofty green mountains that surround
the slim valley. Walking the colourful streets of a small
peninsula, where the faded grandeur of Indochinese

colours clatter like the sage green shutters on the run-down French villas. One such shutter taps rhythmically against the room window under the swirl of a storm that came out of nowhere at the end of a sunny day. Rain hammers on the awning, beating onto the street. A stream of fat, purposeful drops hits the floor outside the hotel room door with gusto.

The woman, relieved to be dry, relieved to have stopped, but feeling little comfort in her capacious room, closes her eyes and pretends to fall asleep. Scents of jasmine and frangipani roll in through the window on the steam from the rain, floating past the decorative tea set on an old chest of drawers under the window to the street, permeating through the gauze netting around the dark teak, simple four-poster bed, reaching the reclined woman.

A silver letter M sinks into the bony hollow of her jugular notch as she inhales the sweet frangipani and exhales deliberately, stirring and testing. Testing to see if she can drift away after the long walk that left her tired; testing herself to see if she can escape the dark thoughts plaguing her; testing to see if there is a predator in the room, whether he'll come out of his hiding place if he thinks she won't notice. So they can catch each other unawares.

If I pretend I'm asleep he might come out.

Because that's preferable to the woman. She would rather know whether she is alone or not by coaxing someone out. It seems so much more straightforward than going to the reception desk and asking the friendly man with a dragon on his shirt to check under the bed, behind the door, or in the Thai copper bathtub.

Unless it's him. Unless he's the man I can hear breathing in my room.

No, the man hiding in the room is more dapper than the man in the dragon shirt. His clothing more formal, his eyes more murderous. So the woman raises her arm, in order to make her slumber look more authentic, resting it on a cream and navy striped cushion. She closes her eyes and concentrates on her stillness, so her lids don't flicker. Within seconds she feels the sure embrace of sleep as it pulls her into the striped cotton of the chair.

I am so very tired.

She arches her arm further up above her head, into the shape of a question mark hanging over her. There the acting stops; her limbs twitch in that state of in between. They are weaker, thinner, paler than they usually are. Her skin is a milky shade despite the sunshine of her travels. Her hair is shorter, wispier, wavier than normal, as if she cut it herself with blunt scissors.

The test she spent all day planning as she walked the riverbank and the lanes has only tested herself. If there is a man in the room, he might just let himself out while she is asleep – and then she will never know. Or perhaps he'll stay and do worse.

Deeper into the cradle, she sinks, as two hands appear at the foot of the chaise longue, curling, snaking, creeping up the stubby legs of it and then the fabric of the upholstery.

A face emerges. Long, grey hair, slicked back straight from a widow's peak to the nape of his neck. If the woman opened her eyes, she would see his: narrow and lupine at the foot of the sofa, as if he were an animal foraging for food. He bares his teeth into a smile. His moves are slow and deliberate. His body rising as if uncoiling from a basket on the cool tiled floor. Rising as his hands stroke her bare feet, past a silver chain on her ankle, examining the edges and lines of her legs. Rough hands, olive skin, move up a once muscular leg that is now fragile, as he inhales every detail, every mole, as if inspecting a specimen in the lab. The man wears a dark suit, the jacket fastened with a single button at the waist, over a white shirt that is open at its deep collar. The woman doesn't know it, but the man looks both respectable yet unhinged; impeccably dressed yet filthy-fingered. His teeth gnash sharply and eyes widen with a smile, salivating at the prospect of what's in front of him, what he's hungered for, what he's about to catch.

He glides his feral fingers up over the woman's chambray shorts, feeling her ribcage under her white vest, over her small breasts and up, onto the bones that meet at the base of her neck. He sees the silver M in its pool, and slides his hands outwards, along the protruding lines of her collarbone, along blue-white skin towards each shoulder, then back, to her neck, her throat. He caresses the tiny M with a dirty fingernail and then taps it twice, as if to turn on an alarm.

Eyes open, pupils shrink, but the woman does not scream.

I knew it.

The man jumps over the back of the chaise longue with athletic ease and sits down next to her reclined body. His legs crossed, his appearance dandy. She is frozen. Proud to have proven herself right, but paralysed in fear as she wonders whether the man will pick her up or pin her down. She looks at him, his eyes excited and deranged, glad that at last they have met, as she waits for him to eat her.

Do it then!

But the man doesn't dig in and devour. He stands up, extends an elegant arm and gives a haughty nod, as if commanding the woman to join him in a dance. She looks at his rough hand, sees the blood-red dirt under his fingernails and wonders what he has touched. Still, she accepts, shakily placing her pale hand in his. A gold ring of flowers spins loosely on her forefinger. The man curls his spine as he leans over to lift the woman and she rises primly, her two hands in his. Their eyes meet and their faces are level.

At last.

The woman can smell meat on the man's breath in their dancers' embrace; she can see the nicotine stains on his sharp teeth; smell the rain and the oil in his hair. He directs her around the orange and grey tiled floors, spinning her in a violent waltz while their eyes are locked and their limbs stretched. They whirl around the four-poster bed, neat and crisp with white waffle sheets and fuchsia petals scattered on the pillows, inviting them both inside the shroud of the voile netting. They storm past the chest of drawers with the tea set on it, past another shuttered window in this grand corner room, that leads onto the garden quadrant where banana and coco fronds break the rain's fall. They move back to the chaise longue and the door to the bathroom, where the copper bathtub refracts a golden glow through the gap in the door. Together they whirl, in a spin, a storm, as they clutch each other's faces, wondering who will be the first to strike.

2

December 2015, London, England

'Happy anniversary, beautiful lady!'

Maya raises her now-empty glass of water, where bubbles no longer leap with gay abandon, and disguises its emptiness with her long fingers and a rectangular smoky quartz ring on her right hand. The central heating in the apartment is giving Maya a savage thirst, but she doesn't want to impose on her best friend, Nena, sitting opposite her, dazed and cross-legged, with a six-week-old baby in her arms.

Maya curls into the grey wing-backed armchair and feels contentment. It's a good chair. It was Tom's only sticking point – after access to his son Arlo – when his ex-wife asked him to move out. If he was being forced to leave the home he had loved, the son he had gazed at in the small hours while his wife refused to talk to him, he was taking his favourite armchair with him.

The chair is made even more comfortable by the reliable thighs of James' lap underneath Maya, as she slinks across him, trying not to take up too much space.

Maya and James are in the living room of Nena and Tom's north London flat, visiting for tea, cake and cuddles on a dark Saturday afternoon.

The flat looked a lot lighter and airier when Maya and James last visited in the summer, but now it's drowning in bouncing chairs, nappies, playmats and feeding cushions. It's why Maya wants to take up as little space as possible, so she raises her empty glass and swallows her thirst.

'Cheers!' Nena raises a bottle of Infacol and a thick, black eyebrow, while she gives the bottle a shake. Gone are the colourful cocktails of yesteryear, the flower garlands that adorned her hair and the glitter that danced across her long eyelids. Now Nena's canvas is blank and her face is tired, but she still shines with a faraway beauty that would be hard to place if you didn't know her father's family migrated from Bahia in Brazil to Britain in the 1980s. Maya looks at Nena and marvels. Two years ago she was a clown by day and dancing on the West End stage by night – using her deft acrobatic training to trapeze three boyfriends on rotation and never drop a spinning plate/ball/man.

'What a difference a year makes!' says Maya. 'No, *two!*'

Tom reappears from the kitchen with two bottles of beer and hands one to James, who extricates his arm from around Maya's waist to switch an empty bottle for a full.

'Thanks, mate.'

Tom puts the empties on the coffee table next to a cake and slumps into the green sofa by Nena's side, peering in on his newborn and stroking her cheek. Maya doesn't want to point out that neither she nor Nena have a drink. Tom rarely gets a chance to sit down.

'Sorry, Tom,' smiles Maya. 'Cheers to you too!' She raises her empty glass again.

'Well, yes, it wasn't just *my* wedding, even if it felt like it,' laughs Nena in mock-diva mode, even though their grand Westminster nuptials, one year before, did have touches of Nena written all over it: from the Brazilian singer to the swing ensemble of her West End friends on the dance floor. But Tom was there, beaming proudly, and he's been present ever since. Leading Nena by the hand on honeymoon to her father's motherland; rubbing her feet as they started to swell; attending every hospital and antenatal appointment with enthusiasm, even though he'd been through it all before with Arlo; working hard to reassure Nena that maternity leave won't ruin her career as a television presenter, in the children's department Tom heads up.

'Yes, dear,' smiles Tom, in mock subordination, still as hooked as he was when he first met Nena, dressed as a clown as the children's entertainer at Arlo's third birthday party the winter before.

Maya raises her empty glass for a third time. 'And cheers to you, Arlo, this is really a late birthday cake for you, sweetie.'

A boy with a shiny brown bowlcut looks at Maya and smiles shyly. The dark gap between his two front teeth almost glimmers as he walks on his knees towards the cake on the coffee table. He edges a chubby, inquisitive finger towards a standing sliced strawberry but stops just before he makes contact. Wide-eyed, he anticipates the look that comes from his dad.

Maya concocted the *fraisier* cake last night in her kitchen at home in Hazelworth. A delicate, decadent creation of strawberries, proud and upright like the soldiers standing in a row on Arlo's T-shirt. The strawberries are doused in vanilla-flecked crème mousseline and framed neatly by a pale Genoise sponge. Atop it sits a disc of light pink marzipan, a glazed strawberry and crystallised rose petals. Maya made it, every single component, all by herself: lovingly painting egg white onto rose petals and whisking up crème pâtissière in a whirl, all thanks to knowledge she gained studying for her *diplôme de pâtisserie* – or going to Pastry School, as she called it. She knew as she was making it that a *fraisier* was a bit ridiculous for a kid's birthday cake, but she wanted to put her skills to good use.

'Well, this is a step up from Colin The Caterpillar, hey Arlimoo?' Nena laughs from her feeding station on the sofa. 'That's what he had on his actual birthday, poor sod.' Arlo smiles. 'But I did have my hands full.' Nena swaddles Ava, their ravenous baby, in her arms and lifts her to her breast.

'Fancier than any cake I had when I was five,' says Tom, stroking his smooth head, his friendly blue eyes gleaming at the creation on the table.

Maya leans away from James' lap slightly, plucks a pristine strawberry from the cake's edge and hands it to Arlo conspiratorially.

'Baker's prerogative,' she winks.

Arlo doesn't know what Maya means, but he likes the gist of it, and his eyes light up again.

James strokes the small of Maya's back tenderly. He saw how hard Maya worked at 'Pastry School', putting her heart and soul into learning new skills. She started with sweet and shortcrust pastry in January, advancing through to choux in February, in time for their first Valentine's together, when Maya made James a love-heart-shaped wreath of rose eclairs.

By March, her Swiss and Italian meringues were peak perfect, and in May she plunged into filo, konafa and Middle Eastern delights, making herself some birthday baklava along the way. June was all about Genoise,

Viennoiserie and *petits fours,* and by July – as James' contract expired on his small terraced rental and he moved into Maya's flat, Maya was up into the small hours in the kitchen, burnt and blistered from spinning hot caramel nests and mastering sugar-work.

When she graduated from Cordon Bleu in September, and they celebrated with a glass of limoncello at their friends Dominic and Josie's Tuscan wedding, her knife, piping and presentation skills were all patisserie perfect. All thanks to hard work, dedication and an unexpected inheritance she received late last year.

Neither Maya nor James minded that they were like ships passing in the night – James would return from shooting a wedding at 1 a.m. to find Maya up to her elbows in matcha macarons, pistachio *saint-honorés* and raspberry *millefeuille* with an icing sugar mist around her brow. James had been working hard, capturing a bride and groom in their best light, taking pride in taking pictures for a living – and he was ever so proud of Maya. And a couple of kilos heavier from all the taste testing. But Maya had done it. She had got her *diplôme* – a distinction no less – of which she was very proud. She would have made Velma very proud too.

Arlo licks the sticky sugar-glaze of the strawberry from his lips.

'Actually, I think we need tea with that,' states Nena. 'Tommy?' she hints.

Tom bounces back up off the sofa.

'We'll cut it in a minute, Arlo,' appeases Nena. 'Daddy's just making everyone a cup of—' Nena cuts herself off with a realisation. 'Holy shit! It's your anniversary too!'

Arlo looks at Maya and James with wide, shocked eyes.

'Oh sorry, Arlimoo, don't tell Daddy I said a swear.'

Arlo blushes.

'Well, yes, there is that.' Maya smiles as James takes a swig from his bottle.

Maya loved James from afar on their daily commute and it took almost a year for her to heed the advice of her elderly friend Velma and give James – or Train Man as he was known among Maya's friends – a note, asking him if he'd like to go for a drink. James politely declined, on account of having a girlfriend and being a loyal sort of chap, so Maya went back to that excruciating, longing commute. Months later, Maya and James finally found themselves both single and both stranded in a snowy station doorway late at night. Maya had been travelling home from Nena and Tom's Westminster wedding when the train stopped halfway to Hazelworth, and in the scramble for taxis (and wearing inappropriately strappy silver sandals), Maya bumped into James, who swept her off her frozen feet.

'Sorry, Sugatits,' says Nena, stroking Ava's bottom as she suckles. 'I'm so caught up in all this shit.' She looks over to Arlo again but is relieved to see he didn't hear her this time. He's too busy zooming a plastic penguin wearing a deep-sea diving outfit along a skirting board.

Maya shakes her head as if to say *don't worry.*

'Are you guys doing anything to celebrate? Please tell me you're going out tonight and that you have a life. It's fish 'n' chips and night feeds for our first anniversary.'

James strokes the back of Maya's hair as she curls back onto him. 'We thought we'd have dinner in town after seeing you guys,' he says. 'There's only so many times we can go to the trattoria in Hazelworth. We're upgrading our pasta tonight.'

'Ooh, where to?'

'Locanda Locatelli, in Marylebone.' James rests his bottle on his jean-clad thigh.

'Sounds delish,' sighs Nena dreamily, believing she's not going out for the next eighteen years.

'It does look really special,' says Maya, turning to James and placing a kiss on his lips.

'Everyone want tea?' asks Tom as he pokes his head around the door.

Nena, Maya and James all nod yes pleases and Tom disappears again.

'So, while I'm anchored here and going nowhere, tell me about your trip. I mean, who cares if Holly, Phil and the Real Housewives of Beverly Hills are my best friends, right? I can live vicariously through you two!'

Maya blushes. She and James have been planning this trip for months now and she feels a little guilty talking about travelling around the world for a year, when her best friend can barely get past the thought of another sleepless night ahead of her. Out of guilt, Maya focuses on making faces at Arlo, still zooming a penguin along the skirting board. James fills Maya's silence.

'Starting in India – we leave on Boxing Day.'

'Nice,' says Nena, gazing down at Ava, as she takes her off the breast, readjusts her top and sits her on her lap.

Maya marvels at the ease with which Nena does the mum-manoeuvre, not realising that Nena feels self-conscious and clumsy.

'We start in Delhi and then travel to Udaipur, where the wedding is.'

'Wedding?!'

Nena looks at James like she missed the memo. Her eyes dart a glance to Maya's left hand, still clutching an empty glass, but the only ring she can see is Maya's Dinny Hall smoky quartz on her right hand.

'Yeah, my old boss.'

Maya feels agitated. 'James' old boss invited us to his wedding,' she adds, although she's sure she told Nena this before. 'All Bollywood luxe in a palace on a lake. You know, low-key…'

James widens his eyes to emphasise Maya's point.

'But James will have to work, so it won't all be fun.'

James nods his agreement.

'James is photographer number four. Charged with doing the reportage pictures.'

'Oh right,' says Nena, trying to bring up the burp that is dancing knots in Ava's hard stomach.

Arlo pads back to the *fraisier* cake. Maya thinks he's been so patient, so she slides down from James' lap to the rug and removes another strawberry for him.

'Here you go,' she whispers, smoothing his shiny hair into place while James resumes telling Nena about their itinerary.

'So, we're starting in India, and then travelling to Thailand and through Vietnam, Laos – maybe Cambodia – Indonesia, Australia…'

But Nena's eyes are firmly on her daughter's back. She needs this burp to come up before Ava starts crying and fretting, and before Nena does the same during another fraught evening and night ahead.

James trails off.

'Here,' says Nena as she stands, defeated, thrusting Ava towards James over the coffee table. 'I can't get her to burp – can you give it a go?'

'We're out of milk!' groans Tom, poking his head around the door again. 'I'm just popping to Sainsbury's.'

'I'll come with you,' says James, bouncing up out of the armchair and forcing Nena to hold on to Ava, who lets out a huge burp over the *fraisier* cake.

'Thank god she didn't puke on it,' laughs Tom.

He and James put on their coats and head out into the dark December afternoon before Nena and Maya have a chance to shout, 'Bye!'

'That went well,' laughs Nena.

Maya had noticed how uncomfortable James looked as he jumped up and threw on his navy peacoat and she can feel Nena's tired eyes boring into her right now, so she keeps her gaze firmly on Arlo.

'How's school then, buddy? You getting on OK in Reception?'

'Yeth,' lisps Arlo. 'My best friends are Loota and Miss Telly.'

'Loota? That's an interesting name.'

'Lu-ca – ca, ca, with a curly ca,' says Nena kindly. 'Lu-ca and Miss K-k-kelly.'

'Lu-ta,' Arlo tries.

Nena doesn't want to push it. She loves being Arlo's stepmum and they have a brilliant relationship, so she can see that if she says it again it might knock his confidence.

'So, tell me again,' says Nena, still standing while she places Ava into the crook of her shoulder and rubs her back. 'I wasn't really listening.'

'I know,' Maya says, giving an understanding smile.

'India first. Then where?'

'It's OK, we'll send you postcards.'

Nena looks a little crestfallen. 'I'm sorry, I've just got so much going on with all...' Nena gestures to the baby.

Maya feels bad that she's made Nena feel bad, so she tries to make it right. 'No, no, no, it's fine. I don't know how you manage it. A five-year-old and a newborn! You're doing amazingly.'

Nena shrugs as she rubs the sleep out of her eyes. 'Yeah, but Arlo's with Kate and Patrick most of the week, I don't even have to do a school run. Perhaps if I did, then I'd make it out of my pyjamas...'

'Yes, but what fine pyjamas they are...' admires Maya, stroking Nena's faded oversized Levi's T-shirt with baby sick on the shoulder.

She has a point. Only Nena could make the tired-new-mum-look chic. Her T-shirt is tied in a knot above her soft belly, where a brown line runs down brown skin; her marl shorts don't look that dissimilar to her usual off-duty dancer look of leggings, long skirts and sweatshirts over vests or one bare shoulder. Her long, straight, jet-black hair is shinier and fuller than ever thanks to the hormone surge, and she hasn't started the new-mum shed yet. And her make-up-free face looks tired yet youthful; her huge eyes shine less brightly than usual, but they are stark and beautiful.

Nena changes the subject. She doesn't like talking about herself any more. 'So, how's it going with Train Man? Do you think you can handle a whole year of just the two of you?'

Maya has been asked this question a lot lately. By her sister Clara, by her old workmates at FASH, by her new baking buddies from Pastry School, although not all of them still call him Train Man.

'You can call him James, you know.'

'I know, old habits...'

'Well, I think we'll be OK.'

'You "*think*"?'

'We've barely seen each other since he moved in. He's been so busy building up his portfolio, doing all these weddings, I think it'll be nice just to catch up, to be honest. To just get on with it.'

'But you live together...'

Maya's face prickles with heat. 'Well, I've been at Pastry School in town in the week... and packing up the flat so we can rent it out since I graduated. And James has been out loads working; shooting weddings most Fridays and Saturdays... Apart from Tuscany, we've barely had any time to stop. And there he was so nervous about being Dominic's best man, he couldn't exactly relax.'

'At least he had a weekend off photography detail.'

'I think he'd rather have been behind the camera than making the speech. But he did a great job.' Maya sighs proudly. Then remembers her protest. 'We'll be fine,' she says, with a slight irritation in her voice.

'Well, you're about to find out. I imagine travelling will be a test: helping each other through the squits... pissing on each other when you're stung by a jellyfish... getting ripped off at every border crossing... arguing over who decided to take the wrong turn... Surely travelling and parenting are the two biggest killers of relationships.'

Maya frowns. 'I hope not.'

'But, hey, if it goes well, you never know what might happen.' Nena holds up her left hand and wiggles four fingers. The gems in her engagement and wedding rings sparkle.

'Oh, shut up, not you too! It's all I get. At Dominic and Josie's wedding; from my sister; from the guys at Pastry School; all this chat about the Bollywood wedding... everyone going on at us and saying, "You're next!" and "Tick tock!" It's all getting a bit tiresome.'

'Well, if he doesn't ask you to marry him, then he'll be missing a trick. He'll have so many sunsets, so many romantic opportunities, it'd be rude not to, if you ask me.'

I didn't ask you.

Maya looks uncomfortable and tries to make things good again. 'Anyway, pass Ava to me, will you?' she says, opening her arms and changing the subject. 'Come to Aunty Maya, you peach of a baby you.'

As Maya takes Ava into her embrace, she closes her eyes and inhales the smell of her small furry head. The sweet clean scent helps soothe out the knot of ill ease in the pit of Maya's stomach, but it can't quite erase the image of James' face as he dashed out of the door.

3

December 2015, London, England

'So, what else is on our to-do list?' Maya asks, before slurping up a strand of chestnut tagliatelle too clumsily for the restaurant they're sitting in. A speck of taupe-coloured sauce lands on the crisp white tablecloth; the beige and white booths in this elegant corner of London feel like a cosy hug on this decadent December night.

'It's just the last of those boxes to go into storage: our clothes, my camera stuff, your KitchenAid... unless you're leaving that for Timo.'

'I am *not* leaving that for Timo.'

'Well, we can't do any of that until Christmas Eve anyway.' James pushes his glasses up his nose and tucks into his black truffle gnocchi. They both mentally count down the days until Christmas Eve and say *five* to themselves at the same time. 'Did you tell the insurance company that the flat needs to move over to rental for the year?'

'Shit, no. I'll add that to my list.'

Maya marvels at how clever, how organised, how *handsome* James is.

James taps a front tooth, signalling to Maya that a short strand of chives has got stuck between hers, and she blushes and smiles from behind her hand. Maya reaches for the compact mirror in her make-up bag, looks into it and removes the offending greenery, thinking how much worse it will be when she gets the squits, as Nena so cheerfully put it.

'I think you have to tell them; it changes something about the building or contents insurance if you're renting it out.'

'Do you think we'll regret Timo taking over the flat?' she asks.

'He'll be fine. He'll have Florian to answer to if not. And me when we get home.'

Maya laughs. James doesn't have an ounce of aggression in him. And her baby brother Florian is a 6ft 5in quiet giant. But Florian's best friend, Timo, is Hazelworth's biggest playboy, and Maya doesn't want to think about how many girls will be passing through the stained-glass door of her lovely, light, first-floor maisonette in the next twelve months.

James looks at Maya reassuringly. Everything about James is reassuring. His warm brown eyes. The dimple in his left cheek. His strong shoulders and soft hands.

'I'd better make a note to call Nationwide or I'll probably forget...'

Maya takes a black Sharpie and a notepad out of her bag – *the* notepad she tore a piece of paper from, more than a year and a half ago, on which she wrote a note for James, asking him if he'd like to go for a drink. First came his crushing rejection, then seven months of longing, not knowing that he too had wished his circumstances were different, before they were thrust together in the most serendipitous of circumstances, in the snow one year ago tonight.

'And phones?' Maya asks, Sharpie at the ready. 'Are we sure we're cancelling our contracts and ditching our mobiles?'

'Yep. Don't need them.'

'But shouldn't millennials always stay connected, even on the Mekong Delta? Shouldn't we be vlogging about this experience in daily updates to billions of YouTube fans?'

'You sound really square, Maya.'

'Just sayin'...' Maya tries to look youthful and sassy, and then remembers she's in a restaurant where she should be looking adult and refined. She smooths down the black blazer over her gold lamé vintage dress.

'Well, not at the price we pay a month – I checked. Laos and Cambodia aren't the kind of countries we can roam for free,' says James. 'Bin them. It'll be liberating. There are internet cafes everywhere now. We can email and Skype and chat whenever we need to. We'd only ever need a phone in an emergency, and we'd be really unlucky to encounter one of those...' James raises one eyebrow hopefully.

'*What's the worst that can happen?*' replays in Maya's mind.

A waitress in a white jacket comes to refill their glasses with white wine from an ice bucket, then leaves again promptly.

'Anyway, enough about dull things like mobile contracts and house insurance...' James lifts his glass and widens his eyes. 'Happy anniversary, beautiful, sweet Maya. I love you so much.'

Maya blushes and beams a sparkling, chiveless smile. She can't believe how she's lucked out. Train Man – *Train Man* – is in love with her. Train Man thinks Maya is beautiful and sweet. Train Man agreed to take a whole year out so they can spend every single minute of every single day together, travelling the world, lounging on beaches, reading books, plotting their future together.

She smiles, raises her large wine glass and hopes their futures are aligned.

'I love you too, baby. And a year!' she sighs. 'It's gone so fast! Although, technically, it's two and a half for me...'

James laughs, and his dimple sinks further into his cheek. He spears some gnocchi onto his heavy shiny fork which then pauses at his lips.

'We're going to have such a brilliant time,' he says, before tucking in enthusiastically.

Maya lets out a sigh of relief. 'Really? You think so?'

James hadn't been all that keen on going travelling when Maya first suggested it. He was worried about how much time he'd spent building up his portfolio through hard work and word of mouth, only to throw it all away by turning down portraits, family photos and weddings. For a whole year. Worse still, he'd have to cancel bookings he had already accepted. But a phone call out of the blue from his old boss at the advertising agency where he had worked with his best friend Dominic had got Maya thinking.

'Millsy you twat, it's Jeremy Laws here.'

'Jeremy, hi!'

James pictured Jeremy Laws, chief creative officer at MFDD advertising agency on Charlotte Street, scratching his red beard as he spoke.

'You're coming to my wedding.'

'Eh?' James had said – surprised to hear from a boss he was sure he'd burned his bridges with.

'I'll pay for your flight and a couple of nights' accommodation... on the condition you take some photos. Priyanka wants that reportage style and Dominic says you're not too bad. So, I'm booking you as well as the official photographer. And the fashion photographer. And the interiors photographer. Jesus, she wants this wedding to be in *Vogue*, *Tatler*, *Elle Deco* and *Grazia India*. It's crippling me!'

James had heard that Jeremy Laws was finally settling down, with a woman who looked like an Indian princess no less, but he didn't expect to be on the guest list, let alone to be part of a wedding in Rajasthan.

'Congratulations, Jeremy, I'm—'

'Do me a favour and just be the reportage photographer. Nice post-Christmas break. I'll pay for your trip over and you do your pictures for free. Deal? I'm not paying another bloody photographer.'

James laughed as he listened to the rasping sound of Jeremy scratching the russet-coloured stubble over his Adam's apple. He hadn't spoken to Jeremy Laws since he quit MFDD just over a year ago, to leave a life of branding, packaging and advertising dog food, craft beer and feminine hair-removal products for a new career taking wedding photographs and portraits.

'When is the wedding?'

'New Year's Eve. Udaipur, India. If you say no, I'll fire you.'

James laughed again while he tried to get his head around Christmas plans he hadn't yet made. A conversation – a commitment – he and Maya hadn't got round to.

'Dominic showed me your website, you're not as shit as I thought you'd be.'

'Thanks. It's going well so far.'

'Bring that new bird of yours too.'

James told Maya about the crazy phone call, thinking she might quite like an Indian escapade after Christmas, before she started looking for a professional role in patisserie, but it planted a bigger seed than he'd anticipated and her eyes sparkled in excitement as it grew.

'Why don't we go out for Jeremy and Priyanka's wedding, and just, kinda, stay there?' she said one autumn afternoon while they read the Sunday papers in their local pub. 'Use a chunk of Velma's inheritance to go travelling. Make a year of it before we... before we get proper jobs and settle down. It'll be perfect!'

Maya's beloved friend Velma, a septuagenarian agony aunt with a penchant for cream cakes, had died just before Maya had given James the note asking him if he'd like to go for a drink. In fact it was Velma who had encouraged Maya, with her adventurous spirit, her twinkle in her eyes, and her 'What's the worst that can happen?' attitude, to make the leap and take a chance. And it was Velma who was still inspiring Maya to live a little and see the world.

James took some persuading. He already had wedding bookings for summer 2016 and he would have to turn them down if they did stay in India and go travelling from there. And he was keen to get on the property ladder somehow – he'd never owned a home and didn't want Maya to think he was riding on her coat-tails. She owned the light and lofty Victorian maisonette they lived in, but he wanted to bring something to the relationship. And then there was the fact Maya would be funding the trip; he wasn't sure how he felt about that...

'Come on, baby,' Maya pleaded. 'We've barely seen each other since you moved in. This way we have a whole year to talk, to travel, to make love, to make sandcastles, to make plans for the rest of our lives together.'

James still looked uncertain.

'Think of your travel portfolio! You could take some amazing photos. I can see it now: Indian kids playing cricket on dusty greens; Buddhist monks walking in a line; or cute Guatemalan kids in colourful artisan clothes – travel magazines love that kind of thing. You could move into travel photography, sell some pictures while we go along...'

James thought about how much he loved photographing people; how he thrived on seeing their stories and the peculiarities of their lives through his lens. And he looked at the excitement and the enthusiasm on Maya's freckled face, knowing she was right. The housing market could wait. People would carry on getting married and would always need photographers.

So he had said yes and scooped Maya up when she flung her arms around his neck and said, 'It's going to be such fun!'

He came round to the idea and started buying guidebooks and researching places of interest, even if it pained him every time someone from the Kaye-French photographer's agency contacted him about a booking he had to turn down, or a bride-to-be contacted him because she had seen amazing pictures he'd taken at a friend's wedding. What pained James most was how terrible he felt when he cancelled the bookings he already had lined up. Brides cried. Grooms said 'For fuck's sake,' and James apologetically returned their deposits. But Maya hugged him, said it would all be OK, and hoped James really was on board.

'You really think we're going to have an amazing adventure; you really think we're doing the right thing?' Maya says, with a hopeful smile.

'Well you talked me into it, so I bloody hope so!'

Maya pretends to wince.

'I know so,' he adds, letting go of Maya's hand.

4

A woman with carmine-stained lips and hair that dances around her ears looks through a bakery window. Above, a royal-blue awning protects her paper-thin skin from the sun, enhancing its deathly hue. She bites her bottom lip as she surveys the offerings from under her furrowed brow. A row of *roulé Normand*. A solitary *abricot-frangi poire panier*. Three *pistache-framboise pliés*. She is neither hungry nor full. She has felt the same for the past few days, and she wonders why, even faced with tiny delicacies she knows she enjoys, she's not moved enough to buy a single one.

A man with a paper bag packed full of pastries opens the bakery door to leave and the pale woman walks slowly through the wooden frame. She doesn't thank the man for holding the door open for her, nor does she notice his chagrin. The man's not even sure she noticed him at all, but he rolls his eyes to himself and tuts.

The woman shuffles towards the counter, where more baked goods await appreciative tummies. Her eyes, wide and light, stare. She does long, slow blinks, as if she's a baby taking in the world.

A kindly man behind the counter nods, indicating for her to tell him what she wants while he puts out oven-fresh delights. As he leans into the glass cabinet that separates them, he notices the woman's bottom half. The way her white cotton vest clings to her flat waist; her blue chambray shorts have a cloth belt of the same fabric; she has nothing on her feet, except for a chain on her left ankle.

Silly tourists, he thinks, still smiling amiably.

The man places croissants in a row behind the sign that reads '*croissants aux amandes*', like little, dappled soldiers, hot from battle in the oven.

Customers sit at tables reading books, maps and newspapers. A small man dressed as Napoleon Bonaparte stands in the corner, waving his arms, trying to catch the woman's attention.

'Pssst! Pssst!' he says, hoping no one else in the bakery cafe will notice.

None of the customers – the gossiping friends, the businessmen nor the backpackers – look up from their crêpes and coffee. The hissing man disturbs only the woman, wide-eyed at the counter.

'Pssst! Pssst! What is your name?' he asks, in an abrasive voice.

'You already know my name,' whispers the woman, with alarm. His craggy, caricature-like face reminds her of an illustration from her past. The man looks like Rumpelstiltskin, hopping on one leg and making a fist, from the cover of the book her father read to her as a child. The face scared her then and it's unsettling her now.

'Ahhh, yes,' he says, rubbing his hands together. 'Man. On. Well. Pay me some attention, Manon, and I will give you good advice,' says the little general in his navy coat with gold brocade epaulettes. He has a mischievous look on his face.

He is bothering Manon and he's enjoying it.

She wonders why he is bothering her when she was minding her own business, seeing if she could arouse a hunger from within her aching stomach by looking at the pastries laid out in front of her, reminiscent of those she loves from her favourite bakery in her village back in Alsace; wondering why no one else has noticed the man in the corner, causing a brouhaha.

Show him my fear and he'll grow. If I am friendly he might go away.

'Aren't you hot in that?' Manon finally gets the courage to ask, turning to the little man in the corner as she says it, but not looking him in the eye. It is a hot and languid day outside. The heat is bringing the scents of tamarind and coconut into the bakery, where they marry with pastries and coffee. It is far too hot for such military regalia.

The baker behind the counter looks puzzled.

'Hot? I'm OK. It hotter out back with my ovens,' he shrugs in broken English. 'What would you like?'

Napoleon laughs. 'Silly girl.'

'What?' she says towards the corner. Taken aback.

'Would you like something to eat or drink?' says the man behind the counter, confused by the delicate-looking woman without any shoes on. He looks at her over the counter now, getting a fleeting impression of her from the floor up, and wonders whether she has the means to pay.

I'm not a charity, you know.

But she looks clean enough. She might just be lower maintenance than most of the travellers who come in with backpacks, long lenses and guidebooks.

The baker looks to the pockets of Manon's chambray shorts and she secretes a shaky, self-conscious hand inside the left one.

Napoleon starts taunting her, egging her on to eat. 'An army marches on its stomach, you know.'

'I'm not hungry!' says the woman irritably.

The man behind the counter puts his palms up submissively, as if to say he doesn't care whether she does or doesn't buy anything, and he slopes off out to the ovens, to check his next batch of cinnamon whirls.

Napoleon laughs. A nasty, goading, belittling laugh.

'I said I'm NOT HUNGRY!' She bellows this time, like a child having a tantrum, repeating the words *NOT HUNGRY, NOT HUNGRY, NOT HUNGRY.*

The man in the corner laughs demonically under his bicorne hat, his Rumpelstiltskin face contorting, until he laughs so hard that he rolls on the floor and starts kicking his little legs into the air like a beetle stuck on its back.

Diners pause their conversations and look up at the woman as she runs out of the bakery and onto the steamy street, towards the curve of the mighty Mekong river.

5

December 2015, Hazelworth, England

'Tell me the route again!'

Herbert Flowers on Christmas Day is a man in his element. He doesn't wear a gaudy jumper with a smiling reindeer and a light-up nose, nor does he wear novelty socks with jingling bells on them. On Christmas Day, Herbert Flowers favours a Nelson Mandela-style shirt, golden, brown and majestic across his wide shoulders, for all the heat he will generate eating nut roast while he tries not to look at the plump turkey sitting on a clementine and sage wreath on the serving platter in front of him.

Maya's father decided to become vegetarian on his sixtieth birthday and often enthuses about a whole portobello mushroom, stuffed with cheese or pan-fried in red wine and garlic, despite looking longingly at the meat resting in front of him. Truly, he is grateful for everything in front of him, he loves a special occasion: having his wife next to him at the head of the table; his four adult children and three grandsons around him – chatting and laughing and mocking each other while he relishes the revelry, red wine and Turkish delight. He is comforted by the clatter of crockery and the production line of dishes filled with red cabbage, Brussels sprouts and roast potatoes, being passed diligently in a row. Herbert is the congenial host, with ruddy cheeks glowing, and he even twirled the edges of his moustache for the occasion.

He tops up glasses from his standing position to the left of the turkey, only stopping when his youngest grandson, Oscar, leans to take a swig of what he thinks is Ribena. His mother, Maya's older sister Clara, intercepts before it's too late.

'Erm, not for you, Oski. Here, have some apple juice.'

Oscar's big brothers, Henry and Jack, look at each other and giggle about the wine, while Maya's younger brothers, Jacob and Florian, shovel more roast potatoes than they ought to onto their plates from ceramic bowls as they pass.

Maya drowns her plate in gravy from the red-and-white jug her mother Dolores only uses on Christmas Day, as she starts the well-rehearsed route.

'India tomorrow. We fly to Delhi, spend a few days there, then travel to Udaipur for the wedding.'

'Ah, now India is a place beyond all others where one must not take things too seriously.' Herbert quotes Kipling to his daughter. 'The midday sun always excepted...'

Maya looks up at her father, bottle of wine in one hand, as red as his cheeks, and Herbert gives her a wink as he smooths his billowing shirt over his rounded tummy. He lifts a satisfyingly heavy spoon and starts to load potatoes onto his own plate. She smiles and continues.

'Then Thailand, Vietnam, Laos, maybe Cambodia – we're not sure yet. Indonesia by summer, then...'

'No, Herbert!' scolds Maya's mother. 'They're cooked in goose fat! Those are yours – I did those ones in olive oil...' She gestures to a small tin at the other end of the table, which Maya's brother Jacob graciously passes, not before Florian has poached one as it passes through.

'Hey, they're Dad's!' snaps Clara.

'Bellend!' mouths Jacob.

Herbert puts the bottle and the spoon down, chuckles to himself and takes ten little roast potatoes from a tin, crisp and golden and not made from any meat product whatsoever.

It's always when Maya or James get to the Indonesia part that people start to glaze over and drift off. Not that people think Indonesia is boring – it looks pretty spectacular from the travel books and blogs Maya and James have been reading – but people tend to switch off when they get too detailed or too excited about their trip.

Except for Amy Appleyard – editor of *Esprit* magazine, Britain's glossiest broadsheet Sunday supplement. Amy had keenly followed Maya's Fifi Fashion Insider column she wrote for *The London Evening Standard*. It ran for a couple of months last winter, as an anonymous exposé about life working on the inside of a fashion retail giant. Everyone was talking about it at the time – from *This Morning* to *Victoria Derbyshire* to *Newsnight* – wondering who Fifi Fashion Insider really was. Amy Appleyard noted Maya's name when she finally cracked and revealed that she was Fifi Fashion Insider, and she called Maya in for a meeting to chat about a staff job on *Esprit*.

When Maya told Amy she was about to go travelling with Train Man, a man she had loved from afar on her daily commute and who was now her boyfriend, Amy was intrigued and asked Maya if she'd write about her travels in a weekly column. Amy even listened to the entire route with interest: India and Southeast Asia for six months, then Australia and the Americas from June until Christmas.

'We'll call it *My Travels With Train Man*,' she said, not giving Maya a chance to suggest any other title.

Maya had got into all kinds of trouble when she wrote the secret insider column about her old workplace, FASH, and vowed never to do anything so underhand or so stressful again. But this was different. Legitimately Maya. An honest and open account of what it's like to go travelling with your boyfriend in your late twenties, when most of your friends are settling down and having babies.

Plus, the column payments would be a little bit of pocket money to boost what was left of Velma's inheritance, after the £17,000 Maya spent on her *diplôme de pâtisserie* at the Cordon Bleu. All Maya needed to do was persuade James that this column was a good idea – he was a shy guy after all – but she promised him she wouldn't write anything too personal.

Maya looks up, already knowing she has lost her audience, and changes tack. Besides, you have to be quick at the Flowers dinner table, *especially* on Christmas Day. There's no time to talk when Florian is sniffing around the roast potatoes – he's often on his second helping before Dolores has finished carving herself a first slice of turkey. 'Thanks, Mum, you're the best. *Bon appétit* everyone!' Maya raises a forkful of petits pois doused in gravy. No time to raise a glass even.

'Happy Christmas!' chime Jacob and Clara.

'Epic spuds, Mum,' mumbles Florian, through a mouthful of Maris Piper.

Henry and Jack, who are eight and six, chink their glasses of apple juice and are scolded by their dad, Robbie, when they splosh it over their best trousers.

Jacob flashes a full mouth of stuffing at Florian, at an angle so their parents can't see. It's a little game they have taunted each other with since they were their nephews' ages – flashing food from their mouths at each other without getting caught or bollocked for it, although now they should know better.

Maya catches sight of sage, onion and saliva in Jacob's mouth and rolls her eyes at him.

I wish James were here.

Which reminds her. There is so much to think about in the next twenty-four hours.

'Did you have a word with Timo about taking care of the flat?' Maya asks, slowing down Florian, trying to save some potatoes for their mother. 'And, you know, that *thing* we talked about?'

'What thing?' Florian says, looking irked. All he wants to focus on is the red cabbage on his fork.

'Spunk on the sofa?' interjects Clara with a childish chuckle.

'Clara!' says their father in a jolly bellow.

'What's spunk?' asks Henry.

'*Lingua*!' shouts Herbert, trying to hide the amused sparkle in his eye.

Dolores frowns, although her dreamy demeanour makes it hard to decipher if she's frowning at the change of tone at the Christmas table or the fact that nobody saved her any gravy.

'He's coming over later to pick up your keys. Talk to him about his spunk then.'

'Why the hell are *we* doing this? Where are those lazy bastards?'

Clara is standing at a sink full of orange-tinged dishwater and greasy plates, annoyed by her brothers. Maya dries knives and forks with methodical pride.

'They're playing Frustration. With Dad and Rob...'

'Oh right, well who the bloody hell is watching the boys?'

'I think they're watching *Frozen*. Mum's having a lie-down.'

'Great.' Clara empties the dirty water from the sink and the plughole belches. She refills it with an irritated shuffle from one foot to another but knows she is getting to the satisfying part where she can see progress is being made in the mess of dirty crockery. 'Well, they can sort the tea and stollen, lazy shits.'

'Who, Henry, Jack and Oscar?' asks Maya in alarm.

'No! Jacob and Florian. They always do this...'

Maya looks at her reflection in the shiny silver knife blade – the knives Dolores and Herbert only get out on Christmas Day – to appreciate her polishing skills more than the fatigue in her face. She examines an eyeball, as if hoping to find that her to-do list is written in the black and orange flecks around her hazel irises.

Keys to Timo, cancel car insurance, double-check both passports are with James, give mobile to Mum...

'Shame James isn't here,' laments Clara as she watches a heavy stream of water push up the rising suds. 'It would have been nice for you to spend Christmas together, given you didn't last year.'

Maya's back prickles. 'We'd only just got together last Christmas...'

'I know, it's just a shame.'

It is a shame. Maya didn't like kissing James goodbye at Hazelworth station on Christmas Eve morning, all his worldly belongings stuffed into his backpack, while she packed him off to Kent to say goodbye to his mum, dad, sister and sister-in-law. She didn't want to be awake at 2 a.m., folding the last of her clothes and jewellery into boxes to go in the garage at 'Flowers Towers', as her family call it, when the only place she wanted to be was nestled into James' neck in their bed. She didn't want to wake up alone on Christmas Day again – she'd rather got used to the warm feeling of waking up against James' arm, even the scent of her morning breath against his skin is sweet and appealing. The last two Christmas mornings, despite James being her boyfriend, were much like most of Maya's adult Christmases. Waking up alone.

Maybe next year...

'Well, he did need to see his family to say goodbye to them,' Maya reasons, with herself more than Clara.

'He'll be at the airport tomorrow. I hope, anyway! You can say goodbye to him then.'

'I guess. And you're about to have a whole year together. Lying on a beach. Lazy cow.' Clara looks at the bubbles and loses focus.

At first Clara was cynical about her little sister falling in love at first sight with a stranger on the train.

You don't know him.

He could be a total weirdo.

What if he has a voice like David Beckham?

All valid points at the time. But now she knows James, she can understand precisely how Maya fell for him. And now even Clara gets a little bit flustered and lost for words when the tall, dark and handsome man who makes her little sister happy walks into the room.

'All those sunsets. All those romantic waterfalls...' Clara says dreamily, envious of her sister's exciting life, but content with the love and the repetition that fills and punctuates hers, as a mother of three young boys.

Clara gasps as she plunges her hand into the water, as if the temperature is too hot. But it isn't – she's just had a really exciting thought.

'Think of all the proposal opportunities he's going to have! Oh my god, Maya, he's *so* going to ask you.'

6

December 2015, Kent, England

'Happy Christmas, James. Happy Christmas, girls,' James' mum says in a small voice as she raises an elaborately cut glass of sherry at the table. It's the most flamboyant Diane Miller gets all year.

'What about me?'

'You too, dear,' she says to her husband, as he scratches his white hair. 'You too.'

James' dad, Stuart, and his sister, Francesca, barely look up from their plates. Francesca's wife, Petra, lifts her wine glass, closely followed by James, and they say 'Happy Christmas' in unison. 'Cheers Diane,' adds Petra. 'Thanks for a beautiful lunch.'

The Christmas dinner table at the Miller home in Kent is quieter than the Flowers of Hazelworth. It is circular, covered by a neat tablecloth with holly embroidered onto it. In the middle, a metal Christmas carousel rotates, where angels chase – but never catch – each other, powered by heat rising from the candles around it. Gold crackers perch uncracked on beige linen napkins, and Diane's late mother's Denby ware pottery all still matches. No one's elbows knock into anyone else's elbows. No one shouts 'SPUDS TO THE NORTH END!' over a clatter of crockery and glasses. Neither James nor Francesca flash a mouthful of food at their sibling. James can imagine it's a lot noisier at the Flowers dinner table, even though he's not yet spent a Christmas there.

It's a staid but loving table, and only gets lively once Stuart and his daughter have hit the mulled cider and fall out over who should have won Sports Personality of the Year; how Stuart voted in the General Election or last year's closely run Boxing Day game of Trivial Pursuit.

Stuart looks at his plate with contentment. Meat and two veg is his favourite kind of dinner, so turkey *and* pigs in blankets is as fanciful as it gets: his favourite meal of the year. Everything is right with the world as Stuart Miller sits down to dinner, but he's a quiet man, so he doesn't say it.

James' mother motions to the window, knife and fork in hand, at the gnarly bare branches of the cherry blossom tree, and notes that the rain held off. No one answers as they enjoy the beginnings of their lunch. Diane is very good at talking about the weather, whether she's at the dinner table, hanging out the washing or playing bridge with their friends. It doesn't seem to bother her if people join in her meteorological observations or not.

'How's Maya getting on?' asks Petra, preening the quiff of her lilac hair. Petra adores James. She finds comfort in the fact he looks so much like his sister. His darkest brown, wide eyes and olive skin. Hair that's almost black, swept to the side in a side parting. She is reassured that the things she loves about James are the things that made her fall in love with Francesca, and perplexed that their swarthy features are so unlike their very Anglo-Saxon-looking parents.

'Yeah, she's busy packing up the last bits that didn't make it into storage. Just clothes and stuff now. And saying goodbye to her family.'

Diane inhales a whimper and swallows it so no one can hear.

'Ahhh, it'll be nice to see her at the airport,' says Petra with a reassuring smile.

'So, what's the route again?' asks Francesca, as she lifts a crystal glass she wouldn't dream of drinking from in her own home.

'Fly to India tomorrow, Delhi first, then the wedding in Udaipur…'

'Franny told me,' enthuses Petra, clapping her hands swiftly before unfolding her napkin. 'What an amazing gig!'

'I didn't have much choice, Jeremy just sort of ordered me to go.'

'Well, I think you should be very proud – how many photographers are asked to fly out to shoot an opulent Indian wedding?'

'Erm, four. I'm photographer number four.'

Diane smiles proudly. Stuart stabs at an undercooked Brussels sprout.

'Well still, I bet your pictures will be the pick of the album.'

Petra is definitely the chattiest person at the Miller table. Probably because she's not a Miller. And it's probably why she and Maya have bonded at thirtieths, sixtieths, Easter lunches and summer barbecues over the past year. And taking James to the airport tomorrow means they get to give Maya a goodbye hug too – as well as extricating them from awkward Boxing Day drinks up the road at Mary and George's house. Their daughter, Kitty, is James' ex-girlfriend, and the last time they bumped into Kitty in Sainsbury's Tunbridge Wells, Petra had a job of keeping Francesca out of the same aisle, she was so worried about the tirade she thought might burst from her mouth.

James puts his hand to his mouth to clear his throat and carries on to the silent room. 'Then from India to Thailand, Vietnam, Laos – maybe Cambodia – Indonesia…'

'Are there more peas?' asks Stuart, giving up his battle with the sprout. They're his least favourite part of his favourite lunch anyway. He only likes to eat a token couple, and only because it's Christmas.

'Yes, dear, just in the microwave...'

Diane gets up from the table and goes in search of peas.

James can tell no one is all that interested in the route so tails off.

'Sounds ace,' says Francesca, not asking him to go on.

'What are you doing about keeping up your portfolio?' asks Petra. 'Your pictures will be awesome, maybe you could move into travel photography. This year *Condé Nast Brides*, next year *National Geographic*?'

James widens his dark eyes, enthusiasm brimming. 'Well, I do like capturing people, whether it's a wedding or not. So maybe...'

Francesca looks up but smiles to herself. Her favourite photograph in the world is one of Petra, taken from the back, half-laced in a corset, her shoulder blades muscular and strong. James took it on the morning of their wedding day and a large print of it hangs in the bedroom of their Victorian terrace in Birmingham.

'That's my biggest worry,' James adds, pushing the black rectangles of his glasses up his nose. 'Letting down all the couples I cancelled next year; getting a bad rep. I'd only just started to get the ball rolling.'

'But you didn't just leave them in the lurch. They have months to find another photographer.'

'I know, but...'

'It'll be OK, I'm sure,' Petra nods. 'As I said, *National Geographic...*'

James looks down as he chases a sprout around his plate. He can't help thinking he might be shooting himself in the foot.

Petra can see the doubt flash across his features. 'And this big Bollywood wedding might open lots of doors.'

'Let's hope so, eh?'

'Anyway, what does it matter if you're a kept man?' says Francesca with a hint of glee.

'What do you mean?'

'Well, Maya has her millions.'

'Hardly millions – she spent a good chunk of the inheritance on her course. And she's going to be working while we're away, writing travel columns for *Esprit* magazine.'

Stuart finally looks up from his plate, impressed, even though he always throws *Esprit* magazine straight into the recycling. High fashion, celebrity wisdom, handbags, homes and recipes are not his kind of Sunday afternoon reading.

'Well, enjoy it I say. Good to see a sister enabling my brother to loaf around,' Francesca says with a raised eyebrow.

'Eh?' James looks puzzled.

Diane walks back in to the dining room with a Tupperware container crammed with peas and tips them into the green serving dish with a matching green and gold domed lid. 'There you go, Stuart. More peas, James?' she asks, blinking fast through glassy eyes. 'Actually, they're petits pois,' she adds, as her voice cracks.

Stuart frowns. He thought they were peas and was very much enjoying them. But he doesn't complain, not when his wife is so *emotional*.

The Millers don't wear their hearts on their sleeves, but James had noticed the sadness in his mother's eyes today.

'Oh, Mum. It'll be no different to the advertising shoots I used to go on with Dominic,' James says, grateful to change the subject from whatever Francesca was trying to get at.

'But you always came back from those.'

'And I'll come back from this trip. This time next year I'll be home. In fact, I'm sure the trip will be over and I'll be back before you know it.'

Diane sits down and replaces the lid on the Denby dish with the petits pois in it. Petra asks Stuart how his allotment is coming along and Francesca steals a pig in blanket from her brother's plate.

'Looks like that cloud isn't shifting,' Diane mumbles, as she looks back out of the window.

My Travels with Train Man

Hi, I'm Maya, I'm 29, and I'm a stalker. Through completely non-grubby means, I have had Bono beckon me for a cuddle, The Hoff has laughed at my jokes, and Tom Cruise has led me by the hand on one of his red-carpet walkabouts. But the stalk of my life, the one I'm most proud of, was the handsome stranger on the train who ended up falling in love with me.

For almost a year after he started getting the 8.21 a.m. to King's Cross, I wore that little bit extra mascara and tried not to stare as he read books I loved. He was so beautiful and seemed like a good soul, but we never spoke. I tried to test if he would notice me by 'accidentally' dropping my ticket, to see if he would pick it up. My heart sang when he did, but I blushed too hard and squeaked too high to say anything more than an inelegant 'Ta'.

It took almost a year for me to pluck up the courage to write him a note – on my birthday in May – and another eleven days for me to actually give it to him. When he emailed me at 5 p.m. to say thanks, happy birthday, but unfortunately he had a girlfriend, I was gutted but decided to cling onto the use of the word 'unfortunately'. Remember, I'm good.

Months passed. Friends told me to move on. I went on the odd date. I even dated the guy I used to slow down for in kiss chase at primary school... but I just couldn't get past the fact that they weren't Train Man. My sister called me 'too picky'. I know I sound like I was taking the fast train to Crazytown, but I really saw myself with Train Man.

Months after I'd given Train Man the note, I was doing a shoot for a newspaper I was working for (you might remember the whole Fifi Fashion Insider furore – yeah, that's me), and who was the photographer at the studio? That's right, Train Man. He didn't get the chance to tell me his circumstances had changed. Stunned in shock and silenced by his beauty, I was too embarrassed to seize the moment. When his ex-girlfriend walked in, I fled the studio with a hot face and a broken heart; I thought they were still together.

Fast-forward a few weeks and I was on the last train home, stuck in the snow at 1 a.m. in a village outpost.

I was about to panic, and there he was in the doorway. He told me he was single; he had been for months. He said he'd noticed me – HE'D NOTICED ME?! – way before I dropped my ticket or threw the note at him. He told me he'd noticed my sparkly eyes. We kissed in the doorway of a closed pub and that night I fell in love for real.

We no longer get the 8.21 a.m. to King's Cross. In fact, we're about to embark on another, bigger, adventure – my long-held dream of travelling the world for a year. And you, dear Esprit *reader, are invited too…*

7

New Year's Eve 2015, Udaipur, India

'YOU AND JAMES SHOULD GET MARRIED!' bellows Josie from across the dance floor. She is teetering on skyscraper heels, in the same oyster hue and with the same satin sheen as her micro dress, clutching a bottle of Moët in her left hand. 'BEING A WIFEY IS AMAAAAAAZING!'

Maya looks at the bright colours and rich fabrics swirling around them, relieved that James isn't within earshot. It takes a lot of noise to drown Josie out, but the twelve dashing men banging out bhangra beats on kettle drums have spared Maya this time around. Maya doesn't have to flush a shade of awkward and James doesn't need to smile uncomfortably and change the subject.

It started three days ago at the *mehndi* ceremony,

when Josie first started asking Maya why James hadn't proposed yet – and if she thought he might. Maya was relieved to be easily able to change the focus of conversation onto Priyanka and her friends, and to lose Josie in the intricacies of floral and geometric henna.

The cringe factor was upped two days ago, after the cricket match that turned into a black-tie dinner. Josie was so giddy that the gang were back together that she had a bit too much fizz and started crying when she tried to explain how happy she was and that marriage really was the best thing she and Dominic had ever done.

On day three of the festivities – a boating trip followed by lunch at a palace on the lake – a tipsy Josie stood up on the sunset boat back across Lake Pichola and started twerking to 'Put A Ring On It', a backing track of which she played on her phone. She even straddled James for part of her routine, shoving her ring finger at him and pointing it in his face. James was not amused. The bride's grandparents were not amused. Dominic was mortified and pulled Josie back into her seat before she capsized the boat and drowned everyone in it.

This morning, over breakfast of kachori and roti, in the palatial gardens that hugged the still lake, Josie was offering up her Italian wedding villa venue for Maya and James to wed in, even though it wasn't hers to loan out.

'Oh, wouldn't it be lovely to go back, Dom?' she mused through faraway eyes.

'Easy, Joze,' replied Dominic, rubbing his droopy brown eyes, sensing the change in the atmosphere, while James scrolled through the photos on his digital SLR and Maya thought *make it stop*.

But it didn't... Earlier, during the flower-filled Hindu ceremony, Josie had squeezed Maya's arm as Jeremy and Priyanka took their seven steps around the fire, leaned in and whispered to Maya and James, 'Oh gawd, you *have* to do this at your wedding.'

Now, surrounded by handsome men in jewel-encrusted kurtas and turbans, and women in saris and Chopard bindis, Josie is *still* banging on about it, and Maya is relieved that James is somewhere else.

What's the obsession with getting married anyway?
Is it because Maya is turning thirty this year?
I don't mind.

Is it all the 'proposal opportunities' Clara and Nena made a big deal of? What's with all the pressure? Why can't people just let them enjoy themselves? Why can't they just... be?

'HAVING A HUSBAND IS AMAAAAAZING!'
Oh fuck off.

Maya feels irked but keeps dancing in her sweeping Erdem dress: black, grey and purple florals sway down to her gunmetal heels.

Maya hadn't been sure what to pack for four days and nights of luxe wedding celebrations, ahead of a year's backpacking. First there was the white Bianca

Jagger-inspired suit for the cricket match; then the black beaded cocktail dress for the dinner afterwards. For boating and lunch at the lake palace, she wore a brown dress with large cream polka dots. For the official ceremony, she wore a sari Nena had loaned her (which weighed a ton) from when she was in the ensemble in *Bombay Dreams*.

And what do you wear for a party where the groom is going to arrive on a white steed ahead of camels and elephants and the bride is carried on a gondola throne made of velvet?

Anything, reasoned Maya. *No one will be looking at me anyway.*

But she did want to look nice for James, to get into the wedding spirit. She was more worried about shipping the wedding week clothes back to England, but Josie kindly brought an extra suitcase. Sequined saris and stoles wouldn't be much use on a beach in Thailand.

I don't want to be anyone's wifey anyway, Maya tells herself.

To distract herself from the disquiet in her stomach, Maya decides to play a round of 'short, shorter, shortest'. It's a game she silently plays to amuse herself when Josie is being annoying or when she feels alone and misses James, so she looks around the room, trying to find someone in a shorter dress than Josie's. Double win if their heels are higher too. Maya is usually ninety-eight per cent certain that she won't find anyone in a shorter dress than Josie's, whichever bar, restaurant or wedding they're attending. Except perhaps for Josie's own wedding in Tuscany, when her dress was decidedly demure. That was until the evening, when she whipped off the bottom half and exposed her petite, dainty legs. Maya thought she might dress the same if her legs were so tiny and shiny, although not here. Only Josie would wear such a dress to a Hindu wedding. In which case, Maya is one hundred per cent certain that none of the five hundred guests will be wearing a dress as short as Josie's, and feeling bad for Josie's cultural faux pas, she softens a little.

'Just being *here* is amazing!' Maya shouts back as she lets an old man with a long grey beard twirl her around. She and Josie laugh, until Josie gets her heel caught in the chiffon overlay of Maya's dress...

Gah!

With booming momentum, the kettle drums crescendo as fire-eaters hail the entrance of the bride and groom in the ballroom, for the final part of the party. Jeremy, uncharacteristically sheepish and smitten, leads his bride in. Gone is his cream and gold brocade frock coat and matching turban from earlier and now he stands with ravaged red stubble and an Armani tux. With a proud face and a sweaty hand, he leads Priyanka onto the dance floor in her four thousandth outfit of the celebrations: a bronze and gold Elie Saab gown that hugs her cartoon-character curves and fans out into a fishtail. Maya thought Priyanka's pink ceremony sari couldn't be beaten – at every costume change Maya has gasped and thought *Wow*. That the last incarnation of Priyanka couldn't possibly be topped. Now, as guests gawp at the happy couple, beyond the men roaring out flames, Maya thinks Priyanka might just be the most beautiful woman in the whole world.

Her beauty makes Maya think of Nena, and she wonders how big Ava is, yearns for the smell of her skin, wonders what she's doing right now. Is she curled in her mother's neck or bouncing in her vibrating chair and letting out a gurgle? She feels a stab in her stomach, right at the point Josie falls into her, and puts the blow down to the impact.

'SORRY!' Josie bellows in Maya's ear, as she regains her balance and returns to whooping and dancing, flitting between a twerk and the Bollywood-worthy moves Priyanka's friends busted out earlier.

Champagne overspills from her bottle onto Maya and the grand ballroom's dance floor.

Not the Erdem! You're battering the Erdem!

Maya looks down at her dress, relieved that the dark florals hide a multitude of Moët, further relieved to see people clearing the dance floor at the behest of staff in colourful kurtas, politely asking guests to make way for the bride and groom's first dance.

It's a timely opportunity to move Josie along.

'Come on, lovely, they're about to do their thing,' Maya says, slipping a hand around Josie's waist and guiding her off the starlight-flecked floor.

Josie teeters, as Maya leads her to the side to watch and props her up, not sure how Josie can stand up in those heels, let alone do the running man in them. Dominic approaches, to take over, and rolls his eyes at Maya with affection.

A DJ in a white tux and black bow tie fiddles with his laptop. Men in colourful sherwani frock coats and matching trousers raise their beaters in the air above the kettle drums and pause.

Maya looks around. It is as if the room has frozen in time as she studies her surroundings to see everyone pausing for this pivotal moment. Jeremy Laws, London's biggest advertising cheese and serial shagger, is finally settling down, deigning to marry the most beautiful woman in the world.

At last.

The lights go down. The room still holding its breath. Paused, but for the couple in the middle. Sweeping strings and the warm sound of Etta James rise while Jeremy takes Priyanka in his arms and five hundred hearts swell across the ballroom as the guests all come back to life.

Maya feels that sharpness in her stomach again, and looks up. Beyond Jeremy and Priyanka she sees the figure of James in the shadows, standing across the dance floor, as he takes the last reportage shots of the night. Despite not knowing anyone at the wedding other than James, Dominic and Josie, Maya hadn't wanted to get in James' way while he worked, so she had ensured that while he was tailing Jeremy and Priyanka around dressing rooms, boats, elephants and palaces, she kept a respectful distance. She chatted to ancient *ammus*, exchanged pastry and pudding tips with chefs in the kitchen (gulab jamun was definitely going into her repertoire) and met many interesting people, who had flown in, from London to Lahore, New York to New Delhi, Manchester to Mumbai. If Maya felt nervous or alone, all she needed to do was look around, to find Jeremy and Priyanka, and there she would see James. Studious and beautiful, his tongue sticking out of the corner of his mouth while he concentrated on getting his shots. His camera his shield and his comfort blanket, glad that no one would be looking at him. Except perhaps Maya. Her glances and supportive smiles had powered James on to the point at which they could start their trip properly. Knowing that when Jeremy and Priyanka's first dance finishes, when the diva stops singing, that James can clock off and they can just *be*.

Through a gap in the newlyweds, James' lens lands on Maya. His heart swells to see the woman he loves, clapping and clasping her hands as she looks on at the happy couple. He looks through the lens, to truly *see* her, but the star lights and dry ice obscure his shot, so he focuses on Jeremy and Priyanka again, getting the final pictures he hopes no one else can.

As the last note fades and the guests erupt into cheers and applause, James lowers his camera and loosens the thick silk of his black bow tie. Maya locks eyes with him across the dance floor and smiles as he strides over to her, shattered and relieved.

'At last,' he whispers, as he holds Maya's cheeks in his palms and kisses her. They press their foreheads against each other's.

'Baby, you did a brilliant job,' Maya says, trying to stay on her tiptoes.

'I hope so.'

'I *know* so. Now let's enjoy the rest of the night. Have a drink. Drink to the year ahead.' Maya peels her forehead away from his and places a kiss on his lips.

'Great idea,' James answers, unbuttoning the stifling collar on his white shirt. 'You know it's not going to be like this forever…?'

Maya furrows her brow. 'What do you mean?'

'Palatial bedrooms, boat trips on the lake, feasting like royalty, free bar, endless chana…'

James looks a little serious for a second. Maya shrugs.

'What are you on about? It's going to be even better.

You. Me. Peace and quiet. Incredible India. It'll be amazing, just the two of us...'

Around them, colourful cloth fabrics rise and swirl, dancers twirl, and Maya and James follow the parade of guests out to the terraces for the firework finale, to see in the New Year over the lake.

8

Manon examines her reflection in a small, rectangular compact mirror. Her blue eyes are circular, like saucers. Her pale nose has a pink patch of sunburn in the middle of it. Her wispy, mouse-brown fringe sits higher than usual, pushed back through exasperation and weariness.

I need to rest.

She lowers the compact but keeps clutching it as she looks around her, to see if she can find a green patch of grass to sit on among the dry, brown brush. The lush green banks she has seen on her travels are nowhere near this part of the river and she laments to herself while she slumps down to sit. She opens her backpack to find the stale boule of bread so she can take a nibble, aware that it will make her mouth even drier. She looks out ahead of her. The river is wide, brown and strong.

She glances left and right and wonders which way is China, which is Vietnam. She lost her bearings days ago.

A little man, dressed in navy blue and brocade, removes his hat and sits down alongside Manon. He looks up at her in anticipation, waiting for her to offer him a morsel.

'The satellites can see you, you know. They can see you not sharing.'

'But you don't need food to exist do you, Monsieur? Not like I do.'

'I might.'

The small figure is so close that she can see beads of sweat starting to form around his hairline. The steamy riverbank is too hot for thick trousers, wool coats and heavy, jangling medals.

'Well, would you like some of my boule?' Manon asks, hoping he will say no. She's so hungry she doesn't want to share, but she's scared of the small man's wrath.

'No, you eat it. You get the dry mouth. You drink in the river water and catch dysentery. I'm fine thanks. I'll watch and I'll laugh and the satellites will catch every moment of it.'

'Leave me alone. I offered you my bread, what more do you want?'

'I don't want your stale bread.'

'So why are you here? Why are you following me?'

'I'm here to guide you, Manon. Make sure you choose the right path.'

'I did choose the right path, didn't I?'

Napoleon Bonaparte gives a wry smile and the eerie face from her childhood frightens her once more. She looks back to the river.

Manon has a thought. Perhaps her mirror will make the man go away. If she looks at him in the mirror, he might dissolve, he might evaporate. She puts her boule on her lap. She doesn't want to rush eating it anyway; she's so hungry, and has so little money, she doesn't know where her next meal will come from. So this she will savour. Her little mirror experiment will help prolong it; it will help defer her gratification.

She opens the compact again and examines her face. It looks passive yet demented, beautiful yet distorted. She angles the mirror to her companion, sitting on the dry brown brush next to her in his little white jodhpurs and small black riding boots, and tries to find his reflection in it at the same time as banishing her own.

'What are you doing?' asks the soldier, suspiciously. 'You're scheming!'

Manon can't see him in the mirror, but she keeps angling it anyway, as she strains her neck to search.

'Trying to confuse the satellites?'

Manon can hear the acerbic voice, but she can't see the little man now.

Perhaps he isn't there. Perhaps I am confused.

Manon moves her head and tilts the mirror, aware that she can no longer see him at all, neither in her peripheral vision nor the mirror. She stands up with cautious feet, so she can search more thoroughly. She spins around. The view in the mirror blurs as she sees the riverbank, she sees reeds, she sees the Mekong, the sand and the dry brush behind her, all spinning spinning spinning…

A frightful face appears over her shoulder, magnified in the mirror.

'BOO!' bellows the man, as mischievous as a hobgoblin, his contemptuous eyes filling the frame.

'Argh!' screams Manon in alarm, before slumping back down onto her bony bottom.

To triumphant cackles and chuckles, Manon realises she has been outwitted. He is still there. The satellites are still watching. This nightmare isn't going to go away.

Manon angles the mirror back to her own face, hoping to seek comfort in her reflection. Hoping her mother's eyes stare back at her, as calm and reassuring as they were when she was alive. She looks at her own wide, terrified eyes in the reflection of the compact mirror, only to see that they are bleeding.

9

Maya wakes with her cheek pressed against a soiled sheet. Bloodstains from hotel guests long departed permeate in brown circles of varying sizes. Her alarm call is no longer the sweet chirrup of a kingfisher on the lake, it's now a wild pig scavenging in what sounds like a corner of her room. She rubs her eyes and sits up, looking around the rickety furniture and threadbare furnishings. To her relief, there isn't a pig in the corner of the room.

Through a tattered curtain hanging on a piece of elastic, Maya sees James on the other side of the long, open window, sitting on the veranda drinking tea. Or at least that's what he asked the kindly hotel worker for.

'Gross,' he mutters to himself, as he spits the tea out onto the hotel gardens. The wild pig looks up at the tea trail quizzically, then looks down again, continuing to rummage through litter in a neglected corner of the plot.

Maya stretches and walks out onto the veranda in her olive-green slip, checking no one else is in the gardens beyond their little decking.

'A room with a view, huh?'

She kisses James' cheek and sits down beside him, wrapping the bobbled blanket shawl on the back of the seat around her.

James looks up from his guidebook, at the pig. 'Yeah, sorry about that. How the mighty fall…'

Maya lifts her bare heels onto the edge of the cold, metal seat and curls into a ball.

'It is a lovely view,' she says. 'If you just ignore this shit bit right in front of us.' She gestures her hands to the wild pig in the litter.

James smiles.

They both look at the view beyond the garden, of Lake Pichola and its morning bathers, boats and kingfishers. If Maya squints, she can see the domed bronzed onions on the roof of the palatial hotel where they spent three luxurious nights.

Sigh.

As the wedding party packed up and flew back to the Punjab, Mumbai, Lahore, London and New York, Maya and James checked into reality: one night in the not-terribly Exotic Happy Heritage Hotel, before their big bus journey to Bundi tonight.

James unfolds a map and studies it, then reads something aloud about Brahmin blue buildings they can expect to see, while Maya rubs the sleep out of her eyes and reaches for the cold toast in the middle of the table. She eschews the little white plastic pack of butter James saved her, thinking there's no point if it won't seep in and melt. Oh how she wishes there were a plate of warm doughy kachori and a glass of mango lassi in front of her.

'We're sleeping on the bus tonight, yes?' she asks through dry toast.

'Yep, eight hours in the sleeper car.'

Sleeper car?

Maya smiles to herself and looks at James.

'I think sleeper cars are a train thing.'

James looks up from his guidebook and map with a thoughtful smile but doesn't say anything.

'Once a Train Man, always a Train Man, eh?'

James pulls Maya towards him, then lifts her off her chair and onto his lap. A pig comes a bit too close to Maya's toes, still polished a shade of Black Cherry Chutney from her pre-wedding prep, and she gives her foot a flick to try to keep the boar at bay.

'Argh!' she gives a repressed squeal. 'Go away!'

Maya rests her head in the space between James' shoulder and his ear, leaning into the curve of his neck and feeling his pulse on her temple.

'I hate this!'

'Shoo! Piss off!' says James, with only slightly more certainty than Maya, before holding her into him.

The pig snorts and shuffles back to its corner.

'This is what you wanted, honey – travelling, backpacking, roughing it with the pigs.'

Maya shuts her eyes and leans in even closer. 'Well, we're most definitely roughing it now, earning our stripes.' James kisses the top of Maya's head. 'I know, I know, I guess it's just a bit of a comedown after being so spoiled all week. Makes it seem even more…'

'Brutal?' they chime.

'Well this place is shit,' reasons James. 'But it's a life lesson. And tonight won't be that bad. I imagine it'll be a wide reclining seat. Like Premium Economy on a plane.'

'Premium Economy sounds good. I can sleep on a wide reclining armchair. Anything's better than that disgusting bed in there,' Maya shudders, as the pig gets his snout stuck in an empty bottle of Thums Up! cola and starts snuffling at an even louder volume.

IO

'A 27-year-old London-based French national has gone missing in Thailand. Manon Junot, who is a post-doctoral researcher at SOAS at the University of London, was travelling the region by herself on an extended Christmas break, but her family raised concerns when she didn't board the Paris-bound flight she was due to return on, on New Year's Day. Now investigators from the Metropolitan Police have joined forces with intelligence in Paris and are flying out to Chiang Rai, the last place Manon was known to be seen, to help Thai investigators in their search. Clarence Meek has the story.'

SCREEN CUTS TO A MAN IN A LINEN SUIT FACING THE CAMERA.

'Manon Junot had been travelling around South East Asia for four weeks over the Christmas and New Year period, but family and friends raised the alarm when she didn't arrive *at Charles de Gaulle airport in Paris last Saturday. After questioning the airline, her family soon learned she had failed to check in, and alerted authorities in Thailand.'*

SCREEN CUTS TO THAI MAN IN MILITARY-LOOKING UNIFORM. A BANNER SAYING 'SOMSAK KONGDUANG, THAI POLICE', RUNS ALONG THE BOTTOM OF THE SCREEN.

'We were alerted to the fact that a French national didn't turn up for a flight in Bangkok five days ago and hasn't made contact with friends or family since. She had travelled in Thailand, Laos and Cambodia over December, and her passport was last registered at a hotel in Chiang Rai a fortnight ago. We're very concerned and are working with our friends on the Laos and Myanmar borders to see if she left the country overland, and also with Cambodian border patrol in the south.'

SCREEN CUTS TO A PHOTOGRAPH OF A WOMAN JUMPING BACK IN LAUGHTER AS SHE FEEDS AN ELEPHANT A BUNCH OF BANANAS AND THE VOICE OF CLARENCE MEEK RETURNS.

'Ms Junot had been in regular contact with friends and family while she was away, posting photographs on her social media pages during her trip.'

SCREEN CUTS TO A WOMAN WITH DYED RED HAIR. A BANNER ACROSS THE BOTTOM OF THE SCREEN READS 'NADIA RUTSCHMANN, FRIEND'.

'At the start of her trip she was posting updates, every couple of days maybe, to her Facebook and Instagram. Nice pictures, of beautiful places she was visiting. We didn't think too much of the posts stopping, we hoped she was having

fun, but to not hear from her and for her to not use her flight ticket home, well that's a worry.'

VOICE OF CLARENCE MEEK RETURNS.

'The academic – who researches economic development of the Asia Pacific region at SOAS in central London – left the UK on the second of December.'

CUTS TO POLICE OFFICIAL KONGDUANG AGAIN:

'We're now talking to other guests at the hotel she was last registered as staying in, to see if they spoke to her in the days before she was due to fly home. Not all hotels and hostels register their guests' passport details, but we are trying to piece together the last two weeks of her trip, when she stopped contacting family and friends.'

'Clarence Meek, BBC News, in Bangkok.'

11

Nena sits on the sofa, chewing a cold crumpet, gazing at the television and the face of a woman feeding bananas to an elephant. She didn't take in any of the news story about the woman, if indeed the story was about the woman. Perhaps it was about the elephant. Nena's too preoccupied, trying to remember if it was five times she woke in the night or six. However many times it was, it's irrelevant.

Either way, I'm shagged.

She changes the channel, to try to find something that will wake her up, as Tom pokes his head around the living-room door.

'I'll leave you beautiful ladies to— Oh, where's Ava?'

Nena scrolls up through channels, before quickly changing back to BBC Breakfast.

'You going already?' She looks up with pleading eyes. Tom doesn't answer.

'She's asleep,' Nena says, pushing the plate with the half-eaten crumpet onto the low coffee table. It's not even this morning's cold crumpet, it's one she made while she was burping Ava after a ferocious 1 a.m. feed. Now it's 8.30 a.m., Tom's only just going to work, in the same building this very news about an elephant or whatever is being broadcast from, and already Ava is on her first nap of the day, having woken again at 5 a.m. and Nena giving up on night.

'What are you going to do today then?' Tom asks cheerfully, as he wraps a grey scarf around his neck.

What am I going to do?

'What do you mean?' Nena's feline eyes look alert and defensive, despite the shadowy pouches beneath them.

'Well, why don't you have a nap while she's napping?'

Nena's spine relaxes a little. 'Oh. Well I can't. This is my chance to eat, to wash up the shit in the kitchen.'

'To watch *Lorraine*?' Tom laughs but sees straight away that Nena doesn't find it funny. 'Leave the washing up, I'll do it when I get home. Oh, I'm collecting Arlo from school remember, so we'll be home earlier.' Tom says this like it's a good thing, but Nena is surprised this doesn't make her happy. She doesn't want Tom to go, but she feels under more pressure to get the flat in a fit state for Arlo's Wednesday night sleepover, in a shorter time, if Tom is doing school pick-up. Sometimes it's easier when Tom is working late.

'Are you seeing that new girl today?' she asks.

'What new girl?'

'My replacement.'

Tom can see Nena is in combative mode, so he slides his bag down his back and comes into the room, slinking into the sofa beside her.

'She's not your replacement. She's additional talent. Anyway, no one could replace Nincompoop Nena,' Tom says as he nuzzles Nena's face.

A smile creeps across her lips. Before becoming a mother, before meeting Tom, Nena was Nincompoop Nena, the best children's entertainer in North London. She wowed divorcee Tom – even more than she wowed Arlo and his friends at Arlo's third birthday party – so much so that he gave Nena a job as a children's TV presenter. Now Nena from *Nena's Tiny Dancers* is stopped by mums and dads further afield than N16. Not that she's been anywhere in a while. Not since their honeymoon last Christmas in Bahia. But even in Brazil, British parents would stop Nena on the reef and say, 'Look! It's dancing Nena!' to their confused offspring.

'Anyway, you'll like Dr Rosa, she's funny.'

'A doctor.' Nena sighs. 'So she's funny and clever. And attractive, no doubt.'

Tom doesn't deny it but raises a diplomatic eye-brow.

'I hate her.'

'Well, I love you – come here...' Tom leans in and Nena reclines a little.

He kisses crumpet crumbs off her lips; she tastes of butter and morning breath. She kisses him back, thinking for a second that this could be nice, if only she didn't feel so knackered or so fat. Or there wasn't the washing up to do. Or she'd sorted out getting her coil fitted. Or that if she tried it out – tried sleeping with her husband – and it failed, it would be the biggest waste of a nap ever.

I have so much to do.

'Go on, you've got to go to work.'

'I can be late...'

'No you can't. Go!'

A cry comes from the bedroom.

'Oh for fuck's sake, Tom!' Nena says, as if it's his fault. She struggles to get herself up off the apple-green sofa.

'I'd better go,' he says, slinging on his bag.

'Can't be late now, can you?' she snaps. Tom looks hurt and Nena softens. 'See you later. Hang on, let me get Ava so she can kiss you.'

Moments later, Tom cradles his wife and his baby in the hallway and goes down the stairs to the door, a little too happily for Nena's liking.

'Right, what shall we do today?' says Nena as she slinks back into the sofa and changes the channel to ITVBe.

12

January 2016, Udaipur, India

In a dusty bus depot on the outskirts of a city, Maya and James remove their pristine backpacks and put them down on a vast expanse of dried, cracked mud. The brown ground is fleetingly tinged pink from the sunset and a wind whips up a whirl of dust and feathers. James throws his large grey-and-black bag down in a more gung-ho fashion than Maya – he thinks grime and dirt will make them look edgier, how 'real' travellers should look – disguising the fact they started their big round-the-world trip in Oberoi opulence.

James used to do the same thing when he was a teen with white, box-fresh trainers – he'd ask Francesca to jump up and down on his feet, to roughen them up a bit and make them look less 'new', to make him look less of a mummy's boy. Francesca always obliged with more gusto than James intended, and the gentle toe taps and foot presses would inevitably graduate to stamps, painful kicks and James and Francesca coming to blows.

Maya doesn't want to put her beloved new Macpac on the ground in case it touches one of the many globs of spit there, thick, gloopy and red from chewed-up tobacco, so she carefully heaves it on top of James'. It was an emotional moment when Maya found the backpack she wanted to buy. She and James had gone to the outdoor shops in Covent Garden to get themselves all the gear they would need for the year ahead, and she tried on different styles, as if she were wedding dress shopping.

Too big.

Too military.

Too Bear Grylls.

Too masculine.

Too feminine.

When Maya found the one that was *just right* – steely grey, sleek zips, and just the right proportions – she looked at herself in the mirror, the long empty backpack stuffed with bubble wrap and tissue, like a koala hugging her shoulders. Aside from it feeling deceptively light, Maya liked how she looked.

I look the part.

Sizing up her reflection, Maya imagined her departed friend Velma, young and adventurous, heading off on one of her trips to Buenos Aires, Paris, or Istanbul, to work in whichever bureau she was to report from. Full of excitement at the prospect of the sights she was about to see, the friends she would make, the food she would eat, the men who would twirl her around, at milongas or in the Moulin Rouge.

Velma would approve of this backpack.

'That's it. That's the one.'

Velma would approve of James.

She took her Visa card out of her wallet and bought her backpack and one James had chosen, grateful to Velma for the inspiration to travel – and the means of paying for it.

So no, Maya won't fling her backpack onto ground stained with spit blobs that were right in front of where people stood waiting for colourful buses to take them beyond Rajasthan's jewels and dunes. Besides, Maya put too much effort into her capsule wardrobe to just sling all her worldly belongings onto the floor.

I might have to put my face against it and use it as a pillow.

Crowds jostle, as a brightly painted bus pulls up, bald tyres skidding in the brown dust. A loud hiss emanates from the back of the bus as Maya and James wait beside it, inhaling a cloud of steam and exhaust fumes as they let the locals get on first. James drags and Maya lifts their packs towards the door, where they politely edge up some steps, cumbersome and cluttered, onto the already crowded bus. James hands two thin white pieces of paper to the driver and gives a hopeful smile.

The driver urges them up from his perch by the door and signals for them to move down the back of the bus.

'Our bags?' James asks. 'Can you open up the side? The baggage storage?'

The driver shrugs, and ushers them on.

Maya steps up behind James and whispers in his ear. 'I don't think there is a baggage compartment. We'll have to take them on with us.'

James looks irritated and pushes his glasses up his nose. 'There isn't room,' he says through gritted teeth.

James surveys the bus. It's entirely full. Eyeballs look back at him with interest, in silence. There are no wide, reclining seats waiting for James and Maya. There are no wide, reclining seats at all.

James turns back to the bus driver. 'Erm, I think this must be the wrong bus. We're meant to be on the night bus to Bundi. Is this it?'

The driver gives a gentle, graceful move of the head and James can't decipher what it means.

Do we get off?

Do we stay on?

A young man with thick sideways hair and white teeth, sitting in one of the six front seats, stands up to make a declaration. 'Dude. I love your shirt,' he says, appreciatively as he eyes the beige cheesecloth shirt on James' back.

'Thanks.'

The man looks pleased with himself and sits back down.

James sees an opportunity – the passenger looks more agreeable than the driver.

'Do you know where our seats are?' James asks hopefully. He shows the passenger the thin white pieces of paper. 'We have sleeper tickets.'

'Ahh, sleeper tickets are up there, sir,' the man says cheerfully.

James and Maya look to the roof of the bus. There is no upstairs.

'There, dude.' He points again to an open compartment that looks more like a parcel shelf than a bed. The shelves run down the entire length of the bus, with sliding doors so passengers' belongings (or passengers themselves) don't tumble out on the winding, mountain roads. Most are crammed with plastic holdalls, laundry bags and bundles tied with string. Maya's sure she can hear a chicken clucking in a compartment near the front. At the back they seem less stuffed.

'That's the sleeping compartment?' James asks.

The young man moves his head and James thinks it's a nod.

Maya gasps. 'James, why is no one else sleeping in the boxes?!'

'Because they're not stupid.'

The bus driver wants to get going; the passengers are starting to get irritated by the dude in the cool beige shirt and his worried-looking companion.

James walks down the aisle, past storage crammed with picnic hampers, more laundry bags, blankets and boxes.

Was that a dog in that compartment?

He turns back to Maya.

Or something else?

'Yep, this is it,' James says soberly.

Maya feels like she's been punched in the stomach.

'You're kidding.'

A woman in a pale blue sari and her son lean towards the window, anticipating that the Westerners' sleeper compartment is above their heads; enabling James to throw their luggage up and into it with a laboured heave.

'You next,' he says, offering Maya a foot up. Maya puts one foot in James' cupped hands and the other on the edge of the woman's seat, careful not to touch her beautiful clothing, as she climbs into the box. There is dirty carpet on the base of their compartment and her nose almost touches the roof as she lies down.

James looks around, without a clue as to how he's going to get into the box without just climbing all over the seat and the woman and her son, who still don't say a word.

He shrugs an apology and gives an optimistic smile, hoping she'll move further. She leans towards the window again, this time squishing into her son and him against the window, making way for James' foot so he can get a leg-up.

The bus lurches forward, making it even more awkward for James to get a foot in without kicking any of the passengers.

'Sorry,' he mumbles, as he pushes himself up and slides into what looks like a coffin made for two. It would be romantic if it weren't so hellish.

Inside, Maya curves into a ball and tries to suppress small sobs. The box is too small for her, how the hell is James – all 6ft 1in and equine legs – going to curl inside it next to her. And their two huge backpacks. But deftly he does, and they lie side-by-side on their backs, their noses touching the roof of the box, their legs feeling amputated by their baggage. The bus engine chugs and Maya and James turn to face each other, knowing this is the part where they have to dig deep. They lie like two coils, fully sprung.

James tries to smile. 'Shall I shut the "door"?' He gestures to the wooden sliding panel at the edge of their box.

Maya doesn't know what's worse, the tinny noise and dramatic sound effects of the 1970s movie that's just restarted in the main cabin or the chug of the throaty engine, hammering into the space behind their skulls. She can't even answer through her stifled tears.

This is what I wanted. This is all my fault.

James sees the panic and desperation on Maya's face, a darkness looms over him and he's reminded for a second of Kitty, his ex-girlfriend, stern and scowling, and what it felt like to care for someone plunged into thunderous darkness.

'It'll be OK, honey – you're my champion sleeper, you are. Just try to get some kip and before you know it we'll be in Bundi.'

Maya breathes rapidly and struggles to speak. 'We'll… we'll suffocate with that door closed.'

'Look, I think that's a window…' James reaches behind Maya's head. 'That'll let some air in.'

James cranks open a small triangular window behind Maya and in flies a cloud of thick black exhaust smoke. Both of them cough, struggling to breathe in the box.

'Urgh, no! We'll choke to death if the exhaust fumes come directly in… I can't really breathe as it is.'

James shuts the window. Tinny Bollywood soundtrack it is.

Maya takes sharp shallow breaths, trying to expel the black fog from her lungs, knowing that her only comfort is in the fabric of James' clothing, the smell of his neck. Her legs start to tingle and shake, as if she's just walked ten thousand steps down a mountain, and they feel out of control.

'Honey, you're shaking…'

Perhaps it's pins and needles.

'Come on, it's OK, hug in to me and take deep breaths.'

But my stomach hurts too.

Maya plants her face further into James' shirt, his chest.

My legs. They're out of control.

James holds Maya into him, but that only stifles her more. She flails onto her back and kicks her legs rapidly, as if she's clawing her way out of the ground.

I'm being buried alive.

'Breathe...'

This is what I wanted.

'James, I have to get off.'

This is what she wanted.

'You can't get off, honey, we're stuck here all night. Just curl into me and try to get to sleep.'

A horn sounds on the cliff-edge road and Maya's heart races even faster.

'I can't, I can't, I just feel so desperately...'

Stuck.

Maya's breathing is sharper and more anxious; she can barely speak through panic and tears and a feeling of being stifled.

And empty.

'I just, I just... I just want to...'

Suddenly Maya finds her voice among the sharpness and the shouts into the chug of the engine, the blaring movie, the horns of passing trucks on the road out of Udaipur.

'I JUST WANT TO GET OFF THIS FUCKING BUS!'

James is alarmed. Mild Maya, who's never raised her voice at him, is shouting in anger and panic and kicking her shaking legs, and he wants it to stop.

'It's OK. You're OK. We're OK…' he says, stroking her forehead. Repeating his mantra over and over again, softly into her ear.

Maya pulls back and looks at James. His wide, lovely eyes are full of such certainty and conviction that Maya can't help feeling calmed. Her breaths regulate and the shaking of her legs slows down. Tears leave tracks down her cheeks, telltale stripes cleansing away the pollution they hadn't realised enveloped them, and Maya looks into James' eyes and lowers her voice, as if this box is a priest's confessional.

'I just want to get off this bus, James,' she sobs. 'I want to get off this bus and go home. I think I want to have a baby.'

My Travels with Train Man

So that stunning wedding I told you about? Turns out not every day in India is like that. Hotel rooms don't all have slipper baths, chocolates on plump pillows and towels fashioned into swans. Life isn't an inexhaustible buffet of pani puri, bhel and gulab jamun, served on silver platters that never seem to dwindle. Men in colourful kurtas don't just break out into a dance. Women in turquoise, fuchsia and saffron-hued saris don't stride in glorious formation on every street corner. Life isn't like a Bollywood movie. The Indian wedding – my introduction to this wonderful, polarising, beautiful, noisy, hectic country – gave me false hope, and the reality is, some days are hard. The noise, the begging, the pollution... just getting from A to B feels like a slog of packed trains and pushing;

English is widely spoken, yet every conversation seems to end in a misunderstanding. And if one more person launches a red spitwad (called paan, apparently, which doesn't make it any more appealing) onto my shoes, I'll cry. It's a good thing Train Man has the ability to make everything OK.

We eventually came down from our kettle-drum-thumping high and checked into what's becoming more standard Indian accommodation – the mid-range hotel. It's cheap, yes, somewhat less palatial than our first experience: more Marigold Hotel than Maharajah's residence – and I admit it sucks a bit having been spoiled. But Train Man has been very gallant about it and is getting stuck into backpacking the way I ought to. And he does a nightly sweep of our past-their-best hotel rooms for bugs, which is both heroic and sexy.

We're now in Agra, where there seem to be an awful lot of bugs, but one thing has made it all worthwhile: a glimmer of our former palatial existence, in the most beautiful palace of them all, the Taj Mahal.

We set our alarms at 3 a.m. so we could see it before the crowds, almost blue in the serenity of sunrise. 'A teardrop on the cheek of eternity,' my dad told me before we started this trip. And that it certainly is. We walked around the shrine built by Shah Jahan as a memorial for his third wife Mumtaz Mahal, who died giving birth to their fourteenth child in 1631. I gazed across at Train Man and wondered if he would do such a thing for me, if we were to ever have fourteen children. It's a bigger ask than clearing cockroaches from our bedroom, I guess, so we walked around in awe before we went to find some chana from a street vendor and to catch up on our sleep.

But two strange things have happened, dear reader, since we came to India. 1) We've both put on weight. This Delhi belly thing is a crock, which means all of the amazing ghee-fried goods we're eating are clinging firmly to my thighs. And 2) I'm clucky. It happened somewhere between Udaipur and Bundi, on a bus journey that was more traumatic than quaint (I'm still too upset to write up the experience of sleeping in a coffin, the feeling of being buried alive for eight hours, but I will one day, I'm sure). But I looked into Train Man's warm eyes as I feared for my life, put my earbuds in my ear and turned on shuffle on my battered old iPod Nano. Kings Of Leon, 'Knocked Up'. First it made me realise I want a baby, then it made me cry all night. Uh-oh.

13

Nena sits in the Nena-shaped hole at one end of the sofa, feeding Ava, and wonders if she's ever going to get up, its gravitational pull is so strong. Not that she's going anywhere in a hurry. Her mother, Victoria, sits at the other end, in the space for Tom or guests, draped elegantly as she gazes at her granddaughter, still wearing her cream wool coat and Gucci loafers. BBC News is muted on the television opposite them.

'Darling, I think you should do whatever you want. It's *your* body.'

Nena kicks off her slippers, accidentally pushing her copy of *Esprit* magazine onto the floor.

'The health visitor was a bit judgy, said she's too young. World Health Organisation says six months. Nazis.'

'Oh, bother to them!' says Victoria, curling her already slightly upturned nose. 'You're her mother, you have to do what's best for you. Happy mama, happy baby, I always thought. Anyway, I'm sure I weaned you around four months. She's almost that.'

Hmmm, not really, closer to three.

Nena rubs her brow but doesn't say anything.

'What does Tom say about it all?'

'Well, he can't even remember how old Arlo was, but Kate says she weaned him at six months.'

'Oh.'

'He wants me to do whatever I want, but I feel bad.' Nena looks at the blue veins running through her light brown breast. 'I just can't keep up with production. She always bloody wants feeding, day and night. Mostly at night.'

'Then don't.'

Victoria puts a pale hand on Nena's grey marl pyjama bottoms. Looking at her mother's elegant fingers, with their familiar lines and rings, gives Nena a sense of comfort. They're the hands that rubbed her back when she was sick as a child; the hands that clapped proudly – if demurely – when Nena was earning awards in ballet, tap and swing. The hands that softly stroked Nena's long black hair when she was crying in hospital about the enormity of motherhood.

'How did you cope?'

'I gave you bottles, darling. I was back at the

Ballet within three months; I had to be fit enough to perform, mentally agile enough to memorise five shows at a time. I couldn't be up all night, surrounded by... this.' Victoria gestures to the mountain of baby paraphernalia, swamping the light symmetry of the Edwardian flat. 'Why don't you give her formula? It really isn't a crime and you've done so well to feed for this long.'

Nena looks down and strokes the eyelashes of Ava's closed eyes as she suckles.

'Formula is much better these days than it was in the eighties, and you turned out fine. I mean, I couldn't have functioned without formula and without help. That's why your father sent for Avó. She was a pain in the backside, but by golly she helped with you.'

Nena thinks of her grandma. Her shapeless floral dresses. The folds on the tops of her arms. Her round tummy and little thin legs beneath it. How she, a Brazilian peasant, and her mother, principal dancer at the Royal Ballet, couldn't have been more different. She smiles and remembers her fondly.

'Ahhh, Ava would have loved her,' Nena says with a wistful smile, as she lifts her baby to her shoulder and tries to bring up a burp.

'Avó would have loved Ava!'

Nena rests Ava on her back against her lap and moves her legs gently in circles, to help ease the wind in her stomach. 'You've got teeny-tiny legs like Avó!'

Ava looks up at her mother, smiles and farts, making Nena jump, but not laugh.

'You surprised me!'

'Good girl, bravo!' applauds her grandmother, still not that keen to get stuck in.

Nena looks at the digital clock on the tickertape on the TV. It's 4.48 p.m. and there's brand new *Real Housewives of Orange County* at five, although Nena is too embarrassed to admit to her mother, either that she watches it or that she punctuates her day by it. *Real Housewives* is her cue to throw on some clothes, to make it look like she's been up and doing, so Tom doesn't worry about her when he gets home.

'Come on, why don't we go for a walk, darling? We could go to the park.'

Nena doesn't want to go for a walk. It's almost 5 p.m. on a cold February afternoon, and the eternal darkness outside is not worth getting changed or a change bag packed for.

'It's OK, Mama. Tom will be home soon. He'll want to hear all about our day, won't he sweetcheeks?'

Victoria arches an eyebrow as she looks around the flat with disappointment and Ava's cheeks flush red as she passes more than wind.

Nena wonders how she can flip from BBC News to ITVBe without her mother noticing. She looks along the green sofa, but Victoria is gazing at the silent news. Another story about the French researcher who's gone missing in Thailand or Laos or Vietnam or wherever it was she went missing around Christmas. When she didn't make her flight home.

'Ghastly news,' Victoria says to herself. 'Her poor parents.'

Victoria looks away from the television and catches sight of *Esprit* peeping out from under the sofa and picks it up. Emma Thompson exudes confidence on the cover under a cool crop of white-blonde hair and Victoria wonders if she's had any work done.

'Oh, how's Maya getting on?'

She starts flicking through the magazine with purpose.

'Good, I think. We haven't Skyped in a few weeks, but it all sounds like a hoot according to the column.'

'Bravo, Maya!' says Victoria, as she flips past Golden Globe beauty, recipes with aubergines, and handbags shot in an American desert before she gets to *My Travels with Train Man*, three quarters of the way back.

'Although according to that she's got clucky,' Nena adds with a doubtful brow. 'Don't know why she wants a baby now, not when she's got the world at her feet. Maybe she just made it up for drama.'

'Must be Ava's influence,' says Victoria, looking from the magazine to her grandchild. 'I know I'm biased, but she is astonishing. And definitely the most beautiful baby that was ever born.'

'Fancy changing her nappy then?'

'No, darling, don't be ridiculous.'

14

February 2016, Kerala, India

'It just would have been nice if you'd warned me,' James says, before sipping through a straw that's jutting out of a raw coconut. 'I thought you weren't going to write anything too... personal... in there. You know, keep it light.'

James sits at the round rattan dining table in the living room of their houseboat, moored into a siding of the Keralan backwaters. Palm trees trim the thin pathways along the wide, flat expanse of dark water. On one side, a red flag with a white hammer and sickle is tied to two posts like an advertising billboard. Frogs leap from lily pad to lily pad; a cormorant airs its wings on a branch.

For three days, Maya and James have been holed up on the *Arayil*, a houseboat slowly navigating the canals and lagoons of the backwaters. It would have been romantic were it not for *Arayil*'s captain, Sumon, drivers Jineash and Manoharam, and chef Pradeesh, all keeping them company and wanting to learn more about Maya and James: what life is like for them in England, whether they also love cricket, what they eat for breakfast at home, whether Leicester City really can win the league. In the evenings, Sumon moors the boat and the crew leave Maya and James to it, not before they roll down the plastic sides of the back deck, in order to minimise the mosquito bites at night.

Pradeesh is such a fine chef, James and Maya were almost tempted to take him up on his offer of moving in with them back in Hazelworth.

'We don't really do that in England,' said James apologetically. 'Not us anyway. Although we wish we could.'

Now the crew have disembarked for the final night, and James and Maya are feasting with their fingers on fried fish, curry, rice, sambal and porotta from banana-leaf plates. They each have a large coconut that Pradeesh proudly hacked down from a palm tree as they moored, from which they're drinking the sweet watery milk.

Maya's face gets hot as she works out how she can keep this conversation light – everything felt so dark that night on the bus – so she shields her eyes with her own large green coconut as she takes a sip.

Maya had been completely blindsided by her overwhelming desire to be a mother. It's not that babies weren't part of her plan: she'd mothered Jacob and Florian and changed their terrycloth nappies when she was just a little girl. She adored her nephews and felt happiest blowing raspberries on their chubby stomachs. And she was nothing but over the moon for Nena when Nena told her she was pregnant – and loved Ava from the first moment she met her. But that all seemed safely stored under 'save for later'. Something she and James might think about if their trip went well. Not once, as she packed and prepped, did she think it would be an issue on a trip she pushed for, and she surprised herself as much as she surprised James during that bleak journey to Bundi.

While she tried to forget about her wobble, she forgot that James is her biggest fan, and when he's in an internet cafe, emailing Dominic or Petra, or his mum and dad, he visits *Esprit* online, to see how the columns look when they're published, given they can't see a hard copy of the magazine on their travels.

Maya had conveniently forgotten to show James that column before she sent it.

'It's not *that* personal,' she says, putting down her coconut and scooping chutney to her mouth from a papad. 'I didn't fully tell the readers how I lost my shit about it on the bus.'

'But you've put it out there, in black and white, that you want a baby; that I don't want one.'

'I didn't say that.'

'You may as well have.'

'But you don't.'

James doesn't argue with that.

Maya can feel beads of sweat forming on her freckled nose. Perhaps it's the chutney Pradeesh warned her about.

'But you make me look like a bit of an arsehole.'

'No I don't. I said you're a hero who gets rid of cockroaches and you have a tendency to make everything right with the world. And you're not an arsehole, I would never say you were.'

James shrugs.

'It was just a blip. I was just inferring that we are unaligned. We *were* unaligned.'

'Unaligned?'

James' eyes look wider and glassier. There is an exasperation in his face that Maya has never noticed before.

'We're travelling, Maya, *you* wanted us to come on this trip. I cancelled all my bookings so we could do this.'

Maya wonders why James is so upset, when really it should be her who's feeling cut up.

'It's fine, we went through this in Bundi,' she says placatingly. 'It was just a wobble.'

'Just a wobble? Honey, you listened to your iPod and you cried all night.'

'I was panicking in that coffin. Look, you don't want a baby and I don't want a baby, so we're all good and all aligned now. And I won't write anything too personal from now on. Not without checking with you first, yeah?'

Maya tries to sound breezy as she studies James' face.

James smiles gratefully, his dimple sinking into his left cheek. Maya can't resist getting up out of her rattan chair and walking round to him. She plonks herself across his lap and kisses the dimple repeatedly, as if she expects to fill it with kisses; to smooth it out. Smooth everything out. James' arms hang down by his side, his topless torso is warm and his skin smells sweet, so Maya kisses that too and looks at him cheerily.

'Anyway, look, mosquitoes aside, we're in paradise, and I've found my stride with this travelling malarkey. Nothing can ruin it for us now.'

15

'It's been six weeks since 27-year-old French national Manon Junot went missing in Thailand and authorities are under increasing pressure to make arrests after releasing Vorapat Tanakrit, the caretaker at the Lemon Tree Hotel in Chiang Rai, where Ms Junot was last registered, without charge. Tanakrit was the last person to be spotted with Ms Junot, after he was filmed on CCTV comforting her in an alleyway in the town on the twentieth of December. There have been no other leads since. Her anguished father and stepmother, who first became concerned when she didn't make contact at Christmas, raised the alarm when Manon didn't make her flight back to Paris on New Year's Day. Today the family made another heartfelt plea at a press conference in their home town in the Alsace region of France.'

A BANNER ACROSS THE SCREEN READS 'ANDRE JUNOT, FATHER'.

'We ask anyone who might have been staying at the Lemon Tree Hotel between the eighteenth of December 2015 and the first of January 2016 to think about whether they saw Manon in or around the hotel, the gardens, or even the town. Whether it was an interaction in the kitchen, or a drink in a local bar… she's a memorable girl, she has a charm and a great way of making people feel special, so we would like to think some other tourists or workers in Chiang Rai or elsewhere along the tourist route might have remembered where she was, what state she was in. My beautiful Manon has a face you don't forget.'

THE MAN BREAKS DOWN IN TEARS. THE SCREEN CUTS TO A BLONDE CORRESPONDENT IN THE FIELD.

'The family are also urging police in Laos to get involved after tourists in the capital, Vientiane, reported a French woman "behaving erratically" in a bakery in the city in December. Thai police chief Somsak Kongduang, who is leading the investigation, believes Junot had left Laos and re-entered Thailand overland at the Chiang Khong/Huay Xai border in the north on December fifteenth but would like to talk to police about her time there.'

THE SCREEN CUTS TO THE FACE OF POLICE CHIEF KONGDUANG.

'Our friends in Laos are reluctant to get involved because Miss Junot had already re-entered Thailand, and border authorities have no record of her leaving the country again,

so I understand they are not keen to open up a grand investigation there. But we do ask for help with information and CCTV, to see if we can learn anything about her time there.'

CUTS BACK TO BLONDE CORRESPONDENT TALKING TO CAMERA.

'With so little help and so few sightings, the Thai police now have to unpick what happened on the days between Ms Junot arriving back into Thailand and her arrival at the Lemon Tree Hotel in Chiang Rai three days later.

'In a transient route that's full of Western backpackers, someone must have befriended a French woman travelling on her own. Who did she meet? And what information might they have about her plans to get from Chiang Rai back to Bangkok? If indeed, she planned to at all. This is Heidi Adler, for CNN, in Bangkok.'

16

February 2016, London, England

Tom walks through the revolving glass doors of New Broadcasting House, a vertiginous curved glass building that looks like it might spin into orbit, swipes his ID pass and saunters through a second set of glass doors. The security guard gives him a nod.

'Morning, Steve.' Tom flashes his friendliest smile before walking briskly up a flight of stairs, two at a time, past a newsroom, where a man sits at a desk talking to camera, through three sets of doors and along a labyrinthine corridor, past soundproof booths and tiny studios, glass offices and along another higgledy-piggledy corridor, out into an open office of hot desks where the Children's department tend to convene. There's a small kitchen area at one end of it, that looks out onto the cul-de-sac of the BBC entrance, and Tom has a quick glimpse out of it, to see the view he so loves in this corner of central London. He looks at his watch and walks back to the kitchen.

It's not even 9 a.m., but already there are brown circles on the cream laminate worktop. Teaspoons wobble in little brown pools. A sign reading PLEASE WASH UP YOUR DIRTY CUPS sits behind a sink housing three dirty cups. As Tom surveys the coffee machine, trying to decipher how it works, he curses himself for not stopping at Caffe Nero to pick up an Americano on his way in.

He looks at his watch again, having not properly registered the time a second ago, realising he doesn't have time to go back out, or to find someone who will get him a coffee, and hopes his 9 a.m. meeting with the Head of Planning will be catered.

Did I ask Nicky to book breakfast?

Did I ask Nicky to book a room?

'Shit,' Tom says out loud, as he searches the coffee machine for clues.

'Need a hand?' says a soft low voice.

Tom looks up to see Rosa Samarasekera peering around the corner, her cheek leaning on a hand that's propped against the kitchen's only wall. Her eyes are ridiculously large, her mustard polo neck making her chiselled face and long angles look like a carved bust. Tom almost doesn't recognise her without her white coat on.

'Dr Rosa!' Tom gives up on the machine and leans back against the sink, crossing his arms but keeping one eye on his watch. 'Thanks, but no. I've realised I'm not that desperate for watery coffee, I'll hold out. How's it all going?' He looks up, his blue eyes twinkling under the strip lighting.

'Great, thank you. I've just been meeting with Props to run through everything for *Headlice*. Comedy giant comb? Check.'

Tom strokes his bald head.

'Yeah, sorry, not much help with that one. But I've watched the rushes on *Poo* and you're amazing. You're doing a great job.'

Rosa smiles. 'Really? You think?'

'Yeah, for sure; you're a natural. I'm so pleased we're going for the second series.'

'Oh me too.'

Rosa lingers on the crow's feet and smile lines around Tom's eyes, and he is too polite and feels too self-conscious to look at his watch again, to check how little time he has before his meeting.

'Actually, Tom, I was wondering if I could have a chat at some point, when it's convenient?'

Tom searches Rosa's face. 'Of course, is everything OK?'

'Yes great, it's just…' Rosa's lashes sweep downwards. 'This is all so new to me – and so different to Guy's. I know my way around A&E, but all this.' She looks up.

'It's wonderful, but it's crazy. I would just appreciate your wisdom and knowledge – a few pointers really...'

Rosa's eyes, dark and glimmering, look hopeful and Tom thinks of Nena sitting on the sofa back home.

'We could go for a *proper* coffee?' she smiles, her white teeth brightening up the dull kitchen area.

Tom scratches his head. 'I think that's a great idea. I'm busy today, but I'll have Nicky contact you. We'll find a time this week.'

'Oh that's wonderful. Thanks so much.' Rosa's cheeks blush pink.

'But really, Rosa, you're doing an awesome job. You're the best.'

My Travels with Train Man

Namaste, India. You have been truly wonderful. From opulent palaces to cows crossing the road; from the colourful ceremonies and funerals at the ghats to dolphins diving into the murky waters at Fort Cochin. You were brutal and beautiful and everything in between – and more than I ever could have anticipated. And despite what everyone had warned us ('Great food, hideous Delhi belly…'), neither Train Man nor I got sick once. Well, nothing that wasn't self-inflicted by too much Kingfisher, Cobra and chana…

So here we are in beautiful Thailand, and getting here felt like going back to the future. We boarded a plane in the beige dust and 1970s décor of the Indira Gandhi International Airport in Delhi (complete with actual piles of paper at the check-in desk and one of those Rolodex flight departures boards that flickers in old movies) and disembarked to change planes in low-lit and futuristic Singapore, which was so clean, so slick and so minimalist, it felt as though we could have been on the International Space Station in the year 3000. Another swift flight brought us to Bangkok, and, wow, what a city.

BKK as it seems to be called on billboards and in bars is majestic yet fun; gilded yet clammy; energising yet tiring – and it has shopping opportunities aplenty. It's been hard to resist looking in the multiple malls many of my friends raved about, but my capsule wardrobe is fit to bursting, and backpackers don't do McCartney or Miyake anyway. Not unless they're fakes. So, we sidestepped the shopping for Wat Pho, one of the most serene of the many temples around the Grand Palace, whose golden spikes prod the balmy skies above Bangkok like spears, whose reflections glimmer in the Chao Phraya river, the city's artery, when the moon is up. Wat Pho is sometimes called the Temple of the Reclining Buddha for its 46m golden statue, which fills a grand room. It's a peaceful world, away from the flying phlegm of India... until us tourists ruin it by trying to get a shot that does the Reclining Buddha justice (trust me, it's impossible).

Bangkok has felt so refreshing. We even went to the cinema. Bollywood gods Amitabh Bachchan and Shah Rukh Khan still have my heart, but we were craving a good high-octane Hollywood movie that wasn't four hours long, so we plumped for The Force Awakens *at the mall. It felt like Date Night – not just because of the double armchair, the big tub of popcorn and the cosy blanket. It was so special, as it's something Train Man and I have barely had the chance to do even before we started this trip.*

Now we're at the beach and I feel like we've finally found our stride. I've got so good at this backpacking malarkey, I've forgotten the hormonal panic that hit me on a night bus to Bundi. I've stopped thinking about how much I wanted a baby – although Thai babies must be the cutest in the world. And it's so idyllic, I'm tempted to suggest we stay here.

Our days are lazy and leisurely, spent lying on pristine sand and eating Magnums – and Train Man is looking even hotter than Leonardo DiCaprio in The Beach *– his skin is as deep brown and as bronze as his eyes, and I'm just so… happy. The only trouble in paradise? Choosing whether to go Almond or Double Chocolate Caramel – and whose turn it is to go to the beach bar to buy them. We're off to a Full Moon party this week. Is twenty-nine too old for fluoro make-up, glow sticks and buckets of SangSom? I'm not sure I have the energy, but I'll report back…*

17

March 2016, Krabi, Thailand

Maya reclines on her back, propped up on her elbows, as she looks out to sea. She has seen some stunning beaches in her almost-thirty years, from Sennen Cove in Cornwall to Bocas Del Toro in Central America, but this one takes the prize. The water flips from crystal clear over pale cream sand the colour of ground almonds to a stripe of mint green that hugs the Andaman Coast. Craggy karsts jut out of the water covered in lush green foliage. A fishing boat laps gently against the shore. Sounds of splashing and chatter provide a tender soundtrack as James drifts in and out of sleep. The only thing missing is the Almond Magnum that Maya and James have become somewhat partial to from the drinks hut at the back of the beach.

I'll go get one in a minute, Maya thinks, as she looks at a young girl, diligently doing cartwheels along the shore, trying to straighten her legs to applause from her proud parents.

Shit. The call.

Maya looks at James' analogue watch as he stirs from his slumber, but she can't see what time it is for the reflection of the sun on its face.

'Baby,' Maya tries to whisper. 'What time is it?' She puts her hand on his wrist and gently angles the face away, but still the sun is too bright.

Relinquishing their phones took some getting used to. At first it felt like they'd forgotten something, like they shut the front door and left their keys inside. But the momentary panic soon passed; they found other ways to fill those moments when looking at their phone screens would be the customary thing to do.

Three months in and the lack of phone is liberating. Although Maya always wonders what the bloody time is. As a result, she's become adept at scouting out clocks in shops, cafes or the corner of the television when she's found a local-time news channel. She's accustomed to glancing at James' wrist, or craning her neck to look at the phone in the hands of the person in front of her in a queue. Most of the time it doesn't matter; James is the timekeeper when there are trains, planes and buses to catch. It does matter now though, when he's asleep and she has an appointment with her editor in London.

James opens one eye and tries to focus. He looks to the sky, pretending to be able to tell the time from it.

'Hmmm, about three? Four?' He stirs, rolls over and sits up, scratching the sweat on his growing stubble. 'I think I need some more sun cream on my back, will you sort me out?' he mumbles.

'No, but what is the actual time? I have a Skype call with Amy Appleyard at three thirty, our time.'

James stretches, yawns and looks at the brown and orange watch on his left arm. It's old and barely splash-proof – its hands don't even glow in the dark – but he likes it. 'Three twenty, you're fine.'

James smiles and Maya melts. His olive skin has gone a gorgeous shade of golden and his smell – he smells as sweet as frangipani – is sublime. Or is that the factor-fifteen oil he's been slathering all over himself which needs reapplying?

Maya stretches and moves across to James' sunbed, drizzling oil on his shoulders and back, before rubbing it in brusquely and wiping her hands on her tummy. She stands and realigns herself, tying her sarong around her white bikini like a bath sheet. She needs to get out of the sun anyway. Her brown hair is saltwater curly and turning golden along the baby fronds at her forehead and the waves at her tips; new freckles are bursting through her skin like popping corn.

'Done. Protected. And you smell edible, I could eat you up.' Maya smiles. 'But I have to go. Amy wanted to chat about "something", which sounds scary. Hopefully it's about using your travel pics…'

Maya ties her hair in a messy bun on top of her head and grabs her sunglasses and purse.

'Want me to check your email too?'

'Nah. It'll only be something I either won't want to take on, or I'll want to take on and can't.'

'Ignore it as long as you can, I reckon,' says Maya, with a disconcerting feeling. She wishes she didn't have to have this conversation with Amy.

James looks skyward and puckers up, so Maya can lean down and plant a kiss on him.

'Love you, honey.'

'Love you too. Be right back.' Maya walks off with a wiggle before stopping to turn around. 'Almond?'

James smiles. 'You read my mind.'

In the small beach hut snack shop, Maya is relieved to see the one computer is vacant.

Phew.

She gestures to it and the man behind the counter nods, so she sits down. Machinery whirls, a fan blows, and Maya adjusts her face in the frame of the screen.

She starts the call. To her surprise, Amy answers straight away; her feathered blonde hair and square face fill the screen. She is sitting at her desk at the newspaper giant's HQ in East London, issues of *Esprit* lining the shelves behind her. Issues Maya has only seen online so far but would love to get her hands on. There's the TV presenter celebrating her fiftieth birthday with balloons and a frou-frou skirt. The pop star opening up over her split with her rugby player boyfriend. The reality show judge getting an edgy makeover. All of the stars face forwards on the cover, all look over Amy Appleyard's shoulder, all peer at Maya as if she's in a bizarre interview.

Amy stares into the lens. 'Maya? Oh, you're there. Hi, how are you?'

Maya feels uneasy about this meeting. She's never had a meeting in a bikini before, so she lowers her head, trying to cut her white bandeau bikini top out of the picture, but now it looks like she's naked, so she adjusts her sarong just to prove she isn't, tying it in a bow at the back of her neck.

It's not like she doesn't know I'm at the beach.

'Good thanks,' Maya says, knowing Amy won't want actual specifics. 'You?'

'Great. So the column's been going well in that we're happy with the mechanics of it, but we need a change in tack.'

Maya nods politely at the camera, trying to measure her face so she doesn't look as anxious as she feels.

'It's all a bit… nice. A bit travelogue. A bit… smug, dare I say? You're getting on too well.'

Amy definitely said 'nice' as if she meant 'dreary'.

Maya tries not to look hurt. 'Oh, sorry.'

'It's just *Esprit* readers really aren't that interested in temples per se. They want to know what chic outfit you were wearing when you went into the temple; how Instagrammable it all looked; whether your new Asian diet is making you feel so smoking hot, you're slinking around that temple like a supermodel on a shoot; whether you and Train Man had a blazing row just before you went into the temple, and the sexual tension was so much, all you really wanted to do was tear each other's clothes off. That kind of thing.'

'Oh,' says Maya, feeling like a disappointment.

Amy leans back and taps her Montblanc pen against her cheek. Maya can now see she's wearing a white shirt with a black pussy-bow tie.

'How are those baby cravings working out for you? Still desperate to make a mini Train Man? He's not ready, no?'

'Erm, it's not a problem any more,' says Maya cheerily, suppressing the urge boring from her belly button to the back of her spine, making her slump into the plastic seat, sweaty under the parts of her thighs the sarong doesn't cover.

'Oh...' says Amy, not hiding her disappointment.

Maya's heart sinks.

'Is there any way we can spice things up a bit? Make it more *Esprit*?' Amy's eyes widen as she has an idea. 'Or could you talk about how much weight you're losing, maybe we go down the body route, make it a health and well-being column if the relationship is too nicey-nicey?'

She definitely meant dreary then.

Maya feels the comfort of coconut curries and Almond Magnums around those sweaty thighs and holds onto that thought.

'Hmm, well I reckon Train Man and I might be the only people to have put on weight in India. All that ghee and gulab jamun – and we didn't even get the...' Maya stops herself.

Amy narrows her eyes and scrutinises Maya. 'Really?'

'Really. Train Man even has a hint of a love handle, and he's always been lean. Never had to think about what he eats.'

Amy widens her eyes again. 'That's it, yes.' She makes a fist and does a little punch in the air to herself. Then turns to the left, where Maya knows Amy's PA, Danni, sits at a desk beyond her open door. 'Danni, can you ask Mirry what the name of that spa was again?' she shouts, before turning back to the camera. 'Miranda, our features ed, went on a press trip recently, to one of those intense Thai spas.'

'Oh right.'

'Poo Camp, she called it.'

Maya's freckles flush red. 'Poo Camp?'

'Yeah, she hasn't written it up yet. And doesn't have time to for that matter. So perhaps we can use it for your column instead. It's this pretty full-on spa on some idyllic Thai island or something. Clay shakes, 4 a.m. yoga. Fasting. Self-administered colonics. That kind of thing.'

'Self-administered whats?'

'I didn't think it would be right for you, but actually, if you're carrying a bit of weight and unhappy…'

'I'm not unhappy.'

'Well, I think this could really work, if you're game. It could be brilliant. You and Train Man, in it together, facing a challenge, trying to slim down and reset your chakras and stuff.'

'Sounds… lovely?'

Amy calls out again to someone off screen, someone beyond Danni's desk. 'Where? Koh what?' She turns back to face Maya. 'One of the islands. I'll get Danni to mail them and set it up. Can you get there this week?'

Amy's assistant appears in the edge of the shot. 'Hey, Maya,' she waves.

Maya waves back. 'Hi.'

Danni walks off.

Maya is thrown. She doesn't like the sound of this, but she doesn't want to lose her column either. She knows she's only getting a fraction of what the celebrity chef gets for his weekly column on the double-page spread after hers, but the pay from her weekly dispatches is a nice bit of pocket money for the trip. And they only wangled the Keralan houseboat for free because she agreed to write about it in *Esprit*. They never could have afforded it otherwise. Plus, there's the hope that Amy might want to use some of James' photos in the travel section…

'Well, we were going to head north, to visit an elephant sanctuary.'

Amy leans forward again and looks into the lens with the 'Really?' gaze of a woman who doesn't have a bleeding heart. She needs to perk up this column, on the newspaper tycoon's orders, and it's too early to can it after just ten weeks. 'Think about it, Maya,' she says bullishly. 'These things cost thousands. People flock from all over the world to change their bodies and their lives, and all in paradise. You and… er, Train Man, are getting the opportunity to do it for free. As long as you namecheck the spa.'

'I guess. I mean, brilliant.'

'Great.' Amy clicks her Montblanc pen and throws it down on her desk, satisfied that she's come up with a solution. 'If you can do a pre-spa column, setting it all up nicely, then a couple from Poo Camp, if you can stretch it out, and then one after, to say how all that hunger almost broke you, but at least you're skinny kind of thing… Could be jolly.'

'Or it could actually break us,' laughs Maya nervously.

'Here's hoping!' Amy says with a laugh.

She's joking, right?

Maya becomes aware of her thighs again, squeezing together on the sweaty plastic seat. Maybe it's not such a bad idea. She's not been able to run as much as she'd like to since their trip started; it was hard to go out alone in India and in some places it didn't feel like the right thing to do – and Pradeesh's feasts – all of the food in India – have made Maya's size 10 capsule wardrobe fit rather snugly. She doesn't have any roomier clothes to relax into. Even James, tall and lean, is getting a little softer. Within the steamy confines of the mosquito net of their hostel bed last night, Maya definitely noticed a novel squidgyness on James' hips that wasn't there before.

'OK, let's do it. Poo Camp it is.'

It can't be as bad as all that.

'Great, I'll get Danni to book it all up and send you dates and details. It'll be wonderful. Although rather you than me.'

At the counter, Maya opens her coin purse to gesture paying for her internet time. A bead of sweat runs down the back of her neck. The man behind the desk looks harangued in his cramped corner as he's joined by his wife and a chubby baby wearing only a nappy.

'Forty baht, miss.'

A woman speaking English with a German-sounding accent walks in and asks for the vacant computer Maya has just finished with, and the man behind the counter turns and snaps at his wife. Or at least Maya thinks he's snapping, but hopes for harmony's sake it's just a cultural peculiarity. The Thai woman walks around the counter and gently but determinedly places her baby into Maya's arms so she can log in and start the machine for the German tourist.

'Hi,' the tourist nods at Maya.

'Hi,' Maya nods back awkwardly, unsure as to what to do with a stranger's baby in her arms.

She looks at the baby looking up at her. Maya thinks he's a boy but isn't sure why. He has a round face, shiny, inquisitive eyes and a tuft of hair sticking up from his crown like a garden gnome wearing a black hat.

'Aren't you gorgeous?' Maya says, resisting the desire to blow a raspberry on his Buddha-soft belly. The baby and Maya both look at each other, mesmerised by the sight in front of them, and search each other's eyes. 'Aren't you lovely?'

The man behind the counter doesn't engage with Maya, he's just waiting for the forty baht, which now sits in Maya's purse on the counter.

The trickle of sweat runs under the clasp of Maya's bikini top and down her spine as her eyes well up. The purity and beauty of the baby in her arms weakens Maya's core, and she has to hold on tight, through fear she might melt into the floor and drop him. 'You are just a treasure!' she says, lowering her face in his hair as she kisses his head, inhaling his sweet scent and hiding her tears.

The baby's mother returns and nods gratefully as she takes him. He kicks his legs in joy mid-air as Maya feels the emptiness of the space he filled. She smiles and looks down, focusing on the money in her purse.

Deep breaths.

'Forty baht was it?'

The man nods.

Maya goes to hand over a note but pulls it back as she spots the freezer compartment next to the till. A happy distraction.

'Oh, and one Almond Magnum please,' she says, wiping an eye as she leans into the soothing chill of the freezer with a white love heart on it. Rummaging blind as she looks up at the ceiling, until she finds the comforting, familiar shape. She grabs one. Then she grabs another.

Fuck it. I need a pick-me-up. And if we're going to go to Poo Camp, we're going out in style.

18

March 2016, London, England

'Maya is SUCH a lucky cow – first the Full Moon party and now a luxe detox spa. *In Thailand*,' says Nena, throwing the magazine on the floor. 'I could so use that right now,' she adds glibly under her breath.

'I know, I read it before CrossFit.' Tom is crouched in front of the shoe caddy in the hallway, putting his trainers back on a rack and searching for his fresh khaki New Balance kicks that are too nice to do exercise in. A patch of hair rises from above the belt of his jeans as he bends over and Nena looks over from the sofa through the open doorway with disdain.

'When did you go to CrossFit?'

Arlo pads into the room with a cuddly penguin and gently rests it on Ava's shoulder. Ava is sitting upright in a bouncy chair, arms flailing at the colourful animals hanging in front of her, so she bats the penguin onto the floor and Arlo scowls. It's Sunday, a weekend Arlo is spending with his dad, Nena and baby sister, and he's chomping at the bit to go out.

'Daddy, can we go to the park nowwwwwww?'

'I'm just getting my trainers on, sweetheart. Can you go and do a wee?'

Nena sighs. 'The Haven it's called. Oh, to be heading to The Haven, hey Arlo?'

Arlo looks up blankly, then pads out to go to the toilet.

Tom pulls up his jeans and brings his trainers into the room to put them on.

'Are you coming, Nen? The blossom's out in Clissold Park. Looks lovely.'

Nena wants to suggest to Tom that *he* take the kids out. By himself. Give her half an hour to turn their bathroom into a haven.

Why don't you just go?

When Nena does galvanise herself to get out of the flat, to wheel the buggy to Sainsbury's, or take Ava to be weighed at the baby clinic, she always sees dads out alone with their progeny, proudly walking with papooses hugging their chests. It makes Nena feel annoyed, angry that Tom never instigates this or even makes such a suggestion. She thought he'd be more hands-on, especially given he's done it before.

Nena looks around the mess of the room, wondering whether to suggest he just go, or do the wholesome thing and join them. Nena sees *Esprit* magazine on the floor and Maya's photo at the top of the column. The picture was shot in a studio in London Bridge before she left, but in it she already looks bronzed and happy and... dare Nena think it, *smug*?

'Come on, sweetheart, Arlo needs to get out, the air will do us all good – the papers can wait...'

The papers can wait?

'Don't judge me, Tom.'

'I'm not judging you. I'm just saying, let's get out, get some fresh air.'

'You're judging me for not getting out enough. You're making me feel lazy.'

Tom is too kind to say it's Nena making herself feel lazy.

Nena doesn't like how she sounds; she doesn't like the look of puzzlement on Tom's bemused and confused face. This whole thing is confusing. They never argued until they became parents, and Nena assumes it must be her fault, because Tom's already been through this.

I'm not a natural.

'I'm not judging you, babe. I just know you're happier when you are out. When you've got some crisp sunshine on your beautiful face. Come on. I've packed the change bag.'

For once.

'Don't be sad,' says a little voice from the toilet, between tinkling sounds.

Tom and Nena look at each other, a smile breaks the tension.

'He's right, don't be sad.' Tom offers his hands to Nena, which she accepts sulkily, and he plants a kiss on her lips. He can tell she hasn't brushed her teeth yet today but decides not to remind her.

'I'm not sad I'm just... *knackered*. I could so use some sunshine on my face!' Nena chooses to ignore Maya, looking up at the room from the floor, and buries her head into Tom's chest. 'Some sleep. Some indulgence. I am so low on the pecking order, I need someone to rub my back. To feed me. And then I read that Maya's biggest problem is she's about to go to a spa for a week. *I* need to go to a spa for a week.'

'OK, I'll take the kids, you have a bubble bath. We'll stop at Sainsbury's and get roast stuff too, yeah?'

Nena feels bad, yet relieved. 'Is that OK?'

'Of course it's OK.'

'I just wish you'd suggest it.'

'I did suggest it! Look, I'll go out – Arlo, grab your moon boots. Take as long as you need. We'll go to the park and the shops, you have a bath.'

Nena lifts Ava out of the Jumperoo and slides her into her thick brown onesie with teddy bear ears, that's laid out among the newspapers on the floor.

'Her buggy's downstairs, yes?'

'Yep.'

Nena lifts Ava, kisses her on the nose, and rubs Arlo on the head. 'Have fun at the park.'

Tom takes Ava and the change bag. Arlo stands on the doormat in his coat and boots.

'Anyway,' Tom says, gesturing to the zip on his quilted jacket so Nena can do it up for him as his hands are now full. 'I read the column. That spa doesn't sound like luxury to me. Self-administered colonics? Sounds like hell.' He kisses Nena's cheek. 'Love you, have a nice bath. Have a rest, yes?'

Nena nods. 'Love you too.'

She closes the door and stares at her hand pressed up against it. The relief that surrounds her, the awareness that this is the biggest joy she's felt in weeks, makes her feel wretched.

19

March 2016, The Haven, Thailand

Standing in the spartan surroundings of their double room, the spa host, a man called Moon, with a shiny round face and a shirt with tigers in different sizes all over it, gives Maya and James the skinny on the week ahead.

'So, have a cleansing dinner tonight in the restaurant from our pre-cleanse menu – you have been eating clean for the past two to three days, yes?'

Maya looks at James guiltily. Last night they went to a Full Moon party on the beach around the bay two boats away and washed pizza and doughnuts down with SangSom and Coke, which they sipped from a bucket through straws. A look between them says Moon doesn't need to know this.

They nod.

'Yes. Eating clean,' they chime.

'So, at 7 a.m. you'll have your first bentonite clay shake; herbs at 8.30 a.m.; another shake at ten.'

'Oh goody,' says James, not completely on board with this whole thing. When Maya returned from the beach hut with the news that they were going to an intense detox spa where they would have to do self-administed colonic irrigations, James could tell she was trying to polish a turd by talking rapidly about how luxurious it would be. But he just about came around to the idea of a challenge.

'After your 1 p.m. shake and herbs, you'll have a lymphatic flush juice, another shake at four, and then straight into the colonic session in... here.'

Moon opens the door to the bathroom for the 'ta-da!' moment. His big reveal. It's what hardcore Haveners come from all over the world to experience: set up against the toilet is a bench, propped on an upturned bucket, leading on a slight decline to a toilet seat. Next to the high, wall-mounted cistern is a tall hanging structure on wheels, that looks like a cross between a triffid and a saline drip, from which hangs a huge bag of dark brown liquid. From the bag, a tube drops almost to the floor and is fastened with a bulldog clip. Luxe clinical detox this isn't.

Moon points to a cup next to the sink, with two plastic tubes standing inside, like toothbrushes. 'One with pink sticker for the lady; one with blue sticker for you, sir. Our staff will set up and clean away after each colonic flush – you will take it in turns – but make sure you use the right tip every time, or you exchange bum-bum germs.'

Maya burps up what feels like a little bit of sick mixed with SangSom, and wonders if she should run to the toilet, but it's right in front of her, making her feel worse.

'Those plastic tubes. In the toothbrush holder. Are they the…'

'Anal inserts, yes, ma'am.'

'And we keep our own anal inserts?' coughs James quietly, so no one else might hear.

'Oh yeah. Reusable. We think of the planet here. But you use your own, each day. We clean and return it back to cup for next day.'

Where will we put our toothbrushes?!

Moon enthusiastically hops and straddles the wooden board and lies on his back. His tiger shirt drapes beneath him a little. 'Staff will have put your tip onto the tube, resting on the colema board, so all you have to do is remove pants and edge down onto the tip.'

James and Maya stand aghast and horrified.

'Edge, edge, edge, until… bingo!' Moon mimes the action through his clothes. 'Then release clip to let the coffee solution fill you up. As your tummy swells, it might cramp a bit. It feels a bit like you need to…'

'Shit?' asks James.

'That's riiiiiight,' smiles Moon. 'Hold organic coffee solution in the bowel until you can't take any more, then...' With his two hands, he gestures an out-pouring.

Maya holds her hand to her mouth.

'When all done, have a look! The basket in the toilet bowl catches the bits if you want to look at them. Then tip them in the toilet and flush away. Ta-da!'

Moon seems to be a man who loves his job, but he's very earnest about it and doesn't seem to see the funny side in his-and-hers poo tubes next to the sink.

'What should we expect to find in there?' James asks nervously.

'Oh, you know. Sludge, some leafy matter, sweetcorn, an old boot...'

'What?' Maya gasps.

'I'm just joking. About the sweetcorn anyway.' Moon laughs, and James almost manages a smile too. 'Same thing for five days. No cheating. No food. Just clay shakes, lymph shakes, herbs and broth. Meditation and yoga will get you through.'

All Maya can think about is last night's pizza and how she hopes that might get her through. It was a dirty pepperoni of dubious meat provenance, bought from a little takeaway shack at the back of the beach, but, in hindsight, it tasted *good*. All the more when she compares it to the herbs and broth to come.

'I give lectures every evening over vegetable broth and wheatgrass shots, it's a good time to meet fellow fasters and exchange ideas.'

Maya knows what James is thinking. He has no intention of meeting fellow fasters and exchanging ideas. It all sounds ghastly to him. And Maya doesn't want to see the contents of her own basket, let alone talk to a stranger about the minutiae of theirs.

'What if I don't want to talk to anyone, Moon?' Maya asks.

'Not even your husband? That fine too.'

Moon leaves the room with a smile and wishes Maya and James a nice evening.

As the door shuts, Maya puts her head in her hands.

'Oh, baby! What have I done?'

'I don't know,' answers James, trying to sound upbeat. 'But we're here now. We'd better make the most of it.'

Maya can't believe it. Two years ago she was pining for this stranger on a train and now she's roped him into joining her in self-administered coffee colonics in their shared bathroom. She doesn't know whether to do a silent fist pump or run away, fast.

20

March 2016, London, England

Nena slumps back on the bench overlooking an empty tennis court in Clissold Park and lifts Ava out of her pram. Ava's cheeks are plump and Nena rests her lips on them, seeking comfort in the kisses she peppers her brown and pink face with. A man in a hat passes by and does a double take: with the baby's back to him, Ava's brown woollen onesie with little ears on the head makes it look like Nena is clutching and kissing a teddy bear. He gives Nena a wry smile, but she doesn't notice.

'Come on, baby, time to wake up or you won't sleep tonight.'

Ava is unmoved and her eyes drop again as she rests a full cheek onto her mother's shoulder. Nena would like to let Ava sleep for longer, it's so much easier when she's asleep, but she can't face another 10 p.m. bedtime or another five times getting up in the night.

Nena sighs and takes in the view. Parents and pre-schoolers play on swings, slides and a wooden balance beam with ropes and pulleys. The children look so old to Nena, so big, and such a world away from Ava. Nena can't imagine Ava being strong enough to sit up in a swing, or being able to walk the balance beam. Or talk even. Or life ever being easier, despite the fact Arlo is a very easy-going five-year-old. She just can't see past the fog, the fatigue.

The boredom.

Nena wonders if any of the other mothers in the park feel as bored as she does. She wonders if their days fly by in a flash of nothing to speak of, no anecdotes to tell their partners. Whether the other mothers understand what it's like to be so in love yet so bored all at once.

One mum pushes a blond boy with red cheeks and a line of snot from one nostril, glimmering in the cold sunshine, on a small reinforced swing. At the next swing, a dad with swarthy skin the shade of Nena's pushes a girl with curly hair. In-between pushes, the mother of the blond boy smooths down her own ponytail self-consciously, while she tries to act cool talking to the handsome man. Back and forth their banal questions fly, rhythmically, animatedly, about baby groups and nursery choices and how little Theodore loves sushi.

They don't look very bored, Nena thinks, seeing a spark in the hot dad's eye.

She looks like she's enjoying motherhood more than I am.

The repetition. Back and forth.

Nena nuzzles into Ava's bear suit while she resolutely sleeps on her shoulder.

'Nena? Nena from *Nena's Tiny Dancers*?'

Nena looks up, not in the mood to chat or sign an autograph, at a woman with birdlike features and a buggy. It was a mission to get out today, to leave the flat. She did it to get off her arse and feel proud of herself; she didn't do it so she could have a selfie taken with a CBeebies fan.

'Or should I say, Nena Oliveira from Bateson Hall! Remember me?'

Nena looks at the woman properly and her face relaxes with relief. 'Emily Snatch!'

She smiles. 'I've not been called that in a long time. May I?'

Emily Snatch was actually called Emily Slaith-Newsome, and she was the sweetest girl in Bateson Hall. She was the flatmate who would field calls Nena and Maya didn't want to take, buy *The OC* boxset for everyone to watch, and who would stand over Nena with a glass of water and a Berocca when Nena was dry-wretching after a big night out. At university, Nena and Maya found the name Slaith-Newsome such a mouthful, among a crowd of other Emilys in their halls of residence, that Maya came up with the moniker Emily S-N. Which Nena soon evolved into Snatch. It didn't suit the girl with the pearl earrings and stripy Oxford shirts, but it appealed to Nena's sense of humour, and Emily Snatch didn't seem to mind. She really was nice.

'For sure,' says Nena, pleasantly surprised by how pleasantly surprised she is to see Emily Snatch, so she shuffles along the bench, teddy bear on her shoulder.

'I'm sorry to disappoint though,' Emily says in plummy tones. 'I'm no longer a Snatch.'

They giggle, aware of how childish they're being with their babies in tow.

'My husband Harry is a Smith.'

'Ahhhh, you'll always be Emily Snatch to me.'

Emily puts the brake on her UPPAbaby buggy and peeps into the bundle lying horizontally.

'So, we both got out of breeze-block hell and made something with our lives, eh?' Nena nods to Emily's buggy. 'How old's your little one?' She cringes to herself. It's chatter she hates hearing other people asking, *back and forth*, and tries not to hate herself for getting embroiled in it.

'Oh, she's six months. Iris.'

'Oh! Ava's five months. How funny,' Nena says, thinking it's not that funny really.

'Your first?' asks Emily, whose face is thinner and her body smaller than the kind and matronly girl she always seemed at uni.

'Yep, my first. Although I have a stepson who's five, so I had a little bit of a trial run with him.'

'Nothing prepares you for this though, does it?' says Emily.

'Nope, definitely not.'

Hot Dad swaggers past with his little girl on his shoulders. Nena wishes Maya were on the bench next to her, so she could stick an elbow in Maya's ribs and appreciate how fit he is, but she returns to polite chit-chat.

I miss Maya.

'Is Iris your first?'

Maya doesn't understand.

'No, I have two older kids, they're at school right now.'

'Oh wow,' says Nena, feeling cheated. The solidarity she felt to meet someone going through what she's going through, something Maya doesn't understand, seems fraudulent; Nena feels like a novice again.

'Sammy is six, Belle is four...'

'Wow, you've been busy!'

'Yeah, do you remember Harry? Harry and I got together in the third year.'

Nena can't for the life of her remember Harry, although she did sleep with a few Harrys at uni. She hopes Emily's Harry wasn't one of them.

'Oh yeah,' she lies.

'Well, we got married after graduation. I've been pretty much knocked up ever since,' Emily says with a laugh.

'I can see! How's it working out for you?'

'Exhausting. Shit. Wonderful.'

Nena warms to her again.

'Well, I guess you know what it's like...' Emily cranes her neck. All she can see is a shock of thick black hair under Ava's bear suit but says Ava looks gorgeous anyway.

Nena smiles, she knows it's true.

'Yeah, weaning isn't going that well for us... I just can't get her off the boob. Can't get her off me at all for that matter; she's a drainer!'

'Ahh, don't worry, it'll happen. I never would have had Belle if it hadn't.'

A few weeks ago, Nena might have sternly told Emily to fuck off with the wisdom, but today she is willing, she is open, she is grateful, to cling onto any nugget of advice that says *this will get better.*

'It gets much, much easier when they're at school!'

That's four years.

Nena wants to cry.

'Which school are your kids at? Arlo, my stepson, he's at St Andrew's.'

'That's Sammy and Belle's school! Which year?'

'Oh, he started in September... is that Year 1?'

'Reception. Belle's in Reception; she's not five until June though.'

'Arlo Vernon. Brown bowl cut, shy smile, super cute.'

'Oh, Arlo and Belle are in the same class!' Emily's birdlike features look both alert and puzzled as she pieces together the jigsaw of Nena from Bateson Hall landing a job on CBeebies – and so now she must be married to her friend Kate's ex-husband, Tom. Kate leaving Tom for Bland Patrick caused quite the stir among the other mums at Baby Group, so Emily is heartened to learn it all worked out in the end for Tom.

'Yeah, Tom is my husband,' says Nena, as if she can read Emily's mind.

Emily marvels at what a small world it is and how surprised she is that she hasn't seen Nena at school at all. Nena is too embarrassed to say she's barely got out of her pyjamas since the school year started. Emily wonders if there is tension between Kate and Nena, although Kate's never said anything negative about Tom's new wife, only that she works in children's...

Of course.

More pieces fit together.

'My kids love your show, you know.'

'More than Dr Rosa?'

Emily looks blank because Dr Rosa's show hasn't started airing yet. 'I told Sammy and Belle that I was friends with you at university and they were very confused, as if it wasn't possible for someone to exist outside of the television.'

'I'm not sure it does seem possible right now,' says Nena with a wan smile. Before realising that maybe she has revealed too much. 'Yeah, it's only on repeats at the moment. I'm on mat leave. And obviously I need to lose about three stone before I go back to work…'

'Nonsense. You look amazing as ever.'

The thought of going back to work makes Nena panic. She has until October. Which seems both an age away and like it's tomorrow. Nena is conflicted by how much she misses work: the energy of it, the pride she has in what she does, the autonomy of earning – and how terrified she is to go back.

It'd be nice to pee when I need to, or drink a hot drink while it's still hot.

'Are you still in touch with Maya Flowers? You two were as thick as thieves.'

'Yeah, she's still my mate, but she's travelling with her boyfriend at the moment, so I haven't seen her for a while. Lucky cow.' Ava stirs. 'You might have read her column about her travels, in *Esprit* magazine.'

'Oh god, I haven't read a Sunday paper in, oooh, about six-and-a-half years?' jokes Emily.

'Well, it's the only thing I do read, to see where in the world Maya is – her emails are getting less frequent the further she gets from home. We must try to Skype soon.'

She won't believe it when I tell her I bumped into Emily Snatch.

Ava wakes up and writhes, little knots of hunger gnawing at her tummy and Nena's anxiety.

Emily peers into Nena's shoulder again and coos.

'Is she sleeping through the night?'

Nena wants to say 'Fuck off,' but remembers the kindness with which Emily held Berocca in her palm.

'No. She hasn't slept through once. I'm still feeding her through the night. Ridiculous, eh?'

'Not really. You have to do what's right for you. So you can stay sane while you're keeping them alive.'

Nena feels a rush of relief.

That's it. All I have to do is keep her alive.

'How do you manage to keep *three* alive?' Nena's thick dark brows crease and furrow.

'Oh, three is easier than a new "one". Nothing was harder for me than going from self-indulgent, confident woman, to suddenly having a newborn. It was hideous. I don't know how I managed.'

Nena looks at her watch, unzips Ava's bear suit a little and puts her under her top to her breast. She's not fed much in public, but for some reason she doesn't feel self-conscious now, and that feels like a milestone.

'Drat, what time is it? I have to get the kids from school.'

'Two forty-five.'

'Ah! I'd better go. Want to walk with me? Oh, I guess you can't,' Emily gestures to Nena's chest.

'No, Kate's getting him today anyway. Tom does pickup on a Wednesday. I sometimes join him,' Nena lies, feeling terrible that she's not met Tom at Arlo's new school once. She vows to remedy that, on a Wednesday soon.

'Well, it's lovely to bump into you.' Emily repositions Iris on the sheepskin liner of her buggy, then hesitates. 'Hey, er, do you go to any baby groups at all?'

Nena looks nonplussed and doesn't answer.

'I go to a really nice baby sensory class, usually on a Monday morning, but she runs a couple of sessions a week. In the side building by the town hall. Fancy meeting there one Monday? They're not wankers.'

Nena doesn't know what to say, she is flooded with panic.

'Well, some are, but we can laugh about them over coffee afterwards.'

Get a grip.

'I'd love to,' says Nena, warmly, as she pats Ava's bottom.

'Great. It's 9.30, so I go straight from drop-off. See you Monday?'

'See you Monday, Emily Snatch,' Nena smiles.

Emily hesitates, seeing a self-doubt in Nena that makes her think she might never see her again. 'Actually, let me get your number, in case anything comes up. It often does with three to get up and out in the morning.'

Nena calls out her digits while Emily presses them into her phone and sends her a text.

'That'll have my details. Right, better go,' Emily mouths as she unlocks the brake of her turquoise roofed buggy and walks hastily on the path out of the park.

Nena looks back at the children's play area and the lake beyond it. It's emptied out now. Just her and Ava. Everyone else dashed off to flirt some more or to collect big siblings, or to get the tea on. Or to just keep their little ones alive.

21

March 2016, The Haven, Thailand

'I'm going for a run,' Maya whispers, as she kisses James' forehead. 'It might be my last for a while…'

Maya knows she sounds melodramatic but is worried that, even in a few hours, she might feel too weak on her diet of clay shakes, herbs and air to do anything as physical as running.

James sits up, rubs the sleep out of his big brown eyes and puts on his glasses. 'OK, honey, go carefully yeah?'

'I'm only going along the beach – maybe the paths at the back of it.'

James blinks behind his lenses, to help him focus. 'It all gets a bit jungly at that far stretch, I'm not sure what's around the karst at the end – I wouldn't go off the shore or the path or anything.'

James has never seemed to worry about Maya running; he's always had confidence in her strength, her common sense, her orientation. But since they've been following the disappearance of Manon Junot on BBC World or CNN, he's become increasingly apprehensive every time she laces up her trainers.

'I'll stick to the beach then,' Maya appeases, before planting a kiss on James' full lips as he clicks on the television with the remote control on the bed.

When Maya packed her capsule wardrobe for their big trip, she knew that one of her footwear items (alongside the bronze Havaiana flip-flops, the red Lulu Guinness raffia wedges and the clunky North Face walking boots she travels in – all bases covered) would have to be her Nike trainers. Running for her was non-negotiable. The freedom to move after being cooped up. The chance to reflect. The opportunity to think about what her next column should be about. The chance to scout out new places to eat. Since Maya's father had encouraged her to take up running by convincing her that it could mend a broken heart, she had never looked back. Slowly building up from a slumpy novice to a strong woman, and now when Maya runs she is Beyoncé outrunning a big cat – she can do anything. Even if some of her runs on this trip were ill-advised.

In Agra, Maya was chased by wild dogs, yapping at her heels before she ran for cover in a surprise branch of Pizza Hut, where she leaned against the glass window and cried while she waited for the dogs to lose interest and disappear.

After their stay on the houseboat in Kerala, Maya ran along the beach at Alleppey, marvelling at the men on their haunches, meditating as they looked out to sea. It was only as she got closer she realised that the men weren't practising yoga, they were using the beach for their morning constitutional, and she scowled as she ran past their neat piles of poo.

Some runs have been beautiful. Lodhi Park in Delhi; Lumphini Park in Bangkok; the beach on the Andaman Coast. Maya still appreciates the curative powers of running, even when the runs are less than pleasant. She pictures Herbert running in front of her, the comforting bob of his bouncy hair, leading the way to safety, giving her strength.

I miss my dad.

The norms of a Thai beach mean Maya can wear shorts and a vest with her Nike trainers today, so she weaves out past The Haven's rustic cabañas, alongside Moon's open-sided common room that they haven't dared venture into yet, and to the shore. While the gemstone-green water is dazzling, the coastline is less pristine here than the Andaman Coast. Seaweed and sticks pepper the sand. The beach here feels more...

raw, which suits the back-to-basics ethos of the spa. Indian opulence this isn't, despite the hefty change-your-life price tag they're relieved they don't have to pay.

Maya breaks into a run, thinking about the man she left behind, rubbing sleep from his eyes and putting on CNN. How supportive he is, of her running, of her baking. How he put his dream career on hold for her so they could go travelling. How she can't mention again the yearning she feels inside.

Her pace quickens as the wet sand on the shore is hard enough and flat enough to tread without the sensation of running through treacle. The beach isn't wide but it is long, and completely empty. There are no tourists dipping in the crystal water. No paddleboarders wading towards the inlet at the end.

Look at this! This is all for me. This is going to be my best run yet.

Maya decides that if it's too barren and too isolated beyond the jungly end of the beach, where the karsts come closer to the shore – they might even jut out of the sand, it's hard to tell from here – she will turn around and do a few lengths of the beach before she goes back to James and starts the brutal business of cleansing. She thinks of a plate of mango, bursting with the zing from a lime squeezed over it, cold from a few minutes in a fridge. Her mouth starts to water.

Shit, I forgot my water.

Maya nears the end of the beach and judges from the time it took her to run it that it must be half a kilometre at least.

Perfect. If it's too isolated and barren beyond, I will turn around and complete 20 lengths.

The end of the beach is getting closer, the rocks that spike out to reach the sky become taller, swamping her, and Maya wonders what lies around the most lush and proud karst at the end, right in her path. Will she be able to snake past to another similar expanse of sand, or will the water come up high and smack the rocks?

She turns to look back behind her, to see how small the buildings of The Haven are from this far end of the deserted beach. And then her head smashes into something she neither saw nor expected. Something that is both hard and spongey. It hurts, and it dazes Maya, who struggles as she stumbles back, trying not to lose her footing and fall in the water. She flails, aware that there is the figure of a man standing in front of her. Confused that her main priority is to not fall onto the sand where the water laps, because if she gets wet, it will be harder to run away.

'Uff!' says the man, whose face she can't see for the stars in her eyes.

Her arms flail further, as her wide, flat feet save her. Balancing her. Stopping her from being dragged onto the sand and into the sea. She stills herself, and puts her hand to her throbbing forehead, shielding her eyes as she regains her composure.

'Ow.'

James was right.

Maya pushes her hand up, over her forehead, and opens her eyes, trying to focus on the man who still seems to be standing tall in front of her, unaffected by their collision, not saying a word.

Maya thinks of Manon Junot and wonders if *she* ran into a man on the beach, never to be seen again. She wonders why this face in front of her looks familiar, like someone from the television or a face from her past.

This can't be right. I must have hit my head hard.

She focuses again, into the sunlight.

But she is right.

'Oh. It's you,' Maya says, rubbing the bump she can already feel on her forehead. 'What are you doing here?'

22

Years of love and harmony unravel and rewind until Maya sees herself lying broken on a bed, crying so many tears that they tumble into her hair, turning it from poker straight to forever wavy.

'Are you OK?'

Maya puts her palms on her thighs and takes deep breaths into the sand. The shore just about laps at the edge of her trainers. Not getting wet was a win.

'Yeah... yeah... I'm OK. Just confused. What are *you* doing here?'

'What am *I* doing here? What are *you* doing here more like?' he laughs.

Jon Vincent is smiling. His glacial eyes are as bright as the sea, but not as warm. His once-shorn hair is now longer, his hairline higher, as an arc of blond rises upwards from a curved widow's peak. Gone is the tennis-ball fluff of a buzz cut Maya used to give him at university. They both look different.

Maya catches her breath.

Those eyes.

'I'm travelling. With my boyfriend,' she adds a bit too hastily to be as casual as she intended. 'What are you doing here? How did you spring out of nowhere? I didn't see you.'

'Yeah, I realise,' Jon says, pummelling the red patch on his chest with one fist. 'I didn't see you either. But this is my morning walk. I love this stretch, especially when it's so peaceful.' Maya and Jon look up and down, surveying the empty beach. 'Although, weirdly, I prefer not to have a beautiful woman run full pelt into my chest.'

Jon's fist opens into a flat palm and he circles his torso to soothe the impact point. Maya doesn't apologise.

'Are you staying at The Haven?' she asks.

'Yeah, I come every year. To kick back. Cleanse. Get out of London and all the…' he waves erratic hands around his face to gesture craziness.

'London? You're still in London?'

Maya was relieved that she had never bumped into Jon after he dumped her. Not once. On the late July morning she last saw him, when she packed him off for the final day of his Shakespeare summer school course at RADA with a muffin and a kiss, she didn't know that he was going home with his Ophelia that night, with just a text to say it was over and that he was sorry. And he never contacted her again. The £5,000 flat deposit was gone; it had paid for Jon's course. Over the summer he had fallen in love with sonnets and someone else, he had quietly and gradually moved all of the things he wanted out of their shared rental flat in Finsbury Park without Maya even noticing. Maya cried and cried until her hair turned wavy, until she got up, moved back to Hazelworth, started running with her father. And she never saw him again.

'Well, London, Stratford, Toronto, LA... Wherever work takes me really. You could say I'm a bit of a nomad.'

Maya stands tall and puts her hand to her brow, to shield her eyes from the rising sun. To check if this is actually Jon Vincent standing in front of her on a secluded corner of a secluded beach in a secluded part of another continent.

Dammit, it is.

'Want to walk?' he gestures beyond the karst at the end of the beach to the next bay around the cove.

I need to Skype Nena. She won't believe it when I tell her I bumped into Jon Vincent.

'OK,' Maya shrugs, to her surprise.

This coincidence is definitely worth a conversation, even if she doesn't know where to begin. Maya doesn't want to carry on running in front of Jon anyway. He's never seen her run and she'll feel too self-conscious in her shorts and vest. Running was something she did After Jon, to cure herself of heartache. Anyway, her forehead is pounding and her knees feel a bit weak. Walking is good.

'Just until I catch my breath,' she says, giving herself a get-out.

23

Maya glances back down the beach, to see if anyone can see her, before walking around the lofty karst to another, even more rugged and undeveloped stretch. She looks up in awe and gasps.

'Wow, gorgeous isn't it?'

'Stunning,' Jon says, looking at Maya.

Maya feels like she's breaking a rule. Leaving the confines of The Haven and its private beach on day one of the detox. Agreeing to go for a walk with the man who broke her heart. She thinks of James, back in their bedroom, and imagines him scrolling through his digital SLR camera roll looking at pictures; his beautiful concentrating face with his tongue sticking out at one corner of his mouth.

'So, you come here often,' Maya states, embarrassed

by how the words come out. She puts her hands on her hips as she walks, hoping to catch her breath, and feels a trickle of sweat running down her spine and into the top of her shorts. She gazes down at her feet on the sand, stealing looks at Jon and what he's wearing as she goes. Cream shorts and a tailored pastel-coloured shirt, open at the chest she bumped into.

'Every year if I can.'

'On your own?' Maya says, trying to sound neither bitter nor hopeful.

'Yeah, I love the tranquillity of this place; I like to come and reset the dials. Escape the intensity of my craft.'

'Your *craft*?' Maya tries not to sound churlish.

'Yes. Acting.' Jon gives a little look as if to say *of course*.

'Oh, you still do that?'

'Well, I'm making a pretty good living from it, you could say...'

Maya wonders which drama he might have ended up being a bit part in, because she doesn't remember seeing him in the *Radio Times* or *Esprit*.

Five thousand pounds well spent then.

'Oh, I've not seen you in anything.'

'Most of my TV stuff is in the US; although I do more theatre lately. I'm still recovering from *Hamlet* at the Barbican, such are the demons of method acting.'

'Oh right.'

'But it's nice to come out here, do some yoga, read some scripts.' Jon looks at Maya and winks, as he waves the ream of white paper he's carrying. She feels a familiar flip in her stomach. 'And it's nice not to be recognised.'

Maya takes her cue to look at Jon's face properly, to see if she can recognise anything from her past. His delicate features are the same, his little nose and thin lips, but his bright eyes have creases and crow's feet starting to form, which suit him because he always did look young for his age. Maya hears Nena's scornful voice in her head and it tickles her; she misses her.

Baby-faced Assassin. I'm going to kill him.

Jon's skin is pale, his face not yet tanned. His hair isn't golden blond, the way it turned when they holidayed in Mykonos and Ibiza. She figures he must have recently arrived too.

'Are you doing the detox? I start today.'

'I'm in pre-cleanse phase. Landed late last night, so I start tomorrow. It's intense, I can't lie,' he says authoritatively. He doesn't know that this is Maya's first time at The Haven, but he assumes it is. He rubs the soft hair at the back of his neck. Maya remembers the feeling of rubbing her cheek against the tennis-ball fuzz. It looks better longer. 'I always drop about six kilos here, and I'm pretty lean to start with.'

'Wow.'

Maya is suddenly aware of her softer frame, although Jon has never seen her so fit.

They carry on down the beach, away from The Haven, away from James.

'So, what do you do?' asks Jon, putting his script into a plastic bag from 7-Eleven.

This is it. This is Maya's time to shine. To prove that she got over Jon and fell in love again. This time with the love of her life, and that her new career as a trained patisserie-chef-slash-travel-writer is pretty amazing thankyouverymuch. In the panic of her nerves and the racing of her heart, she doesn't realise that that's exactly what happened. Her life doesn't need polishing.

'Oh, so you know I went to work at Walk In Wardrobe?'

Jon looks a bit vacant but nods.

'Well, I was there a couple of years, then I went to FASH – you must know FASH – and then...' She wonders whether to tell Jon about Fifi Fashion Insider, or assume he already knows. Her face was *everywhere* for a week around the big reveal. That it was a girl called Maya Flowers writing an anonymous newspaper column about life on the inside at FASH. People were talking about *her* on *Question Time* and *Woman's Hour*, surely Jon would have noticed. 'Do you remember about eighteen months ago, there was this story...'

As they stroll in the morning sunshine, Maya loosely explains and Jon looks slightly puzzled.

'Maybe that's when I was Stateside. I did a legal drama most of 2014. On location in Canada.'

Maya feels a little crestfallen and can't be bothered to go into more detail. Nor is it worth mentioning *My Travels with Train Man*; she doesn't want to give Jon the satisfaction of saying he's never heard of that either. 'Ah, well long story short, I left fashion and moved into baking.'

'Baking, wow? What do you do, like, little cupcakes?'

'Patisserie.'

Maya feels a puff of satisfaction from saying that. Rustic Maya and her rough-around-the-edges bakes are now polished and refined – and she worked bloody hard at refinement too.

'But I've packed away my KitchenAid and my palette knife. James – my boyfriend – he and I are travelling. For a year.'

'Wow, Maya, you sound really happy. I'm glad you're happy.'

They stop again and turn to face each other on the sand as the waves gently lap Jon's bare toes and Maya's trainer heels.

Maya looks at Jon's face. Half of her is like jelly. The other half of her wants to punch him for sounding so bloody patronising.

Maya wants to ask Jon whether he has a girlfriend. An actress wife or a poor Juliet or Rosalind back in Blighty, waiting for him to get back from Thailand or wherever he buggered off to go and find himself again. He doesn't have a ring on his wedding finger; there is no tan line from where he might have taken it off.

As they approach the end of the next cove, Maya feels relief. Relief that her forehead has stopped hurting, relief that there is nothing else to say right now, relief that this walk has reached a natural end. All she wants to do is run and get back to James. Her dark, tanned, reliable boyfriend, waiting in the bed they made love in last night – before self-administered colonics in a shared bathroom kill any chance of romance thereafter.

'Look, I'm going to get going – I was meant to drink my first clay shake at seven, and I'm worried I'll lose any power left in me once I stop eating actual food.'

'It's really not as bad as you think.'

'OK, well, I don't believe you, but thanks,' Maya smirks, before turning around.

'Nice to bump into you, Maya. Literally.'

'Weird to bump into you, Jon.'

Maya gives him a salute and breaks into a gentle jog, to get back to her thoughts, her column, her love.

That was *weird*.

There were so many levels of weird about the encounter that Maya can't think about what her next column should be, or how much she wishes she could have mango for breakfast. She's not even panicking about the colonic later. All she can think about is how weird that was; to physically bump into Jon Vincent;

to see him after all these years; that neither mentioned the elephant in the room or on the beach: how Jon took Maya's flat deposit and broke her heart.

'See you in yoga!' he shouts after her.

Fuck it, Maya thinks, as she breaks into a run on the sand towards the karst that separates this cove from the next, aware that Jon is watching her. She feels the slight wobble of cellulite in the back of her thighs, sees the curve of her upper arms in her peripheral vision. She runs like Beyoncé.

I am strong.

24

'Our correspondent, Clarence, is live in Bangkok with the latest. Clarence, there's been a slight change of tone in the investigation, hasn't there?'

'Yes, Anna, it's now been three months since Manon Junot was last seen in Thailand, and yesterday – what was her twenty-eighth birthday – was seen as an opportunity for the family, who have met with the police in Thailand, to make a fresh appeal. They released some interesting new information pertaining to Manon's well-being that they hope will help the public and in turn help the investigation. Her elder brother, Antoine, and sister, Valerie, joined the now-familiar face of Police Chief Kongduang in Bangkok, to plead with the public for help again. Here's what they had to say.'

CUTS TO A PRESS CONFERENCE FROM BANGKOK WITH A SAD-LOOKING MAN IN HIS THIRTIES AND A YOUNGER

WOMAN IN HER TWENTIES, SITTING ALONGSIDE POLICE CHIEF KONGDUANG. THE FRENCH MAN TALKS TO A BANK OF MICROPHONES.

'The police are aware that our sister does have a history of mental health problems, for which she has been treated and we have cared for her for many years. She was managing with this and able to lead a very normal and fulfilling life around this with her work in London, but we are mindful that Manon might have had a relapse.'

CAMERA CUTS TO THE SISTER.

'We just want to say to Manny if she's watching, or if anyone is with her and can tell her, that we love you, we're thinking of you on your birthday, and we will celebrate you – and keep celebrating you – until you are home. Until you are safe back with us. We love you.'

THE GIRL BREAKS DOWN IN TEARS AND COLLAPSES ON HER BROTHER'S SHOULDER.

CAMERA CUTS TO THE STUDIO WHILE THE ANCHOR TALKS TO THE CORRESPONDENT ON A SCREEN.

'Clarence, what can the police tell us about Manon Junot's mental health, and what effect does that have on the investigation?'

'Yes, it's strange that the family and the police chose to release this information now and not before, but they didn't go into any detail – and we're not sure what Ms Junot's mental health history is – but it does throw a new sensitivity to the search: might she be suffering depression and could that be the cause of her disappearance? Are the police *looking into suicide, for example? Police Chief Kongduang wouldn't be drawn on that – but it feels like this investigation has changed tack. The conversation seems to be less about an abduction or random attack and more about whether Manon Junot had a relapse in her health and whether her state of mind affected choices she made, where she went and what she might have done. Her sister, Valerie, alluded to her being with someone, in asking people to pass on a message. Might they think she's been kidnapped or being cared for? It's hard to tell. For now, they hope their latest appeal will be enough to find Manon safe and well and to bring her home.'*

'Clarence, thank you.'

25

James turns off the TV from his position propped up in bed and continues scrolling through his photos. One arm is raised behind his head, the other is holding the camera and pressing arrows on a circle while he zooms in on a shot of Maya diving into the sea. Her white bikini bright against her tanned skin.

Beautiful.

The moment of peace is broken however when Maya bursts through the door, sweaty and bothered, with a red mark and a small lump, slap bang in the middle of her forehead.

James looks up through his black rectangular glasses. Sexy as hell, but for the empty long glass of grey sludge he's just picked up.

'I made the clay shakes – yours is by the TV.' He winces. 'You OK?'

Maya rubs her forehead and furrows her brow. 'Just about. I wasn't looking where I was running, but I'm OK.'

James sits up. 'You want some ice? I could get some from the kitchen block, I'm sure.'

'No, it's fine. I was rather hoping for a mango lassi or a banana milkshake.' Maya rolls her eyes.

'Sorry, honey, you got us into this mess. If I'm drinking it, you have to.'

'What does it taste like?'

'Clay.'

'Oh.'

'It's gross. But think of it acting like a magnet and sloughing out all the shit as it passes into your tummy.'

'Have you been talking to Moon?'

'Hahaha, no, but I think visualisation is the only way to get through this. Imagine its healing properties. Or that it tastes of mango lassi.'

'Oh, the mango lassis!' Maya sighs. 'OK, visualisation... Does that help?'

'No, I gagged.'

Maya picks up and examines the tall glass of grey sludge by the television and contemplates one last treat before she dives in. Except she doesn't have any treats. The last sweet treat she ate was a Crunchie on the boat from the mainland, which tasted like it was way past its sell-by-date. She's been craving Green & Black's since they left home in December.

Maya plonks herself down, sitting next to James on the bed, and takes the cocktail stirrer from his glass to awaken the sludge at the bottom of hers. She looks down, into the grey abyss, then raises the glass to her mouth.

I have to do this. The column depends on it.

'So, here's a weird thing,' she says, stopping before her lips touch the liquid, hoping to delay one uncomfortable thing by mentioning another.

'That looks really sore.' James beat her to it. He rubs her lightly freckled forehead with his thumb.

'Ah, well there's a funny story there…'

Maya looks nervous. James sits up higher and concentrates, he's not used to seeing her like this and has no idea what she's about to say.

'Are you OK?'

'Well, you'll never guess who I literally bumped into on my run?'

James pauses. He has no clue. They are on the other side of the world and they haven't made any new friends here. They mainly have no friends because they're antisocial buggers who tend not to mingle with other, younger backpackers. They prefer private rooms to dorms, rummy for two to naked Twister at a Full Moon party, and quiet nights drinking Singha and SangSom on their terrace to Kumbaya around a campfire with travellers who are ten years younger, teens who like to hop in and out of each other's bunks at night – although thankfully none of that is happening here at The Haven.

'Wasn't Manon Junot, was it?'

'What? You're obsessed! The media are obsessed. I bet they wouldn't be so obsessed if she wasn't so gorgeous. Anyway, I reckon she's in China by now.'

'Why China?'

'I dunno. Thailand, Laos, Cambodia... why not China?! And I dreamt it the other night.'

James looks baffled.

'But anyway,' Maya is suddenly worried that she sounds too excited about this gossip, so she checks herself and looks back at her clay shake, stirring it three times clockwise. 'It wasn't Manon Junot, silly.'

'Who did you bump into then?'

'It was Jon,' she pauses. 'Jon Vincent.'

James looks a bit blank. Jon and Vincent next to each other are two names that don't mean that much to him.

Maya feels even more awkward having to spell it out. 'Jon Vincent, my ex-boyfriend. You know, the twat who squandered my flat deposit on acting lessons and ran off with Lady Macbeth.'

'Oh, right,' James says, a bit disinterestedly, although he really wants to ask loads of questions. 'What's he doing here?' is the only one he has the courage to ask.

'Same as us. Detoxing. Loafing. Not writing about it, mind, like I have to… He has a pile of scripts. Apparently he made it as an actor. Which is a bit annoying really, giving he stitched me up, surely he owes me fifteen per cent of everything he earns. On top of that five grand. And there's seven years of interest…' Maya laughs nervously, seeing that James is disconcerted by her wittering.

'What was his last name again?'

'Vincent. Jon Vincent.'

'Nah, never heard of him.'

'He probably uses a stage name. Jon Vincent is not the kind of name to go stellar. Actually, did you know Vin Diesel is called Mark Vincent? Jon probably took his cues from Vin and has a much more exciting stage name.'

I won't give him the satisfaction of asking though.

'How do you even know Vin Diesel's real name?' James' expression looks somewhere between horrified and impressed. Maya does have Excellent General Knowledge skills. They helped her win a gameshow once.

'Maybe he's calling himself Vin Power or Vin Petrol?' Maya chuckles nervously to herself. 'Although, no, that's not his style. He's more charming British luvvie than American action hero. Vin Grant?'

James frowns.

Shit, did I just say 'charming'?

Maya knows how ridiculous she is, and that this clay shake isn't going to go away, so she whips the stirrer around one last time before facing the inevitable.

'Right, here goes...'

26

March 2016, London, England

'Thank you so much for finding the time to have a drink with me. I know you're a very busy man.' Rosa touches Tom's forearm gently before pushing her fingers through her neat bobbed hair. He feels the imprint of her on his skin and is surprised by her boldness, despite the fact he just hugged his boss a warm farewell.

Coffee was swapped for a quick drink in the Groucho, where Tom had a 4 p.m. meeting with the Controller of Children's and thought it might be nice for the two women to coincide before Charmaine McCourt had to get her train back to Manchester. Introduce the chief to the talent, and hopefully make Rosa relax a little by feeling like a valued part of the team. The new star signing.

It's now 6 p.m., and Rosa is looking relaxed enough, slinking into a curved lilac velvet booth that's perfect for two, while she twists her flute of Cucumber Fizz on its stem with ease.

'No problem. It was great for Charmaine to meet you too. I know she's going to love you as much as I do.'

With a long finger, Rosa lifts the garnish out of her glass – a cucumber peeling that's been fashioned and coiled into the shape of a rose – and eats it.

'Starving,' she says.

'Do you want to grab some food?' Tom asks, pointing his thumb over his shoulder towards an area where people are dining. 'The buttermilk chicken is top-notch.'

Tom regrets suggesting it as soon as the words come out. Nena knew about his big meeting with his boss but won't be expecting it to go on into the evening; he doesn't want to get home late.

'No I shouldn't,' Rosa says, smoothing down a silk shirt that's too expensive to eat buttermilk chicken in. *Phew.*

Suddenly reminded of the time, Tom moves things along. 'So, you wanted to chat. What's troubling you?'

'Yes... well... It's just—'

'Go on...'

'This TV world. It's all so new to me – and I'm so so grateful for the opportunity. I just want to make sure I'm doing everything all right. Better than all right in fact. I want to be exceptional. I'm just not very confident.'

Tom looks at Rosa's face in the rabbit warren of the private members' club. Her eyelids are glossy and her face is intelligent – she looks more like a newsreader than a children's TV presenter. The neediness jars with the polished exterior Rosa Samarasekera exudes.

'Well, your producer thinks you're doing exceptionally well, and, as I said, the rushes look brilliant. So, whatever you're doing, keep on doing it. Don't change a thing.'

Rosa blushes. 'Thanks, Tom. Sorry,' she says, turning her glass again. 'Always the head girl! In academia and medicine, you're always graded; you have regular feedback. Empirical data. Talking to a camera in a darkened studio in MediaCity, well, it's hard to know whether I'm an A star or an epic fail.'

'You're an A star, Rosa, trust me.'

'Thank you – I really appreciate it.'

Tom has a flash of an idea: he could put Rosa in touch with Nena, she could give her some tips – then he realises that would be a terrible idea and washes the thought away with a sip of his rhubarb gin and tonic.

Rosa sinks her Cucumber Fizz.

'Time for one more?' she says, looking at her watch.

'Erm…'

'Doctor's orders,' she commands, with one raised eyebrow.

'Pardon?'

'Doctor's Orders: Martell, Strega, Merlot and lime juice – it's a cocktail, here, on the menu.'

Tom's face relaxes into laughter and he rubs his five o'clock shadow with his palm. 'Oh. Well, it would be rude not to then. One more...'

Tom beckons a woman with a short black fringe and thick winged eyeliner, and she takes his order, before he stands to go to the loo.

'Back in a second,' he nods, as he winds through the room, pressing hands and patting friends on the back as he passes the bar and heads to the basement toilet. As he goes, Rosa surveys his tall frame, gives his anatomy a once-over. He looks more dapper than usual. His cords and cable-knits have been replaced by a navy blazer, a crisp white shirt and chinos. Tom always exudes an air of authority, of competence, whatever he wears, but smartness suits him.

Nice bum.

While he's gone, Rosa looks around. At the soap star who recently got back from the jungle; at the comedian with the hangdog expression and the dirty coat; at the actress who's been misbehaving here since she was a teen. She watches the pianist play 'As Time Goes By' and sees Tom pat him gently on the back as he walks back towards her, past the piano with a Union Jack painted on it.

A waitress puts two blood-red cocktails and a little bowl of Twiglets on the table.

'So, Charmaine was asking after your baby. How old is she?'

Tom's eyes light up. It's easier for his eyes to light up than Nena's. He's in the Groucho having a drink, excited to get home to his baby; knowing he's not been tending to her every whim all day; knowing that he will sleep through the night undisturbed because Ava's cries don't terrify or wake him the way they do Nena. She always bounces out of bed first; Tom often doesn't wake at all, even when the cries persist and Nena tries to ignore them.

'Yes, she's almost five months.'

'Ooooh, tough times,' Rosa curls her nose.

'No, it's wonderful! I have a five-year-old too.'

'Oh right,' says Rosa, thrown.

'Yes. Arlo's easier; Ava's a little madam – not a sleeper. It's a good job she's so beautiful.'

Rosa looks at Tom, Doctor's Orders bringing a glimpse of confidence and a flash of a determined look.

Like her father.

'Like her mother. She's got this shock of black hair and bright blue eyes…' Tom stops short of getting his phone out. He's a senior figure at the BBC and Rosa is new talent. She doesn't need to see his baby photos.

'Your eyes are the brightest blue – I've never seen it before – they must come from you.'

Their eyes lock.

'So, do you have kids?' Tom asks, changing the focus, suspecting not.

'Gosh no! Between the hospital – this – and my busy social life, I don't have time for anything else. I'm too selfish anyway. I like late nights and long lazy lie-ins.' Rosa purrs, and gives her cocktail a little stir. 'I'm enjoying life too much to be anchored down anyway at the moment. I'm not even dating. Not exclusively anyway.' She looks up at Tom and he feels distinctly flustered.

Now it's Rosa's turn to change the focus, she doesn't want to overstep the mark.

Yet.

'Oh, so I received an invitation today, for some big Children's party next month.'

'Oh yes, the Bertie & Betty sixtieth anniversary.'

'That was it!'

'That's great you've had an invitation – should be fun. Bertie still comes to loads of events. He was even at Camp Bestival last year. He's almost ninety; he was camping too!'

Rosa scrunches up her face as if to say, *How ghastly*, but Tom doesn't notice.

'Such a trouper. But it'll be a brilliant opportunity for you to meet loads of other Children's talent: producers, editors, assistants, poets, artists, writers, contributors...' Tom doesn't mention that he hopes his wife will make it to the party.

'Can't wait,' Rosa whispers, slinking deeper into the embrace of the plush lilac seat.

'Hey, so I had better go – see my daughter before Nena puts her down.'

Rosa doesn't acknowledge that she knows who Tom's wife is, lest she give away the fact that she googled it, so she finishes her drink in one slurp and licks her lips. 'Yes. I'd better get to my shift.'

'Shift?'

Tom looks at the drink Rosa has just drained.

'Yup, I'm doing nights for the next three days. Well, for the next three nights…'

'Wow,' says Tom, hoping Dr Rosa doesn't need to use a scalpel in the next few hours.

'Oh, it's fine. I'm on top of my game,' she laughs, accidentally revealing that she had no doubt she's doing brilliantly on *My Brilliant Body,* the medical show she's the star of. 'And I'm more of a night owl than day. I come alive at night.' She sticks her tongue out and winks.

They stand and grab their bags.

'I'll get you a taxi,' Tom says, as he guides Rosa out, careful not to touch her back as he follows her through the cosy club.

As they put their coats on in the plush green and leather of the lobby area, a man with frameless spectacles stops and squeezes Tom's arms.

'Tom! How are you?'

'Nick – great thanks. How's News? How's Xander?'

'Both good thanks. We're off to Washington in a few weeks actually, going to be based there for the election.'

'Oh wow – sounds great.'

Tom is aware of Rosa, prim, preened and ready by his side. 'Oh, Nick, this is Rosa Samarasekera, she's currently filming a new show for Children's.'

'*My Brilliant Body*,' says Rosa, as she shakes Nick's hand.

Tom does a mental sigh of relief that Nick will be out of the country when *My Brilliant Body* airs, so he won't see just how well Rosa would fit in his News department.

'Rosa, lovely to meet you. Tom, it'd be great to catch up before we leave.'

'Yes let's. Oh, and well done on the BAFTA nom – I take it you're not leaving until after that?'

'You know me, I turn up to the opening of an envelope.'

'Well, let's hope the envelope opens your way.'

'Thanks, Tom.'

The men loosely hug and Rosa smiles tipsily, as she and Tom head out into the stir of Soho, where he swiftly hails a black cab from the corner of Old Compton Street.

'Where are you going to, is it Guy's?'

Rosa is as tall as Tom in her gunmetal grey wool coat, sharp black tailored trousers and leopard-print stilettos. Their eyes meet and she nods.

'Guy's please, mate.'

The taxi driver nods and Tom opens the car door for Rosa, frightened by the fire in his belly.

She bends her slim legs to ease herself in, the bones in her feet are visible as she elegantly swings her knees in and shuts the door. She opens the window and gazes up at Tom, looking dashing on the pavement.

'Thanks again.' She gives him an assured smile.

'My pleasure. See you at work.'

Businesslike.

Tom taps the edge of the curved cab roof twice to indicate the driver to go. He needs to get out of this quicksand fast. He slings his leather satchel across his body and strides up Dean Street towards the lights and the buses of Oxford Street, with a spring in his step.

'"Not very confident"?' he smiles to himself. 'My arse.'

27

March 2016, The Haven, Thailand

'Hey, brother, that was inspirational,' gushes Jon, clasping Moon's hands in his and giving him a solidarity hug.

Moon smiles and releases his hands so he can tuck his parted floppy fringe behind each ear.

'Thank you,' he nods, before calling out to the room. 'Broth will be another fifteen minutes, so have a look at some of the reading materials, talk to each other, share experiences. We're all in this together, remember, so take comfort and good energy from those around you.' Moon gives a sage nod as he excuses himself from the open-sided bamboo lounge and heads down some steps to the kitchen block, further down the path.

James stands to stretch his legs, kicks out his rolled-up blue jeans and holds his hands out to help lift Maya.

For forty-five minutes, Maya and James sat cross-legged on a rug while the night breeze from the sea generated a tinkle from a chime made of shells – a gentle soundtrack to Moon's lecture on how to support the lymphatic system. As Maya drifted in and out of listening, trying to pay attention but distracted by thoughts of Green & Black's, she looked around at Moon's disciples and tried to gauge how far along they were in their 'healing journey', as Moon called it; to see where she fitted in all of this. The small Australian woman with sparkly eyes and sinewy arms was definitely a pro. The overweight Canadian called Justin asked a lot of questions, while Maya tried to count how many other Canadian Justins she'd heard of (two). And there, sitting opposite Maya on the carpet, nodding enthusiastically at Moon's sermon, was regular detoxer Jon, catching Maya's eye every now and then. After Moon finished talking, guests shared their progress notes and observations, exchanged stories about what brought them here and divulged details of the contents of the little sieve baskets that caught all the matter they had flushed from their bowels.

After the afternoon Maya had, taking turns with her hot boyfriend to do self-administered coffee colonics, she didn't want to relive or share *any* of the details or any of the trauma, thank you. Let alone in front of her ex-boyfriend. So Maya and James sat and listened to the group; to stories of excess and enlightenment; to Moon.

James is a good listener, but he's tired, so as he helps Maya up and she smooths down her purple Roxy beach dress, he gives her The Look that reminds her of the pact they made: that they would listen to Moon's talk, politely look at some leaflets, drink their broth and go with the codewords 'Shall we catch the news?' when one of them is ready to leave. Both Maya and James thought it would be a handy exit strategy if things got awkward with Jon, although neither said that aloud.

Maya ignores James' reminder about their pact, that it's almost time to go, she wants her broth first.

'That's him,' whispers Maya, sticking an elbow in James' rib and nodding towards Jon, standing chatting to the Australian with sparkly eyes. Maya feels a stab of something in her tummy, but maybe that's the after-effects of the colonic – it has been gripping ever since 'That Experience They Don't Want To Talk About'.

'I know,' James says, trying not to sound irritated. Even if he hadn't noticed Jon looking across at Maya during Moon's talk, he would have guessed that he was Maya's ex. It wasn't the actor's arrogance, his Omega watch or his impeccable quiff. Nor was it his puffed-out chest, or piercing eyes that irked James while he looked at his girlfriend. It was the feeling that Maya was looking back.

Maya casually pretends to peruse the leaflets on the table, wondering how she's going to introduce James to Jon, knowing she has to at some point; wishing she had a mobile phone to snap a photo of this crazy coincidence and send it to Nena for reinforcement. Maya didn't go to the internet room and get online today, she was too tired from her run, from the clay shakes, from the herbs, from her headache, but she needs to in the next couple of days to file her column, and she knows first stop will be a gossipy email to tell Nena that she ran into the Baby-faced Assassin, who isn't so baby-faced anymore.

She's gonna flip.

'I know, right?!' the Australian says with playful eyes, as she runs her fingers through her hair. She looks up intently at Jon. 'But the chia seeds make *all* the difference – they are so worth it. I'll give you the recipe.'

Chia seeds?

Maya's trying, but she can't help feeling that the clay shakes, the herbs, the psyllium husks and the vegetable broth will make her so miserable, none of this will make any positive difference to her life.

I don't want to be thin and angry.

James is trying a bit harder. He did go first with the clay shake and the colonic. He did listen to Moon's sermon without looking around the room and daydreaming about everyone else's back stories, and he is walking over towards Jon and the Australian woman with an extended hand.

'Hi, I'm James.'

'Good to meet you, James. Jon,' Jon nods, with a bemused smile and a confident handshake.

The Australian extends a tiny hand and says she's called Kimberley, while Maya pretends to read about the beneficial properties of lemongrass.

Get it over with, Maya.

Maya sidles over to James, Jon and Kimberley and slips her arm around James' waist. She smiles a hello at Kimberley, who excuses herself to go to the loo.

'Wish me luck!' she laughs, while James, Jon and Maya all smile and wince internally.

'Great to meet you, Jon. Maya tells me you two used to go out.'

Wow.

Maya is surprised and impressed by James' uncharacteristic forwardness.

Jon's cheeks flush a very English shade of red and his arrogant air drops.

He looks slightly cagey.

James loops his arm around Maya's waist and she feels his thumb gently rubbing the small of her back.

'Yes, the university years. "Time doth transfix the flourish set on youth, and delves the parallels in beauty's brow..."'

'Pardon?'

I don't recognise you, mate.

'Shakespeare. Sonnet 60.' Jon clears his throat. 'You're a very lucky man, James.'

James smiles as if to say *I know*. Stubbornness has edged out irritation, the dimple in his left cheek sinks and his tanned and amiable face looks comfortable, confident, friendly. Maya is blown away by how much cooler James is than she would be if she had to be at Poo Camp with James' ex, Kitty Jones.

'So, Maya tells me you've been through this before then?' James' smile belies the fact he's trying to suppress the image of Jon's hands on Maya. 'When will I stop craving Nando's?'

Jon looks visibly relieved. 'Day three. I promise.'

The two share a laugh while Maya picks up a leaflet about chakras. She can still feel James' thumb stroking her, reassuring her that everything is going to be all right.

Moon walks in with the first tray of broth.

Maya turns to James.

'Shall we eat this and then catch the news?' she suggests.

My Travels with Train Man

Train Man's just come out of the bathroom and I've asked him what colour his poo is. It's not the most romantic conversation we've had in the year and a bit since we got together, and I'm not feeling terribly proud of myself either, but there are extenuating circumstances, so let me explain.

Yesterday we arrived at The Haven – the intense detox spa I told you about last week in a stunning and secluded corner of Thailand. And, apparently, talking about your faecal matter is the norm round these parts.

After last week's hedonism at the Full Moon party (I've recovered btw), my body and my mind felt ready for a little detox. I know this is a first-world problem, but it turns out travelling in 2016 makes you somewhat lardy. I knew all that gulab jamun and ghee was going to catch up with us sooner or later, but so too have the SangSom buckets, the Magnums (Magni?) and spending all day sunbathing at the beach. It's even caught up with Train Man – the only man I know who genuinely looks good in skinny jeans. Or at least he used to.

So we checked into The Haven and set about eating a tasty pre-cleanse menu of tropical fruit and sumptuous salads before we dive, head first, into fasting.

It's a hippie, holistic kind of place, and our appropriately named spa manager, Moon, welcomed us, weighed us in (I am half a stone heavier than when we left home) and gave us the tour – which included a (clothed) demo on how to self-administer a coffee colonic. As we watched, I felt so guilty about what I'd badgered Train Man into that when Moon said the word 'anus', I started giggling nervously. I soon stopped when he handed us the rubber gloves and advised rummaging through our colonic sieves after the event, to see what we might find in there.

'Knowledge is power,' is one of the many wise mantras Moon likes to repeat, and I think we're going to hear a lot more of them in the coming days.

But one of the many things I love about Train Man is that he is a trouper. So here we go, with seven days of sun salutations, clay shakes, herbal pills and the thing I will struggle with most: fasting. If you've read my column before, you will know I am sixty per cent water, seven per cent blood, and the rest is all sugar. Not eating pastries, chocolate, brioche and cake might just kill me – but I won't let it.

I'll check in with a progress report next week, dear reader – I am hoping to shift that half-stone and have skin that's more akin to Audrey Hepburn than ET (the sun hasn't been kind to my ever-increasing wrinkles), but what was Train Man's answer to my icky question?

'Bright green, honey. Oh, and I'm sure that Matchbox car I swallowed when I was three was in there.'

Now the bathroom has been refreshed (Those. Poor. Cleaners!) and it's my turn to get on the board. Wish me luck!

28

'You'll never guess who I bumped into!' Maya and Nena say in unison, and then laugh.

The screen freezes and Maya can only see Nena's face stuck in time, from a few seconds ago. Caught in amusement at the coincidence of having said the same thing, mixed with the slight confusion of a tiny time delay and a bad connection, wondering if what the other said was in fact their own echo. Nena's eyelids are half closed as she is frozen on her sofa, her tired face dimly lit by a lamp at one end of it and the glow of the television behind the laptop.

Maya can tell from the smaller window, with her own face in it, that she looks a different sort of tired. Her eyes are narrow and sleep-ridden from having woken at 5 a.m., so she could file her column and Skype Nena before sunrise yoga – although Nena thinks Maya looks tanned and invigorated and said as much when they logged on.

The connection resumes, the frames unfreeze and both women move again.

'You go first!' Nena says.

'No you!' replies Maya, knowing her anecdote will take some beating.

Nena looks around her living room and keeps her voice low, so as not to wake Ava in her cot in the bedroom. Nena *really* needs Ava to sleep, even though part of her is desperate to show her off. She hasn't spoken to Maya in weeks and could do with someone other than her friends inside the TV to talk to. The television is muted and Tom is working late, so Nena speaks her news in hushed tones.

'Emily Snatch! In the park, the other day. So weird. She looks the same.'

'Oh weird,' says Maya. 'How is she?'

'She's a baby factory. Churning them out.'

'Oh.' Maya feels a surprising stab of jealousy but brushes it off her lap and onto the white tiled floor of the 'IT suite', a basic rectangle that's more of a stark classroom for two than a modern tech hub.

'Yeah, she has three kids, one of them is in Arlo's class. She lives near me. We're hoping to meet up…'

'Cool.' Maya has loads of questions about Emily Snatch but feels the sands of time ticking before the sun rises; before Ava needs Nena's attention; before the connection goes again. So she doesn't ask any of them, and knows that's fine with Nena.

'You go next. Who could you have possibly bumped into out there?'

'WELL...' Maya thinks of James, who she left stirring in bed so she could get online before yoga, and feels oddly guilty about the excitement of her news. 'It's another blast from our university past.'

'Oh god, who?' Nena winces, wondering which of her exes it could be.

'Jon Vincent.'

'WHAT?!'

She wasn't expecting it to be Maya's ex.

'Yes.'

'The Baby-faced Assassin?'

'The very same.'

'Mother—' The screen freezes again, but unfreezes almost immediately. '—ucker. What's *he* doing there?' she says, with a crease of her nose.

'Ooh, I'm so annoyed, Nena. He's here between filming. He's only gone and bloody made it as an actor! He comes to Thailand regularly to "reset his dials".'

'Urgh, gross.'

'I literally ran into him on the beach looking all Hollywood. Actually, come to think of it, I reckon he's had his teeth done...'

'I've never seen him in anything, and I watch a lot of films.' Nena remembers her current reality is reality television – of *course* she wouldn't have seen Jon in anything she watches.

'I don't know about films, I think he alternates between Netflix dramas and theatre. I googled him before I called you, to have a little snoop – he must work under another name because the only Jon Vincent on IMDB is a sound engineer.'

'What does he look like?'

'The sound engineer?' Maya says with a half-smile.

'The Baby-faced Assassin.'

'Annoyingly, he looks good.'

'Arsehole. Married? Kids?'

'Not sure. Don't wanna ask.'

'Damn, Maya, if only you knew his stage name, we could find out *everything*. Maybe he has a bonkers actress wife.'

Maya feels another surprising stab of jealousy. 'Yeah, I don't want to ask that either. Don't want to give him the satisfaction.'

'What did Jon say?'

'Not much – we're kind of avoiding the whole issue – we're avoiding him really. Although James has been really cool about it.'

'Go, Train Man.'

'We're about to do sunrise yoga though, and I noticed Jon's signed up for it too. So that might be awks.'

Maya wonders why there's a fizz in the hollow of her stomach. Or is it the excitement of talking to Nena? She misses Nena.

'How long's he there—'

Maya thinks the connection has frozen again, but actually it was the jagged move of Nena's head turning towards the living room door and freezing intently, to hear whether Ava is crying.

'Shit, she's awake.'

'Get her! Let me say hello.'

'I don't want to stimulate her, she'll be super-awake and hard to settle.'

Oh.

Nena sees the disappointment in Maya's freckled face and thinks *Fuck it, she won't sleep anyway.*

'Hang on, I'll go get her…'

While Maya waits, she looks out at the palm trees swaying in the dark. The computer suite feels a bit creepy when she can't see much outside it, knowing that under the strip light and stark walls she is visible – and visibly alone – to anyone outside. She thinks of James again and wonders if he's got up, or whether he's fallen back asleep.

Nena returns to view with a chubby Ava in a patterned sleepsuit, snaffling into her mother's neck. Maya's fear levels abate as her heart fills with love and longing.

'Ah!' Maya gasps.

'She's a bit snuffly, I wonder if she's teething.'

'Oh look at her! She's grown so much.'

Nena's tired face nods. 'I might have to feed her.'

'And her hair! There's so much of it.'

Maya's coos are enough to pique Ava's interest, and she turns her ruddy cheeks out from her mother's neck towards Maya, who she is confused to see on the screen.

'Hello, my gorgeous girl. It's so good to see you!' Maya marvels at the monitor and waves.

Ava's furrowed brow squints back and she turns her body further. Just as she reaches out a hand, the screen freezes again.

'Oops, you've gone,' Maya says, waiting for the connection to resume. 'Hello? Can you hear me?'

The screen stays the same. An image, stuck, of Nena on the sofa, obscured by Ava in the foreground. Maya can now see the pattern on her sleepsuit is of little whales shooting water from their blowholes. Her soft black hair frames her bright eyes. Her mouth is a circle of determination and intrigue. Her hand has chubby creases below the wrist as if someone left an elastic band there, and she's reaching out to touch Maya through the screen.

'Hello?'

Maya puts her hand to the screen, to touch Ava's.

'Hello?'

The connection fails. The screen doesn't move. And Maya bursts into tears under the strip lighting.

29

'We store a lot of anger in our thighs, so open them out and let that resentment flush forth from your pelvis,' says the compact Californian yoga teacher with pecs for boobs. As embarrassing as this is for Maya, the notion of releasing anger from her thighs is preferable to an earlier instruction about letting her anus blossom.

Maya opens one eye and sees James on the mat to her right, exhaling with a sigh as he struggles to keep his legs crossed. He rearranges himself, trying to tie his feet in a bow, but his stiff limbs keep getting tangled in the roomy white kurta pyjamas he took from the Indian palace hotel.

Maya closes her right eye and opens the left. Jon is on that side, a hand resting on each knee, each forefinger and thumb making a circle, his eyes closed as if he's sleeping sitting up. He looks at peace. He looks in the zone. He looks like Sting might be his dad (he isn't). On mats beyond him sit Kimberley and an even more lithe woman, who has fishtail plaits and, like Jon, has obviously done this before.

All five disciples sit cross-legged in a line, facing the open front of the thatched studio, waiting for the sun to rise. As peach shards start to poke out of the darkness and a hot blur appears on the horizon, Maya hears the sizzle of Jon's steady, deep breath.

He's good at this.

She wonders if Jon has opened his eyes at all during the past forty-five minutes. Surely he must have looked at the women to the left of him, in their spaghetti-strap vests and tiny skintight shorts. Maya is wearing her rather less sexy running gear.

'That's it, go deeper...' the teacher says, as she gently presses limbs and pats shoulders encouragingly as she walks barefoot on the decked floor. She's had to pat James' shoulder a lot more than anyone else's in the class. Maya wondered if the teacher – who Maya thinks is called Jess because she has a beaded necklace spelling out the name above her muscly chest – fancies James, but concludes it's probably just because James has clearly never done yoga in his life and needs the most help. A yoga teacher wouldn't fancy anyone so inflexible.

Jess walks along the line.

I wish I were better at this.

Maya wonders why her thighs still feel angry as she tries to bring her crossed knees closer to the mat.

It was just an internet connection.

'Give your body up to the earth, lift your chest a little so it connects with the rising sun.'

Ava looked so beautiful.

'Give up any tension you can by offering it to the world. Trust in the universe. Let it fill you up.'

But I feel weirdly empty.

As the sky turns from peach to orange, and nature's straight lines cut through wispy clouds, Jess asks the class to stand. 'Now you've made the sun rise – you've trusted the earth – we're going to remind the earth to trust us. So let's finish with *vrikshasana*, or tree pose,' Jess says, trying to swallow her loud voice into something more sedate. 'Gently uncross your legs, crouch, and roll up to standing.'

James stands up in a shot and untangles his giant pyjamas. 'What Indian guy is *that* much taller and *that* much fatter than the average man?' James had said when he first tried them on. Maya thought he looked as sexy as Sidharth Malhotra, her favourite Bollywood discovery, and told him to keep them, but now they do make him look kind of clumsy.

Maya rises more gently, and Jon, eyes still closed, does an elaborately slow and precise roll up. James shoots Maya a look that says he thinks yoga is bollocks and Maya tries to suppress a smile. As the class wait for Jon to unfurl, open his eyes and appreciate the sunrise, Maya tries not to appreciate his chest. He's wearing only pale grey yoga pants under his beading bare torso and Maya can see each vertebrae stack as he stands tall.

Jon finally opens his eyes and realises everyone is waiting for him, he has an audience. He runs his fingers up through his messy blond morning hair. 'Sorry about that,' he shrugs. 'I went somewhere special.'

Jess gives an understanding smile.

Jon coughs politely into his fist. '"I have more memories than if I were a thousand years old",' he says, taking in the view, flabbergasted by its beauty.

'Beyoncé?' asks Maya.

'Baudelaire,' confirms Jon.

Under Jess's instruction, the class stand on one leg, with one foot pressed against the inside of the opposite inner thigh, their palms pushed together above their heads. They look like a row of fence posts – some more rickety than others – as they take in the lines of orange, blue and white stacked in front of them in the sky above the sea.

Maya looks out to the horizon, feeling less sad about the aborted call than she did an hour ago but still confused by the internal conflict she feels in paradise.

'And rise, rise, rise out of the floor, ready for another day,' says the all-American yogi, ending with a 'Namaste.'

'Namaste,' Jon replies, closely followed by the rest of the class.

James wobbles on one leg as he tries not to lose his balance, but dizziness from the lack of calories and the inflexibility of his limbs makes him fall to the mat with a 'Fuck!' As James breaks his fall with his palms and gives up, Kimberley lets her anus blossom and accidentally releases the fart she'd been battling to hold in for the entire class. Maya's inner child finally enables her to relax and she and James stifle a giggle.

30

'Receive one thousand for your thesis,' James reads from the board.

'Oh, don't mind if I do!' says Maya, taking a crisp pink bill from the bank and puffing out her shoulders.

Maya and James are on their small terrace, playing the battered old Game of Life from the box they borrowed from the common room, seeking solace from the midday sun. It also helped distance them from the tasty food smells coming from the restaurant kitchen.

James winces as he spins the wheel. Even the soft click and whir of the little plastic prong on the number wheel is bothering the dehydration headache that's starting to creep across his temples.

'Nine,' he says, while he pushes his brown Wayfarers up his nose and advances a plastic yellow car around a track. He lands on a red rectangle. 'Get married,' he says sombrely. 'I don't know what that means.'

Maya feels frustrated. They went through this when they played yesterday.

'Spin the wheel and I give you money depending on the number you land on,' Maya says begrudgingly. She's already annoyed that James landed on 'journalist' – the career with the biggest salary apparently – and he gets 20,000 every pay day.

James spins again and works out how much his wedding gift will cost Maya. Maya doesn't make the obvious joke and ask James who he's marrying, she's not in the mood, but she rummages in the small plastic bag of colourful cars and pink and blue pegs, takes out a pink peg and flicks it across the board at him.

'That's 2,000 please.'

Maya frowns and hands over the money, then spins the wheel for her turn.

James tries to lighten the mood. 'So Nena was OK?'

'Yeah fine.'

'Tom all right?'

'For fuck's sake! Teacher. Salary 8,000.' Maya rolls her eyes. 'No, he was out, it was just Nena.'

Maya doesn't mention Ava.

'She seems OK though.'

James spins and Maya watches life's lottery favour him again.

'But it cut out, we didn't really talk for long.'

'I guess you told her about running into Jon.'

James moves his car along the board.

'Yeah, weirdly she bumped into an old uni friend in Stoke Newington,' Maya is relieved to counter. 'Not quite the way I did.' She rubs her forehead.

'Twins!' James laughs. 'Take two pegs and receive 2,000 from each player. Hang on, is that 2,000 per twin?'

Maya frowns again while James rummages in the small plastic bag. The sound of his fumbling for pegs agitates Maya and she bites her lip.

'What shall I have? Two boys, two girls, one of each?'

'I don't fucking know!' Maya snaps, standing up to go inside and find a can of Coke on the bedside table. Except there is no can of Coke on the bedside table, they're detoxing, so she comes straight back out. She wants something, but she can't face her lymph flush juice yet.

James looks confused and rubs his temple. 'What's the matter?'

'Nothing!'

Maya throws the money across the board and James gives a conciliatory look.

'Look, why don't you go for a run, you seem like you could do with it.'

'Don't patronise me, Jame—'

'I'm not, you just seem like you need to—'

'It's too hot to run!'

'OK, I was just—'

'I can't anyway. I feel awful. I have zero energy. I won't do sunrise yoga tomorrow.'

James is relieved to hear it as he has no intention of ever doing sunrise yoga again.

'And I'm so hungry. I need chocolate.'

Maya's neediness softens her, which in turn softens James.

'Me too. My head's hurting.'

Maya and James give each other consolatory smiles and hold hands across the low table they're hunched over. The sound of Bob Marley coming from the restaurant helps defuse the discord.

'Let's finish this, eh, and have a nap,' James suggests. 'Sod it, maybe we just sleep through the next few days.'

'We've got colonics at three, remember?'

James scrunches up his face.

'Your move then,' he says, a competitive glint in his eye that irks Maya and she lets go of his hand.

She spins the wheel of misfortune and moves her red car along. When they played yesterday she cheerily sang 'Little Red Corvette' as her piece wound around the bends on the board. James can tell that won't happen today.

'Five,' she states. 'One, two, three, four, five.' Maya cranes her neck to read what's on the board. 'Honeymoon over: pay 10,000 for overdue bills.'

James shrinks into his rattan chair.

'For fuck's sake!' Maya says, pushing the board away as she gets back up. There still isn't a can of Coke in the bedroom.

31

'Mind if I join you guys?'

Jon stands topless and proud, his strapping legs in stripy tailored shorts and his bare feet beige from the sand. He holds his lymph flush juice in one hand and a wedge of bound paper in the other.

Maya is somewhat thrown. And mortified. It's day three of their detox and, having just done her third colonic of the week, she and James decided to leave the sanctuary of their bedroom – too close to the scene of the atrocities in the stark en suite (no Matchbox car today for James, just green sludge; Maya's had a greyer hue) – and escaped to the cafe area with a mural made of shells on the wall behind the bar. Maya doesn't want to go through the contents of her bowels with Jon. Yesterday's yoga was awkward enough. Today she's even less keen for another such encounter, and James has become unusually grumpy.

It's a good job Maya filed her first column before she Skyped Nena, her head is now way too fuzzy to write anything Amy Appleyard would deem acceptable copy. In fact, all she and James have been able to manage is to lie on the beach or play board games on the terrace by day and watch chick flicks in the common room before an early night, without the energy to even touch each other.

Despite his growing migraine and malaise, James has been trying: gamely attempting the reverse warrior at dawn; lightly chuckling at romcoms with Maya, fifteen women, and Canadian Justin (who is shrinking by the day) at sunset. James even welled up during *The Devil Wears Prada* last night, but when Maya asked him if he was crying, he blamed the lack of carbs for making him emotional.

Jon hasn't partaken in early-evening chick flicks. He's preferred to stick to mindfulness and meditation; using the downtime to read scripts in the bar or have a massage on the beach. He's always had a charming smile for Maya and James though, as they pass each other in the common room or on the shore. No one has mentioned That Thing They Haven't Talked About.

Maya and James look up at Jon with slow moves and sallow cheeks. They feel so tired and listless that their eyeballs hurt. Even the turquoise sea at sunset isn't lifting their spirits: James has the worst headache he's had in years. And it's not even alcohol-induced.

'You said it got better by day three,' Maya scolds. 'My chocolate cravings have never been worse.'

James gestures for Jon to pull up the vacant chair, even though he doesn't want him to.

Jon laughs as he puts his glass on the table and pulls the chair back, not realising that the scraping sound of wood on wood is boring into James' head.

'Yeah, sorry about that.' Jon turns the chair the wrong way around so he can straddle it. 'Works for me by day three. I'm a day behind you, so just you watch. Tomorrow I'll be cartwheeling through here. Maybe it's tougher your first time, I can't remember.'

Maya studies the menu wedged into a wooden block on the table. One side has raw food delights, the other is Thai vegetarian. There is no menu of course for those who are fasting, so they both nurse a bottle of water, wishing they could order a 'rawsagna' – even though layers of courgette, fermented almond cheese, aubergine mock bacon and fig pâté would ordinarily make them heave.

'Well, in two days' time we can move onto the raw menu, baby,' Maya says, as she clumsily leans into

James' arm, just to make it clear it were he she were calling baby. The impact of Maya's nudge makes James look like he might fall off the table. Or throw up.

'I can't look,' he says, slumping his head into his hands. 'I don't think I can even face broth tonight. I might just go to bed.' He rubs his hands up through his brown hair, making him look more despairing.

Maya feels panicked. She doesn't want to be left alone with Jon, but she doesn't want to miss her broth. She's looked forward to it all day, which is saying something.

'But what about Moon's lecture?'

James shakes his head gently.

'And *Miss Congeniality* starts in twenty minutes, you'll like that one.'

'Nah, I can't, honey. You have my broth. Double helping; you'll need it. I feel like shit.'

James stands and scrapes his chair back, cursing himself internally for doing the exact same thing Jon did and making his head even worse. He goes to kiss Maya on the lips but misses as she turns her head up at the same time. They are both self-conscious under Jon's gaze, but James is too poorly to care.

'Shall we catch the news?' Maya asks, but James looks puzzled.

'Huh?'

'Want me to come with you?' Her eyes widen as if she's trying to tell James something.

James frowns. Now he's irritated, as if there's a reason he shouldn't leave Maya alone with Jon.

'No, you're fine. See you in a bit.'

James snakes down the path from the bar to the sea and turns left up another path to find their room between the trees. He feels so wretched, he walks slowly, swaying like a man trying to conceal he's drunk.

'Poor guy,' Jon shrugs, throwing his ream of paper onto the table with a thump. He rests his chin on a palm, propped on his elbow on the table, leaning further in towards Maya, who is still watching James walk away. 'I guess some people can't tolerate it as much as others – it's insane how every person's detox journey is different.'

Maya gazes, from the trees in which James disappeared, back to Jon, to the stack of paper on the table.

'What are you reading?'

'Oh, it's something I'm writing actually.'

'Writing?'

'Yeah, a script I'm writing. I had Hiddleston in mind for it at first, but then I thought fuck it, it's perfect for me.'

'Oh right.'

'Weird isn't it – I was writing this character – a slightly damaged spy, gone a bit rogue but finding the right path – and I connected with him so much I thought "Dammit, this *can* be me!" It's so good, I can't give it up. So I have to go back to the producers to drop the bombshell, persuade the heavies in Burbank to take a chance on me. I'll do it when I'm back.'

'Oh, OK, good luck with that.'

Jon picks up his lymph juice and takes a sip. 'Thanks,' he says with a deep green moustache, before he wipes it away on a bare arm. 'Hopefully I can make them understand. My passion will speak volumes.'

Maya looks at his arms and remembers how they held her.

'I'm sure it will.'

Jon looks at Maya, her kind and encouraging eyes, and smiles.

She smiles back, ruefully.

'Strange isn't it? Sometimes the best and the most obvious thing is right under your nose. It takes a while to see it.'

Maya unscrews the lid of her water and takes a sip, looking out to sea beyond her bottle, as if it's a telescope scrutinising the horizon. She doesn't notice Jon looking at his fancy watch.

'Anyway, shall we head over to the common room for the movie?'

'I didn't think you liked chick flicks.'

'No, but I *love* Sandy.'

'Sandy?'

'Bullock. Met her at an amfAR event in New York. She's a *hoot*. I'd watch anything with her in.'

Maya shrugs as if to say OK.

'Come on then, better get a good position...'

32

Three hours later, Maya and Jon are back at the bar, dimly lit with twinkling fairy lights, only this time they're sitting on stools facing the shell mural behind the bottles. The sea laps gently beyond the open-sided restaurant behind them, and Aphex Twin piano notes plink plonk through the stereo. Maya's not sure if it's the music pulling at her heart strings or the tequila – they are pissed after their third of the evening. They stayed on after *Miss Congeniality*, to listen to Moon's lecture and to drink their broth – double helpings in Maya's case. Jon suggested they go for a chat and Maya couldn't help herself, so when Mabel, a young Kiwi worker with purple and grey hair in two buns on the top of her head, flashed them a bottle of Cazador from under the counter, Maya thought it might be what she needed to brace herself for battle.

'Is this a test from Moon?' she asked, before turning to Jon. 'Does Moon always do this? Am I being tested?! Are you his spy?'

Maya already felt a bit drunk and giddy and couldn't work out if it was the delirium or something in the broth.

Jon shrugged.

'I'll cheat if you cheat,' he said, with a twinkle in his eye that roused an anger and a sadness in Maya. So she sat up on her stool, nodded to Mabel, and met him at his challenge.

Three shots later and she's got the giggles, as they reminisce about their university days.

'No, but do you remember that night in the Bombay Express when Dave Mitchell went CRAZY because you ate a bit of his naan?' laughs Jon.

Maya throws her head back and cracks up. She'd forgotten all about the twenty-year-old man having a temper tantrum because someone took a tiny bit of food from his plate. Maya grew up with a family for whom everything was a free-for-all at the dinner table. Everyone dug in and shared. She soon learned not everyone came from a Flowers type of family, where you had to be robust and you had to accept that someone might just steal a bit of food from your plate. And Dave Mitchell lost his temper.

'Oh yeah! He said he didn't like sharing because of the whole germ-spreading thing, so in my defence you picked up the rest of his naan and licked it.'

'Funny. As. Fuck,' says Jon proudly.

''Cause that helped!' Maya laughs, then stops when she has a thought. 'Oh, hang on, what if he had OCD or something? Shit, actually were we really mean?'

'No, he was just tight-fisted. Should have learned to share, the elf-skinned bull's pizzle.'

Huh?

Jon laughs about how funny he is and his glacial eyes gleam in the fairy lights reflected on the shells and the shards of the glass in the mural. Then it hits her. Maya finally realises where that colour comes from. Jon's eyes are the same colour as the water around the Thai coast. She'd never realised it until now. How funny to bump into him then, here of all places.

They giggle at the memory of Dave Mitchell losing his shit in the curry house and pause, looking at each other in the dimly lit bar, only to be interrupted by the screen lighting up from a notification on Jon's phone. Maya jumps, like a rabbit caught in headlights. Jon scrambles for his phone, as Maya sees the backlit wallpaper, a photo of a baby.

Shit.

Jon reads out a news update.

'Police investigating Manon Junot disappearance say they have reason to believe she was suffering paranoid schizophrenia in the run-up to her going missing.'

Maya's eyes widen.

'Not really news. Not worth a push notification anyway,' says Jon, turning his phone face down on the bar.

'You have a baby?' Maya asks coolly.

'No, not mine. It's Charlie's boy. My nephew.'

'Charlie's a dad?! I can't imagine!'

'Yes, he's still a twat, he's just a twat with a kid. Not sure how he had such a cute baby. His partner is pretty hot though. All comes from her.'

'What's his name?'

'Geronimo.'

'Geronimo?'

'Yeah, he is just awesome. So funny. Makes me proper clucky.'

'Clucky?'

Maya's heart starts to race. She really shouldn't have downed three tequilas on an empty stomach.

'Yeah,' Jon nods, regretfully, looking into Maya's hazel eyes.

The shell mural on the wall behind the bar starts to mutate and the room around them begins to spin. The emptiness in her core and the racing of her heart makes Maya feel somewhat bilious.

He wants a baby.

Her eyes narrow, her moves become lumbering, and she leans into Jon, their foreheads almost touching.

'Why did you do it?' she whispers.

Jon leans away slightly, taken aback by the sudden change of topic; surprised by a blunt and candid side of Maya he doesn't remember.

'Why did I do what?'

Jon shifts on his bar stool.

'You know.'

He shrugs his shoulders, then leans back in. Their temples almost touch now.

'I suppose it's because I wasn't good enough for you. I felt inadequate.'

Maya inhales sharply.

'So why didn't you just break up with me? Why didn't you just end it? Say you weren't feeling it.' Maya goes to twist the ring on her right hand but remembers she took it off earlier – it was getting a bit loose and she didn't want to lose it. 'Why did you piss our money up the wall? *My* money? I had to move back to Hazelworth. Shelve my dream of buying a home for another, I dunno, five years...'

Jon puts his hand to his other temple, to create a shield from the bar, make a bubble for he and Maya, and he looks remorseful. 'I genuinely don't know what to say.'

'There's nothing you can say really, it's done. I just never understood why you did it so callously. Taking your things little by little. Sending me that text. I was so good to you.'

'You were.'

'It was a total dick move.'

'It was.'

Mabel comes back to top up their tequilas with a wink and some added green juice, so their glasses look like wheatgrass shots. She gives Jon a knowing smile and walks off to flirt with another customer.

'Looks like it worked out for you though, you and…'

'James.'

'Yeah, that's right, James.'

'It did.'

Maya thinks of running behind her father, looking at the criss-cross lines of the back of his pineapple neck. Of her brothers helping her move into her new flat. Of the day she first saw Train Man walk up the platform to get the 8.21 a.m., and how she fell in love at first sight. She smiles with heavy lids but just can't help herself from picking the scab.

'But why? *Why* did you do it? *Why* did you cheat? If you felt so inadequate – you could have just told me.'

'Because it was easier to break up with you if you hated me. I was so in love with you, Maya. Talia meant nothing to me, we didn't last ten minutes, but I just knew I wasn't good enough for *you*. I wasn't enough for your amazing imagination, for your brilliant, crazy family. For your career dreams. I was just an actor bum. I didn't know I was going to make it big then. I thought I'd do you a favour and set you free, and I knew I had to make you hate me or you would never get over me.'

'I did hate you.'

Jon looks sad. And uncomfortable. He looks very uncomfortable in their bubble, but he's trying.

'I'm just so fucking sorry, Maya.'

33

James kicks his legs out in discomfort and rolls over. Nothing feels right. Without a sheet, he shivers; with a sheet, he sweats – and when he's underneath it, he feels stifled by frustration and the toxic hum of a sickly scent.

Where is she?

He turned CNN off an hour ago. Even with Anderson Cooper on mute, to keep him company and to prevent Maya from having to turn on the stark, burning light when she came in, so she could see where her things were and find her way around, James could hear a high-pitched buzz of electricity that tore into his brain like a drill going through his eyeballs. The tickertape on the TV said it was midday in New York; 11 p.m. in Thailand, so James decided to not be so considerate, to not leave a gentle light on. He turned off the TV and rolled over. Sweat, roll, roll. Taunted by the rattling of the air-con unit until he turned that off too. Taunted by the sound of the water gently lapping on the shore through the open window. Taunted by the sounds of digital dance, jazz and low laughter coming from the restaurant bar in the corner of the cove. He stopped fidgeting for a second so he could listen, and see if he could place Maya's laugh out there. He wanted to work out if she were in the bar or the common room, with new friends or old, and listen for clues to see if she'd gone to late-night yoga with Jon.

In the silence and the sweat, James lies, thrashing in the heat, his skin smelling of chemicals, his brain hallucinating. His hair damp. His chest clammy. He thinks he can hear Maya's feet on the gravel path leading to their room, but the sound fades out and disappears, deeper into the woods beyond the kitchen block, beyond the furthest rooms. James lies with his arms above his head and kicks his legs. He hears giggles, he hears whispers, rising and falling through the window. He hears a door, he hears a stumble and a crash, and then, finally, he sinks into a feverish slumber.

34

March 2016, London, England

Nena brings the buggy to a standstill outside the unassuming 1960s building with pebble-dash render. It doesn't sit well adjacent to the Art Deco town hall, but it serves the community with jumble sales, ballet lessons and baby sensory classes. Nena had to google what baby sensory actually was, after Emily Snatch told her about it. She soon learned it was all about developmental play through sight, sound, smell and touch, but still didn't really get it.

'Throwing jelly about? Foam parties?' she scowled at Tom's laptop screen. 'I have enough food and shit thrown at me at home.' He hugged her and said it sounded great. So, this Monday morning, Nena asked Tom to watch Ava while she got dressed and brushed her teeth. She even combed her long black hair before putting it in a messy ballet bun. And she made it to the community centre, a whole ten minutes early.

Triumph.

Nena sighs and thinks of Emily's reassuring birdlike face. How she always looked like a mother hen, even when she was eighteen, wearing her lady shirts and wielding a first-aid kit around. So if mother hen goes to baby sensory classes with her third baby, it must be better than some of the classes Nena has scoffed at.

It'll do Ava good.

Nena eschewed the NHS Baby Group at the health centre after just one meeting, telling Tom all the other women were arseholes. She smiled politely when the health visitor handed her leaflets about Tumbletots and Music Train, then tucked them into the recycling. And at baby weigh-in clinic she always keeps her eyes down.

It'll do me good.

Nena looks at her phone. It's nine twenty-one, so she decides to grab a coffee from the Costa next door to ease her apprehension.

I'm not sure I can be bothered.

Nena thinks of Maya and imagines what Maya might be like as a mother. She knows Maya would try really hard. Maya would probably have gone to all the baby groups, all the classes, and made loads of friends. Maya is a doer and a trier.

I've never had to make an effort.

This feeling is so alien to Nena, she feels discomfort in the pit of her stomach. She looks up at the coffee menu on the wall to try to calm herself with familiar fonts and colours; trying to distract herself by pondering the vast array of choice, when she knows all she wants is a milky latte.

What's wrong with me?

Before Nena became a mother, she would turn up at parties alone and know she would make five friends that night. She would happily walk into any room and confidently make conversation – usually with the most handsome or most damaged guy in it – and more often than not she'd end up naked with him, then breeze out of his flat the next morning, leaving him hanging.

Nena sees her reflection in the flat stainless steel of the back of the coffee machine and doesn't recognise the brown-skinned girl with an unusually pale face. She isn't familiar with the nervous eyes looking back at her.

'Half-shot latte,' she says, swaying rhythmically, gently back and forth, against the buggy without even noticing. Comforting Ava, comforting herself.

She looks out onto the high street and sees a drizzle start to form on the windows.

Sunshine, I need sunshine.

Nena thinks of Maya again, lording it up, all freckled and tanned, at the luxe spa in tropical Thailand. Free and fit and entwined in Train Man, all tanned and strong and ready to take on the world – and Jon Vincent – together.

She pays for her coffee and wheels the buggy to the end of the barista's bar. As she waits, she looks out of the vast window again, idly out onto the high street, wondering how wet she will get ducking next door to baby sensory.

Shit.

Nena sees the woman she disliked most from the one and only NHS Baby Group session she went to. The woman is walking cheerfully through the drizzle, her baby in a sling on her chest as she pulls open the heaving door of the hall, ready for class. She's the mother who dominated the session, trying to beat everyone as if they were playing birthing Top Trumps, regaling the group with the horrors of her fourth-degree tear.

I didn't want to hear it then, I don't want to hear it now.

Nena picks up her half-shot latte and wheels the buggy to the door, hitting the automatic open button with her jean-clad hip. She steers the buggy out of the coffee shop, lowers her sunglasses despite the rain and walks past the pebble-dash community centre, towards home.

35

March 2016, The Haven, Thailand

Maya stirs to the sound of pottering and packing. She can hear footsteps padding around the bed. Zips opening. Clasps fastening. The sound of nylon straps being pulled and tightened. The sound of intention and movement. She opens one eye and James comes into focus. Top off. Cargo shorts slung low around his slimmer hips. He looks more spritely than when he shuffled off to take his pounding head to bed before the sun set last night.

James, relieved that it has passed, yet packing with purpose, must have sweated out every toxin, every bug, every last bit of clay and clag, to rise like a phoenix from the ashes – before having a much-needed shower. Jon's day three is obviously James' day four, and only now does he feel like he's come through the worst.

Maya feels like it's the Day Of The Dead, her head is throbbing at the front and the taste of bile and tequila rises from her stomach.

He's packing?

The ill feeling in Maya's head is echoed by the atmosphere in the room, and it forms and lingers like a black smoke snaking around her heart.

'What are you doing, baby?'

Hurt and sadness fill James' big brown eyes. It's a look Maya hasn't seen before – except maybe fleetingly on the train, when she didn't know that his own heart was hurting as much as hers. The unfamiliarity of it is disconcerting. Knowing that she has caused it makes her feel wretched.

'Packing.'

'Where are you going?'

'Away from here.'

Maya sits upright and clutches the sheet to her chest. 'What? You're leaving?'

Horror crosses her face.

'Yep, I'm not staying around here.' More zips, more straps, all pulled with stern precision, not anger. 'It's up to you if you come with me or not.'

James sounds so callous. Maya has never heard him sound anything like this. She hopes he's bluffing, that he does want her to go with him really, but the sick feeling in her stomach and the guilt in her heart make her realise, she deserves this.

'But we have… three days left.'

'I'm done with it.'

James' face is more beautiful than ever, which in turn makes Maya panic even more.

I can't lose him.

'What?'

Maya has that terrible feeling she's being dumped.

'I'm done with it, Maya.'

Maya shakes her head as if to say no, and a boulder rattles inside her skull. 'James, please…'

'You've made me look like such an idiot. I didn't *want* to drink clay and stick a tube up my arse. But I did. For you. For your column. I didn't *want* to hang out with your ex-boyfriend, but I did. For you. And, if I'm honest…'

'You didn't want to come travelling?'

James finally meets Maya's eye. He doesn't answer.

'I want to get to Vietnam. Keep moving.' He puts his backpack on the floor by the door. 'Last night I felt the shittiest I've felt in ages. I was sick. Sweating. Awful. And where were you? Breaking all our hard work in this bullshit, getting pissed by the looks of it.'

Maya feels terrible and nods a gentle nod.

'With your ex-boyfriend too, I imagine?'

Maya's silence says it all.

James remembers the laughter rolling on incense from the bar to the bedroom.

'Nice one, Maya, nice to know we've got each other's backs.'

'Oh no, I'm so, so sorry.'

Maya jumps up onto the mattress, determination to salvage things overriding her nausea, the sheet still wrapped around her, and touches James' bare shoulder. He shrugs her off, takes the T-shirt that's hanging from the chair and puts it on. It feels unkind and alien to James to shrug Maya off, he just wants to wrap his arms around her, but he can't.

'Look, nothing happened with Jon. We went to the common room, watched the movie, listened to Moon, and then... he asked if I wanted to go to the bar.'

'And you did. You wanted to go and get pissed with him rather than check on me.'

'I wanted an apology. That's what I really wanted.' Maya is shocked by how angry she sounds. It's enough to make James stop and look at her. 'I'm sorry, I should have come back sooner, to see if you were OK, but I wanted to look him in the eye and ask him why he did it.'

'And did he? Apologise?'

'Yes. He did. I needed to hear it, to be honest, so I could draw a line under everything.'

James widens his eyes as if to give a sarcastic thanks.

'Look, let me get showered and dressed, I'm coming with you, it's not even a question.'

James feels relief but doesn't show it. That it was what *he* needed to hear.

'Baby, I hate this place. I hate him! I was just doing it for the column. So they didn't sack me, so I didn't...'

'So you didn't what? Lose your career? Whether it's newspapers or patisserie, I've supported everything you do, Maya.' James shrugs.

'I know. And I don't want you to think I'm not supporting you. You're an *amazing* photographer. This time next year you'll be overrun with bookings and commissions.'

Maya edges towards the side of the mattress and stands, still wrapped in the sheet, level with James, still looking downbeat.

I'm such an idiot.

'Look, I'm sorry. But I cheated on the detox, with tequila, not on you, with Jon. And I shouldn't have done it, I should have come back and mopped your brow.' She smooths his hair to the side of his forehead and kisses it. 'I'll do anything to make it up to you.'

Maya wraps her arms around James' neck.

'Anything?' he asks.

'Anything,' she says with a twinkle in her slightly yellow eyes.

'Get dressed, and let's get out of here.'

Maya nods.

'I don't want to rummage in my shit, or for broth to be the culinary highlight of my day. And I don't want to see your ex-boyfriend, who treated you awfully, fawning over you and parading around like the Big I Am because he's a hotshot actor who can do the lotus position better than me. He might know loads of A-listers, and I'll always make nice and be polite, but I'm never *not* going to think he's a prick.'

'*I'm* never going to not think he's a prick.'

'Good. Then kiss me and pack.'

Maya likes this commanding side of James. He's usually so amiable and placatory. But feisty Train Man is hot.

Maya moves her kisses up James' neck until she plants one on his lips.

'You stink.'

'I know!' she laughs, and jumps down, untangling herself, so she can shower, pack and get the hell out of Poo Camp.

Maya stands at the table with all the leaflets on top of it and steps out of her bronze Havaianas, ready for her weigh-in. Or weigh-out, rather. While she waits, she ponders how she can let Moon down after The Haven kindly offered this trip to Maya and James for free, for a write-up. How can she write it with the tension Amy Appleyard wants (*Well done, Amy, you got your bust-up*) without letting *Esprit* readers know she royally messed up?

As Maya waits for Moon, she looks at a leaflet about crystals, and considers which small and polite fib she can tell, to explain why they're leaving three days early.

Another member of staff, a man Maya hasn't seen before, walks up the wooden ladder steps to the common room and comes in clutching the scales.

'Mister Moon is in the main office. Big hoo-ha. Guest leave without paying.'

Maya gasps. 'Really?'

'Yeah, it happen every now and then. But we track 'em down and kill 'em.'

Maya gasps again before seeing the smile on the corner of the man's mouth.

'Well, I'm sorry to hear that. But if you can let Moon know everything was wonderful, thank you, and sorry that we're leaving halfway through, we've just had a family matter come up.' Maya hopes her excuse sounds less flimsy to someone who doesn't speak English as their first language. 'I'll write up a glowing review.'

'Here to please you, ma'am. Hope you return to The Haven again soon.'

'We will,' Maya lies, knowing she will never voluntarily not eat for a day ever again.

'Always our raw restaurant,' says the man, as if he can read her mind. 'Not everyone come to fast.'

Maya blushes and takes her cue to step on the scales while James walks their luggage to the little wooden boat waiting at the shore. He already clocked a loss of 4kg this morning. As Maya rises barefoot, she steps up onto a cloud of relief. She's relieved to be leaving; relieved to be putting Jon well and truly in her past; relieved that the weight of betrayal is now lifted from her shoulders.

My Travels with Train Man

If you're looking for the elixir of life, I'm afraid to say clay shakes is not it. We've just left what rapidly became known as 'Poo Camp', and while my skin is sparkling with radiance and freckles, and I am lighter and leaner than I've felt in ages, I am also desperate for some spring rolls.

It's been a strange few days here. The daily meditation, lectures, sunrise yoga, late-night yoga (which isn't a euphemism, it's actually a thing) were all just the tonic after getting bogged down by long bus trips, too many Magnums and a lazy lifestyle at the beach. But I won't mind if I never have to do another self-administered colonic again. Or any other kind.

The embarrassment and hunger made for a tetchy few days between Train Man and me. I'm not very good at not eating sugar; it makes me really grumpy. So much so that even being in a Thai idyll couldn't stop me acting like a total bitch over our nightly vegetable broth. If there were chocolate on the premises, trust me, I would have found it. So this, our biggest test, has only confirmed what I suspected: that Train Man must be the most patient man on the planet.

Poor guy. He has gamely watched Legally Blonde, Dirty Dancing and The Devil Wears Prada in a common room surrounded by women (he was rooting for Anne Hathaway in her cerulean blue cable-knit, mind); he had to get onboard the (enema) board to fill his bowel with a coffee solution and even offered to go first so he could tell me the dos and don'ts of it; and he didn't love me any less when he heard me discussing the contents of my basket with Moon (no Matchbox cars for me, but I think there was a Creme Egg wrapper in there somewhere). He even forgave me when I cheated on him and broke the detox for a couple of cheeky tequilas and a bowl of wasabi peas after I bumped into an old friend in the bar (go figure).

Anyway, in a world where 'rawsagna' is cheating, you know you're in for an intense few days. But our stats speak volumes. Train Man's brown eyes are glowing like Oscar statuettes. And I have lost more weight than I've put on during this trip and can even see the outline of some muscles on my stomach (if I say six-pack out loud then I'll think of Tunnock's Tea Cakes, so best I *don't). But I really, really, want a plate of spring rolls. And a Crunchie.*

So, with a gleeful heart, we say goodbye to beautiful Thailand and head to Vietnam, where we will take in a motorbike tour around the north of the country, eat spring rolls in Hanoi and have clothes made for us at the famous tailor shops of heavenly Hoi An.

Train Man and I feel closer because we've overcome our first true test, and I never have to do another self-administered coffee-colonic. We'll never speak of this again.

36

March 2016, London, England

Who's the twat buying the kale? Nena thinks as she idly stares at the conveyor belt in front of her. The middle-aged woman sitting behind the checkout with a badge that says Sandra gives a sympathetic smile, to half apologise for the customer in front, who just nipped off to 'get one more thing' before Nena got in line. Nena doesn't smile back, instead she rhythmically rocks the pram, hoping Ava doesn't wake in Sainsbury's. She studies the shopping on the belt in front of her and compares it to her own meagre bag of pears, the single butternut squash, a bag of salted peanuts and a box of Mikado. Judging from the customer in front and the abundance of buckwheat, flaxseed and sumac, she must be much more wholesome and much more organised than Nena, but Nena knows she can – she *will* – always come back tomorrow. It's pretty much the only place she goes.

Ava lets out a little gurgle to announce that she is awake.

Shit.

Nena was hoping that Ava would stay asleep until they got home, so Nena could wake her by getting her out of the pram at the bottom of their flat stairs. Every nap has an optimum length, depending on the time of day it falls. Not too short or Ava will be ratty, not too long or the night will be even worse than usual. Nena seems to punctuate her day by trying to get Ava to sleep, then trying to wake her up.

'Sorry!' says a tall man with thick ginger stubble wielding a packet of organic brown rice, as he deftly slides back into his place in front. 'Almost forgot this!' he says, shaking it with glee like a child with a box of Tic Tacs. Strapped to his chest is a young baby, clinging like a koala in deep sleep, its tiny fingers splaying out against the man's proud chest.

Sandra smiles as if to say 'Don't you worry at all', because Sandra is more tolerant than Nena and Sandra loves babies, although she failed to coo at Ava in her buggy.

The man proceeds to put his groceries into his mustard-coloured Fjällräven backpack, as if he is stacking building blocks neatly into place. He is obviously a very efficient packer as well as a wholesome eater.

Surely he's not feeding the baby all that yet?

'How old?' asks Sandra, gender non-committal, as she swipes the barcode on a box of puy lentils.

'She's five weeks,' says the man, in an unnecessarily loud voice, as he packs with a flourish.

No, she's definitely not eating polenta and puy lentils. I bet he's going to rustle up something nutritious for his tired wife for dinner. Wanker.

Ava gurgles and Nena tends to her, propping her seat up a little so she can see and straightening her blanket.

'Shhhh, shhhh,' she soothes, hoping Ava isn't so hungry that she creates a scene. 'Nearly there.'

The man pays for his shopping, slings his backpack onto his broad back, gives Sandra a wink and Nena a nod, and saunters out, without his baby even flinching.

Nena wheels the pram forward.

'Awww, what a good dad...' says Sandra, favourably, with knitted eyebrows and glassy eyes.

Nena can't even think of a response as she puts her four items in the shopping basket under her pram.

A good dad?

Nena wants to ask Sandra what she has to do to be deemed a good mum? No one calls her a good mum when she does the shopping with Ava in a sling. Does Nena have to have nailed sleep, weaning, potty training, walking, bed-wetting and GCSEs by six months to be deemed a good mum?

'Yeah, great,' Nena replies, trying to bury her sarcasm into her leather jacket as she rolls her pram away, feeling even more unremarkable.

What do I have to do to be remarkable?

37

'Backpackers in the Vietnamese city of Hanoi are claiming to have spotted missing 28-year-old French scientist, Manon Junot. 19-year-old Elleke Sloof and her 20-year-old boyfriend Jaap Melis, who are students from the Netherlands, believe they spotted Ms Junot by the lake in the heart of the city in a confused state. Ms Junot has been missing since New Year's Day when she didn't board a flight homebound for Paris.

'Our Asia correspondent Heidi Adler has been following the story and is live in Hanoi. Heidi, what credibility do these claims have?'

SCREEN CUTS TO A BLONDE WOMAN STANDING IN FRONT OF A LAKE LIT AT NIGHT AS SHE FACES THE CAMERA.

'Well, Rita, Elleke Sloof and Jaap Melis aren't the first people to claim to have sighted Ms Junot since she was last recorded on that CCTV footage from Chiang Rai, Thailand, in mid-December. But this couple are being listened to, and their account is enough for the Vietnamese authorities to have said they will open enquiries into it. Why? They're keeping tight-lipped at the moment, but this sighting took place before the family released further details of Ms Junot's mental health, so parts of their description of Ms Junot's behaviour might concur with what the family have experienced in the past.

'Ms Junot's father, Andre Junot, released more details this week of his daughter's mental-health history, including an episode of paranoid schizophrenia while she was studying at the Université Sorbonne in Paris in 2010.

'Here's what Miss Sloof and Mr Melis said at a press conference back in Amsterdam today.'

SCREEN CUTS TO DUTCH BACKPACKERS IN A PRESS CONFERENCE AT AN AIRPORT. THE YOUNG FEMALE SPEAKS.

'We were just taking a stroll around the lake when we saw a woman matching Manon Junot's description – she had the same clothes even: the blue shorts and the white vest; they looked dirty, as if they were her only clothes. She even had an ankle chain on her foot. We couldn't believe it. She was walking with a local man, he kept putting his arm around her. We walked behind them for a while, trying to keep up, and it was only when Jaap called out her name – he shouted "Manon!" and she looked around – that we thought, "That's it, it's her!"'

THE MALE BACKPACKER SPEAKS:

'That's when she started behaving erratically. She looked panicked, and was breaking into a run, looking back at us. The man was struggling to keep up with her. Shouting things at her as he tried to stay with her. She looked pretty savage, wild in the eyes. We didn't want to alarm her further, so we went straight to the police.'

SCENE CUTS BACK TO HEIDI ADLER, STANDING IN CENTRAL HANOI.

'So, Rita, police here in Hanoi are now going through CCTV footage from the central district of the city, and following up with hospitals and asking questions to see if it was indeed Manon Junot, and if so, who she was with. We know from the 2010 incident that Ms Junot was reported missing by her friends but was found in hospital two days later. It's now been 100 days, and the family say they're heartbroken. Perhaps this sighting will give them fresh hope. Rita, back to you.'

SCREEN CUTS BACK TO THE STUDIO.

'Thanks, Heidi. That's Heidi Adler, in Hanoi with the latest.'

38

April 2016, Northern Vietnam

'Maya. Maya. MAYA! Wake up! You're falling off!' James' cries are frantic and frightened – and barely audible above the throaty chug of a Soviet Minsk motorcycle, brown and dirty with splats of mud. But the sudden twist in James' body and the panic in his voice startles Maya enough for her to open her droopy eyes. She sees a man and a woman overtake on a moped with a pig bound in netting, strapped horizontally on a little shelf above the back wheel, and wonders if the pig is dead or alive. Or if, indeed, she's dreaming.

The pig must be dead or it would put up a fight.

The soporific pull of the engine lulls her under again, and her body starts to slide away from James.

'MAYA!'

Just as she's perilously close to that last release of her hand around James' waist, close to coming nose-to-tarmac with the potholed road, Maya jolts. The slip was enough to scare her awake. She sits upright and tightens her grip on James' middle as she watches the pig weave in and out of traffic and accelerate off ahead.

'Honey, you have to stay awake!' James shouts at the top of his voice, but so much of it is lost in traffic. 'Hold on! You're falling asleep and slipping off! I can't drive and hold you up!'

Trucks, vans, motorbikes and cars fly in and out of undesignated lanes on the broken highway. The lush valleys, mossy karsts and wavy green rice terraces have given way to flat lands peppered by thin grey concrete buildings, and Maya realises they are nearly back to base.

For the past three days and nights, Maya, James and an Irish couple called Dee and Lenny have been navigating Vietnam's northern countryside, stopping at markets and monkey sanctuaries along the way; sleeping under mosquito nets on the creaky wooden floors of high, stilted houses; welcomed into the homes of hill-tribe families.

As the group loaded up their panniers and set off from tour leader Cuong's workshop in Hanoi, Lenny, a tall but stout man with silvery blond hair, pink cheeks and mischievous eyes, introduced himself to James, while Maya wriggled uncomfortably in the waterproof trousers she'd just been given by Cuong. An old army helmet, thick sweatshirt, charcoal waterproof overtrousers and biker boots was not her go-to outfit.

'Lenny. Good to meet you, pal,' he said, as he extended a large hand. As James shook it, Lenny's girlfriend marvelled at the motorcycles, all propped up on their stands in a line.

'Things of beauty!' she said, stroking the curved body of the fuel tank, black and shiny like a beetle. 'They call them "iron buffaloes". Difficult to start, but once you do, they can run and run. Such strength!'

James, Maya and Lenny all looked at Dee, marvelling at her beauty, her strength, more than the Minsk motorbikes – her enthusiasm was intoxicating.

'They wouldn't pass emissions tests back home, but jaysus, they are a-mazin'!' Dee said, caressing the seat of the one she hoped would be hers. She walked over to Maya and James, raised a hand and smiled. 'I'm Dee.'

Maya and James already felt ashamedly English for not having made any friends on their trip (Jon definitely didn't count), so they were relieved, on the first evening, 150km out of Hanoi, at a rustic dinner table, to hear Dee and Lenny hadn't made any friends either, and they'd been travelling for a month longer.

'But you're Irish. You make friends wherever you go!' said Maya in surprise.

'It's all kids getting pissed up and jumping into each other's bunks after a foam party, isn't it, Dee?' said

Lenny, with a roll of his eyes as he watched James, Maya, Dee and Cuong sprinkle dried snake bile into some rice wine.

'We've kept ourselves to ourselves too,' replied Maya, as if to make Lenny feel better, although it was actually true.

The Dao hill tribe they were staying with brought out fish, soups and spring rolls that left a lingering taste of mint and holy basil that was so pure and sensational, Maya said she would happily survive on them for the rest of her life. Lenny asked the proud cook if he had any chicken wings he could rustle up, but he settled for fish when the answer was no, as long as Dee took out all the bones for him first.

On the second day, they stopped at a village to watch silk weavers at their looms and then sat by a river while Cuong poured boiling water into four bowls of pho, made by one weaver's mother. As Maya, James, Dee and Lenny sat watching their noodles come to life, Cuong unwrapped a foil parcel with a baguette inside.

'What are you having?' asked James, bewildered as to why their guide wasn't tucking in to a pho of his own.

'Sandwich,' smiled Cuong, carefully straightening the foil out as he opened his lunch.

James craned his head to ask what culinary combination was inside the colourful baton.

'Peanut butter, salami, honey, tomatoes, cucumber, Laughing Cow...' Cuong answered, taking a hearty bite.

James laughed.

'I like Western food,' Cuong added with a shrug.

On the second night, Lenny dared to try the dried snake bile sprinkled in rice wine, and it made him relax a bit more about there not being chicken wings on any of the menus among the cornfields and karsts of the verdant Vietnamese countryside, where there always seemed to be life burgeoning from out of the rich soil. The drink made Maya lean into James, kiss his neck and wish she could grow something inside of her.

Now, with the loud throaty chug of the Minsk motorcycle making Maya yearn for bed, she's ready to get back to Hanoi – find a hotel with a decent mattress and a proper shower, clean some of the mud off her – although, boy, were those waterproof trousers a lifesaver! Maybe she'll take a run around the centre of Hanoi. She's looked on Google Maps and there's a path you can run, all the way around Hoan Kiem Lake, that's about a kilometre long and looks safe enough, being slap bang in the middle of the historic centre.

A truck weighed down under a mountain of grey slate toots its horn as it overtakes the three Minsk motorcycles; the loud blood-curdling beep making Maya jump and scream. She's certainly awake now. James doesn't hear her scream among the rattle and din, even though her chin is resting on his shoulder and her mouth is just behind his ear. She cowers and buries her face into James' back, to protect herself from flying debris.

'You awake?!' James shouts again, urging Maya not to be asleep.

'Yes. Yes, sorry!' Maya yawns.

The motorbike tour, the peace of the countryside, making new friends – it's tiring, but it all feels so new. So liberating. This is what Maya had in mind when she pictured her and James travelling. Not crying in a coffin on a night bus in India, or comparing their poo or arguing about bumping into an ex.

This is what it's all about, Maya thinks, as she dodges a shard of slate and is grateful for the helmet that she knows her brothers would say makes her look like 'a total helmet'. If only they could see her now.

The group has listened to the wisdom of tribal elders while hugging their great-grandchildren – chubby babies with smooth faces and gleeful eyes – shared anecdotes under the stars, eaten the most delicious, nurturing and tasty food of their lives, and cut through devastatingly beautiful countryside. Maya hasn't even missed chocolate. This is the happiest she has been on the trip so far.

I am so very lucky.

The only downside is that the chug of the engine, and the comfort of clinging on to James' waist, means Maya finds being a passenger on a Minsk motorcycle very hypnotic. She'd never even been on a moped before, and thought she'd be terrified to be so vulnerable on the open road. Turns out the biggest danger to Maya is herself and her sleepy head.

Now, Cuong, quiet and knowledgeable, is guiding them back into the traffic fumes and the multi-lane chaos of the outskirts of Hanoi.

'Please don't fall asleep again,' James pleads, khaki green helmet tilted wonkily on his head.

'It's OK, baby. I'm awake now.'

Maya squeezes James' stomach to reassure him. Despite the danger, the horrors of the overloaded trucks flying past so close, riding on the back of James' motorcycle feels like the safest place in the world.

Cuong speeds on up ahead and indicates with his arm to turn off. James, steady and reliable, follows suit. Dee and Lenny follow behind, Dee driving at the front, while her boyfriend sits, bolt upright, his white knuckles and terrified teeth visible every time Maya turns around to check they're still there.

James and then Dee indicate off, following Cuong into the outskirts of Hanoi as the light starts to fade. Down a few quieter roads to an industrial area, Cuong pulls up outside what looks like a Chinese restaurant.

'Dinner,' he says, with a faint smirk on his face.

James kicks down the stand on his bike and removes his helmet, his brow furrowed, his mind troubled. Maya almost melts off.

'Honey, it's so dangerous, you falling asleep like that.'

'I know, I can't help it. You're just so… cosy.'

'If you slump off the back at 50mph on the motorway you'd be flattened by a lorry. It's chaos!'

Maya plants a kiss on James' lips. Even in panic mode he has an air of calm.

'Well, dinner will wake me up, I'm sure.'

'Hmmm,' says James doubtfully.

The third motorcycle pulls up and quietens the deep rumble of the engine. Dee pulls off her helmet with a satisfied smile, letting her thick black curls spring out, tall and proud.

'Which way round is it again?' James whispers to Maya under his breath.

James can't get his head around which name belongs to which person, despite three days of conversation and confessionals. He thinks both Dee and Lenny are names that would suit either a man or a woman, and both work in a spoonerism, which adds to his confusion. He looks at Maya with his baffled, handsome face.

'*She's* Dee, *he's* Lenny. And neither of them are called Lee or Denny.'

James nods compliantly.

But he could be a Lee.

It didn't take long after getting together for James to find out about Maya's Special Memory skill. She knows the digits of every car number plate her parents have ever owned; that the capital of Honduras is Tegucigalpa;

that she can recall every meal of their trip so far, where they were when they ate it, and what rating out of ten she would give it. She also remembers which way around Dee and Lenny's names go, and for all of this, James is in awe.

They only met Dee and Lenny three days ago in the workshop in Hanoi, but the long drives and shared experience – plus the laughs over rice wine at night – make it feel like longer. Dee and Lenny are good company: Dee is brave and bold and her loud punchy laugh is contagious; Lenny is an endearing rounded teddy bear, who always looks to Dee to concur with him after every sentence.

'Wasn't our scene, was it, Dee?'

'I don't really like fish, do I, Dee?'

'She's the better driver, aren't you, Dee?'

Dee, with far-apart eyes and a gap between her two front teeth, just nods a 'Yes, dear' and Lenny, with sparkles in his besotted eyes, is content knowing that Dee is in agreement, even if she might not have been listening.

Maya and James are heartened by how different they are, yet how well they work. They're not as tactile as Maya and James – not as tactile as Maya anyway – but they seem completely unified, as if one couldn't survive without the other to look after. Well, Lenny definitely wouldn't survive without Dee to remove his fish bones.

They've got along so well, they've decided to carry on travelling together down to Hoi An. But James does need to get their names right first.

'Well, that was amazin'!' Dee says with glee, as she kicks out the stand and jumps off the muddy Minsk. She walks around, stretching out her legs, a jubilant sparkle in her eyes.

'No no no no no!' laments Lenny. 'Please, Dee, please tell me that's the last of it; we don't have to get back on.'

Dee looks to Cuong, who's patiently waiting, as he has done for much of the trip.

'Just a little ride back into Hanoi.'

'Oh no!' Lenny clasps his face.

'Relax!' Cuong says. 'First, dinner...'

James pats Lenny on the back and Cuong extends his thin arm towards the dark wood, red and gold restaurant, and slings his leather jacket over the seat of his motorcycle. He wears a black T-shirt with 'In Minsk We Trust' emblazoned in red across his heart in a *chû nôm* script. Maya is delighted to jump out of her overtrousers, and the hungry, weary travellers walk in.

A man in white chef aprons gives Cuong a loose hug.

'Guys, this is my friend Nguyen, this is his snake palace.'

They speak to each other in Vietnamese.

'Did he just say snake?' Lenny attempts to whisper to Dee. She pouffes up her hair and tucks her fitted checked shirt into her tight jeans.

'You'll love it, Len.'

Maya looks at James and gives a nervous smile. Excited by what awaits. Comforted by Dee's voice. Maya loves how her soft Dublin lilt jars with her beautiful brown skin. James puts his arm around Maya as they follow Cuong and Nguyen into the restaurant, past a row of urns covered in cloth tied with rubber bands. Past the open kitchen, wall-to-wall in pots and pans, with searing fire rising to the ceiling.

Nguyen is more affable than quiet Cuong, the effusive host wanting to impress the tourists. He reaches an arm out to present the table that awaits – white linen and plates all set – and Maya notices he is missing the thumb from his left hand.

'This restaurant has been in Nguyen's family for eighty years,' says Cuong. 'It's a traditional snake restaurant – a delicacy in our country.'

Lenny gasps and holds his hand to his mouth, making it into a fist with the melodrama of a pre-teen girl, not a thirty-five-year-old man.

'It's OK, babe,' says Dee, squeezing his other hand.

'No need for menu here,' says Cuong, while Nguyen nods profusely. 'There are ten dishes, plenty for everyone to share. It all comes out at different times.'

'Do you have any chicken wings?' asks Lenny, shuffling in his seat as another man approaches the table, carrying an urn. His question goes unanswered.

The man pulls off the cloth and shakes a long cobra onto the floor, which lands with a slap, writhing and rising in anger at the table.

'Oh jaysus, Dee!'

Cuong sits at the top of the table with the calm demeanour of a man who has seen this before; watching with a gentle smile as Maya, James, Dee and especially Lenny all recoil and lean away from the cobra at the table, the spectre at the feast. The cobra rises fast, flaring its neck high and wide. Just as it's about to lash out, the man standing next to Nguyen, the one who brought the urn, slits the cobra's throat in a flash. Maya and Dee scream while Lenny repeats, 'No no no no no!' in anguish.

Maya can feel James' hand on her thigh, squeezing her, urging her to be OK, excited by this new experience.

A third man appears at the table with a little bottle perfectly placed to collect the snake's blood as it drains from its body, while the man who slit the cobra's throat cuts out the snake's heart and puts it on a little plate between James and Lenny. Only James and Cuong look close enough to notice that the heart is still beating.

Over the next two hours, and much to Lenny's disdain, Nguyen proudly brings out snake soup, a snake bile shot, snake pieces fried in green leaf, snakeskin crackers (Dee likes how they look like snakeskin prawn crackers and suggests to Maya that they wear them as a fashion accessory), snake spring rolls, shredded snake teeth fried in herbs, BBQ snake, a second snake soup, and rice fried in oil from the snake.

'All from that one cobra?' asks James.

'All from that one cobra,' Cuong replies with a puffed chest. 'In Minsk We Trust' expands.

Maya leans in and lowers her voice. 'What happened to Nguyen's thumb? Was it a snake?'

Cuong laughs quietly. 'No, he chopped it off cutting vegetables,' he replies with a quick wink.

'No no no no no,' laments Lenny, traumatised by the whole evening.

39

April 2016, London, England

'Pleeeease, baby girl, please eat something,' Nena begs Ava, who just stares back at her before giving a long and sassy blink. Ava has thick black hair like her mother's, although it swirls in loops and whirls like the black ink of a fingerprint. Tom's imprint is left in Ava's sparkling blue eyes, which are dulled slightly by the current impasse. Ava's mouth is clamped shut, her stubborn cheeks fill out, so her face looks like a puffin, and she turns her head away from her mother, towards the kitchen door, as if to say *I am not interested in your boiled potatoes.*

Nena tries not to cry.

Or your fish fingers.

Weaning isn't going well.

Or those orange sticks you tried to trick me with before.

Pureed foods didn't go down well. Ava spat out the carrot, the parsnip, the mushy peas and even the pear, all of which Nena frantically scooped up and ate herself. She wasn't going to let the peeling, the steaming, the pulverising, the sterilising, the freezing and the defrosting of little ice cubes of organic food go to waste. The cool sweetness of the pear felt like the most nourishing meal Nena had eaten in ages. Then she pressed a tea towel to her mouth to stifle a loud sob, so as not to alarm Ava.

With that, Nena decided enough was enough and she had to take action to stop both of them losing their shit at every mealtime – to get Ava off the breast – so she went to baby weigh-in clinic, concerned that Ava wouldn't be gaining weight – or worse still, dropping it – through her reluctance to get off milk. Nena's reluctance to breastfeed had been growing ever since Ava cut two bottom teeth and had taken to biting Nena's already-sore nipples.

A matter-of-fact health visitor called Tina recommended baby-led weaning as an alternative to the dejection of unwanted puree.

'What do you even mean?' asked Nena, trying not to let the wobble in her voice grow into something undignified.

'Offer her manageable chunks of what you have: potatoes, chicken, broccoli, whatever you've cooked for yourself – give her some of your roast dinner – it'll enable her to copy you. Monkey see, monkey do,' Tina added cheerfully.

She's not a monkey.

Nena was dumbfounded.

'I don't cook roast dinners.'

I don't have the fucking time.

Nena wasn't sure she'd ever cooked a roast dinner – it was Emily Snatch who made her soup in Bateson Hall; Maya who looked after them in their houseshare the two years after by cooking her signature roast chicken with chickpeas and chorizo; her mother Victoria who made comforting feijoadas when Nena went back to her parents' for some nourishment; and it's Tom who sorts a leg of lamb for Sunday lunch while Nena keeps an eye on Ava and Arlo.

'Well, weaning is often a power struggle,' Tina elaborated, looking over her half-moon spectacles. 'But baby-led weaning gives Baby the power to answer her own inner hunger cues.'

Or throw expensive organic chicken on the floor.

Nena looked blank. The past dazzle in her eyes dulled by night feeds and day feeds and having her nipples bitten. The health visitor didn't know what else to suggest, so she brought the encounter to an end so she could see as many people as possible during her clinic.

'See how you get on,' she said, breezily. 'But you *can* keep breastfeeding, you know. Just because she's six months doesn't mean…'

Here we go again.

'Actually, I'm thinking of stopping breastfeeding,' admitted Nena matter-of-factly, as if she was spoiling for a fight.

Tina stopped perusing a plastic folder of leaflets and looked up. 'Oh.'

'She's draining me. She's biting me. I can't take it any more. I've tried formula, but she wouldn't have it. I've gone to the pump to get a bit of distance. Even the act of feeding her has been driving me mad.'

The health visitor studied Nena's face. 'Driving you mad?'

Nena waited for the lecture.

'I've done it for six months,' she said defensively.

'Are you OK?'

'Whether I stop breastfeeding or not, Ava needs to start eating food; humans eat food.' Nena tried to laugh to lighten the oppressive feeling on her chest. Was it a tightening within or was it Ava wriggling on her lap?

'You've done a great job. Her weight is fine. But remember, once you stop there's no going back. It dries up, it's gone.'

She's judging me.

'I just thought expressing milk would be a good halfway house.'

Before Tina could find the leaflet she was looking for on baby-led weaning, Nena got up to leave, muttering something about a washing machine being delivered.

She didn't give Tina the chance to end the encounter how she would have liked, but still she pushed her glasses up her nose and called the next mother in.

As Nena wheeled Ava's buggy up the winding ramp path that led out of the health centre and onto the road packed with buses, cars, mopeds and a fruit and veg stall gathering pollution, she burst into tears and sobbed, knowing that her crumpled crying face looked the same as her daughter's.

Ava blinks slowly now, defiantly, mouth still clamped, staring at the baby bouncer hanging from the door frame to the hallway.

'Come on. This is a Taste The Difference fish finger. Do you know how good a fish finger is? Let alone a Taste The Difference fish finger?!'

Ava picks up a piece of crispy crumbed cod in her chubby fist, extends her arm and opens her hand out ceremonially. Flakes of fish fall to the already smattered tiles of the kitchen floor.

Nena taps the plastic plate with a fingernail as if she's about to make a speech, to alert Ava to the boiled potato and carrot baton under her nose. Ava fidgets irritably in her seat, arching her back and extending her soft tummy. Then she hammers her fists down onto the table tray, picks up the plate and drops the whole thing onto the floor. The plate spins as if a clown has just dropped it in a deliberate act of slapstick. Nincompoop Nena doesn't find it very funny. Her chest tightens again and the kitchen walls seem to shrink a little around her.

'What's WRONG with you?!' Nena bellows, as she bends down to pick up the plate. 'For fuck's sake,' she adds with a quiet inhale of breath.

Ava arches and contorts and cries, shocked to have been shouted at by the face she most trusts, and Nena feels deplorable for shouting at her baby so aggressively, in such anger. She picks Ava up out of her highchair and whispers into her ear, soothing herself as much as Ava.

'I'm sorry, I'm sorry, it's OK, it's OK... Shhh...' Nena rocks Ava on her hip as she sways from side to side. 'It's just you need to eat or you won't get through the night. I can't carry on like this... Shhh, shhh...'

Nena can't take another sleepless night. Bedtime fills her with dread; not knowing what's coming or just how many times Ava will wake makes her feel sick as night-time looms. Every time Ava does wake, it's Nena, with closed eyes and a heavy heart, who pads into Ava's nursery, feeling like she's being deliberately tortured.

Tom can't do the night shifts, he has to be at W1A early most mornings for breakfast catch-ups with schedulers, studio visits, meetings with production companies, discussions with talent... talent like his wife used to be before she went on maternity leave. Tom has to get up and go to work so he can hang out with Dr Rosa, and Nena goes to bed knowing that she won't sleep for more than an hour or two. That it'll be her getting up five times a night. And she's just so. Fucking. Tired.

'You can't drink milk all your life, you know,' Nena says, walking into the living room and slumping onto the sofa in defeat.

Ava flicks her head and widens her eyes on hearing the word milk.

'Sixteen-year-olds don't survive on milk.'

Nena looks into Ava's eyes, blue and alert and excited by the promise of milk, and Nena is disarmed by her daughter's beauty.

'OK, baby,' she concedes. 'I just need to express.' Nena knows Ava won't have a clue what she's talking about, but still, it's what she does. She has no one else to talk to.

'I'm just changing your nappy.'

'Let's run you a bath.'

'Mummy's just getting some water.'

Nena commentates on her every move as she talks to a void. Ava doesn't answer. The Real Housewives of Beverly Hills don't answer.

'I'm putting you on the mat, so I can express, OK?'

Ava says nothing, but both are calmed by the prospect of a solution. A plan.

Nena rests Ava on her back on the playmat to check she can still roll over, whether the lack of food in her diet means that she might have forgotten her milestones, but she does, straight away. Nena leans to turn on the television.

'I'm just getting a bottle from the steriliser.'

Ava seems placated and she seems to understand that milk is coming at least, even if the delivery format is less preferable to her mother's breast.

Nena walks back to the kitchen, picks up another boiled potato she missed off the floor and lifts the lid on the steriliser.

Thank god.

She's relieved to see there is one sterilised bottle left. Had the oval plastic contraption, that Nena already bemoans takes up too much space in the kitchen, been empty, she might just have picked it up and thrown it out of the window.

Nena takes the bottle and goes back to the living room. There's a catfight on the TV. A woman in sequins points her finger in another woman's face. Nena smiles.

Excitement at last!

Ava rocks on all fours, captivated by the argument. She turns her face towards her mother for comfort.

'It's OK, baby, standard Housewives bitchfight. They'll be shopping in Neiman Marcus by the end of the episode.'

Ava blinks. Big blue eyes like a baby big cat.

Nena slinks into the apple-green sofa, into the space that's a bigger version of her bottom, and attaches a funnel-like piece of plastic to her nipple. At the end of the tube is the sterilised bottle, empty now, but she hopes for a good yield. She turns on the pump and the hum of the electronic whir makes a sound like a cow's moo. Her breast starts to tingle, her nipple hurts. Nena hoped pumping breast milk, creating a production line of bottles in the fridge door, would help wean Ava off her. Get her off the comfort of suckling day and night. Give Nena a break from the feeling of being drained all the time, the pain of the occasional bite – and Tom could be more hands on.

But the moo of the breast pump also drains and depresses Nena in a way she didn't expect. And Tina the health visitor was right – her stores are starting to deplete.

There's no going back.

The suction is taking longer and the bottles are harder to fill. And still, Ava's waking in the night wanting bloody milk, even if it's expressed.

Why won't she take formula?

Ava rocks backwards and forwards on all fours on the mat.

The pump groans. Pitiful drips hit the floor of the plastic bottle. Ava starts to cry.

I need to pick her up.

The cry loudens.

If I detach myself, if I put the bottle down, will the bottle still count as being sterilised?

'You're hungry, baby! Why didn't you just eat your dinner?'

Ava's cry grows louder and more distressed and her tired arms weaken, giving way underneath her, sending her cheek crashing down to the mat.

Thump.

Shit.

Nena pulls the sucker off her nipple, switches off the pump and carefully balances the bottle on the arm of the sofa. She scoops Ava up and cuddles her as they both cry.

'I'm sorry, I'm sorry, I'm sorry,' she repeats.

I'm just not very good at this.

Nena and Ava sob into each other's cheeks, Ava's blotchy and red from the impact and her tears, as Nena turns in a circle in the middle of the room. Real Housewives laugh and the bottle teetering on the arm of the sofa, not even a quarter full, topples over. Watery milk trickles slowly over the arm of the apple-green upholstery, and Nena starts to wail.

40

In the foyer of the Hoi An Happy Homestead, Maya, James, Dee and Lenny are tired and relieved: relieved to be static; relieved that tonight they can sleep in a bed, in a room, and not on a tatty train. It's the morning after a night spent in a four-berth sleeper car travelling south on the Reunification Line from Hanoi to Danang, the nearest outpost to this UNESCO town of Hoi An – a pilgrimage for people in search of peace, pho and finery. And, as funny as Lenny is at a sleepover, it makes for a tiring day after. As they bedded down for the night and the train tooted its horn out of Hanoi, Lenny regaled Maya and James with the story of how he wooed Dee, a personal trainer, by telling her he wanted to get in shape and train for the Dublin marathon.

'Will ya train me up?' he said, as he did an impression of himself stopping Dee while she was stretching with a client in St Stephen's Green.

It wasn't until four months later, when Dee joined Lenny for his longest training run, and they talked candidly and breathily, as running companions do, that Lenny admitted there was no marathon place with his name on it. He had no intention of doing another twelve kilometres on top of the thirty he had gradually built up to in order to impress Dee. He confessed he'd seen her in the park and thought she was so beautiful, her brown skin and strong arms glistening in the summer sunshine, that he decided there and then to conjure a story as a ruse so he could spend time with her.

'He had to pay me!' Dee added with a laugh, flashing a gap-toothed smile as she, too, listened while Lenny told their story.

After that longest run, three hours in the autumn sunshine, Lenny leaned against a horse chestnut tree and panicked at the prospect of having to go any further, both in his lie and in kilometres. With red cheeks and a breathy laugh, he said, 'Here's a funny thing...' and told Dee about his cunning plan. Fortunately he was too tired to be embarrassed.

Dee chipped in as Lenny retold the story on the train.

'I said, "Well, you may as well run it now, ya eejit!" A mate of mine from the gym had dropped out – hurt his knee – Lenny went white when I said he could have his place!'

'I did go white, didn't I, Dee?'

When marathon day came, Lenny ran, powered by the runs he and Dee had shared as the seasons changed, and heartened knowing she would be cheering him on along the way. No one was more surprised than Lenny when Dee planted a kiss on him at the finish line and said, 'G'wan then, I'll let you take me for dinner.'

Maya clapped and cooed from her top couchette. James smiled from his underneath.

'I didn't know you were a runner – we could have gone together on some of those runs I did up around the rice terraces. Would have been nice, Lenny.'

'Ahh, he's no runner!' Dee guffawed.

Lenny blushed. 'I've not laced up my trainers since. Why should I? I won gold that day.'

Maya told Dee and Lenny the story of how she and James got together, Irish eyes smiling in their bunks at every turn, every longing, every rejection, every disappointment… until the fateful night they were both thrown off a train in a snowy village outpost. When Maya got to the punchline, Lenny clutched his heart and said, 'Good for you, Maya.'

As the train started to weave through Vinh, past the corridor to Thailand, Myanmar and Laos, Lenny made everyone laugh with stories about his life as a travel agent. Of the scouting trips he'd been invited on to check out new resorts around the world; of the eccentric customers he books holidays for; of the high roller who always travels first class while his wife and kids go economy; of how he directs honeymooners to Mauritius and the Maldives because he can't pronounce the word 'Seychelles'. ('Ahh, you don't wanna go there, the Maldives are much better...' he mimicked – Lenny is very good at doing an impression of himself.) At 2 a.m., Dee said, 'Shut up now, Len,' from her top bunk, and he obediently went to sleep, enabling the rest of them to as well. They woke to sunrise over the green rice terraces and temples approaching Hue, before arriving at Danang and taking a taxi to Hoi An.

It was a long night. It's a relief to arrive; they don't even mind the hotel's padded red velveteen décor of the interior walls and the welcome desk.

The four friends slide their backpacks down their bodies and drop them to the floor, Maya still less gung-ho than James, despite her backpack starting to look rather well-travelled.

A small woman with an eager smile asks for the travellers' passports.

James and Dee unzip pockets, wallets and document holders and lean against the soft desk, while Maya and Lenny stand near the luggage, watching the bicycles and the slow hum of people going about their business on the street outside. Maya yawns. She is both annoyed at Lenny for keeping her awake for most of the night and fond of him for being so bloody entertaining. She doesn't know whether to hug him or punch him on the arm.

Then Lenny has an epiphany. 'So I shared a dorm with the famous "Train Man" – on an *actual* train. I can't believe it, Maya. That's a cool story.'

Maya smiles proudly as she looks over at James checking in. His black T-shirt has faded to grey and his blue jeans are sagging a little around his bottom. Maya's heart pounds.

So handsome.

'I know. Cool, heh? There's definitely a story you could sell there, Lenny.'

'What, "TRAIN MAN TALKS ABOUT PHO IN HIS SLEEP!"' says Lenny, waving his arm across an imaginary headline. 'Or, "TRAIN MAN SNORES LOUDLY ON THE HANOI EXPRESS!"'

'How about "MY NIGHT OF PASSION ON THE LOVE TRAIN WITH TRAIN MAN!"' adds Maya with her own arching arm and sweeping hand.

Lenny's eyebrows knit together. 'Ick, Maya, you took it too far.'

Maya winces an apology and looks over to James and Dee. James and Dee are both the fixer halves of each couple. The sorters. The checker-inners. Maya doesn't relish being bundled with Lenny as the least competent of a pair, not when she's so resourceful, when she's Excellent at Remembering, but actually she's so tired this morning, she's happy for James to be giving passport details and credit card deposits.

And Lenny is good company.

'So, what are you going to have made?' Maya asks, changing the subject, atoning for a joke that didn't go down well.

'Ah well, our Aidan's getting married at the weekend, it's why we're going back home now.'

'Oh wow. Baby Aidan's getting married?'

'Yep, wee Aidan. Although he's six-foot-five,' Lenny says with a proud twinkle, as he puts his hand across his brow and pretends to look up, as if he's Jack about to scale a beanstalk. Lenny's hardly small himself.

'Oh I have one of those, Florian. Only we're four siblings and not fourteen. But Florian is a baby giant too.'

On the night train from Hanoi, Lenny also kept Maya and James awake with tales about the many Mullens, his thirteen brothers and sisters, and in which order they fall. Maya's Special Memory skill means that if she concentrates really hard, she can remember them all.

Martin, Anne, Brenda, Gavin, Deidre, Lisa, Orla, Michael, Niamh, Marian, Leonard, Eve, Ciara, Aidan.

She silently congratulates herself.

'Ah well, my baby giant is getting married – can you believe it – before me?' Lenny gives Maya a wink. 'Anyways, I need a suit for the big day – a good one too, I'm his best man.'

'Ahhh, how lovely, Lenny! Have you got your speech sorted?'

'Nope. You know me, Maya, I won't be short of a word or two.'

'Hahaha, no, that's true. Any idea what kind of suit you'll have made, you know, to look the part?'

Maya tries to imagine what Lenny would look like in a suit – she's only ever seen him in grubby T-shirts, three-quarter-length cargo pants or biker overtrousers.

'I'm thinking of going out there. Having something a bit fancy. Light blue maybe. Show off me tan. Or teal. Dee says I look nice in teal.' Lenny puffs up his chest like a proud peacock. If Dee were standing next to him, he would have looked to her for affirmation. 'Not that any bugger will be looking at me. Plus our Aidan got all the looks.'

Maya laughs. 'Oh really?'

'Yep.'

'Fourteenth-time lucky?'

'Yep. A *lot* of Irish hearts will be breaking this time next week, that's for sure. Tall. Handsome. Clever. He got all the bloody brains too.'

'He sounds lovely!'

Lenny rolls his eyes. 'Anyway, what about you, Maya? What will you have the tailor stitch ya?'

Maya thinks back to her FASH days. Working for an online clothing giant meant she crammed her wardrobe full of mass-produced voluminous skirts and cotton summer dresses, all at forty per cent off. Since she was fired over a year ago, she has only bought one pair of shoes, travelling kit aside – a pair of grey patent brogues for starting her patisserie course in style – fast fashion all seemed so wasteful and throwaway having worked inside it. Faced with the famous tailors of Hoi An, Maya wondered if it's better to *not* have anything made. Make do and mend. Then she thinks of the Miu Miu dress she tore out of an issue of *Paris Vogue*, left in a cafe in Hanoi. The lilac velvet bodice with small buttons down to the waist. The fifties skirt in navy net. Perhaps she could be persuaded by a nice trip to the tailor shops, ship it home in case there are any fancy events to go to next year. Seemingly there are always weddings.

'Hmmm, maybe a dress,' Maya says, coming round to the idea. 'I do miss my dresses.'

She thinks of the wardrobe at the top of her Victorian maisonette and how it used to look before they packed up their clothes and Timo moved in. Ninety per cent of the wardrobe was crammed with Maya's dresses, ten per cent James' jeans and shirts.

'I did see this nice dress in *Vogue*. Strapless. Kind of in at the waist and out again…'

Maya notices Lenny zoning out as he looks into space beyond Maya's shoulder, out of the door into the late-morning sunshine. She can tell he's not interested.

'I dunno, we'll see,' shrugs Maya. 'I wonder what Dee will have made, she'd look stunning in *anything*.'

Maya's attempts to reel Lenny back into the conversation fail as she realises he's gone. His attention is fully on the street outside the Hoi An Happy Homestead. She's tempted to turn around.

Lenny's friendly eyes narrow. His shoulders rise.

'Lenny? You OK?'

Maya turns around and sees people cycling past; families breaking for lunch; a child with a Paw Patrol schoolbag on her back, almost as long as her; a trader wearing a conical hat carrying a stick across his shoulders, selling something from the baskets dangling low at either end as if he's a human set of scales.

Maya turns back to Lenny, now craning his head as if to catch a better look of the street.

'Lenny? Are you all right?'

'Sorry, Maya. I'm not being funny, but there was a fella in the doorway, checking you out a bit too long for my liking. Thought I'd give him the Mullen mad-eye,' he says, with a wink.

'Huh?'

'I'm just kidding witcha. I'm a peaceful man. But there was a fella there checking you out through the door. I wouldn't be happy if a man was looking at my Dee like that.'

Maya turns around again. A woman cycles by with a toddler in the basket of her bike. Whoever it was isn't there any more.

'Maybe the guy was checking *you* out, Lenny,' Maya winks back.

Lenny rolls his eyes as if to say, *That would be just my luck*.

'Right,' says Dee, heaving her backpack up off the ground. 'Come on, Len. Room 410. Fourth floor. They're 510 above us. No funny business, you kids,' Dee says matter-of-factly as she marches off up a flight of stairs with red velveteen carpet.

James looks at Maya's puzzled face and kisses her on the forehead in offer of a remedy.

'You OK?'

'Yeah sure...' she says, looking back behind her, thinking it's probably not even worth mentioning to James.

'Room 510. Up the stairs.'

Maya strains to lift her backpack as the others go off ahead to find the rooms, but she can't shake the ill feeling as she glances out to the street one last time.

4I

'Which way you dress, sir?' A small man in a brown satin short-sleeved shirt presses a tape measure to Lenny's groin. Blushing and uncomfortable, the big teddy bear sweats a bit more in his three-quarter-length trousers.

'Emmm...' Lenny is rarely lost for words but calls across the crowded tailor's in a loud whisper. 'Psst! Dee! Which way do I...?' He looks down and gestures his hands towards his legs, giving a little nod towards his crotch.

'Left, Len!' Dee shouts across the shop, where she is standing with her arms out so a woman with a tape can measure her ribcage. 'You hang to the left, babe! Most men do,' she adds with authority.

Lenny rises on his toes a few centimetres, looking like he's just passed an exam.

'The left,' he says proudly.

The expressionless tailor continues measuring Lenny for his pale blue suit while Maya and James exchange a look across a table full of cloth and magazines and suppress a smile. The shop is drowning in rolls of beautiful fabrics: cotton, silk, shantung, organza, corduroy and tulle... in every colour of the rainbow and everything in between. There are patterns too: paisley, polka dots, even a fabric with toucans all over it. James did try to convince Lenny to go for a leopard-print suit, but Dee shot that idea down when she could see Lenny might actually be getting on board with it.

Maya's measurements have been taken for her Miu Miu-inspired dress, and it's James' turn. He wasn't going to have anything made, but the tailor's dog-eared copy of *GQ* had a Tom Ford advert in it, in which there was a model wearing a tuxedo James loved – not that he has any reason to wear such a suit. He showed it to Maya while she was having her waist measured. She glanced at the advert. A rakish model pouting in a midnight-blue tux with black silk lapels and slim-fit trousers. The thick silk bow tie harked back to old-Hollywood glamour. Maya knew he would look stunning in it. Perfect next to her fake Miu Miu dress.

'You'd rock it,' she said with a smile.

Not that we have anywhere to wear it.

Now James is being asked which way *he* hangs and Maya is feeling tired from the sleep deficit. She looks hazily, at James, Lenny and Dee, stiff like scarecrows guarding the shop: their arms out to the sides, their lips pursed while they diligently do what the tailors tell them to do, as they imagine what their fanciful new threads will look like.

Maya looks to the door and rubs her eyes. Bicycles. There are always bicycles pootling past in this languid, sleepy town. Merchants in conical hats. Off-duty models 'doing Asia' in shorts and ribbed vests. Children with little pigtails. Babies wrapped around their mothers' backs. Men dreaming in doorways.

And then Maya sees her. A woman whose face she has seen on the television for months. On CNN and Star News and BBC World; in hostels from Bundi to Bangkok, Haad Rin to Hanoi. She is wearing a white vest and blue chambray shorts. Her soft brown hair is bobbed and wavy. The woman walks on.

Maya gasps and turns to James. Standing like a statue. Crippled by Tom Ford.

Too slow.

'I just saw…' Maya pauses. 'James!' she calls across the shop, before thinking twice. 'I'll be right back.'

Adrenaline awakens her. Alert and alive, she rushes out into the street and turns left into the sunshine, scanning the scene for the woman whose face she feels she knows.

It can't be.

She sees a glimpse up ahead. A silver ankle chain catches the sunlight.

Is she alone?

Maya hastens her pace, past a little girl licking a milk-coloured ice cream. The girl looks up at Maya and gives a quizzical smile.

She was spotted with a man in Hanoi.

Maya weaves, rushing a bit faster, but the woman's pace must have quickened because the gap between them isn't narrowing.

Was it Hanoi? I can't see anyone with her.

Her frame is about right. Petite and pale and so very... *French*. Maya doesn't want to draw attention to herself, so she uses her spy learnings from *Miss Congeniality* to keep a low profile while absorbing as much information as she can.

Her hair is longer than it looks in the photographs.

Her clothes don't look very dirty; the Dutch backpackers said her clothes looked dirty.

An old man with a curved spine blocks Maya's path as he walks slowly in front of her, his hat obscuring her view. She cranes her neck and attempts to weave around him, but an oncoming bicycle makes her pull in.

Maybe it isn't...

At the junction where four streets meet, Maya finally darts around the ancient man.

But what if it is?

She scans all three options: up ahead, to her left, to her right.

I can't see her!

The off-duty model cycles back along the street facing Maya and catches her eye as she passes.

Did she see her? Is she wondering if it's Manon Junot too?

Maya looks over her shoulder, at the tourist on the bicycle with the long lean legs, going the other way. Unperturbed or ignorant, she's not sure which, and looks back ahead, scanning three horizons for the pale European woman in the short blue shorts.

I've lost her. I've lost Manon Junot.

A tuk-tuk whizzes across the road in front of her, heading left towards the glassy Thu Bon River.

Did she go along there? To the river?

Maya scans the street. Her gut tells her to turn left, down the smaller side street that curves around the water's edge. The woman had been walking on the left of the street, it's more likely she zipped off down there, given Maya can't see her up ahead, or on the road out of town to the right.

A moped pulls up on the pavement in front of her, rolls of fabric stacked horizontally, like colourful logs ready to topple off the back. Trunks of orange, pink and red, creating a barrier to the street that was her best shot.

Shit.

Maya is irked. Irritated she might have lost the girl from the news, worried that she might have worried James by disappearing. She huffs in irritation, cursing under her breath. The man on the moped kicks out his stand and shrugs an apology, as Maya does a limbo under shantung and cotton. She regains her poise, tucks her hair behind one ear, and continues along the graceful winding street towards the river.

She must have come this way. If she didn't then I've lost her.

Maya walks past tightly packed wooden buildings that were once tea emporiums and Japanese merchant houses but are now boutique hotels, bars and tailor shops. She looks back behind her, questioning her choice, and bumps into an old woman selling buns shaped like pillows, hanging from baskets balanced on a stick across the back of her shoulders.

Maya nearly knocks the woman over.

'I'm sorry, so sorry,' she says, as she props the merchant up and bows subserviently.

'*Banh dau phung*?' says the woman with a hopeful smile, as she offers Maya a puff of thick pastry with a look that says *It's the least you can do.*

Maya puts her hand in her pocket and pulls out a 50,000 dong note. She stuffs it in the old woman's hand with a smile.

'*Dung lai!*' shouts the woman, tugging on Maya's arm and halting her in her tracks.

Maya turns around, cursing herself through a forced smile, and takes the proffered bun, stuffing it in her mouth for lack of anywhere else to put it. Her cheeks inflate, her mouth fills and the comforting sweetness of coconut and peanut oozing from deep-fried batter powers her on. She ups her pace again.

It was Manon Junot. I swear.

In this dreamy outpost, Maya is hopeful she couldn't have got far.

Hurrying further, throwing her all into her hunch, Maya stops to look left down a road that's more like an alleyway, between two thin buildings. She narrows her eyes and sees that the alley opens out into a bright courtyard that has been taken over and turned into a cafe; young couples take tea and buns at small, circular wrought-iron tables dotted in the sunshine.

Maya looks back to the road that leads to the river, but stops and glances back down the alleyway. For some reason, she's drawn to the courtyard at the end of it; her hunch reeling her in. She walks towards the bright beam of sunshine, the light that highlights the cool darkness of the alley, in more of a saunter now than a frantic rush. She's committed to it. If Manon didn't turn down here, then it's too late, she's lost her. If she did and it's a dead end as it looks, she's not going anywhere.

This way.

Maya has the sensation that this is the right path to take, the feeling that something is pulling her. At the end of the alley, as she's just about to step out into the sunshine of the courtyard, another swathe of fabric suddenly unravels in front of her, blocking her way. This time, an elderly tailor with skin like withered root ginger and brown stumps for teeth holds one end, smiling. His daughter – no, she must be his granddaughter or great-granddaughter – holds the other end proudly, so the Westerners taking tea in the courtyard can look at their colourful wares.

The vibrant fabric barrier is awash with colours of crimson red and midnight blue, rippling in the wind that's started to whip up. It feels like a finishing line luring her in, as if it's been held up specially for Maya to cross, to reach her prize. She so hopes Manon Junot is on the other side of the colourful cordon, and she strains her neck, showing her eagerness to pass.

'Sorry,' the tailor's granddaughter or great-granddaughter giggles as she lets go of her end of the swathe so Maya can pass. The fabric billows towards the old man and Maya crosses into the courtyard, startled and frozen by the face unveiled in front of her, looking at Maya as if her arrival was anticipated. Through the red and blue barrier she just crossed. At this precise time. In this sunny courtyard. In an obscure and tiny corner of the world.

'You found me.'

42

April 2016, London, England

'Black decaf Americano, how you like it, yes?'

Rosa Samarasekera perches on the desk and crosses one thin leg over the other under a black leather pencil skirt. Tom is sitting at a desk in New Broadcasting House, trying to get as much work done as possible ahead of a busy day. Runners walk by, taking guests to radio studios, scripts to the newsroom, purchase orders to the finance department, cheese and ham toasties to their bosses.

'Oh, thanks! Saved me from that godawful machine again,' Tom says, barely glancing up as he frantically types, trying not to lose the autumn strategy document he was working on, in which Rosa features heavily. He presses save and minimises the document. Then looks up, giving Rosa his full attention.

Tom studies her face and wonders how long it will be before News try to poach her.

'Well, I was going to get you caffeine but don't want you to peak too soon. Gotta pace yourself, right?' Rosa raises a long, arched eyebrow.

'Yes, of course.' Tom takes the proffered coffee and sets it down next to his laptop. Rosa's bottom is so close to the charge cable he notices she accidentally pulled it out of its magnetic grip. 'Although Nena can't make it.'

Rosa has a look of *I didn't ask if she was coming*, while Tom remembers how he left his wife this morning. In bed in their loft room with Ava suckling on her dummy next to her. Neither of his girls had seemed keen for much interaction. Nena less so after Tom had urged her to come to the Children's party tonight, the party to celebrate sixty years since the first ever *Bertie & Betty* show.

'Bertie Baxter himself will be there!' Tom had enthused.

Nena shrugged. It made no difference to her.

'It'll help you transition back into work – see all the faces who miss you, everyone who's asking after you.' Tom tried, he really wanted Nena to get back to her usual self.

Nena had shrugged again and looked up out of the skylight, noticing how dirty the drizzle had made it. From the look on her face, work seemed like a closed chapter of her life.

'I could ask your mum and dad to babysit…?'

Nena shook her head, and finally spoke, while still looking at the tiny circles of grey pollution on the Velux windows. 'I can't face it. Plus, you'll be networking, I'd hold you back.'

'I'll be stronger for you being there.'

'Tom Vernon's wife,' Nena said glibly.

'Nincompoop Nena's husband,' Tom protested.

'No. I wouldn't know what to wear. I don't want to leave Ava anyway,' Nena said in a way that indicated the matter was closed.

Tom felt voiceless, knowing that the best thing for Nena would be to get away from Ava for an evening. To put on her old clothes and make-up. To work a room again. It would be the best thing for *her*, regardless of how useful it would be for her career, regardless of how it would save Tom answering awkward questions.

Rosa notices the detached cable and raises one buttock. 'Oops, sorry.'

She plugs it back into Tom's MacBook with a spark, and a lightning flash appears on the screen.

Tom laughs and rubs his head.

'Anyway, what's the dress code? I didn't quite get the whole "Bertie & Betty" theme. I don't want to dress like smelly geriatrics, I treat enough of them at Guy's…'

Tom looks at Rosa's face, trying to work out if she's joking. Intrigued, he rubs his head again and answers the question in hand.

'Well, I think the idea is to dress as if it's Bertie &
Betty's heyday. Fifties, I guess. But I'll just wear a suit. I
have a vintage Liberty tie of my grandad's – let's just say
it's from the 1950s even if it isn't.' Tom gives a cheeky
smile.

'Yah, I'm not really a 1950s sort of person, but I have
a stunning Victoria Beckham dress that might suit the
Savoy.'

'Perfect!' says Tom, raising his eyebrows and having
no clue what a Victoria Beckham dress might look
like, hoping it isn't like the Union Jack one Geri wore.
Hoping even more it's not a black skimpy minidress,
because now he's imagining what Rosa's tits are like
and he needs to get on.

He puts the blue cardboard coffee cup down and
strikes a key on his laptop to awaken the screen. *R.*

'I'll let you get on,' Rosa smoulders.

'Great – yes – I need to finish this document before
tonight. Autumn planning. Charmaine will be there, I
know she'll be pleased to see you too.'

Is he flustered?

'Great,' Rosa smiles. 'Enjoy the coffee.'

'Yes, coffee. Thanks for that, that's really sweet of
you.'

'My pleasure.'

Rosa propels herself off the desk, smooths down her
skirt and walks away in skyscraper stilettos towards the
newsroom.

Tom looks up as he types, watching Rosa slink away as he sinks into his seat and lowers his head behind his laptop. He looks at the coffee cup next to him, inhales the comforting aroma and notices Rosa's Pillow Talk lipstick imprint on the white plastic lid.

43

April 2016, Hoi An, Vietnam

Maya steps back, wondering if the elderly tailor and his granddaughter might catch her fall in their fabric.

'I wasn't looking for you.'

Sea green eyes glimmer in the sunshine.

'What are you doing here?' she asks.

Jon doesn't answer. Instead he stands and pulls out the other wrought-iron chair at his table in the middle of the courtyard cafe, offering Maya a chance to join him. A small cup of coffee sits on the mosaic tabletop, a ream of paper is anchored by a mobile phone, protecting it from the breeze swirling off the river behind the buildings.

'Well, this is freaky,' he smiles.

Maya stands awkwardly, looking behind her, at the fabrics, the alleyway, the street.

'You have to stay for a coffee at least. What are the chances…?'

'I can't really, I've left James and some friends in a tailor's shop a few streets away. They'll wonder where I am.' Maya sounds like she's convincing herself more than Jon.

He doesn't say anything. He just looks up, hopeful, enchanted.

Leonardo DiCaprio in a fish tank.

Maya thinks of her first crush, how much she loved him, and suddenly feels somewhat flummoxed.

'I thought I saw…' Maya realises how silly she's going to sound in these most silly of circumstances. 'Oh, it doesn't matter.'

'Please,' Jon smiles, his best Oscar-winning smile. 'The coffee in this place is amazing.' He clicks his fingers and gestures to the waitress to bring two more. 'Better than any expresso I've had anywhere in the world.'

It's espresso with an s.

'I can't be long,' says Maya, disarmed by his enthusiasm, forgiving him for expresso, admitting that this is rather an exceptional coincidence.

She pulls the small, heavy seat out further. Iron scrapes on concrete and makes Maya's chest hurt. She looks at Jon as she sits down. He is more tanned than he was when she left Thailand, so the rest of his stay must have done him good. His bright eyes jump out against his skin and his blond hair, pushed upwards, looks even fairer. Jon checks his phone then flips it over, giving Maya his total attention.

'Look, sorry I didn't get to say goodbye to you at The Haven,' he laments. 'Had a sudden message about a callback, so I headed straight home to London.'

Maya looks puzzled, then realises Jon doesn't know she and James left first, or that they disappeared as soon as they could to get away from Poo Camp, to appease James and prove to him that nothing had happened that night she and Jon got drunk in the bar. To run away from old feelings.

'Oh, don't worry, I think we might have left by then anyway. Decided to sack off the detox and head straight to Vietnam. That hangover! Wow, I mean, it hurt. Anyway, I couldn't face disappointing Moon.' *Or James.* 'So we made up some family emergency and left the next day.'

Maya curses herself for saying too much. She always says too much when she's nervous. Always plays her hand too early. She didn't have to say anything, didn't have to justify herself to Jon of all people.

'Yeah, that was brutal, eh?' he says with a twinkle in his eye. 'Note to self: never go on a detox with Maya Flowers again. You always were the best tequila partner.'

They lock eyes.

Jon relaxes back in his chair. 'So, what do you know, I go all the way back to London for the callback, get the gig, and we're straight into production, on location in…' He opens his arms as if to say 'ta-da!'.

Maya looks blank.

'Southeast Asia!'

'You're *working* out here?' Maya looks at the stack of paper on the table, to see what his big gig is, but his phone obscures the title page. 'Wow,' she adds with a small voice, trying not to sound impressed.

'Yep, a new le Carré. With Damian Lewis. Shot in Vietnam, among other places. And I bump into you. What are the odds?'

Maya shrugs.

Damian Lewis?

'Weird,' she concurs.

The waitress brings two tiny bronze cups of coffee and Maya realises that her mouth is parched from eating the sweet coconut and peanut bun so quickly. She thinks of asking for a glass of water but is really keen to get back to the tailor shop.

'Thanks,' Jon nods, working that Hollywood charm like Bradley Cooper on a talk show.

'So, what's your role?'

'Damian and I play brothers… bit unlikely…' Jon gestures to his hair. 'But he's a *great* guy. And it's nice to bury the hatchet after *Homeland*.'

'*Homeland*?'

'He just pipped me to the lead.'

'Surely you were too young to play a middle-aged US Marine turned rogue.'

'Make-up is a wonderful thing, Maya.'

'What's your stage name again?' Maya asks casually.

'Look, while I have you, I really did want to say sorry.'

'Oh please, Jon, we went through that at The Haven.'

'I know but...'

'And really, you have nothing to be sorry about. I got my happy ever after.'

'No, I meant I'm sorry for fucking off the next day, we had *such* a fun night. I shouldn't have left without saying goodbye.'

'Oh, look, don't worry, we left the next day, really, we didn't notice. If you feel bad, I should be feeling bad.'

'Boy, did I feel bad. You're a bad influence, Maya. I've never broken a cleanse before I broke it with you.'

'What can I say, I'm a maverick.' Maya laughs. And blushes. The realisation that she's flirting makes her down her coffee swiftly. The hit of rich nutty caffeine makes her mouth feel even more parched and her senses sharpen. Jon gazes deep into her eyes.

'Listen,' he says, stroking his hair upwards. 'Don't go off again before giving me your digits.'

'Oh, I don't have a phone any more. We gave our phones up before we left the UK.'

'Your email then. I was kicking myself about not getting it before. It was just too serendipitous to have bumped into you, Maya. At this stage of my life.'

'What do you mean at this stage of your life?'

Jon looks at Maya intently, his smile fades.

'OK,' she says, to break the silence more than anything. She scribbles down her email address on the front of his script.

Jon looks at the familiar scrawl and remembers letters sent to his parents' house full of heartbreak.

'We're staying at the Hoi An Happy Homestead.'

I said too much again.

'Can we meet later for a drink?'

'Only if you bring Damian Lewis,' Maya says with a smile as she walks off. Her conflicted heart making her forget about Manon Junot; an umbilical cord of colourful cotton drawing her back to James.

Once is a coincidence, twice is a... charm? Is that how it goes?

44

'Do. You. Have. Any. Chicken wings?' Dee asks loudly and slowly, as if that'll make her more easily understood. The waiter looks perplexed. It's not that he doesn't understand English, he just can't understand why the woman is being a stickler about chicken wings in this, the restaurant with the most sought-after tables in central Vietnam.

'We have calamari tempura, tuna ceviche, pork and shrimp crispy rolls...' the waiter replies in perfect English with an American twang. Lenny has the face of a hopeful puppy. 'But no chicken wings I'm afraid.' Lenny's face drops. 'The chicken pho is tiptop though.'

Maya squeezes James' leg under the table. Whether they were eating with hill tribes or at snake palaces or in modern fusion restaurants, Dee's relentless quest to find chicken wings for her man, just the way he likes them, is endearing, if a little embarrassing. They'll miss Dee and Lenny when they head home for Aidan's wedding tomorrow. Not before picking up their new clothes in the morning.

Dee looks back down at her menu in a panic. 'Babe, why don't you have the chicken pho? It's like your mam's chicken noodle soup. Only a bit more flavoursome.' She strokes the back of Lenny's neck.

'No no no no no,' he frowns. 'I just wanted some chicken wings.' He looks up at Maya and James in despair. 'I'd even take a plum dip or something fancy, just so I could have some chicken wings.'

'I know, babe,' comforts Dee.

'You'll be home soon,' James consoles.

'Ahh,' says Lenny with a twinkle in his eye. He can almost smell the sticky BBQ glaze from his favourite place on Montague Street.

'He'll have the chicken pho. But hardly any liquid thanks. Can you make it more like chicken noodles than soup? And I'll have the calamari tempura please.'

The waiter nods.

'Right, so that's one green papaya salad, one red snapper, a calamari, a chicken pho without the pho, and, for you, sir?' The waiter turns to Jon.

'What do you recommend, my friend?' Jon sits looking polished and proud: pomade slightly darkens the blond hair it pushes upwards; an Omega watch sits heavily on his wrist; a pressed white summer shirt with tiny geometric squares on it makes him stand out in the darkened restaurant. His clothes are ironed and expensive-looking. He is clearly The One Who Isn't A Backpacker.

The waiter shrugs. He doesn't have much time to schmooze; this table has already taken long enough to order. 'The five-spice marinated beef is good,' he says nonchalantly, looking around at the other tables all needing his attention in the vibrant waterside venue.

Maya sips from her mango margarita while Dee and Lenny put down their menus and gaze adoringly at the actor at their table, waiting to hear what soliloquy will come forth from his lips. The waiter is as unimpressed as James.

When Maya made it back to the tailor's shop, flustered and out of breath, James, Dee and Lenny were sitting on the pavement outside, so she had no choice to explain what had happened. James wasn't sure if he believed the Manon Junot part – it did sound ludicrous – and wondered if Maya had just seen Jon passing and wanted to pursue him. Later, when they bumped into Jon on their way to dinner, James was even more irked when Dee and Lenny invited him to join them, and James had to pretend that this guy didn't rattle him.

'One of those please. Blue.'

'It comes how it comes. Grilled.'

Jon smiles. 'However it comes will be wonderful, I'm sure.'

The waiter is already halfway to the kitchen.

Now that the issue of chicken wings has been put to bed, Dee can't wait to grill Jon on what he's been in, which celebrity gossip he can tell her, who his famous friends are... She keeps glancing at his phone and wonders which A-listers' numbers are in his contacts.

'Sooo, tell me what I've seen you in,' she says, rubbing her hands together. A row of shiny bangles jingle up her arm. She wraps an arm around Lenny but drapes off him, leaning open-mouthed towards Jon. Maya holds onto James' leg.

'*Hamlet* at the Barbican?'

'We're from Dublin,' Dee and Lenny say in unison.

'Of course,' Jon blushes. 'I had a run in *Hamlet*. With Cumberbatch,' he says, putting a fist to his mouth and clearing his throat politely.

James' spine rises. Maya plays with the mango twist in her cocktail and inspects the barman's impressive fruit topiary. It's a handy way to hide her own impressed face. She doesn't want to fawn like Dee and Lenny, who definitely recognises Jon but can't place which show he saw him in.

'I've done TV dramas you might be more familiar with.'

'*Casualty*?' asks James.

'A long time ago, my friend.'

You're not my friend.

Maya wonders how long ago it was in the timeline of their lives. How far his star has risen since he dumped her.

Perhaps I held him back.

'You might mock *Casualty*, but it's where many greats have cut their teeth. Winslet, Ecclestone, Bloom...'

'I wasn't mocking it,' says James, holding up his hands.

Prick.

'What's that fella's name who plays Charlie Fairhead?' asks Lenny. 'Now, he's a legend.'

James gives a little laugh into the mouth of his Bia Hanoi bottle.

'He's Irish,' Lenny adds, with authority.

'Do you know *Our Girl*?'

'Ooh, I like *Our Girl*!' says Dee, her bracelets jangling again as she claps her hands in a quick and short burst.

'Do *I* like *Our Girl*, Dee?'

'Yes, babe, it's that programme with whatsherface in.'

'Ah yes,' says Lenny.

'Well, I just had a small part in that, a cameo. I was a major in the field.'

'Oh, tell them about the legal drama you shot in America,' interjects Maya, trying not to sound keen.

'Canada. Yah, I did this really big-budget legal drama, *The Truth*. Have you seen it?'

Dee nods in agreement, love hearts in her eyes.

I've not heard of it, thinks James.

'I've not heard of it, pal,' says Lenny, as he takes a sip of his beer.

'It must be recent if you shot it two years ago—' says Maya, before stopping abruptly again.

Dee wonders why Maya keeps checking herself every time she speaks.

'So how do yous two know each other then?' she asks, her eyes narrowing.

'Uni friends,' says Maya.

'Ex-boyfriend,' chimes Jon at the same time.

Dee looks between Maya, Jon and James and sees the awkwardness of the situation.

'Jon and I went out for a little bit, at university.'

Love notes in the library flitter through Maya's mind's eye, before the image of her crumpled and crying on a bed.

'Wow.'

The waiter returns with five bundles of cutlery and some dipping sauces as the table goes silent.

Maya strokes James' leg under the table with her thumb.

'So, Damian Lewis,' says Maya, changing the subject. 'What's he like then?'

'Yeah, and where's he eating tonight? He shoulda joined us!' says Dee.

'Now, he *looks* Irish…' Lenny thinks aloud, before slipping into a daydream about the chicken wings he's going to order when he gets home.

45

James puts a contented arm around Maya as they stroll along the riverbank. Paper lanterns rise like weightless pumpkins in the night sky from the edge of the Thu Bon River, glistening against their twinkling reflections as they leap into the air. Maya and James' eyes take in the spectacle, their tummies full and satisfied.

'Must be some kind of festival,' he says.

Lenny's eyes light up and his top lip beads with a sweat he had worked up eating his chicken noodles. 'Wow, all this for us? You shouldn't have!' he says, with a mischievous grin.

'Well, you know, Lenny, we wanted to send you off in style,' Maya replies with a wink.

'It looks magical. Doesn't it look magical, Dee?'

Dee smiles and nestles into Lenny's chest.

Jon walks ahead of them, hands in his pockets, as if the promenade is his stage; the artist's swagger giving him a confident stride. He keeps his head up, taking in the lanterns, seeing if anyone recognises him.

Further up the flat walkway hugging the water's edge, crowds converge, and more lanterns are lit and launched. Gasps rise as each one makes the daring jump, like popcorn popping in a pan, just hitting the right temperature. Children eat chicken from a stick and cotton candy from a bag. Some of the lanterns fail and plummet into the Thu Bon, where they are swept along and bob away like mystical and magical fish.

James releases his arm and takes his digital SLR out of the camera bag around his neck. This scene is too enchanting not to photograph.

'I'm just going...' James gestures, pointing to the river's edge.

Maya smiles. She can already envisage the photographs he's going to take. Children's faces lit up by lanterns and glee. Old men and women with laughter lines so craggy they are impossible to date. They could be fifty-five, they could be one hundred and five. Lights twinkling on the river and the reflection of those paper lanterns that did make it.

Maya looks around in the crowd, remembering again that she thought she saw Manon Junot this afternoon, so she scans pockets of people all along the riverbank, hoping she might see her. The disbelief in James' eyes hadn't gone unnoticed, and Maya wants to prove she hadn't walked off in pursuit of Jon. She surveys the throng, feverishly.

No, it couldn't have been.

Jon stops strolling and looks back at Maya, to see if she'll take his invitation to catch up with him, to enjoy some intimacy among the crowd. It's what actors crave after all.

Maya doesn't notice; she's searching for Manon Junot.

What if she's here now?

Maya looks around, watching people watch people; seeing James, with his tongue sticking out of the corner of his mouth while he politely takes photographs. She looks at other tourists, at families in their finery. She sees Jon's hair above the Viet people. Blond and sunkissed. She catches his eye, then looks back to James crouching by the river, trying to get his shot. She sees Lenny drop to one knee.

'Dee! Oh Dee! I can't help myself, Dee.'

'What are you doing, ya eejit? Get up!' she says, cackling with laughter.

'I don't have a ring, I was hoping to get some Haribo at the airport and propose with a sweet on the plane home. As we took off, you know…'

'What?!'

'But this is too special. These lights are too brilliant. It's meant to be. Here and now.' Lenny's top lip gets sweatier the more he witters.

'What?!'

'Desiree O'Shea. You are the light of my life and I want to make you my wife, to be the mother of my little ones. My partner in crime. Will ya, Dee? Will ya marry me?'

Heads turn. Silence ensues. People freeze in anticipation. Lanterns almost seem to freeze in anticipation.

James looks up from his post, crouching down by the sparkling river, and catches Maya's eye, before hiding swiftly behind his camera. He lifts the lens, poised and ready to catch Dee's response.

'G'wan then, you idiot. I'll marry ya!'

Maya silences her sick feeling with a cheer and some whistles.

'Yay!' she claps.

Paper lanterns continue their journey skywards.

Maya cheers and whoops some more.

James lowers his camera but keeps his eyes firmly on the back of it, checking his shots on the little screen. His discomfort is eased by how pleased he is to have captured such expressions on faces he will miss.

Jon saunters back to Maya, warmly clapping and whistling for a couple he's only just met.

Friendly strangers – locals and tourists – join in and cheer; some pat Lenny on the back.

In the chaos and the whirl of congratulations and launching lanterns, Jon leans in and whispers to Maya. She feels his warm breath on her neck and arches her ear to listen.

'When the shoot finishes, when this craziness is all done, come home with me.'

'What?'

'Come home with me and have my babies. You know it's what we both want.'

46

'Weird about Dee and Lenny, eh? I didn't see *that* coming.' Maya looks in the wonky bathroom mirror, swiping emerald eyeshadow and black mascara onto a damp cotton pad; embarrassed by the telltale sign of how much effort she made with her make-up tonight.

'I did,' James says flatly from the bed. Shutting the conversation down. In hindsight he realises he might have sounded cold, so tries to soften the mood as he flicks through his photos. 'I got a few nice shots though. I'll email them to Dee and Lenny when we're next online.'

There is a silence as Maya methodically washes in the well-worn en suite, staring at her reflection in the mirror; looking deep into her irises and questioning herself as her face becomes increasingly naked.

James leans his head back against the red velveteen headboard. 'Plus he'll have a wedding suit in the morning... maybe that's what he had in mind.'

Neither Maya nor James mention James' own suit, currently being stitched by a proficient hand in a tailor's warehouse across town.

Maya knows that marriage – Dee and Lenny's, or anyone else's for that matter – is something James isn't keen to talk about. He wasn't keen to talk about it in Tuscany; he wasn't keen to talk about it when people made jokes about them eloping on their travels; he wasn't keen to talk about it at Jeremy and Priyanka's wedding back in Udaipur. Every time someone mentions marriage or weddings or anything associated with a declaration of forever love, James does what he did by the riverbank. He avoids Maya's gaze. He looks away.

I get the message. I don't want to either. Honestly.

As Maya looks in the mirror and wonders what James would make of what Jon whispered to her – whether that might change his feelings, his ability to talk – she replays Jon's words in her mind and how they felt as they tumbled into her ear, making goosebumps rise in her neck; making her yearning to be a mother fly down the river and scream back in her face.

How could he say that to me?

Maya swipes the last trace of potion-green glitter from her lashline as her eyes fill with tears. She splashes her face with cold water, wishing the feeling would pass; wishing she too were going home tomorrow.

47

April 2016, London, England

'It's so wonderful of you to remember her like this,' says Bertie Baxter, with a shaky hand and a tear in his eyes as he stands on the chequerboard tiles of the Savoy.

'It's our pleasure,' coos Charmaine McCourt, head of Children's television. 'It's an honour to celebrate Betty, to celebrate *you*, and to celebrate everything you have done for the millions of children you have entertained over the years.' Charmaine steadies Bertie's hand by cupping it in hers. Bertie Baxter, a man with the face of a perplexed dinosaur, a man who looks like he used to be tall but has shrunk into his brown suit, is unsteady on his feet, but flanked by Charmaine on one side and Tom on the other, he's standing tall. They're waiting in a line-up of the big players in Bertie & Betty's current format. The photo call with Bertie and every living presenter has already been done. They stand under a balloon arch in front of a huge wrap poster with the Bertie & Betty logo on it – the one that's been made to look modern with edgy lines and zingy colours. Hugging in for the photo is current series editor Louise and presenters Kezza and Billy. Tom, with his arm politely around Bertie's shoulder, is mindful that Kezza and Billy's shouty voices and Camden-cool clothing might be a bit overwhelming for a man who is almost ninety, so he creates a protective shield for him with his tall and reassuring body. Like Rosa, Kezza and Billy didn't stick to the 1950s theme, but Charmaine and Louise did; their attempts to be elegant waning after a long afternoon.

Photos were taken. Kezza Instagrammed the shit out of it: the balloons, the children's choir, the sit-down dinner... all with her face in them, and *Bertie & Betty* was given a fitting celebration for a show of such esteem.

Bertie Baxter was born in 1927, making him only minutes too young for conscription for the Second World War, which he spent much of looking after his siblings at their grandparents' house in Carmarthenshire. After the war ended and the children returned to London, Bertie went to Cambridge, where he met Girton College student Betty Ward at the university lawn tennis club. Betty was one of the first women to receive her degree at Cambridge, wearing college gowns men had worn for hundreds of years and not just quietly receiving a certificate in the post. Betty continued being an accidental pioneer. For women in the workplace. For women in television. For women who always knew that they didn't want to have children, even though they knew they were *supposed* to want to. It was a question she answered with confidence and a polite smile every time it came up; every time someone said, 'But you're so good with children,' or, 'You'll change your mind.'

When they graduated and returned to London, Bertie took a job at the BBC in Alexandra Palace and told Betty about the many female engineers the corporation had recruited during the war.

'That sounds jolly,' said Betty, who used her economics degree to take a job in the finance department, so she soon joined Bertie on the morning commute from their flat on the Finchley Road to Ally Pally. As austerity gave way to prosperity, Bertie and Betty would spend Sunday afternoons taking high tea at the Savoy. They became so attached to eating cucumber sandwiches under the elegant glass atrium of the Thames Foyer, they decided to have their wedding celebration there in 1951. And it's where, in early 1956, as they ate scones and watched children reading politely at tables, they came up with the idea of a television programme *for children.*

Over the years, Bertie & Betty invited schoolchildren, authors, naturalists, politicians and animals into the studio – the Harrods lion famously ran amok after chewing through a camera cable in the 1960s, making the programme go off air for fourteen minutes. It was the most popular children's programme for decades, chock-full of ideas of things to make and bake, stories from around the world, and ways in which children could rule it, all of which were ahead of their time. Wednesdays at 4 p.m, *Bertie & Betty* was always reliably on air. Always presented by Bertie and Betty Baxter, who aged as children grew up and their children started watching.

When Betty died of a heart attack in 1986, Bertie decided to retire: his grief too much, his heart too broken, and feeling too old to interview a new wave of guests he didn't connect with. Betty had always been happy to evolve. She was funny and bold and always had a mischievous glint in her eye. She would have known what to say to soap opera actors, sporting sensations and Australian pop stars. Bertie was lost without her; he still is, although he gamely turns up to Camp Bestival or industry parties so Betty is remembered.

Kezza and Billy are the twenty-second and twenty-third presenters respectively, hosts who are more comfortable around children of the digital age. Now those children have gone to bed and the party is winding up. Bertie is back in his apartment on Portman Square. Charmaine has left to get the last train to Manchester. Louise is giving Tom a kiss on each cheek.

'We MUST get you and Nena round for Sunday lunch. I'm going to die if I don't meet that baby of yours.'

Tom blushes. 'Sure thing – give me some dates, Nena and I are pretty free!' he laughs, as he rubs the five o'clock shadow on his chin.

'Will do. Before Ava's sixteen preferably.' Louise is clipped and purposeful; her curtness veiling her warmth. 'Lovely to meet you, Rosa, good luck with your show – we'll have to get you on B&B when you launch.'

Rosa, slinking low in a red leather booth in the American Bar, smiles gratefully, but doesn't stand up. 'That would be wonderful – thank you.'

Louise waves her hand as she throws a boxy coat over her shoulders and heads out to her car. Tom sinks back into the booth and looks at Rosa, her champagne glass tilted elegantly in her hand; hoping she's not on call or about to start a shift tonight. He doesn't say anything, he just looks at her as he smooths down his pale blue paisley Liberty tie.

'Gosh, Tom, you knew everyone here. That must feel pretty amazing.'

Tom feels puzzled not amazed. Knowing everyone isn't something he usually puts a successful evening down to. He's just relieved the sixtieth anniversary party went well and that Bertie hung on and made it, even just for an hour or two. Just as importantly, he's relieved that they got great shots of it for the press.

He laughs it off.

'Yeah, I'd rather not know those two clowns right now—' Tom gestures to Kezza, rolling on top of the grand piano while Billy tinkles 'Like A Virgin', badly. 'I think they might regret that in the morning.'

'But isn't that wonderful?' purrs Rosa. 'Their youthful abandon. Ripping up the Savoy in their ripped jeans.' She gives Tom a sideways glance. 'I'd like to do something I might regret in the morning.'

Rosa moves in closer and Tom feels her leg press against his thigh through his suit. Her cream wrap dress plunges between her small breasts and is right up against the fabric of him. She puts a hand on his knee and strokes his inner thigh under the table.

Tom doesn't move. He's tired. Ava has drained him too and now he just wants to feel good again. He looks at Kezza, being told by the night manager to get off the piano, and he feels fatigue, not shame.

Rosa's hand moves to Tom's crotch.

'You're so fucking sexy, I want you inside me so badly.'

Tom looks at Rosa. He wants to kiss her so badly. Make it all go away.

48

'London, this way, Luang Prabang, that way,' says Dee authoritatively, crossing her arms in different directions.

James concurs as he looks from the gate number on his boarding pass back up at the signs in the international departures lounge. The ever-evolving itinerary has changed again, and he and Maya decided to skip Ho Chi Minh's mausoleum and leave Vietnam for Laos. Jon seems to have that effect on James, making him want to move on entirely.

'Come on, Desiree, let's go find some Haribo.'

'Erm, or better still, a proper ring,' she says, elbowing Maya to point out the row of Tiffany, Cartier and Chopard shops Lenny seems not to have noticed.

Maya smiles and there's a pause. It's one of those pauses when people realise it's time they should say their goodbyes. Time for Dee and Lenny to fly home for Aidan's wedding with an announcement of their own. Time for Maya and James to board their flight to Luang Prabang, before heading to Indonesia and the last part of the Southeast Asian leg of their world trip. After that: Australia, Central America, home.

Home.

Home seems so far away. Maya looks at James, feeling bad that she feels homesick, that she's envious of Dee and Lenny going back to the bosom of their families. She strokes his almost-black hair to the side of his forehead and forces a happy smile.

I wanted this.

'It's been fun,' says James, always rendered a bit awkward by a public display of affection from Maya; awkward as only an Englishman can be in goodbye situations like these.

'Come here, fella,' says Lenny, pulling him in for a bear hug. He pulls Maya in too.

'Hey!' protests Dee, before she bundles in.

Maya inhales the sweet smell of coconut oil in Dee's soft curly hair and it galvanises her for the Equator, the tropics and the Pacific ahead. She breathes in the comfort.

'It's been so cool travelling with you guys, we'll miss you. And we're *definitely* coming to Dublin.

That's if we ever leave Hazelworth again after this trip.'

'There's always a bed for yous two in Dublin,' says Dee.

James pulls out and realigns his backpack.

'Enjoy those chicken wings, buddy.'

Lenny's eyes light up. 'Oh, the chicken wings. We're having chicken wings for dinner tomorrow night, aren't we, Dee?'

Dee doesn't answer but leans in to give Maya another, more sisterly, hug of their own.

'It was a pleasure meetin' ya, Maya.'

'You too, Dee,' she squeezes back.

Hugging Dee makes Maya realise how much she misses Nena. How much she misses the girls at FASH. How much she misses Clara, and all of her sisterly support network; how it would be quite handy to talk to them at the moment. She squeezes Dee one last time before releasing her into the wilds of Bangkok Airport Duty Free.

'Right, come on, Len,' Dee says bossily. 'Let's put a ring on it.'

At the shiny metal internet terminal in the large and airy departures lounge at Bangkok airport, Maya leans into the lens and concentrates on what her editor is saying – it's hard to hear with the bustle around her; the announcements on the tannoy; the whoosh of aircraft taking off and landing.

'The snake restaurant was funny, it went down well – apart from with our vegan readership, who were pretty vocal... But we're *still* not getting much on the relationship element, Maya. Do you know what I mean?'

Amy Appleyard ends a lot of sentences with, 'Do you know what I mean?' It's a clever way of taking the shit sandwich and launching it right back at Maya to catch.

The trouble is, Maya knows exactly what Amy means. She knows deep down that in writing columns about crazy dining experiences or her capsule clothing wardrobe, she's evaded all of the relationship niggles between her and James. All of the woes she's felt in the past four months. She's dodged tension and honesty. She didn't even really mention bumping into Jon. Twice. Only that she had bumped into an old friend. And bumping into Jon has been a gift for a juicy plotline and rising tension.

Hang on, did Amy engineer that?

Maya looks around the busy departures lounge, wondering if Jon might be here now...

Of course she didn't engineer it. He's shooting a glossy TV spy drama. With Damian Lewis.

Amy continues. Maya can tell she's looking at herself on her desktop Mac, not at the box with Maya's face in it. She has the air of someone glancing in the mirror to check her hair while she talks, and she keeps giving her head a little shake. 'We had the baby tension, and the cringe of Poo Camp, which were great glimpses and I hoped for so much more. But really, Maya, what's going on beneath the surface? *Esprit* readers want to know the nitty-gritty. Do you two never fall out? About anything?'

Maya thinks of the stress in the coffin on the night bus. She thinks of James' sad face when he wanted to leave Poo Camp. She thinks of all the times she's wanted James to put his hand up and say he wants a baby too, even if it's not now. She thinks of her old friend Velma – and knows she can't really sustain this column if she's not being true to herself.

I've been here before.

'Do you want to call it a day, Amy?' Maya surprises herself by asking the question, by saying it out loud. 'I totally understand if you do. I'm not sure I can bring enough drama to the column. Not the kind of drama you want.'

I can't sell James down the river.

Amy clicks her Montblanc pen rapidly and looks out of the window over Tower Bridge, then back to the screen.

And I'm not willing to make things up.

'No, I'm not giving up, not yet anyway. To be totally transparent, I am having a few conversations with some other writers, a few test columns.'

A man lingers over Maya's shoulder, hoping she'll finish her session so he can sit down and check the scores.

Maya feels the blow and her cheeks flush red. The man at her shoulder gives her an uncomfortable feeling and an urgency in her bladder.

'Oh, right. Who?'

'There's a vegan vlogger – you know, keep things fresh – I can't keep running from the particular uprising. And there's an interiors woman who has some genius ideas about gold being a neutral or something – we're playing with the flatplan, with an idea where we shift your column – *whoever's* column – further back, in Homes rather than Relationships...' Amy's mirror face drops, and Maya knows she's finally looking at Maya, rather than herself. 'But I'm not ready to give up on you just yet, Maya. I think big drama is right around the corner for you.'

Maya smiles, gratefully, although she's not sure she should, and sinks into her chair. She wants to stick two fingers up at the man behind her, making an already tense situation feel worse.

'So, thanks for column seventeen. I'll read it and get back to you with changes. The fashiony one worked OK last Sunday – it went into our spring-to-summer special, but Miranda did have a few things we had to run past Legal. Something about the Miu Miu fakes.'

'Oh, I didn't realise.' Maya mentally slaps her forehead.

'OK thanks, Maya. Have to go, I have a lunch, ten minutes ago. Speak soon.'

The little window Amy Appleyard filled turns black before Maya has a chance to say 'Bye,' and she looks out of the vast glass window, at the planes lining the runway and taking off towards the low and looming moon. Lights and flashes illuminate the inky evening. Maya thinks of what London looks like right now; London at lunchtime. She wonders what Amy Appleyard eats at a lunch meeting. She thinks of the chargrilled sweetcorn and green chilli fritters in her favourite cafe in Hazelworth, and feels a pang in her stomach.

Home.

But first, a new country. And another twelve if they make it, before they eventually fly home on Christmas Eve. The man huffing and puffing at Maya's shoulder is appeased by a Thai woman logging off and vacating the terminal on the other side of the tall metal pillar.

Phew.

Maya looks at the clock on the departures board and speedily types in James' email address and password to check his mail for him. A message from Petra he can open in his own time. A generic banking newsletter from HSBC. Something from a Kaye-French email address, the photographer's agency James used to shoot for. Maya knows none of it will be urgent and their flight is about to board. She logs out and hastily types in her own email login. Cursing her clumsy fingers for getting a few digits wrong and having to retype it twice.

There he sits. In her inbox, as if the past seven years didn't happen. Jon Vincent. Subject: I meant it.

Maya can't face reading it now. It's all too confusing. So she leaves it there, like a grenade, and logs out.

49

'Police in Thailand leading the search for the missing French academic Manon Junot say they are now looking for a body. Ms Junot, whose disappearance was alerted when she didn't board her flight from Bangkok to Paris on New Year's Day, has been missing for four months now. With no new leads, police in Thailand say it's most likely she has died. Our Asia correspondent Clarence Meek sent this report.'

SCREEN CUTS TO A PICTURE OF MANON JUNOT ON HER TRAVELS.

'It's nearly five months since Ms Junot was photographed with this elephant at a sanctuary in Northern Thailand, and almost as long since her family last heard from her. Now they are heartbroken at the news that Thai police have changed tack and are searching for a body, rather than a missing person.'

SCREEN CUTS TO POLICE CHIEF SOMSAK KONGDUANG, WHO IS SURROUNDED BY MICROPHONES AND FLASHES.

'It's with sadness that we're turning this into a different type of investigation, a different kind of search. But in this... this digital era of regular contact and surveillance, we have reason to believe that Ms Junot is sadly no longer alive.'

SCREEN PANS TO CLARENCE MEEK, STANDING A FEW METRES AWAY FROM THE POLICE CHIEF WHILE HE TALKS.

'The family in Alsace gave a press conference this morning with their reaction to the news, saying they are heartbroken by the suggestion and they will not give up hope of finding Ms Junot alive.'

SCREEN CUTS TO MANON'S BROTHER ANTOINE AND FATHER ANDRE, AT A PRESS CONFERENCE IN FRANCE.

'The Thai authorities have made no allowances for Manon's mental-health condition. It was me and my father, a beekeeper not a police officer, who traipsed around hospitals and mental-health wings and asylums in their country, showing photographs of my sister to staff, photographs they hadn't been shown before. We searched for her among their units, the police haven't, and if they are not searching properly, we refuse to believe that Manon isn't alive.'

SCREEN CUTS BACK TO POLICE CHIEF KONGDUANG.

'We are disappointed and disagree with what the family say, that we're not searching. Thailand has spent a lot of money and used a lot of resources in turning every stone in the search for Manon Junot. It's a very difficult thing to disappear in 2016; even people who want to disappear struggle to. So, with great sadness, we have to change the focus of the investigation and be realistic about what it means when someone doesn't contact home, doesn't use their bank account, doesn't use their devices. We are just being realistic.'

SCREEN CUTS TO REPORTER WALKING TOWARDS A CAMERA DOWN A BUSY STREET IN BANGKOK.

'So what does this difference of opinion mean? What's next in the search for the body? The police say they're going to return their focus on Chiang Rai and scrutinise rubbish sites, tips and industrial areas, to see if they can find clues in the town in which Ms Junot was last seen alive. The family in France are appealing to their government and the new French Minister of Foreign Affairs for help sending investigators out to Southeast Asia, saying they can't afford to do the search alone. The family, and the world, wait with bated breath. Clarence Meek, BBC News, in Bangkok.'

50

April 2016, Bangkok, Thailand

James closes his copy of *National Geographic* without looking down as he watches the TV screen on the wall with a lump in his throat.

How does that even happen? How does someone go missing without a trace?

Maya walks across the airport lounge, pulled by the thread that always leads her to James, her heart pounding as she sees him on the bench with his daypack between his feet. He pushes his glasses up over mournful eyes, staring in a daze at the television.

I can't tell him.

'We're boarding,' Maya says, pointing to the screen next to the TV. 'We'd better get to the gate.'

'Everything OK?'

'Fine. She didn't fire me. Although she told me she's considering it.'

'That's nice of her.'

'Well, you know. I see her point. Fashion and frivolity didn't really work out for me before, did it?'

James gives a shrug as if to say it worked out in some ways; her undercover *London Evening Standard* column about fashion and frivolity did play a part in bringing them together. Maya sees what he's getting at and backtracks.

'Well, what I mean is I can't make it up, I can't invent drama just to keep a £175-a-week column going. Even though £175 a week keeps us in phad thai and spring rolls.'

'It is a lot of spring rolls.'

Maya urges James to stand up and get moving with a sigh. As she sighs, she thinks of the wasted storyline in her inbox; the one she can't bring herself to write about; the one she can't even tell James about. She can't let him down.

I love him so much.

So she keeps it light.

'Oh, you had a couple of things in your inbox. A banking thing. Something from Petra and Francesca. And something from Kaye-French. Do they even know you're travelling?'

James stands and lifts his daypack onto his shoulders.

'I'll check it when we get to Luang Prabang.'

James looks back up from the TV to the flight departures screen next to it.

'Final call for London – they're off!'

Maya drops her shoulders, lifts her neck and smiles. She is not going to let Jon Vincent ruin the best thing that ever happened to her, so she wraps her arms around James' middle as he raises his to let her in.

As they walk in tandem to the departures gate, to a new country, James puts his arm around Maya's shoulder as she rests her ear against his heartbeat.

'Just you and me again,' she says.

'Just you and me.'

My Travels with Train Man

Think of your typical holiday packing as you lay it out on your bed: cute flippy dresses, Ibiza-luxe kaftans, black pleather leggings for party nights on the beach, the capacious straw bag, bikinis you've worn so much they're getting a little threadbare around the buttcrack. Bikinis you'll never wear but you thought they were a good idea at the time (I blame Love Island*). Denim cut-offs, vests and a few frou-frou skirts and retro tees... Well, now that packing pile is teetering in your head. Halve it. And again. And again. Keep the one bikini you know you'll wear. Now take out the pleather leggings and your favourite skinny jeans and swap in some cargo trousers (1998 called – turns out they're very good for travelling). Take out your heels and throw in Havaianas and some North Face Hedgehogs (not pretty, but damn* *they're comfy). Take out the satin bomber and chuck in a daggy rain jacket. And a wool scarf and gloves as it's going to get chilly in the southern hemisphere in summer. Take out any gorgeous 50s dresses you used to love to wear to parties and throw in one jersey halterneck that never creases, because, let's face it, the only party you'll be going to is a foam party if you join the Kiwi Express, and fancy dresses are wasted on drunk teens and cheap beer. Take out your bags and statement earrings because your daypack is the only bag you're going to need and... Bingo! You have a capsule, all-season wardrobe, fit for backpacking for a whole year.*

Trouble is, it's a wardrobe that doesn't feel very... sexy.

So what's a girl to do when she arrives in tailor haven Hoi An for just forty-eight hours (the tailors here are fast)? She's going to flick through a copy of Esprit *or* Vogue, *that's what, and find her favourite dress. And then get it aped.*

It's what we did within hours of hitting Hoi An, this beautiful town in central Vietnam, where paper lanterns of all colours hang from the rickety wooden shopfronts of old trading posts.

Train Man and I stood like scarecrows, arms out and rigid, while tailors measured us up so they could cut the fabric we'd chosen into stylish shapes to fit our bodies perfectly.

The next morning: boom. Good enough to be guests at George and Amal's wedding. Train Man looks epic in his midnight blue 'Tom Ford' tux: his olive skin, black hair and emerging traveller's beard making him look too cool for the red carpet. I have a Miu Miu-style dress that is feminine, sexy, playful, and only about thirty quid. And I love it! Shame we don't have any occasion on the road to wear our threads to. And they don't fit in our backpacks. So we're shipping them off and sending them home. Happy that they cost so little, delighted that when we get home, the first invitation we receive, we will be wearing those bad boys. Tom and Miuccia at a children's party? So be it! As long as my nephews don't put 'dinosaur poo' slime on my dress. For now, it's back into the Hedgehogs and cargo trousers, and back on the road. Next stop: Laos and the beautiful city of Luang Prabang.

51

April 2016, London, England

'Nena... you awake?' Tom slopes into the bedroom in his hoody, joggers and Mahabis slippers because it's Sunday, and that's what he wears on a Sunday. A Sunday in spring anyway, although they haven't shaken the chill of winter quite yet, even though the sun is streaming in through the Velux windows and onto the bed. He places a cup of Earl Grey on the bedside table and sits on the edge of the low bed next to Nena, who's lying face down. He strokes the dark brown skin exposed on the small of her back, the space between her checked pyjama bottoms and a pink ribbed vest. Skin that evokes the tropical scents of the Costa dos Coqueiros and their halcyon honeymoon there. He wants to put his cheek to her skin and for everything to be OK.

Nena faces away from Tom, gazing into the middle

of the bed, and wonders if she should pretend to be asleep. Her eyes are wide open. Ava is having her morning nap in the cot against the wall.

'I'll just leave this tea here for you,' Tom whispers.

He doesn't expect a reply and she doesn't say thanks. But he kisses the small of her back anyway, strokes her bottom and stands.

I'll leave her to it.

'Why am I so shit at this?'

Tom is taken by surprise in the doorway.

'What?' He scratches his head and turns around.

'Why can't I do the one thing I was instinctively meant to know?'

'What are you talking about?'

'I can do an Arabian double front flip on a crowded dance floor…'

Tom smiles, relieved at the hint of humour in the air, although he knows Nena's mood is serious; that he needs to tread carefully.

'I can look into a camera and talk confidently without panicking.'

She lifts the duvet over her, over the exposed small of her back.

'I know all the words to "U Can't Touch This". And I can do the Hammer dance.'

Tom feels allowed to smile.

'But I don't know how to stop her crying; I can't feed her.'

Nena's humour shield evaporates around her and she starts sobbing into the bed. Tom rushes over, back to his perch on the edge of the mattress, and puts his arm along Nena's top arm.

'Nena, that is not true.'

He kicks off his Mahabis, climbs onto the bed and spoons her.

'Anyway, look at her now, happy and sleeping and dreamy.'

'But why can't I do this? Why do I dread the nights? And then the days after them. She's six months old and I still don't know her cues. I should have instinctively known what she wanted when she was born... and I still don't.'

'Nena—'

'I worry day and night. I sob every time I watch the news, so I avoid it. I can't breathe when I think about the world she didn't ask to be born into.'

Nena's body starts to shake and she sobs uncontrollably.

'Babe, you're doing brilliantly.'

'No I'm not. I'm just not cut out for this.'

Tom turns Nena around so they're nose-to-nose in the bed and holds her face with both hands. 'Are you kidding me?'

Her tears are flowing stronger now.

'You're AMAZING. You carried her with such strength and beauty. Watching you dance with her in your belly was the most powerful I have ever seen a woman. Watching you birth her, I was gobsmacked. And look at you – you're keeping our baby alive. And happy. Every day! And just because she's a shit sleeper or a pernickety eater... do not let that make you question the power of you. You're an amazing mother. You're winning at this.'

'You would say that. You need to say that, so I can function, so you can go to work.'

'No I wouldn't.' Tom sounds on the verge of indignant. 'I would never say anything I didn't mean. You're a brilliant mum, Nena. You and Ava are the two most beautiful women in the world. You light up the world for me and for Arlo. You *are* our world. And you don't even know how instinctively and naturally wonderful you are.'

Nena shakes her head, as if to make the lies stop.

Tom takes a deep breath. He knew Nena was struggling, but didn't anticipate this – how low she would still be at six months.

'But this *isn't* you. This is fatigue. And fatigue is breeding self-doubt. This is demanding Little Miss keeping you awake all night. This is me going to work. This is you not leaving the flat. This is you needing to get support – and I will help any way I can.'

'You think I need help? You think I can't cope?' she says with hurt eyes.

'No! I think lack of sleep and Ava draining you is making life fucking hard for you. I think you need support, help, whatever you want to call it. I think you need a plan. I think *we* need a plan. And needing a plan isn't failure. Look—' Tom releases himself and rolls over, to pull open the drawer of his bedside table. He takes out some leaflets. 'Tina the health visitor called around when you were asleep on Friday, just after I got home.'

'What?' Nena looks suspicious, as if there's a conspiracy against her.

'She had been worried and thinking about you since your last visit to clinic and she thought you might benefit from some of these? Some are rubbish, but there are networks and support, and if you feel it'll take more than that, then we can go see Dr Barratt. Ask for help.'

'You think it's that bad?'

'Actually, no. I think we need to start by getting her off the boob. Cracking sleep. Sleep will make the world of difference. I'll do a few nights in a row and you go stay at your parents' – come back in the morning when I go to work.'

'I can't be without her.'

'Then stay here, wear earplugs and sleep in Arlo's room.'

'Why didn't you offer to do this before?'

Tom is silenced by guilt and thinks for a second as he looks out of the skylight and watches a seagull fly over Stoke Newington.

'I guess I didn't realise how serious it might be until Tina dropped in.'

'Tina is a witch,' Nena says with a half pout.

'Tina gives a shit. She was on her way out for her anniversary dinner, all dressed up, when she dropped these off. It's stuff about support groups, activities around here, something on weaning... Some useful, some bollocks.'

'Why didn't you tell me?'

'I was trying to find the right time. And you don't need leaflets to tell you how to be a good mother. You already are. Ava is the luckiest girl in the world.'

Nena smiles, and speaks through the snot. 'Not just saying it?'

'Not just saying it.'

Ava stirs and Tom pulls his wife in closer and kisses her bare raspberry-red lips.

'Anyway. You *don't* know the lyrics to "U Can't Touch This". You always get it wrong, but I think it's cute.'

'Huh?'

'It's two *hype* feet, not two tight feet.'

52

April 2016, Luang Prabang, Laos

'I'll leave you to settle in,' says the man with a friendly face and a dragon on his shirt, as he brings two long, thin doors together to close them behind him.

Maya and James look at each other, their eyes excited, as they listen to footsteps peel away on the tiled floor of the old French villa.

'Wow,' smiles Maya, stroking the simple lines of the elegant four-poster bed. Fuchsia petals are scattered across white waffle bed linen, giving Maya the urge to jump right through the mosquito net voile and onto it with childlike abandon. 'If we do ever open that hostel of ours, this is how I want it,' she says, picking up a china cup with pansies on it from the teak chest of drawers under the window. 'Not too many frills, yet understatedly fancy.'

James pushes his glasses up his nose and heaves their backpacks onto the chaise longue that divides the bedroom area from the bathroom door.

Maya winces. 'Don't put them on there, it'll ruin the fabric.'

Upholstery plus dirt is a bugbear of Maya's. It used to bother her when she commuted on the less salubrious seats of the 8.21 a.m. to King's Cross: years of hair and skin and gum and matter, pressed into blue faux-velveteen seat covers. It feels even worse to contribute to the sullification of such an elegant chaise longue.

James looks over his shoulder, tries not to roll his eyes, and drags the big backpacks down the stripy blue and cream upholstery and onto the tiled floor.

Maya bites her tongue. She doesn't want to sound like a nag any more than she already has. She particularly doesn't want to ruin the moment and the feeling of relief to have arrived at their destination and to be staying in a Nice Room.

Maya and James have stayed in so many rooms on this trip, to such varying degrees of hospitable. Some opulent, some squalid. Many in between have been beige and boring and of little note. They've experienced so many types of accommodation, bed and bathroom – and they're not even halfway through their trip – that it's become a talking point on planes, buses and trains. Maya and James discuss what the dream hostel they'll never open might be like, in which unspecified

location, in a faraway future. Maya likes the sound of
Peru. James favours the Alps. It's an evolving dream.
Their hostel will be clean, of course. It'll have little
luxuries like the crisp white waffle bedlinen juxtaposed
with rustic antiquities, like the decorative tea set. High
ceilings are a must. No carpet. And, *wow* – a roll-top
bath like the one Maya has just opened the bathroom
door onto would be gorgeous.

'Look at this, baby!'

White brick tiles and a large, round, vintage train-
station clock contribute to making the lofty walls,
copper taps and long bronze radiator the perfect
supporting cast to the large Thai copper roll-top bath,
shimmering and golden in the middle of the room. By
the time James walks in to check it out, Maya is reclined
in the empty tub, fully clothed and smiling.

'This is it. This is the bath we will have in *our* rooms.'

James laughs and walks back out again.

'Come on,' he says, 'Let's get some dinner.' He closes
the sage-green shutters of the bathroom window and
looks at the big clock. 'Before the restaurants close.'

Maya looks at James standing over her with his
outstretched hands. Always reliably and dependably
there to lift her up. Always reliably and dependably
wanting dinner by 8 p.m. Always reliably and
dependably changing the subject so as not to talk about
their future.

53

Maya digs the flat sharp edge of her oar into the sandy riverbank and leans on its handle, almost hanging over the yellow canoe she's sitting in. She takes a moment to catch her breath as she watches James battle a patch of white water. His pink canoe is fighting the flow, scared that if he goes down the ramp of a mini waterfall, he will be projected far down the river, too far away from Maya, leaving her alone, hanging on her oar stuck in the embankment.

'Baby, it's OK!' she hollers across the wide expanse. 'I can catch you up! Just stop further down!'

It seemed a good idea at the time. A great way for Maya and James to orientate themselves with this new part of the world, by spending the day kayaking along the Nam Khan river; the tributary of the mighty

Mekong it meets at the top of Luang Prabang. A good way to reconnect after the past few weeks of travelling in Dee and Lenny's company. A good way to shake off the appearance and reappearance of Jon, which they still haven't really talked about.

Kayaking has been great fun so far. A guide called Liko went with them for the first hour, to show Maya and James how to negotiate the green and brown snaking river bends and what to do if they rolled over. Maya was scared at first, but by the time Liko left and they stopped for lunch under the Tad Sae waterfall, she felt like she'd found her stride.

Maya and James ate baguettes perched on the edge of a turquoise pool and stole kisses from each other before other tourists arrived to kill the moment and they decided to get back in their kayaks. Now their arms are tired and their faces feel tight after five hours of paddling in the sunshine, past merchants with boats heavy under the weight of rice sacks; past children running along the river's edge shouting out at Maya and James to wave; past Asian elephants, majestic and curved, wading through the water; past derelict cabins and huts hidden in the tamarind, coconut and mango trees. Now they are ready to go back to their shabby-chic room, to crash out on the four-poster bed, but they're in a bit of a pickle.

James struggles, his arms rippling in the battle against the break, his teeth gnashing as he fights to not be separated from Maya on this otherwise peaceful expanse of bright water, highlighted green by the reflection of the sunshine in the lofty and lush trees on the riverbank.

'I will find you!' shouts Maya, like Daniel Day-Lewis in *The Last Of The Mohicans*. She laughs to herself, but sees the struggle for James isn't funny.

'Arghhhh!' he grunts and paddles with all his might as he rises upstream, over the top of the mini waterfall and across to Maya at the Nam Khan's edge.

James wedges his oar into the riverbank parallel to Maya's, panting heavily as he catches his breath.

'Shit. That was tough.'

'Oh, baby, you poor thing. You could have gone over, I'm sure I would have caught you up.'

James doesn't speak. He just breathes heavily, rapidly. Droplets of sweat form in little bubbles on his olive skin as he regains himself.

'Are you OK?'

He nods and pants some more. His teeth no longer bared. His black hair wet from the frenzied paddling. Blinking frantically to realign his contacts and regain his vision.

'Come on...' he eventually says. 'Let's get back to town. I've got that Skype call in an hour. I'm wiped out.'

Across the river, in a wooden boat obscured by reeds, a still and silent figure watches.

54

Rosa Samarasekera sashays towards Tom's table in the Groucho, teetering on cocktail-stick-thin ankles, her royal blue Roland Mouret dress not doing much to restrict her enthusiastic stride.

'Tommmmmm!' she gushes, as she outstretches her arms for him to take her.

'Rosa, hi,' says Tom, as he stands and smooths down his shirt.

Rosa gives Tom two kisses and takes her Mulberry bag off the crook of her elbow, to place it on the leather wing-backed chair on the other side of Tom. She doesn't want it to get in the way. He inhales her musky perfume and remembers the other night and then he thinks of Nena, crying in his arms about being a bad mother.

'What would you like to drink?' he asks. Businesslike, formal.

Rosa looks around. At the sports broadcaster holding court at the bar; at the theatre director who just won an Oscar; at the former *Bertie & Betty* presenter who is coked up to the eyeballs and Tom is relieved not to have been spotted by. He leans back in his chair.

'Cheeky Dog,' she says with a wink.

Tom looks at the menu. Copper Dog whisky, Appleton rum, apple juice, lemon juice and ginger ale.

'Sure,' he says with a smile, as he calls a waitress over.

Rosa's face is studious. Her gaze intent, as she watches him order, and they both watch the woman walk away.

'Look, about the other night,' Tom says, shuffling in his chair against the glossy petrol-blue wall behind him.

Rosa's face lights up. She was hoping she could get his attention, to see him again, in another intimate corner of London. To be close to him again.

'You made a mistake?' she asks, raising one eyebrow and giving a little laugh.

'No, really. I didn't,' Tom says, looking seriously into Rosa's knowing eyes.

Rosa sighs and decides not to beat around the bush. She lowers her long hand and strokes Tom's crotch. He feels her imprint and looks at her with pleading eyes.

'I meant what I said.'

'Come on. Don't be such a tease, Tom. Honestly! Making me beg...'

'I don't want you to beg. In fact I don't want any part of it.'

'What?'

Rosa leans back and checks Tom's face to see if he's joking.

'I meant it at The Savoy and I mean it now. I'm a happily married man and I don't want to have sex with you.'

Rosa is so shocked, she lets a little gasp escape out of her glossed lips and removes her hand. Her face looks as wounded as her ego. She has never met a man who hasn't wanted to sleep with her. Whether it's the men she's set up with on blind dates, enthusiastic junior doctors taking her from behind during a night shift, or consultants who shower her with luxurious gifts. She has never been turned down before. It is Rosa who says no. This has never happened, and she's completely thrown. She tucks her neat hair behind her ear.

'What are you talking about? You know we both want it. I can feel the chemistry, Tom, I know you can too.'

'Rosa, you're a beautiful woman, and I'm sure I'm extremely lucky – in fact I'm flattered that you would even look at me like that, but I'm just not interested.'

'I thought you dragged me here—'

'I hardly dragged you.'

'*Invited* me here to put the other night right, to have me slide onto you. We could be doing that, Tom. I thought we had a connection.'

Rosa tries again, pressing her hand into Tom's crotch under the table, stroking it more vigorously, more aggressively now.

'Well, you thought wrong.'

Rosa's face becomes petulant as she realises it's not working.

'And if you don't take your hands off me, I will speak to HR about unwanted sexual attention and harassment.'

Rosa backs off sharply and laughs. 'Are you serious?'

The waitress arrives with a Cheeky Dog and a sparkling water.

Tom picks up his glass and looks into it.

'When was it a crime to tell someone you find them attractive? I can't help the passion I feel for you.'

'I didn't invite you to touch me. I wouldn't expect to touch you uninvited.'

'You can! I won't tell if you don't...' Rosa gives a sultry smile.

'Please, Rosa, let's not make this any more awkward than it already is. You're doing a great job on *My Brilliant Body*, I don't want this to get in the way of a bright career you have in broadcasting.'

Rosa stands, leans over the table and grabs her Mulberry tote, before throwing her Cheeky Dog in Tom's face as she strides out.

'What the—'

'Bastard,' she sighs under her breath.

As Rosa Samarasekera storms out through the low-lit and opulent bar, she makes eye contact with the sports presenter who's holding court.

He wants me.

55

April 2016, Luang Prabang, Laos

'Hi James. Looking good.'

Brooke, the bookings editor from the Kaye-French picture agency, is peering into the camera, her piercing blue eyes surveying James from under a heavy black fringe as she marvels at his tan. The last time she saw him, at their offices in Shoreditch, James had a winter pallor; he looked thin and slightly sallow. Now he is bronzed, his hair a bit longer, and he has the look of a man who is enjoying life out of the rat race, even if his kayak-tender arms are drooping at the keyboard.

Last night, after eating river fish stuffed with pork and herbs on a lantern-lit veranda, followed by ambling around the night market to orientate themselves, James checked his emails. He was too intrigued to see what the message from Kaye-French was about; even more so when Brooke said she had something super special he wouldn't want to turn down. James replied straight away, hoping to catch her there and then. When she didn't reply, he suggested a Skype call the next morning – 10 a.m. for her, 5 p.m. for him. All night in the four-poster bed, and all day on the Nam Khan, James couldn't shake the feeling of intrigue, the seed of excitement, wondering what this job could be, hoping it might be something out in the field, to conveniently coincide with their travels.

'Thanks,' he replies, pushing his matte black rectangular glasses up his nose. He took his contacts out as soon as they got back to their room since the muddy Mekong water had got trapped behind them, but Brooke likes a man in glasses. The dimple in his left cheek sinks a little as he blushes.

'So, I thought you wouldn't want to pass this one up without hearing more at least.'

'Go on…'

'English film director and his supermodel wife. Apparently her make-up artist was at some wedding you shot in India – which we at the agency knew nothing about of course, but let's not dwell on that…'

'It was a friend's wedding, I wasn't paid.'

'Well, anyway, the make-up artist said you were a dream to work with, and the supermodel *loved* the images she showed her.'

Is she sure they were my images?

'So her assistant did a little search on you, got past all the Train Man stuff and – boom – found you through us. They want to meet with you asap to discuss.'

'OK...'

'It's a two-parter. An English country wedding in the Cotswolds, followed by a party in a chateau in the south of France. Johnny Depp's house or something. Lots of NDAs to sign. Very exclusive. But it'll open so many doors. If done right.'

James sighs and slinks back into his chair, his hands behind his head and his tired arms swelling. Inside he wants to do cartwheels, even to have been asked is an honour, but James isn't a cartwheeler; his triumphant fist pumps are quiet and internal.

He looks around the internet cafe guiltily, as if he's cheating on Maya by even asking questions, and drops his arms to his sides again.

'When's the wedding?'

Please say it's next year.

'July.'

'Next July?'

'This July. They want to meet you in the next few days. At their home in Fitzrovia, to discuss details, what they want et cetera.'

'Wow. Do they want me to be the photographer's assistant, or do the reportage pictures?'

'No, James, they want you to be the photographer photographer.'

'Shiiiit.'

This is big.

This is really big. James had been getting by, shooting upscale weddings that were being featured in the glossy bridal magazines – he'd even done some editorial fashion and celebrity shoots, but it wasn't exactly lucrative, he was still very much making a name for himself when he and Maya booked their round-the-world tickets. But a celebrity wedding. An A-list wedding.

Johnny Depp's house?!

'Where are you now?'

'I'm in Luang Prabang.'

'Where the hell is that?'

'Laos.'

'Nope, none the wiser.'

'Let's just say it's far from Fitzrovia. Near Thailand.'

Brooke's face drops. 'Oh. Disappointing.'

'Look, can I just chat to my girlfriend and get back to you? We're heading to Indonesia next and she had her heart set on it.'

'Are you serious?'

'No, I need to speak to her.'

'I'm pretty sure Testino would ditch backpacking for this gig. And we haven't even discussed the fee yet.'

James holds up his hands to his ears. He doesn't want to know how bountiful the fee is if he can't do the wedding. 'Don't tell me.'

'Really?'

'Don't tell me. Let me just talk to Maya, see what she says.'

'OK, but I can't tell them you have to think about it, that's embarrassing. I'll try to stall, but get back to me in, say, three hours?'

James' heart sinks.

Brooke doesn't look like she fancies him quite so much.

'I need to get back to them by the end of play today with an answer, otherwise it reflects badly on us too.'

Fuck.

'OK cool.'

'In the meantime I'll fire off some info for you, so you have the offer written down, a bit more detail about locations and timings and things. I'll redact the fee part, if you really don't want to know. And we'll reconvene in three hours, yes?'

Brooke's blue eyes bore into the lens.

'I'll get back to you by then.'

'Great. Oh, and James?'

'Yep?'

'Don't be a dick.'

56

James picks up his camera by its sturdy lens and pays the teenage boy behind the counter, a boy with big ears and an eager smile, before weaving out into the street. The dusk light in the pink sky over the historic centre illuminates lantern-festooned streets and alleyways, and it feels like a perfect time to get some pictures.

Three hours.

Vendors arrive and start to set up their stalls for the night market, laying out their fabrics and wares, some on tables, most on the floor, all on large squares and rectangles of colourful cloth under bright red and blue canvas gazebos.

James sees a child, quietly winding herself in three multicoloured shawls that her mother is hoping to sell tonight, playing hide-and-seek on her own. James raises his camera to the mother, to ask if he can take a picture. The woman nods. The little girl, her black wayward hair tamed across her head in a low side parting tucked behind an ear, looks at James. Through his glasses, through his camera lens, he sees mischief behind the shyness. He gives her the pain au chocolat he had bought Maya from the bakery on his way to the internet cafe, and she devours the pastry as if it's the first thing she's eaten all day.

All around James are colourful paper lanterns and fabrics – in pale lilacs and soft yellows – shades more muted than the brightness of Hoi An – backlit by the pink sunset, seducing him on his walk, distracting him from the conversation he's dreading.

I need my wide-angle lens. I'll go back for my wide-angle lens.

James walks past a temple, along a quieter street at the edge of the town and up the wide steps of the faded French villa, past the reception area and the man with the dragon on his shirt. He knocks twice on the thin double wooden doors before opening the right-hand one.

'Maya…?'

He hears a trickle of water and sees her bare back through the open bathroom door, her skin illuminated by the copper bath.

'In here!'

James closes the door and flips the shutters on the window, protecting Maya from agile eyes and cicadas that might be lurking as night arrives.

The trickle of water, a constant hot stream, fills the deep bath and eases Maya's tired limbs. James walks around the bed quietly, towards the open door to the bathroom. He sees Maya's spine, her freckled and bronzed shoulders, the white marks around the back of her neck where her bikini top is tied. He can smell the frangipani and jasmine on the air as if it's Maya's skin emanating such aromas. He sees the line of her collarbone kissed by the wet tips of her wavy chestnut hair as it unravels from its tie.

It's not her fault.

Click.

James photographs the woman he loves and his heart breaks. He so wishes they wanted the same thing.

She turns around and looks up, the freckles on her face lit by the golden shimmer of the tub, the slow hum of the ceiling fan offsetting the heat she's feeling from the steamy water.

James walks in and lowers his camera.

'Anything interesting?' she asks.

James is disarmed. He wants to slump onto the closed lid of the white toilet and cry. Just looking at Maya makes him feel wretched.

'No, nothing worth the Skype call,' he says mysteriously.

I'm not trying to break your heart.

'I'm going to go back out, get some shots, I've just come back to get a lens.'

James doesn't tell Maya that the light is enchanting out there; *was* enchanting out there – he knows that when he opens the room door again, the sky will be completely different, yet equally mesmerising.

'I'll come with you.'

'No! You finish your bath, you look so beautiful in there. And it'll do you good after today.'

James lifts his lens and takes a few more shots of Maya as she sponges her shoulders. Through the lens, he sees her, yet he can't see what she really wants.

I know it's not what I want.

'I need to go and have a wander. A think.'

'Are you OK?'

'Yeah, sure.'

James doesn't look sure. He looks downbeat and cagey.

Maya has a feeling of dread in the pit of her stomach.

She glances at the old station clock on the bathroom wall; thick black hands power through a face covered in steam, almost in a straight line.

Six o'clock.

James kisses Maya's head.

'I won't be long. I'll be back so we can get some dinner, yeah?'

'OK,' Maya says in a little voice, examining her toes stretched out in front of her.

In almost five months since they left home, James has never shown any preference to be by himself; to go off for a walk on his own. Every time Maya said she'd go to the 7-Eleven to buy a bottle of water or a Crunchie, James got up to put on his flip-flops too. Every time she said she wanted to climb a hill or walk along a wall or seek out a local pastry shop or go to a chemist to buy tampons, James wanted to go too. If either of them had ever craved some alone time on this trip, it was Maya, which she would conveniently achieve on a run. Have some headspace and get it out of her system; walk back through a hostel or hotel-room door sweaty and relieved but comfortably aching to see James again. James hasn't once shown any desire to go off, to be alone. Until now. And his solemnity is making Maya feel distinctly uncomfortable.

'See you in a bit.'

The long wooden doors click shut together and Maya looks to the room beyond the bathroom door and the chaise longue. The simple four-poster bed. It's voile mosquito net moving in the gentle breeze despite James having closed the shutters. The teak chest of drawers neither James nor Maya bothered to put their clothes in. The vintage tea set on top of it. A peep of a backpack stuffed under the bed. Maya can't tell whose backpack it is in the shadows, just that it looks like the shape of a person.

Stop winding yourself up.

Maya looks back at her toes and turns off the tap. The molten water is brimming high against the edge of the bath and Maya feels a flash of guilt about the self-indulgence. But it's a good bath.

I needed this.

Her limbs were tired from the kayaking, her feet already crinkled from a day spent in water. Maya rubs her toes for one last clean, deep red nail polish looking weathered around the cuticles and the edges. Her runner's feet are both tired yet revived. Maya stands in the tub and reaches for the large white waffle sheet she left on the floor, and wraps it around her like a bridal gown.

I'll touch up my toes while he's out, she thinks, looking down at her feet.

Maya reaches into her washbag next to the sink for a shade of nail polish called Temptress and plants herself, in her towel, on the chaise longue. She's mindful not to let any drips of blood-red polish go anywhere other than her nails, and mindful of feeling alone for the first time in a long time. The knot in the pit of her hungry stomach, which is weighed down by a secret, grows. She is unnerved by the shape of a figure under the bed.

57

As she sinks deeper into the gravitational pull of the chaise longue, Maya is startled awake by a smash. Her eyes widen, her pupils shrink. Her body is cold and damp. For a split second she thinks she fell asleep in the bath but realises she isn't seasick, she isn't drowning, she's just startled. A bloody trail oozes on the floor and Maya looks at it with alarm, to see a small glass bottle is smashed into three pieces against the orange, beige and grey pattern of the old tiled floor.

'Shit.'

Maya jumps up, clutching her white waffle towel loosely around her, then screams when she spies a figure under the bed.

It's just a backpack.

Standing firm to regain her balance and her composure, Maya reconfigures the towel so it is tight like a bandeau dress, then pads barefoot into the bathroom, admiring the precision with which she painted her toes; anxious that the polish on the floor doesn't seep and stain the beautiful tiles.

I have to clear that up.

Maya grabs a loose roll of toilet paper and looks up at the clock face, no longer obscured by steam, and hurries back to the bedroom.

It's 8.40 p.m. and James has been gone for over two hours.

I was asleep for ages.

Maya looks to the door, before crouching down and smearing the thick droplets of drying enamel across the tile, turning it from deep scarlet to brown. She tries not to cry as she knows she's making it worse.

This is so unlike him.

Maya throws on her jersey dress, and then unzips the front pocket on her small daypack, takes out a Sharpie and looks around for a piece of paper.

Nothing.

She doesn't want to tear a page out of her precious notebook, the Liberty one with trip jottings and column ideas and notes on what makes a hotel bedroom lovely – so she goes back to the bathroom and takes another few sheets of toilet paper. She walks back to the chest of drawers and writes, although thick black pen bleeds onto the thin paper:

Gone to look for you around the night market. It's now 8.45 p.m. I'll come back here if I can't find you... Mx

Three sentences. More desperate than the three sentences with which Maya first caught James' attention. A note. *The note.* In this note, panic stifles hope.

Maya grabs her coin purse and room key and steps into her bronze Havaianas. She gives one more look around the room before she leaves. Standing at the threshold and glancing back over her shoulder, the room feels eerie, not enticing. She curses herself, sad and hungry to the core, lamenting that decision to not bring phones with them on this trip.

Where is he?

58

Weaving among the stalls of the night market, treading carefully so as not to step on artisan textiles, batik bags, hippie-chic clothes and low-lit lanterns, laid out proudly and orderly on colourful blankets on the floor, Maya looks at a merchant, a young mother, and smiles. The woman smiles back, before scolding her daughter, who is twirling around in a whirl of colourful scarves and shawls.

Has she seen James? Might he have photographed her? She has a face he would have liked to photograph.

The merchant looks back at Maya, hopefully, and proffers a dress she thinks Maya might like. Plain yellow cotton with a band of little lilac flowers like forget-me-nots dotted around a width above the hem. Maya takes the offering, stroking the dress, pretending to be interested, plucking up the courage to ask the woman if she's seen a Western man with a camera around his neck. But she knows she probably won't understand her question.

Maya feels the soft cotton dress, stroking it with her thumb. She pictures herself in a not-distant future and thinks it would look lovely in Ubud or Borobudur, from pictures of towns she has looked at, places she and James are meant to be heading to next. She nods and smiles at the vendor, as if to say it's lovely, looking from the woman to her daughter and feeling terrible that now is not the time to buy a new dress, before giving a look of apology. As Maya releases the fabric from her tanned and tired hand, she hears a voice whisper, low in her ear.

'You'd look beautiful in that.'

Maya inhales sharply, and spins around.

'What the actual—?'

'Can I buy it for you?'

'What are you doing here?'

Maya's arms hang by her side in defeat.

'Same as you.'

'What?'

'It's one of the most beautiful places in the world, so stunning and serene. I'm here to see Luang Prabang. And you. Please, Maya, please let me buy you that dress.'

'Jon, no.'

The vendor looks confused.

Maya's brow knits as she looks up at Jon, smiling down at her.

'What are you doing here?' she tries again.

'Third time a charm? Isn't that what they say?'

Maya looks around the low labyrinth of the night market. She can't see James, tall and reassuring and ready to rescue her again. Maybe he isn't going to rescue her this time.

'This isn't a coincidence, is it?'

'Would you believe me if I said it was? That it's serendipity.'

Maya thinks for a second, and opens her mouth, but words fail to come out.

'Well, I think it's serendipitous we're both here, in another beautiful place, bumping into each other again. Star-crossed lovers, if you will. But I did make it happen this time, I have to confess.' Jon holds up his palms in submission. 'I've come for you, Maya.'

'Come for me?'

The little girl, her hair swept in a low side parting, messy and sticking up behind her ears, steps forward, to watch the white couple in front of her in fascination, as if they are something from a soap opera she once saw on her friend's television.

'Just hear me out please.' Jon brings his palms together. 'I skipped the le Carré shoot to find you. I'm going to get in all manner of trouble with my director, but I'm not going back to finish filming until I've said this to you.'

'Jon, don't.'

Maya puts her finger to his lip and she remembers how they felt on her neck, where his whisper still lingers.

Jon moves it away gently, putting his hand around Maya's wrist. 'When we wrap, I want to go home, I want to go back to London, with you. Home means nothing without you. My life has meant nothing without you for the past seven years. Please.'

'Jon, why are you saying this?'

'I'm in love with you, Maya, that's why.'

She examines Jon's face. He looks tanned. Blonder. More relaxed than he did in Thailand or Vietnam. His pressed, pale pink linen shirt is open to the chest. Perhaps this is the epiphany he was searching for all his life. Perhaps she is the one for him, and he her.

'Come for a drink with me, there's so much I have to explain...' Jon takes Maya's hand in his.

Completely dumbfounded, she lets him lead her away, to see if this is really happening, because it all seems terribly unreal.

59

Jon lets go of Maya's hand and carefully pulls out a chair for her at a table on the veranda of a restored villa. Blackboards on white shutters list gin brands and poetry nights. Maya takes her cue to sit down, imagining Graham Greene might have drunk a Martini on this very deck.

'Two gin and tonics,' Jon says to the waitress, as if he's a regular, even though he's never been to this country before. His confidence astounds Maya. How he can sit at a table with such command, as if it's always been *his* table.

He looks at Maya, a flash of contentment in his pale blue-green eyes.

Maya looks back as if to say, *What now?*

'Look, I'm thirty, you'll be thirty in what, a month?'

He remembers.

'We both want the same thing. We want stability and babies and a *fucking* nice life we've worked *fucking* hard for.'

Jon takes Maya's hand across the table, and she lets him.

He wants me.

She twists the ring on her right hand and pretends to study the brown rectangular smoky quartz, so she can avoid his gaze. His eyes are too disarming.

He wants babies.

'Yes. We do want the same thing,' she concedes. 'But I want it with James.'

'He's going to let you down.'

Maya shoots Jon a look and withdraws her hand. She wonders where James is, if he has already let her down.

This is so unlike him.

'I saw the look in his eyes, back in Hoi An, when your friend proposed. He looked almost... embarrassed.'

Maya knows that face.

'He's not for you, Maya, I can see it.'

Jon weaves his soft fingers back into hers and Maya feels completely confused.

The waitress returns and Maya pulls back and sits up, happy for the distraction. Maya watches the woman who has a beautiful face and a knowing smile, as she places a square paper napkin in front of each of them, and on top of it a gin and tonic. A lychee bobs among the ice cubes Maya can hear cracking, as they swirl and enjoy their moment during the pause.

The cracks ring in Maya's ears and she feels guilty. Caught out by the waitress as she takes a sip from her cold gin and tonic, as she sits intimately with Jon on the veranda. The drink quenches a thirst she forgot she had and reminds her of the turquoise waterfall she and James stopped at earlier in the day, how thirsty she felt when they stopped for lunch. How much she loves him.

Am I so vain that I need to hear him beg?

'Look, I have to find James, he went for a walk a couple of hours ago and said he'd be back...'

Maya knows she sounds like a cliché.

Jon makes a face as if to say *I told you so*, which in turn angers Maya, and makes her stand up.

'This isn't like him.'

Jon opens his mouth to speak, but Maya cuts him off.

'James has *never* let me down,' she pauses. 'You did.'

Jon plays with the chunky watch on his left arm and looks back up at Maya. Those eyes, standing out against his palest pink shirt and his tan, staring into her.

'Go find him – if you can, that is. Ask him if he wants what you want. And then come back to me. I'll wait here. All night on this veranda, if I have to. I fly back to Vietnam in the morning. Come with me. Watch me on set. *Inspire* me to be the best I can be. Then I'll take you home. I'll give you the life you want.'

Maya walks off, past the other tables on the narrow veranda, apologising to couples for making them pull in, down a short flight of wooden stairs, weaving through the market to get back to the hotel, to see if James has returned. A million thoughts flying through her mind.

60

He's not back.

The room is unchanged, the note is on the middle of the bed where Maya left it. It has neither been picked up nor glanced at, Maya can tell. She stands, blinking and thinking, wide-eyed and wide-mouthed, gobsmacked and heartbroken.

In the tall lush valley beyond the river, Maya hears a rumble of thunder. The clock ticks heavily on the wall of the bathroom.

The clock.

Maya rushes into the bathroom – she has no watch – and without a phone she has come to rely on seeking out the time in whichever airport, bus station or shop she can. It's one of the first things she notices when they arrive in a new room. Usually it's an LED bedside table clock radio, or the time on the tickertape of Star News, BBC World or CNN, with a little added mental arithmetic to cater for time differences. Maya looks at the grand clock on the wall. It's 9.50 p.m.

We never eat this late.

They've never *not* gone out to eat by this time. This is so unlike James, who can tell the time from his hunger, to not come back, to not think about what they might have for dinner. Why does he want to be alone?

What was it he had to think about?

Fat drops of rain start to thump on the awning outside the room.

What changed?

Maya walks around the bed to the window that looks out onto the street and twists the fastening that opens the glass panel, enabling her to reach the shutter. She opens a slat. A flash of lightning illuminates the street outside; a rat scurries for cover into a drain.

I don't know what to do.

Maya shuts the slat, the slam creating a frantic, pained echo in her eardrum as she locks the window in front of her. She sees an umbrella in a stand in the corner, between the door and the other window, the one that looks out onto the hotel courtyard. She lifts the umbrella out of its stand, like a musketeer going into battle. A flash of lightning illuminates the fronds in the garden courtyard and Maya screams at the shape of a figure, standing destitute in the rain. Was it a figure or was it a tree?

Is that James out there?

She presses her nose to the window and waits for the next flash of lightning.

Nothing. Just rain. Flora and fauna. A monkey perhaps. Or was it a large palm that had fallen in the storm?

I have to go and find him.

Maya grips the umbrella in one hand and grabs her purse and room key with the other, as she heads out into the rain. To see if she can find an answer to at least one of the questions tormenting her.

Maya heads towards Sisavangvong Road, past white walls and swaying palms, lit and creaking in the storm. She opens out the umbrella to discover it's a golfing size, with words from another, bigger hotel from another, bigger country emblazoned across its outside edge. Still, it offers Maya protection, from the rats and the rain, as she hurries towards the night market.

The colours of the royal blue and pillar-box red pop-up gazebos are dulled by rain, as vendors huddle underneath them, protecting their families and their wares. Even now, the Laos temperament to sit and smile shines through, as locals huddle without complaint, used to storms that follow peaceful days. Those merchants without a canopy above them scrabble to keep their handicrafts dry. Maya sees a man deftly pull four corners of a pretty cloth, with all his wares sitting on top of it, into a big colourful bundle with one tug of a drawstring. The man saunters away through the emptying market, his goods on his back like a giant snail shell of a thousand colours, only he moves with purpose and agility.

Paper lanterns wilt. Dresses flop. Everything soaks up the steamy sweet scent of the rain. Maya weaves through the muddle, under the large black golfing umbrella, trying not to knock into people as they pass; her hair soaking wet from the brief flashes she's uncovered as she moves her umbrella to let someone pass. Her bare shoulders of her halterneck dress are shiny and wet. Searching, searching, searching as despair rolls on the steam of jasmine and frangipani.

Everything's ruined.

And still, James is nowhere to be seen.

61

Maya walks into an internet cafe, suddenly cold and her hair bedraggled.

'Can of Coke please,' she says to a teenage boy with big ears and a skinny frame, who she assumes is serving. He smiles and grabs one from the fridge behind the counter. 'And a computer if you have one?'

The boy gestures to the machines, although neither he nor Maya can tell if there's one free.

Maya props her umbrella behind the door and sees that there is one vacant terminal among the two banks of computers. All the others are occupied by local teens or backpackers taking shelter from the storm, and Maya has to ask two men with bushy golden beards if she can squeeze in to the spare machine, where one of them is taking up too much space.

'Sure,' grunts one in an American accent, sizing up Maya as she passes.

The teenage boy leans in cheerily over Maya, types in a password she tries to read but can't and fires up the internet connection. The computer makes such a whir, Maya wonders if it is powered by gutter rats in the drain below the ground, running frantically on a wheel.

She logs into James' email first, searching for clues as to what could have happened; what made his demeanour change when he went to talk to Brooke from the Kaye-French agency. She's hoping for at least a trace of evidence in his emails, or perhaps to discover something that might have been troubling James for longer, going further back than this afternoon.

Did he see my message from Jon? Might he have seen me hold Jon's hand tonight?

There's the message from Brooke at Kaye-French yesterday, a new message from his bank, and that email from Petra, now opened, to say she and Francesca are sending a parcel out for Maya's birthday to Poste Restante in Sydney, so that Maya can pick it up in May. Maya smiles to herself. The kindness of her sisters-in-law. They obviously don't know anything about what's troubling James.

They expect us to be together next month.

There's an amusing GIF from Dominic that means

nothing to Maya. There are newsletters from the *British Journal of Photography*, See Tickets and Fantasy Football. Something from the electoral register about proxy voting, so James can vote to Remain in the EU. There's another email from Brooke, sent a few hours ago but already opened and replied to. Subject line: More details. Maya reads it.

> So, the Linden/Jolly wedding, Cotswolds July 9th. They want you at the rehearsal dinner the night before at Chiltern Firehouse. They've booked out the whole place. Then the wedding itself in the Cotswolds. They fly the party to Nice on the 11th for all the villa shits and giggles. And fee, I know you didn't ask the fee, but I think we could charge £25,000 plus expenses, minus our 20% of course. So that's your flight home covered and then some. But Ashley Jolly wants to meet you in London on Tuesday, before Hugo Linden flies to Jamaica – he's shooting there for three weeks, so all very tight. Speak soon. Bx

He's gone home.

Maya feels a stab in her stomach and her eyes start to burn. She opens the cold can of Coke and its hiss and release don't help her, nor do the cold bubbles that almost burn her throat.

Fuck.

She scrolls down to see James' reply, sent two hours ago, after he left her in the bath and walked off.

Her heart breaks.

62

I have to speak to Nena, I have to speak to Nena. How can I speak to Nena?

In another tab, Maya logs into her Skype account and clicks on the little circle with Nena's face in it. It's an out-take from her BBC headshot photos, where she's ditched her CBeebies smile and is sticking two fingers up at the camera. The call rings. Maya sits, agitatedly tapping the keyboard with her fingernails, waiting for something to happen on the screen, wondering why James didn't come back to their room. Wondering where he is.

No answer.

Shit.

Maya looks at the clock on the bottom left of the screen. Ten o'clock. It must be mid-afternoon in London. Where would Nena be if she wasn't at home?

I wish I had my phone. I wish we hadn't given them up.

Maya looks around the internet cafe, to see if there's a phone station or a booth. James' voice rings in her memory.

'*We'd only ever need a phone in an emergency…*'

There is no phone in the internet cafe. Maya doesn't remember seeing a phone in an internet cafe since she bravely went travelling, from LA through to Ciudad Juárez, Central America and Bogota, all by herself, aged eighteen. Public phones are clearly a thing of the past, even in Laos.

I need a phone now, I have to talk to Nena. She'll know what to do.

There is no phone. Nowhere to place a traditional old-fashioned phone call. She thinks of asking the American man next to her, the one who was checking her out, if he has a mobile phone – and if so can she use it. But she doesn't know Nena's number by heart anyway; there's no point asking.

'Are you done with that?' says the man with the golden beard, the one she was just thinking of asking to use his phone. He's already half sitting at her desk space and he looks a little put out.

'Oh sorry, I didn't realise you were about to use it.'

'I wasn't, but if the rain ain't going away…'

'Hang on, I just need to do two quick things. Then I'm done.'

Maya types with urgency and then logs out of James' email and into her own.

She checks her messages. The one at the top of her inbox, the most recent, is from Nena. Subject line: Good gossip.

Hey Sugatits,

You OK? Gotta be quick – am about to try out a new class. Well, my only class to be honest, but hey... It's one Emily Snatch recommended (I told you I bumped into her, right? Well, sometimes we hang out on a park bench, only this time with babies, not cheap Tesco's vermouth). But I HAVE to tell you something.

ANYWAY, when I told her you'd bumped into the Baby-faced Assassin in bloody Thailand and Vietnam and that he's only gone and made it as a big-shot actor, the blood drained from her face.

Do you remember Jon's old housemate Adam?! Well, Emily bumped into Adam in hot yoga last week and Adam's LIVID with Jon because Adam's sister, whose name I don't know – but let's call her Eve (bit weird...) had a baby with Jon.

Jon has a baby?

I don't think they got married or anything, and I'm pretty sure she's not that Titania slut Jon ran off with when he was with you, Adam's too nice to have a slutface sister – but they were definitely together, maybe married, and had a baby a couple of years ago. Anyway, wait for this – they called her something terroristy like Isis or Boko or something. His choice apparently, thinking he was being all poetic, actually it *was* Isis cause Emily Snatch said it was just before ISIS became a 'thing' – lol! (FYI, Adam is super embarrassed about this of course, as her uncle, but says luckily she's cute enough to wear her terror moniker well).

Was the baby on his phone a girl? He said it was his nephew Geronimo.

ANYWAY, I digress. Adam's really fucked off with his Baby-faced Assassin brother-in-law natch, not just because he gave his niece a shit name, but also cause he's buggered off and left his sister broken-hearted. And he's racked up SHITLOADS of debt living a faux-lavish lifestyle and owes Adam's sister (did we say Eve?) and their parents THOUSANDS in credit-card debt. Oh and he ain't no actor – he's a total fantasist! Can't even get a job playing the Gruffalo at Chessington. Emily said Adam was super upset because Jon has cleaned out what was left in Adam's sister's bank account, buggered off, and left her and their poor terrorist daughter in the shit. I told Emily you bumped into him in Thailand of all places! She's going to tell Adam. Can you believe it?

I can't believe it.
Baby? Actually that baby could have been a girl.
Damian Lewis?!

Maya thinks of the sharp shirts, the tailored shorts, the weighty watch, the shoots in Canada, the name-dropping… The customer who left The Haven without paying.

I'll give you the life you want.

Maya looks at the computer screen, her eyes filling with water, and wants to choke. She takes another swig from the cold can, bubbles waking her up, making her think.

'*I told Emily you bumped into him.*'

'Bumped into him?' Maya says to herself quietly. The American man with the golden beard gives Maya another glance, but she ignores it, and continues to read.

ANYWAY, better go – gonna brave this class, then go for coffee with Emily afterwards – she can't make it as she has to do the school run (she has older ones, did I say?). She's been amazing actually. Wish me luck! Love your face.

Nx

63

The steam on the windows of the internet cafe and the smell of rain on damp clothes and matted beards feels oppressive in Maya's throat.

I can't breathe.

She pushes back her chair, picks up her can of Coke, and leaves a 20,000 kip note on the counter for the boy with the big ears, before grabbing the umbrella and escaping out into the rain.

It's now coming down heavily, even thicker than before, and Maya realises there's little point shielding herself now – she's already soaked. Her midnight-blue jersey halterneck clings to every curve of her tired body and her Havaianas slip as she struggles to get a good grip in the floodwater. She closes the umbrella and lets the fat drops drum into her skull as she walks determinedly through the emptying streets with difficulty. Maya's hair has turned its waviest, as she marches back through a town she doesn't really know, towards the now-deserted night market. Still scouring left and right as she looks for his tall frame, his comforting neck, his olive skin. But there isn't a single man looking through the lens of his camera; there isn't a sight worth photographing.

Did James see me holding his fucking hand?

Maya turns right and diverts to the bar, where Jon is still sitting under the white awning on the veranda, nursing a Beerlao now, reading Bukowski. He looks up and sees her. His eyes light up and he stands.

Maya flies up the short wooden stairway to the decking, to the table. To her utter surprise, she lifts the umbrella as if it were a rifle and pushes the tip into Jon's chest, pinning him down to the seatback of his chair.

'How did you find me?'

Her shoulders are tanned and goosebumped; her eyes are fiery and fierce.

'HOW?' she shouts louder.

A couple at the end of the decking, the only other occupied table now, stop their hushed longings and look up.

Jon's face turns tomato red.

Maya lowers the tip of the umbrella, from his torso to his belly button, and leans in a bit harder, more threateningly. Jon winces, and raises his arms in submission.

'How?' she says, more quietly and composed this time. Maya is surprised by the fear on Jon's face, but she can't see the rage on her own.

Jon thrusts his palms forward, to assert his compliance. 'Please, Maya—'

'How?'

'Let me explain…'

The penny drops and they say it together.

'The column.'

The column. Maya's jolly, glossy throwaway account of her travels with Train Man, without going into any real detail of their relationship other than their journey, their route, their plans. Her baby pangs.

He found my weak spot and exploited it.

'You motherfucker.'

Jon looks down at his deck shoes on the veranda, palms still in the air, wondering why Maya is still pressing the sharp end of a hefty umbrella tip into his navel. He looks back up, his eyes dulled by the fear that he has failed. He tries harder. This is his one shot. He really has to dig deep into the intensity of his craft if he's to convince Maya now.

'I read your column one Sunday, about how you were going travelling. I wanted to know where you were and how I could find you. To go to the ends of the earth to tell you that I loved you.'

Did I ever mention Velma's inheritance?

'The actor thing is bullshit, right?'

Jon looks ashamed.

'Look, Maya, it was the biggest mistake of my life. Can't you see the lengths I've gone to – the lengths I will go to – to put it right?'

'What was the biggest mistake of your life, Jon? What – cheating on me? Dumping me cold-heartedly? Clearing me out? Or doing it to your wife and baby?'

Jon's gaze turns steely.

'Or perhaps it was stalking me at The Haven? Doing a runner without paying? It was you who fled that morning, wasn't it? You were no friend of Moon – he'd never seen you before in his life.'

Maya leans on the umbrella and presses it further into Jon's belly button. He winces and sweats, looking less comfortable on his perch now.

'You knew I had money, didn't you? Did I mention my inheritance in the column too?' Maya rolls her eyes and calls herself an idiot. She tries to think but can't remember, there's too much swirling in her brain, all underpinned by the despair of having lost James.

Did I say I had money?

'What were you going to do to "put it right"?' She drives the umbrella in further. 'Because that sounds like a lot of mistakes to me. Which of those was your biggest mistake? Because they all seem pretty fucking epic.'

Jon can't think of an answer – he knows he has lost – so he stares out to the rain beyond Maya's shoulder.

To the lofty green valleys above the now blood-brown river. He says nothing. He has stage fright.

'What was your best-case scenario? That I'd go with you and you'd clean me out and leave me at the airport? Or wait until I had a baby before you emptied my bank account? What was your plan, Jon?'

The charming man is undone, and his smile has a hint of menace at the corners of his mouth now.

'You following me around, making these gross promises, might have just ruined the best thing that ever happened to me.'

Jon hears the wobble in Maya's voice, sees that she's about to crumble, and swipes a hand to grab the umbrella, to free himself from her interrogation. But Maya is too wired, too enraged, too heartbroken. Too quick. She lifts the umbrella away from him, as quick as the rising cobra at their table in Hanoi. She holds it like a baseball bat over her shoulder.

'You're a failed actor and a lowlife.'

She thwacks the umbrella and hits Jon in the side of his ribs.

'Argh!'

He takes the blow with a cry and pants heavily as he clutches his stomach.

'That's from me.'

Jon stands, trying to get out of the way, but Maya strikes twice more. He falls back into the chair with a high squeal.

'And that's for your wife and baby.'

The couple at the end table try not to laugh. The waitress with the beautiful face and the knowing smile comes out of the bar to shoo her away.

'Go! Not here!' she says, as if Maya is the rat.

Maya turns around, striding not scurrying, while Jon whimpers in his chair. She walks down the steps, umbrella under her arm. She walks the deserted streets back to the hotel room, where she lets herself in, locks the door behind her, goes to the bathroom and puts the largest towel around her like a shroud. Even under the towel she can hear the fizz of James' contact lens solution bubbling as it cleanses them in a little pot, as it has since they got back from kayaking. From the open bathroom door, Maya sees the note is still there, unread and untouched. She walks over to it and falls through the voile net into the middle of the bed and sobs.

64

April 2016, London, England

'Hi, I'm Nena, this is Ava.'

A circle of friendly female faces smile. The babies on their laps all look in different directions.

'Hi Ava!' shouts the woman at the head of the circle, with a long yellow ponytail and a loud voice. 'I'm Jenny!' Nena imagines Jenny talks at that volume regardless of the proximity to which she is standing or sitting by someone. 'And how old's Ava?' she booms, without taking her face off the baby, doing friendly squints with her round, blue eyes.

'Just over six months.'

'Well hello, Ava! Welcome, Nina.'

'It's Nena.'

'Sorry, Nena. HELLLLLOOOOOOO!'

Jenny makes an exaggerated wave like a children's

TV presenter, only the real children's TV presenter is nervous and speaks gently.

'Hey, Jenny!' says Nena as if she's a ventriloquist, waving Ava's arm. Ava looks puzzled.

'And how did you hear about Baby Sensory?'

'My friend Emily comes with her little one, Iris. Although she can't today… I think she comes to your Monday morning class.'

'Ahhh!' shouts Jenny. 'We know Iris!' Her encouragement is lost on Ava, who has never been awake when Iris has been in her company, but Nena knows she doesn't need to mention that.

A few of the women nod and smile, as if to say *ah yes, Emily is OK, so you might be OK too*. Nena feels a sigh of relief whip up like a mini tornado around the room, escaping through the 1980s-style office blinds of the open community centre window. Beams of sunlight poke back through, creating a grille of straight lines on the floor.

'Well, I'm not sure how much Emily has said, but today is all about fun, games, wonder and exploration – all helping Ava and her new friends develop through their senses.'

Nena looks around the circle, scouting for new friends among established friends, trying not to feel scathing. One mum wears a grey marl T-shirt with Femme Forever in a red retro font. Another has a shaggy fringe and a nice face.

Nena feels a mild panic in her stomach but quashes it by remembering that today she woke up feeling a bit different. The view from her loft bedroom seemed brighter: Ava was stirring happily in her cot, talking to Dandy Lion, her favourite cuddly toy, when Nena woke at 6.35 a.m. The spring sunshine felt healing, beating down through the Velux window onto the bed. She showered, threw on her black skinny jeans and a blush pink jumper, the same colour as her ballet flats, and walked with Tom and Arlo to school for drop-off, Arlo proudly showing Ava off to his friends. After Tom kissed Nena goodbye at the Overground station, she walked around Clissold Park and Ava watched the world from her buggy. They went to Sainsbury's and bought falafels for Ava to try for lunch, and meatballs for them all for dinner. While Ava napped in her cot, Nena took joy in sending Maya a gossipy email; and felt comforted after she pressed send, went into her sent items, and re-read it. The voice in her email was her old one. She sounded like herself again. And while she was tempted to stay at home and watch *The Real Housewives of Beverly Hills*, *Orange County*, *Sydney* or wherever – she didn't. She finally plucked up the courage to go to a baby sensory class. And now, looking around the room, at the eager mothers and their indifferent babies on a Thursday afternoon in spring, Nena doesn't feel cynical or hostile. A few of them even look like women Nena might hope she can go for a coffee with afterwards.

'Right, so we're going to start with "Driving My Tractor", everyone, that OK?' The other mums widen their eyes and open their mouths, some clap excitedly to their babies, and Nena realises straight away that this is a Popular Song. Jenny presses play on her iPod dock, repositions herself so she's upright for singing, and mouths to Nena, with a wave of an arm, 'Don't worry, you'll get the hang of it!'

And Nena smiles back, knowing that she will.

65

April 2016, Luang Prabang, Laos

Maya wakes to a metronome in her head and wonders if it's the crestfallen beating of her heart or the clock ticking on the bathroom wall. It's not the rain. Those dense and thick drops stopped somewhere in the middle of the night, during one of the many frantic and fretful times Maya woke, sat up and looked around the room. And it hasn't yet returned.

She had sobbed into the mattress and then curled into a ball, crying and curling and eventually mustering up the effort to get under the bedlinen. Maya lay and cried, clinging to the empty space where James had slept the night before, willing herself to fall asleep so she could see if it were a nightmare when she woke up; and if it weren't, that she might never wake up.

But she did wake. And every time she rolled and lolled and looked around the dark room at the posts around the bed that always made her jump, she realised it wasn't a nightmare. He still wasn't back. He had gone.

As deep night started to lift through a crack in a broken shutter slat, Maya went to the bathroom to pee.

Tick. Tock. Tick. Tock.

The clock taunted her. The fizzing of the contact lenses taunted her. She didn't know how to remove the clock battery and it was too heavy to take off the wall. So she went to put on the television, to see if Anderson Cooper, Stephen Sackur or Christiane Amanpour might bring comfort and company, or even news of James. Then she remembered this room didn't have a television. She flicked the switch of the old bathroom light and crawled back to bed, jumping the last step and almost ripping the voile with an urgent leap, so the man who might be underneath the four-poster wouldn't grab her ankles.

As the sun started to rise, it dawned on Maya that something terrible might have happened, something worse than James leaving without saying goodbye; he wasn't the type of person to just walk off. With a thump of her fist on the pillow, she realised she needed a plan of action.

Do I tell the police? Do I call Francesca? No, Petra would be better. Do I contact Dominic to see if he's heard anything?

Just as Maya was engaging her practical mind and trying to come up with a plan – just as she was giving up on night – fatigue and trauma pulled her under again, as if trying to stop her finding him.

Now Maya is awake, listening to the metronome in her head, and knows she has to do something. She crawls out of bed and wonders at which point in her most terrible of nights, she put on her olive-green slip.

I don't even remember.

Maya feels the cool tiles of the floor beneath her Temptress polished feet, unlocks a window, and peers through the shutters, trying not to knock any of the china in the tea set as she leans. She wonders how long it will be before the internet cafe opens; what constitutes a missing person; how she can find out where the police station is.

If only we had brought phones.

Out of the window, Maya sees the tendrils of early morning – a cartoon-like mist is cut into a swirl by a peaceful parade of saffron-robed monks, wafting gently through the streets in an orderly line to collect their alms.

He wouldn't miss this for the world.

Maya throws on her cargo trousers and James' jumper. His nicest jumper. The aubergine-coloured one made of merino wool that he wore on the flight from Bangkok and then cast on the chair at the desk under the garden window. It smells of him.

He would have taken his stuff if he were planning to leave me.

Maya remembers how Jon removed all his possessions without her even noticing.

He wouldn't have just *taken his camera.*

'And his passport?' Maya whispers out loud, to no one.

Maya pulls James' large backpack out from under the bed and slides it across the smooth patterned floor, before realising it's more likely to be in his daypack. She releases black clips and fastenings, presses a toggle and opens a zip. Sounds Maya associates with James. The purposeful opening and closing of buckles, the punctuation and the soundtrack to packing and unpacking, taking off and landing. Maya rummages, searching inside to find James' brown leather travel wallet. A gift from his sisters for Christmas, to send him off in style. Maya opens the wallet to see credit cards, insurance cards, immunisation records. James' forehead peeps out of the slot housing his driving licence. There is one passport in the zip compartment, not two.

Maybe mine is in my backpack.

Maya slides her fingers in so she can take out the passport. On the back of it are barcodes and luggage labels, digits and codes.

Sometimes I just don't give it back to him, at least his is here.

Maya opens the passport on the thick page towards the back.

Maya Elizabeth Gloria Flowers. Her serious face in the photo looks up at her serious face in the room. She doesn't even smile at how James always laughs about Gloria.

He's gone.

Maya laces up her walking shoes, grabs her coin purse and room key and puts them in the small bejewelled bag she bought all the way back in Udaipur, not stopping to smooth her hair or clean her teeth.

Maybe he's out there. He must be out there. Why would he go home without his stuff?

Maya steps outside and brings the long thin double doors together behind her. Click.

Or has something terrible happened?

66

Adolescent monks walk barefoot, their wide yellow belts swinging around the waist of their robes. At their hip is a drum-like satchel, in which to collect their alms. Laotian men, women and children, and the more gung-ho tourists, line the pavements on their knees, making offerings without making eye contact. Maya, her own eyes puffy and swollen, is comforted by the invisibility the parade affords her.

She walks into a French bakery, set back slightly from the road, to buy a boule of bread. Her offering. While Maya waits to pay, she looks out of the windows, still searching, to the empty veranda of the now-closed bar next door. She sees the table at which she sat last night with Jon and wonders whether he is still in town or whether he flew back to Vietnam to *not* shoot a pretend spy drama.

Did James see us holding hands?

Maya feels the sick taste of deception in her mouth and just wants to get back to James, to have his hands on her; his arms around her. For him to be safe.

She reaches the counter and hands a middle-aged woman 30,000 kip. The woman nods but doesn't speak.

'Excuse me please, can you tell me where the police station is?'

The woman looks up but doesn't understand.

'Police station?' Maya repeats hopefully. 'Do you know where the police station is please?'

The woman shouts to the back of the bakery and a teenage girl pads through a dark wooden beaded curtain.

Maya tries her luck, hoping the girl might have picked up some English in school, but she is mindful not to shout; not to speak to the girl as if it is she who is stupid.

'Please can you—'

Her voice is drowned by a roar outside, something sounding like thunder, only more foreboding. The girl looks startled, and turns to her mother, who shrugs.

'Oh, don't worry...' Maya says quietly to herself.

Everyone in the bakery looks to the window, to the sky. The deep rumbling noise at the head of the peninsula, echoing in the valley, starts to ripple down the street, and Maya can tell from the mother and daughter's faces that this isn't usual at dawn, during alms-giving, or at any other time. The baker cranes her neck to look out of the front window as she puts Maya's money in the till.

Maya gives a small smile that goes unnoticed and blinks through sore, puffy eyes, to say thank you as best she can, as she heads out into the street where the mist is lifting and the sky is morphing from blue to orange, as if the monks might be painting it with their robes.

It's not raining, I don't think it can be thunder.

The young monks continue their parade; the alms givers are unperturbed by the growing, pummelling noise in the valley.

Maya hands a small boy in the crowd her boule of bread, so he can share it out, as she retreats to the pavement. To watch. To look for James across the street or on a corner, to see if he is weaving through the crowds, taking photographs.

The rumble by the river is getting louder, more thumping, more disruptive. Tourists, who'd risen in the dark to witness or take part in the alms-giving spectacle, look around and tut. Their faces are furrowed and disgruntled, with looks that say, *If this isn't nature's force, it's mighty disrespectful.* The locals kneel with serenity, unmoved by the unusual din in the near distance.

Maya walks along the pavement, parallel to the monks, with less grace and more urgency as she scans the crowd.

What's going on?

A yearning in her stomach draws her to the deep and pulsating noise, so she carries on along the pavement, towards the river, scanning scanning scanning the small pockets of Westerners, mostly taller than the Laos people, to see if James is one of them.

She can't see his thoughtful face looking through a lens; she can't see his tongue sticking out of the corner of his mouth while he rounds his shoulders and watches people watching people.

The noise grows louder and more thumping, like the beating of her heart, as Maya hurries her pace along the road to the tip of the small promontory, to the river's edge where the Nam Khan and the Mekong converge.

As Maya stands on a precipice and looks up at the steep mossy karsts on the other side of the river, she sees the water swirl, a wind whips up her hair, her eardrums hurt from the raw sound, and a helicopter rises in front of her as if the river itself belched it into her face. Startlingly loud and black, like a giant scarab beetle flying right at her, Maya screams and ducks, shielding her face with her arms as her scream disappears into the rotors. The helicopter makes a turning circle in the air and hovers back over the river.

Is he in there? Is he dead?

Maya runs down a winding river-edge road, past French colonial guesthouses and rosewood verandas, past white pillars and pink bougainvillea and plum blossom, around the end of the promontory on a road that curls back towards the centre of the town. Her breath is short and her heart is racing. She has never run like this before.

I have to find the police station.

Maya uses every ounce of the little energy she has to run in her cumbersome cargo pants and walking shoes, her small jewelled bag slung across her body, as she sweeps into a side street and cuts through a tiny alleyway that she hopes will lead her back into the historical centre, because surely the police station would be in the centre of town?

At the end of the alley, Maya rejoins Luang Prabang's main road. More bakeries. Bars that have battened down their hatches until opening time. Some fancier hip hotels. On a crossroads she sees a flash of orange, as the monks curve around a far corner, their oath to Buddha more powerful than the commotion in the sky.

Maya looks left, back towards the river, only a couple of hundred metres away, and sees the helicopter rising again. This time it hovers above a crowd; it looks like the helicopter is trying to tail or contain a crowd of people that seems to grow as it strides and surges towards Luang Prabang's centre. Towards Maya.

What the hell?!

The helicopter looms, the wind thick and throaty under its blades. The group of people charging below it cling on to their hats and flatten their hair as they pace towards Maya, standing open-mouthed and astounded halfway down the road. Children look up and gasp. Bystanders break away from the alms-giving to see what the furore is all about in this lazy and lackadaisical town.

The crowd marches, continuing to swell under the surveillance of the helicopter's roar. Lights flash and a siren starts to scream as the group gets closer, seemingly larger with every step of their approach, as townspeople, tourists and dogs all gather, to try to see what is at the heart of it, and join it as it grows.

Then Maya sees him. Through her puffy cried-out eyes. James is the eye of this storm, flanked now by what must be a hundred people, as he carries a pale woman in his arms, her head turned away as she leans into James' chest. Maya sees dark blue shorts, she sees a rusty chain cutting into a bruised ankle. She doesn't see the terror in the woman's eyes, only the horror of James'. One is swollen shut. Both are cut, bruised and bloody, and his glasses have gone. James' hair seems to have grown longer in an absent night. His arms expand with one last push.

'James!' Maya shouts through a gasp.

Maya!

He can't speak.

She runs to him and puts her hand on his face, mindful of the woman in his arms, examining him as if he were not from this planet.

'Oh my god, oh my god, what's happened?' Maya tries to hold back her cry but can't, the sight is too horrific, but still she digs deep, so she can switch to survival mode.

The crowd slows under the groan of people joining it and shouting, but James says nothing. He can't say anything. His mouth is cut and voiceless.

Maya searches James' open eye for direction, to see what she needs to do, and she gives him a quick and reassuring nod.

'OUT OF THE WAY! LET THEM THROUGH!'

Maya can see that James' cracked mouth is too sore – he is too shocked – to speak, so she does it for him as she waves her arms to clear the path ahead. Swimming on land, treading water, under a helicopter that seems to be trying to push them under.

'Hospital! Police! Where are the police station and the hospital?' Maya bellows to the crowd around them. An excited boy with a shaved head takes pride in leading the pack, beckoning Maya with a small and hurried pace, leading the way in his little sandals.

Maya looks up at the helicopter above them, urging it to take flight, shaking her head angrily at the pilot, before looking back to the woman in James' arms.

'GIVE HER SPACE!' Maya shouts.

No one can hear under the thunderous roar, but everyone gets the gist of what she's saying. Ahead of them, people join the little boy in guiding the way, each wanting a role in the commotion; a story to tell their families over fish soup or *laap* tonight. The wind and the noise of the helicopter make it hard to hear all the different directions and instructions being shouted, so Maya takes her lead from the boy, his small round head bobbing in front of them as he runs as fast as he can.

'This way!' Maya says, as she follows the boy.

As they hurry, as James struggles to keep up, Maya steals glances at his face, to assess his injuries, to dare to take a look at his swollen eye and cut, cracked lips; to peer into his tired, swollen arms.

To see what the face of Manon Junot looks like in real life.

67

The little boy brings the charge to a halt at a modern-looking pagoda on the corner of two streets. Its walls are made of breeze block, its triangular roof of orange terracotta tiles. An orderly rolls a bed trolley down a ramp onto the street, and a woman in a white coat and a North American accent dashes down the steps.

'You speak English?' she asks without hesitation.

'Yes, we're British. I don't know what's happened!' Maya despairs. 'He can't speak easily.'

'Dr Wong,' says the woman. 'This is the Chinese hospital. We'll take them from here. GET RID OF THAT THING!' She waves up at the helicopter, which obediently rises and turns sharply, heading back to the river.

The orderly approaches, proffering the bed, and James slumps Manon Junot onto it with both care and clumsiness, just at the point he was about to drop her. He leans onto Maya and breathes heavily, in relief. She holds him tight and he winces. His arms tired from rowing, from fighting, from carrying. His beautiful face bloody and cracked.

'It's OK, baby, it's OK,' Maya says, bringing James in, putting her forehead to his, stroking his hair. 'It's OK, it's OK...'

'Papers please,' says a man in a sand-beige shirt. His matching trousers have a crease running from his hips to his shiny boots. Mirrored aviator shades conceal most of his face, but Maya can tell it's a face of authority. Another man in beige uniform appears on the other side of James, offering to hold him up even though he is much smaller. The little boy continues to jump up and down in excitement, but the man in the mirrored aviators gestures to swat him away like a fly.

'It's Manon Junot!' Maya tells the policeman. 'Someone tell the French ambassador! My boyfriend has found Manon Junot.'

'Papers please,' says the first man again, this time more sternly. He lifts and replaces his peaked military cap while he waits for compliance.

'English! English!' shouts the little boy, who gets a clip around the ear.

James slumps between Maya and the second officer.

'Passport…' James whispers breathlessly to Maya, finally daring to open his mouth. 'My passport should be in my back pocket, from the flight the other day, but I don't know…'

Maya fumbles around James' body. His camera bag has gone. There is no digital SLR dangling proudly around his neck. She feels in the back pocket of his faded black jeans and finds a wet passport. She slides it out and opens it, careful not to tear damp pages while the first police officer snatches it out of her hands.

'Hey!' Maya protests. She gives the man a hard stare, but he doesn't notice, as he thumbs through soggy pages until he finds the one with the photograph on it.

'James Alexander Miller, come with me please,' says the officer.

'What? He needs medical help! You're not taking him away!'

'Come with me please, we need to talk to you.'

'Get the French ambassador, get the British ambassador, and get my boyfriend some medical help!' Maya demands, standing nose-to-nose with the man, seeing her lioness face in the reflection of his glasses. 'Please,' she adds, quietly.

'This man isn't going anywhere until we've looked at him,' Dr Wong steps in, putting a protective arm around Maya and James. 'Nurse!'

The doctor speaks to the police officer in Lao and he in turn replies, before looking to Maya and James and slipping into broken English.

'Very well,' he nods. 'But then we take him to the station, we have lots of questions.'

'Of course,' nods Dr Wong, ushering James and Maya in through the white and weathered glass doors of the clinic. 'Asshole,' she mutters under her breath.

Maya turns around and sees the little boy who led them there looking up at her. His dirty yellow T-shirt has a blue cartoon elephant on it. His trousers are too short for him.

'Thank you,' she says. Stuffing all the kip she has in her purse into his shaky little hand.

He smiles, and runs home in his sandals, to tell his parents tales they won't believe.

On the other side of the hospital doors, a man rushes to a halt with a wheelchair. James turns around and slumps in it, while both he and Maya wonder where Manon Junot has been taken.

'Don't worry,' says Dr Wong, as if reading their minds. Her pristine white coat and competent, made-up face give her a reassuring gravitas. 'The woman you brought in is being seen to urgently – my colleagues are first-class.'

Maya opens her mouth, to explain to Dr Wong who the woman is. 'She's—'

'I know who she is,' she says, putting a reassuring hand on Maya's arm. 'I have a friend who works out of the French embassy in Vientiane. I'll put in a call to make sure they know, but I'm sure the police will. Let's just get them seen to first, yes?'

'Yes,' nods Maya. 'Thank you. I'm just thinking of her family.'

Dr Wong starts shouting orders for saline and drugs and other things Maya doesn't understand and James is too tired to take in.

Outside the clinic, a formation of police officers jog in perfect unison towards the river and the monks file back into the temple, to return to their morning prayers.

68

Maya perches on the edge of the copper roll-top bath and softly wipes James' skin, olive brown and bruised, with a sponge that looks like soft honeycomb.

'Ow!'

'Sorry, baby, I'm trying to avoid the cuts, but some do still need cleaning. There's dirt and mud. I'm not sure they looked you over well enough.'

'They stitched my eye; they would have said if anything else needed it.'

James speaks gingerly, almost through his teeth, so as not to tear the cracks at the edge of his mouth.

'But this looks nasty, there's still dirt in some of the cuts!'

Maya gives a sigh, unhappy with Dr Wong's 'first-class' team. Her brow is sweaty and her cheeks are pink.

She took off James' jumper and her thick cargo trousers, thanks to the steam she worked up cleaning him in the bathroom, so she leans over the bath in her lace-trimmed marl vest and knickers. Worried and exasperated, and trying to remember to be relieved. But she's tired too.

'I'll be fine. I can't face going out there right now.'

He looks up at Maya, one eye purple and red and swollen shut, while old-fashioned needle-and-thread stitches hold his straight dark brow together. Maya tries not to show the horror she's feeling as she looks at him; her love, back from a traumatic and violent night he hasn't yet told her about.

Maya rests the fuzzy, honeycomb sponge on top of the copper taps, dries her hands on a white waffle towel that's hanging on the radiator and walks over to the window.

'Uff!' she says, opening the latch to let in some air. She gently unpeels a slat, cautious so no one sees her in her underwear, peeping out to see more people gathering outside than when she last looked. A white news truck with red letters on it pulls up. Maya knows there will only be more arriving as time goes on. She shuts the slat with a slam.

At least they don't know he's right here.

At the Police Office Xiengthong Group – a modest white building with brown shutters and not much in the way of security – James was taken away, fingerprinted, swabbed and interviewed. Maya sat nervously on one of the plastic chairs in the waiting area, smiling occasionally at the woman in a beige shirt and trousers sitting behind the desk; anxious that James might be being accused of something; wondering if he had a voice, if he could even speak – if he could even see – or if he needed her to help him. Thinking of how to contact the Foreign Office or speak to the British Ambassador in Vientiane.

What do people do in these situations?

'It's all taken care of,' nodded the officer at the desk, with small teeth and a pretty face. 'Phone calls being placed.'

Maya wasn't allowed to be in the room to hear James' statement, but her panic was abated by the noisy hauling in of a local man with wet, wavy hair to his shoulders and a moustache, flanked by officers with machine guns. He too had a bloody and bruised face.

James hadn't been flanked by officers with machine guns. This was heartening.

Even more heartening was when the most stern of the police officers walked James back into the waiting area with the plastic chairs and pressed his passport into his hand and patted him on the back.

Maya stood up and flung her arms around James, to another wince.

'We'll speak again when the ambassador arrives,' said a translator with large gold-rimmed glasses. 'But for now you go back to your hotel and get some rest, Mr Miller.' She gave him a sympathetic nod.

'It's getting busier out there,' Maya says as she pads back to the bathroom. 'Shall I see if someone from the hospital can come here? I don't think they cleaned you up as well as they should.'

'It's fine, they were focusing on getting samples and stuff first. Cleaning later.'

'Really? Why?'

'It's fine, really, they did enough.'

James sounds more irritated than anything but looks up at Maya in the doorway and tries to calm himself.

'I'm hungry more importantly.'

Maya smiles, her shoulders relaxing a little. 'I'll go out and see if I can get some food, maybe some antiseptic cream. There isn't any in our first-aid kit. I mean, what kind of first-aid kit doesn't have—'

'No. Don't go yet,' James says through his teeth.

Maya stops and sits down on the closed lid of the toilet. She looks at James as he moves his hair to the side, as he did that first day Maya saw him walking down the platform at Hazelworth station. When she was a stranger to him and she could only dream of being away with him; comfortable enough to bathe with him; the person who would make him right again. If she can, that is.

Maya nods. 'It can wait. I might have a cereal bar squirrelled away somewhere... I'll look in a bit.'

She gives him a reassuring smile and turns to reposition his passport, hanging next to her on the radiator, trying to dry out the pages that got so wet she doesn't know how. She takes the sponge from the taps and plunges it into the bath again and holds it gently to James' forehead.

You're back.

Water trickles from the large holes of the sponge, down James' face, his straight nose swollen and bloodied at the bridge.

I was so worried.

'What happened?' Maya whispers.

'I don't know where to start.'

'Start with last night. You left me. Here, in the bath.'

James looks mournful, and sinks back, low into the hot water.

'Why did you go? Why did you want to be away from me?'

'I didn't...'

Maya turns on the tap, to top up the bath with hot water, busying herself while James has a moment to think.

'I had a job offer, when I went to Skype Brooke. A pretty fucking amazing job offer too.'

Maya smiles acceptingly.

'I needed to think about it, I...'

She spares him. 'I know, I know about the job offer.'

'You do?'

'I checked your email when you didn't come back to the hotel. I was so worried...'

James' puzzled face looks as though the whole debacle with the job offer, his dilemma about whether to accept it or not, was all a lifetime ago, as he struggles to remember the minutiae of what happened before It happened last night.

'I was too worried to tell you. I didn't want to cause problems, to rock the boat. So I went for a walk, to take some pictures, mull it over.'

Did he see me and Jon?

Maya takes a deep breath and exhales towards the ceiling, steeling herself for what's to come.

'So I went back to the internet cafe, I emailed Kaye-French and I turned it down.'

Maya sponges James' chest. 'I saw that too.'

She lets him carry on.

'I went back to the market, to take some more shots: the colours and the children and everything, they were so beautiful. I needed to remember that it was the right thing to do, turning it down... That I wanted to keep travelling. Keep seeing these amazing things. Keep having these mind-blowing experiences.'

Maya reaches for a dark brown bottle and squeezes a teardrop-shaped blob of shampoo into James' hair, gently making a lather with one hand.

'I was taking photos of the night market when, through the lens, I *saw* her. I saw Manon Junot. I thought I must be going mad, so I looked up. I was sure I saw her – with a man – but I lost her in the crowd.'

James' voice wobbles and he holds his breath and plunges under water, to rinse his hair, to gather himself.

'No no no! Don't get your stitches wet! They said not to if you can help it!'

James rises but doesn't care. He just continues.

'I couldn't see her, in the crowd of the night market. So I looked at the last photo on my roll, I figured it must have been a picture with that woman in it, so I scrolled back and zoomed in. And it bloody was! She was even wearing the clothes they described on the news. But they were dirty, she didn't look well.'

Maya nods, wide eyes encouraging him to go on.

James ducks under again and rises back up, his hair now slicked back, water sloshing onto the tiled floor.

She strokes his exposed forehead, trying not to touch the cut next to his eye.

'By the time I'd looked back at the picture and was sure it was her, I'd lost them. So I went running through the night market, trying to find her again. It started to rain, it was chaos, and people were packing up… People were appearing and disappearing out of nowhere.'

Maya remembers the fat drops; her hair still smells of its residue.

'I'd seen she was with a man. But they didn't look right, they didn't look like a couple. She looked like a child with a grown-up, a parent – she was so small and so skinny. I searched in the direction I thought they were most likely to have gone and I couldn't believe it, I saw them up ahead.'

Maya inhales a brief gasp before talking. 'It *was* her James, you found her.'

'Yeah, and I followed her. I followed *them*.'

'Where to?'

'Down by the river, right near where we finished kayaking. She saw me following and looked wary, like she was scared of me, not him, so I thought I might be being ridiculous, and I almost turned around. She put her arm around him, as if to tell me to go away, so I hung back. Pretended to take photos. But I could see fear and this weird look in her eyes. Like a catatonic, lifeless look. It wasn't right, and I thought if it was her, if she *was* Manon Junot, then this wasn't something I could walk away from. I shouldn't have walked away from it.'

'You *didn't* walk away, you rescued her!'

Maya turns off the tap and lets the steam roll up and over James' wounds, sweat and salt helping cleanse him. Her cheeks glow pinker as she leans in.

'What did he look like, the man? Was it the guy from the police station?'

James shrugs. He didn't see the man being brought in under armed guard, flanked by a formation of men with machine guns, shortly before James was allowed to leave.

'He was older than us, about fifty? I dunno. Dirty. Curly hair, wet with the rain, or maybe it was greasy. And this moustache.' James both sweats and shivers, as he draws a moustache on his face with his fingers. 'I followed them along the river. It must have been for hours. Through the thick trees. I kept tripping on roots and vines. I went all along the bank we kayaked past, I couldn't believe it. It was getting darker and darker...' James eases his palms over his face to galvanise himself as Maya leans on the edge of the bath, elbows out, her chin on her flat hands. 'I was having to follow quite a way behind them so they didn't see me. She looked back a few times to check I wasn't there.'

'Maybe she was checking you *were* there?'

James raises his eyebrows and his stitches crinkle.

'Maybe...' he winces, through gritted teeth.

'So where did you end up?'

'It was dark and I was tripping over the tree roots. All these roots were everywhere. And I was so worried about getting back to you. I knew you'd be going crazy and be so worried – I'm so so sorry. But it was Manon fucking Junot!'

'It's OK, it's OK. I survived.'

Now isn't the time for Maya to tell James that it was the most frightening night of her life too.

'So I walked, kind of slowly, knowing I could be losing them. But I didn't want the twigs or branches to snap, and in some places it was really quiet, you couldn't even hear the river – when the rain stopped, it was total silence. But I had to keep up too, to not lose them. I didn't know where we were heading.'

'You're so brave.'

Maya gasps, thinking about what might have happened to him – what did happen – and the hideousness of the notion of life without James. The insight into it last night was horrific enough.

'They stopped at this brick hut, really small, must have been halfway to the waterfall we went to, and a light went on inside, so I sat against a trunk trying to listen. Wondering what the fuck to do. Trying to catch my breath, get some energy. I was knackered, to be honest.'

Maya strokes the curve of James' arm. 'Poor baby.'

'So I sat there for ages in the damp and the dark. Mosquitoes buzzing in my ears. I could feel all these things sucking and biting me...' James points to tiny circles of blood on the skin around his ankles. 'I needed to hear whether she was being held against her will, or whether she'd chosen to go missing. I needed proof before I went charging in there. I still couldn't believe it was her. What if she'd just wanted to check out? What if she just wanted a quiet life and everyone had got the wrong end of the stick?'

'No, of course not. Of course that wasn't it.'

'Well, I didn't know what to do. But I remembered her family; her mental health. She didn't look like a happy woman, or a woman in love, or a woman who might have chosen this – she was thin and dirty. Her eyes looked both alert and dead at the same time.'

'I saw them,' Maya concurs. 'As you put her on the trolley at the hospital.'

'So I sat and listened and wondered what to do. Tried to rest to get my energy up after the kayaking and the walk, but I could feel the leeches; the rain was making me shiver. I thought "What are you waiting for?" There was no right time. It was dark, they turned out the light, and I couldn't see *anything* above the canopy of the forest. So I waited for the moon to get higher, so I had my best chance of light, but it just wasn't showing through. Maybe it had peaked. I couldn't work out what time it was. I couldn't see my watch. It was pitch black.'

'You need a new watch. We should have kept our phones!'

'Well, it doesn't matter now.'

'So what did you do?'

'I told myself to stop being a coward.'

'You are *not* a coward.'

'She needed me. You needed me. So I knocked on the door.'

'What happened?'

James grits his teeth. 'He opened it and just punched me, right in the face. Smashed my glasses and my eyes. He must have known I was coming.'

Maya cries as she dabs James' less swollen eye with the sponge, bright pink and red where blood has congealed around a smaller cut.

'My baby.'

'She was there, sitting on the floor, chained to a little bed, like a kid's bed. She looked neither afraid nor relieved.'

James winces.

'Ow!'

'I'm sorry.'

'I was on the ground, I fell back even though the guy was smaller than me, but he was strong, so I had to get back up and fight. I couldn't leave without her. By then I had no choice.'

'Why didn't you come back, call the police?'

'Another few hours to get back to town? I don't know what might have happened. I had no choice. He was feral and angry and holding her captive. I had to fight. I've never had a fight in my life.'

'I know…'

'But I was taller than him. I was younger than him. I hit him, Maya. I hit him, and he was punching me back.

But I kept hitting until he fell back on the bed and I had enough time to get her out.'

'Shhh, it's OK, the police have him. I saw the man you described, he was dragged into the police station. He's locked up.'

James takes a little comfort from this, and continues.

'She put up a fight too – tried to kick me away – but she had no strength. She passed out on me as I carried her, she was flimsy but also heavy, it was weird.'

'Shit.'

'And all the time, as I was carrying her back – in the dark, and I couldn't see – I thought I was about to get it, a blow to the back of my head. I was just waiting for it, waiting to be struck – all the way back to town.'

James sinks underwater again to cleanse his sorrow.

'It's OK,' Maya says with a smile, pushing him back up with a hand pressed to his hair-smattered stomach. Stroking his swollen nose with her finger. 'You did it. You found Manon Junot! You rescued her, and now her family can hold her and hug her and get her the help she needs. *You* did it, James. This will be news all over the world soon.'

James looks to Maya, horrified. 'I can't go out there. I just want to sleep.'

'That's fine, you sleep. The ambassador might be hours, we don't know. I won't let anyone talk to you until you're ready. I've got your back.'

James shuts his eyes in relief and the swelling of his closed eye seems to subside a little, as relaxation creeps over his face.

Maya grabs the towel above the passport, also warming on the radiator, and holds it, crisp and taut at each end.

She changes her tone. 'It wasn't the right thing to do you know.'

He opens his eyes – or tries to – and looks at Maya.

'What wasn't?'

'Turning down the big A-list wedding. I mean, *Hugo Linden and Ashley Jolly* want James Miller to photograph their wedding?! Film director Hugo Linden, who must know shitloads of camera people, cinematographers, set photographers – and they want you? It's amazing. You were trying to convince yourself that staying here, with me, was the right thing to do. When it wasn't.'

'May—'

'It's OK. I accepted it for you.'

'What?'

'I emailed her back. Brooke. Must have been a couple of hours later, pretended I was you.'

'What did you say?'

'I said, "Sorry, had a moment of madness, but rethought it and if it's not too late…" kinda thing. Said, "I'd really love to do it – where do I sign?"'

'You did?'

James' face brightens.

Maya nods.

'What did she say?'

'She messaged right back. Said, "get your arse on a plane asap".' Maya looks up at the clock. 'There's still time – although hopefully even a supermodel diva like Ashley Jolly would understand you being waylaid...'

James rubs his eyes. 'Wow.'

'I'm sorry I held you back. I know it's what you want. Not this self-indulgent trust-fund backpacking malarkey.'

'I don't know what to say.'

'It's OK, I get it.'

James looks up sheepishly at Maya, through his one good eye. 'I don't want to go back without you. But I don't want to hold you back either.'

Maya lets go of the corners of the towel and lets it fall to her lap. 'We want different things, James. I thought this would be a good idea, a great thing to do: go travelling, get it all out of my system before we went home, I got a dream job with my diploma or something, and maybe we tried for a baby...'

James exhales across the bath, towards his crinkled toes, causing a ripple in the water.

'But I could see you flinching every time I mentioned travels – or our life after it – but it's OK.'

'It's not that I didn't—'

'It's fine, I totally understand. I am a bit full-on...'

Maya stands up from the closed toilet seat and perches on the bath's edge. She opens the towel out again, so James can get out, get some rest. So he can go home.

He looks up at Maya's freckled face, sees the tension in her knuckles as she clutches the towel corners taut. And he knows he has to be brave again.

69

'It's not that... It's not that I didn't want this. The trip has been ace. Well, mostly,' he shrugs, woefully. 'It's not that I don't want to have a baby...'

A tear rolls down Maya's cheek and into the bath. She's been so sad and so shocked and so scared and so hurt and so relieved, all in the space of just a few hours, and now she's about to be so heartbroken.

'It's just that—'

'You don't want to have them with me?' she asks.

'I guess I'm just more of a traditionalist than I realised.'

Maya is confused.

'I do want to have babies, Maya, just not yet.'

Maya takes a deep breath and dries her eyes on the corner of the towel. 'I know, I know. It needs to be the right time, right place, right girl...'

'I want to get married first.'

'What?'

'But every time wedding talk comes up, I see you flinch, Maya, you recoil. You shrink away from me.'

Maya teeters, still clutching the towel on the edge of the bath, only their ends are no longer taut. 'Are you kidding?' she asks, searching James' face, trying to look into his eyes, which is pretty difficult given the state he's in. 'You think I *don't* want to marry you? You think I *don't* want to marry Train Man? James Miller? Saviour hero of Manon Junot? Best, most tolerant, most handsome boyfriend in the world ever?!'

James' face lights up in the reflection of the bronze bath and his eye widens. As best it can anyway. Relief rolling over him with the steam.

'Oh my god, I so do! I've wanted to marry you since the first day I saw you on the platform. I thought I would sound nuts if I ever said it. But I do I do! I just thought *you* thought it was too...'

James stops Maya by pulling her into the bath with a kiss, her lace-trimmed knickers and vest soaking.

'Then let's do it,' he says, entwining his legs around hers, pulling her towards him from under her bottom. 'I don't have Cartier or Tiffany or Haribo, but Maya Elizabeth *Gloria* Flowers...' he says with a smirk.

'Watch it!'

'Will you marry me?'

'Yes!' Maya laughs, relief washing all over her as they wrap their legs around each other and she gently kisses James' cracked lips.

'Ow!'

70

May 2016, London, England

'Surely Prince Harry or someone is due any second,' says Francesca, nudging Petra's waist and pointing to the bank of photographers. Petra looks up from under her lilac fringe.

'They're here for James.'

'Shut up are they for James!'

'No, really.'

In the airy arrivals hall of Heathrow's Terminal 5, Francesca and Petra wait, marvelling at the press pack leaning against the thin metal barrier, unaware that on the other side of the photographers and cameras and reporters, Herbert Flowers holds an A4 piece of paper with 'Maya Flowers' written on it in hieroglyphic-style handwriting only she will understand.

A young man in a suit stands to Petra's left, taking a briefing from a woman in a more expensive looking two-piece.

'Do they all have breaking-news permits?'

'Yes, ma'am, I checked.'

'And you know what to do to get them out afterwards?'

'Yes, ma'am.'

'OK great, concierge will accompany him through. Remember there will still be hundreds of other passengers trying to get through. We have Jeddah, Frankfurt, Tokyo and Nice in there at the moment, as well as Bangkok, so try to keep it brief or keep it contained. Apparently he will talk, but doesn't want to for long. And he doesn't want the conference room.'

'Very well, ma'am.'

'When I give you the nod, start ushering them out. I suspect you'll be doing him a favour as well as us.'

'Yes, ma'am.'

The woman looks at the iPad she's clutching on top of her box files.

'Dubai and San Diego are incoming too.'

'Yes, ma'am.'

'Oh look, there's her dad!' shouts Nena, as she hurries into the hall with Ava on her hip.

'I'll check the screen,' says Tom, looking around and scratching his head.

'Herbert!'

'Nena, my dear! How wonderful to see you.'

'Didn't know you were coming.'

'All the world's a stage, my dear,' Herbert declares, leaning in to stroke Ava's button nose. 'And all the men and women merely players...'

Nena laughs.

Herbert leans in further, conspiratorially. 'They have their exits and their entrances,' he adds, sweeping his arm towards the big black letters that say INTER-NATIONAL ARRIVALS.

'And one man in his time plays many parts?' replies Nena, with a question and a wink. Herbert chuckles behind his bushy beard. His rosy cheeks rise. 'This is Ava! Ava meet Herbert. He's Aunty Maya's daddy!'

Ava looks at the man with the bushy grey beard and hair the shape of a clover, bouncing in three little grey clouds above his head. She gurgles and tries to grab his soft grey-and-white chin.

Tom returns. 'Landed. At baggage reclaim.'

'Tom, this is Maya's dad, Herbert.'

'A pleasure to meet you, Tom. I've heard only wonderful things about you.'

Tom smiles and matches Herbert's effusive handshake with his, then both look back to the stream of weary travellers arriving from distant parts.

'Isn't this incredible?' Herbert marvels, as if commercial flight has just been invented. He's only flown a couple of times in his sixty-five years, and he watches like an enchanted child as he waits for his daughter, wondering where in the world the people streaming through behind trolleys might have come from, puffing with pride that their trips won't have been as heroic as his daughter's turned out to be; what a fine man his daughter's boyfriend is. He straightens his A4 piece of paper.

Nena points to the doors and whispers into Ava's ear. 'Through there. Aunty Maya will be coming through there any second now.'

Petra and Francesca try to eavesdrop on the conversation between two people in front of the barrier. A man with a Foreign Office lanyard around his neck and a security guard talk to the same woman in the expensive suit clutching an iPad. They know their brother's arrival is imminent, and Petra smooths Francesca's dark hair and tucks it behind her ear. They give each other excited smiles before looking back along the line. There is nothing to say now, all they can do is quietly wait.

Correspondents clutching microphones nod into cameras, taking silent instruction in their earpieces, punctuated by the odd, 'Yep', 'Uh-huh', and, 'Sure'.

Drivers holding whiteboards, with names written messily in black pen, await clients and the M4. Solitary-looking people crane necks to see what the commotion is about; they're just here to pick up someone they missed, or someone they didn't miss but said they'd do a favour for. Some look a bit put out by the crowds, getting in the way of their day. Others are intrigued as to who the politician, the royal or – even better – the film star might be, whose arrival is clearly imminent. A man with a single red rose smiles to himself as he looks down to his battered Converse, hoping his girlfriend will think he arranged the welcome party for her. Anticipation in the air is thick and exciting.

The doors open, the stream continues, and in the middle, leaning on the protective shield of a baggage trolley, their backpacks lying across it (one more sullied than the other), emerges James, bruised and bashful. At his side, Maya squeezes his waist and tells him this will all be OK.

Bulbs flash.

The reporters swell upwards.

The concierge at James' side, with a walkie-talkie in his hand, encourages other passengers to continue around them, as James approaches the barrier as instructed.

'James! Rhianon Robathan, Sky News!'

'James! Kathleen Kiernander, ITN!'

'James! Laurie Dubois, France 24!'

'James! Gerle Koch, RTL Germany!'

'James! Vinamra Gupta, ABP!'

'James! How does it feel to have rescued Manon Junot?'

'James! What state was she in when you found her?'

'James! How is Manon Junot doing now?'

'James! How are your injuries? Are *you* in pain?'

'James! Have you spoken to Manon Junot's family?'

'James! Who is your companion?'

'James, Clarence Meek, BBC World News...' James looks away from the blur of the press pack, towards the man with a beige face and light ginger hair, down low in the middle. It's a nondescript face but the one he recognises; there is something comforting about him, about his voice. 'James, how does it feel to be home?'

Maya squeezes James' arm and holds it, almost propping him up.

He sees Petra and Francesca waving at him, to the right of the press pack, gives a calm smile, and looks back at the correspondent. 'It feels good. I just want to get home really. Back to work. To get on with my life; grateful that Manon Junot can now get the help she needs to get on with hers.' James nods, giving his cue to the concierge, the airport director and the FCO representative, that this is enough. He can't really say any more right now.

'James! Who's your companion?'

Maya looks up and sees her dad standing next to Nena, Ava and Tom. She sees the crap sign Herbert wrote with her name on it and her heart soars.

All lenses turn to her, content and grateful, now holding James' hand, clutching each other harder than they realise.

'This is my fiancée, Maya.'

Whispers of ahhhs and shouts of, 'Is that Maya with a y or an i?' and 'Isn't that Maya Flowers who was that fashion insider?' and 'When's the wedding?' before the airport director steps in and enables them to move forward.

My Travels with Train Man

I tried to protect him. To give Train Man a bit of anonymity, so these dispatches weren't too embarrassing for the shy guy with a dimple in his left cheek. But the secret's out. Train Man has a name. He is called James Miller.

You'll have heard that name a lot recently. You'll know what James Miller looks like now too. Tall, dark, handsome-without-knowing-it. Deep brown eyes and a quiet smile. You will have seen that smile on the cover of every newspaper. You'll have seen his face on televisions from London to Lisbon and Lima to Lagos. You'll have read the exclusive interview with him in the Sunday broadsheet this fine magazine accompanies. You'll know that he battled leeches, a forest and an angry psychopath – safely behind bars for now – and he put his own life at risk because he knew he needed to save somebody else's. You'll know he lifted Manon Junot from her months of misery and carried her to safety, so she could get back to her family and get better. Having lost him, for one night, made me experience a fraction of the pain Manon Junot's family must have been feeling after a hundred nights like it. And I knew I couldn't live without him.

You might have already put two and two together and realised it was Train Man who saved Manon Junot. If you've been reading this column, you'll know about most of what we got up to on our trip. What you won't know, is that our trip wasn't always harmonious. I didn't mention that there were issues deeper than whose turn it was to have the aisle seat or buy the Magnums, or if I did, I breezed over them.

Deep down, I was harbouring upset. I felt annoyed at myself for wanting the cliché of marriage and babies when I had the world at my feet. I didn't write about how – as annoyed as I was with myself, I was even more annoyed with Train Man – with James – for seemingly not wanting the things I desperately pretended I didn't.

My friends and family helpfully pointed out all the lovely places (temples, beaches at sunset, waterfalls...) and scenarios in which James could, but didn't, propose. Miscommunication and resentment bubbled, and when a shitbag from my past tried to tell me he wanted those things with me, I even wobbled. For half a second.

But I didn't waver because I knew James Miller was a hero way before the world did. He is kind and puts other people first every day. His unshowy, thoughtful reticence means he won't assume someone wants to marry him. It's the same trait that makes him get embarrassed every time he's asked to recount the story of how he rescued Manon Junot.

Because of his unassuming manner, I didn't realise he did want all the same things as me. He does want to get married and have children – he wants the fairytale too – he was just cautious about telling me so. And when he did ask me to marry him, we didn't need fireworks, flowers or a filter. It was just us, bruised and drained, as we hid from news crews and he pulled me into the bath.

We're slowly settling back to reality and James is back at work as a photographer. Getting on with the commission he was offered before this story went global; with new bookings he's made since. I'm spending evenings unpacking our home, running, re-tuning and baking. Who knows, you might even see me in the food section of Esprit *in future. But for now it's goodbye. It's been an honour to share most of my travels with you (and to have made the cover this week!) but I sign off and say thank you to everyone at Esprit, but mostly to you, dear reader. I'm sorry I kept so much from you on the trip, but am so glad to be able to share it with you now. Better go, I have a wedding to plan.*

Epilogue

Under the glass and iron atrium of the Royal Opera House cafe, Nena stands in a shaft of sunlight, dazzling like a multicoloured zebra, in a sequin jumpsuit of vertical rainbow stripes. Arlo clutches one hand, Ava wriggles on her other hip.

'Do you want to put her down? We could just get you with your son...' asks the photographer with a sympathetic smile.

Nena can already tell the sleek silver-haired woman is a mother herself.

'No, it's fine. If I put her down, she'll run straight out the door! She can wriggle, but my arms are strong.' Not yet one and Ava Vernon, with her thick black hair and bright blue eyes has already learnt to walk – and with it she can run amok. Arlo takes his role at the photocall seriously, his side parting and sincere face sitting atop a paisley blue bow tie.

Nena is holding onto her children on a little raised oval platform bathed in the light pouring in through the wrought-iron arches of the Victorian hall, to celebrate the return of *Nena's Tiny Dancers* to the autumn schedule. Patrons taking afternoon tea marvel at the swirl of TV presenters they're not quite sure they recognise around them: the woman who likes to craft, the man who talks to puppet cabbages in a pretend garden, the scientist who makes mints explode, the doctor who explains how bogies form – they're all doing their bit to talk up their shows under the crisp September sunshine – although Dr Rosa plays her part with a sullen pout.

In May, as sunshine and spring blossom brought Nena a confidence to counter every tricky baby milestone – and Ava started sleeping through the night – Nena decided that she did indeed want to return to work, but she wanted to do it on *her* terms. By June she was shooting, only this series she got to take Ava to meetings and into the studio with her – with Arlo joining once school broke up for summer. Ava and Arlo would waddle, wiggle and dance alongside other inquisitive children, filming and following Nena on her adventures around the world via green screen, to tell the stories and origins behind dance traditions; learning foreign words and new steps, encouraging pre-schoolers to get moving. In July, a dyspraxia charity asked Nena to be their patron, which she heartily accepted, and as soon as the shoot wrapped, the Vernons went on their first family holiday to Bahia.

Now it's September, and Charmaine McCourt is throwing a party to launch the new season of children's television, and she's buzzing about, directing photographers, broadcast press and newspaper TV critics as to whose pictures to take, who to talk to next, speaking in soundbites, while always keeping one eye on Nena, the jewel in the corporation's crown. The poster girl for flexible working – something Charmaine was happy to support, having not been enabled when her children were young.

'Did you engineer this?' Nena whispered to Tom as he stepped in to straighten Arlo's collar.

'Not at all!' he protested. 'Anyway, I tried to talk Charmaine out of it,' he winked. 'I know how you hate to be the centre of attention…'

Actually Nena meant the sunbeam beating down on her – she knew she had earned the plaudits herself – but she smiled proudly and playfully all the same.

Nena the clown, now in designer multicolours and polished make-up. Dancer. TV presenter. Wife. Mother. Tom looks at the three loves of his life, happily, if wriggly, huddled together as they have their photograph taken on the podium, and his heart swells with such piercing pride it hurts.

Maya and James hurry into the former floral hall holding hands, their coats flapping open in their rush through the autumn chill, hoping to catch Nena's big moment before they go for dinner. They sidle up to Tom, their fingers still interlocked.

'Just in time!' Maya says, letting go of James and bringing her palms together in a silent clap. 'Wow, she looks amazing.' Maya blows a kiss and gives Nena two thumbs up.

Tom turns around.

'Hey!' He kisses Maya on both cheeks and shakes James' hand firmly.

'Hi!' Maya and James chime.

'I haven't see you since the Hugo Linden wedding. Nena said it was *insane*.'

James gives a knowing look. 'You could say that.'

'Lots of inspiration for you guys?' Tom smiles as he scratches his chin.

'I wish.' Maya rolls her eyes. 'Alas, I have neither the bank balance nor the legs for Ashley Jolly's dress.' She pulls a false grumpy face but immediately breaks it when she spots Nena's mum talking to a former Royal Ballet colleague at the champagne bar. 'Ah, Victoria!'

Maya leaves James to provide gossip on the A-list wedding: the supermodel demands; the superstar chateau in Provence; the impromptu pool party and ruined frocks; the Hollywood action man who made a pass at James, while his heavily pregnant actress wife was stuck back in LA... and dashes over to Nena's mother.

'Maya, my darling!' she gushes with a glorious smile, as she extends both her hands for Maya to take and Nena joins with Ava and Arlo, ready for Granny to take them off for a sleepover. Maya leans in to kiss Ava's head and feels nothing but gratitude.

A short hop across Covent Garden's cobbles and Maya, James, Nena and Tom are sitting on brass-studded burgundy leather banquettes in a French brasserie. As they await their starters, nicotine paintwork and mirrors that have seen a few reflections in their time gaze down on them as they raise their glasses.

'Cheers!' they chime, all nodding towards Nena.

'They do weddings at the Opera House, you know,' Nena deflects as she smooths her sequins into one direction. It's nice being the centre of attention again, but she might have become accustomed to playing second fiddle now.

Maya and James look at each other as though they have news.

'Actually, we've booked it,' Maya says, while James tucks a wave of hair behind her ear.

'Ace! Where? Please tell me it's King's Cross. And you'll have a Thomas The Tank Engine cake.'

Maya smiles.

'Fat Controller doing the formalities?' asks Tom, raising an intrigued eyebrow.

'Actually no...'

'Oh, hang on. Somewhere exotic!' begs Nena. 'Please say it's a destination wedding and we can pretend to be annoyed about how expensive it is, while actually getting super-excited about being forced to go on holiday in Turks and Caicos or Cape Town or something.'

Maya looks at James, then to Nena apologetically.

'Well, we did consider Indonesia, given we never made it there – Bali and Ubud looked amazing, didn't they?' James nods. 'But my family is too big; they'd be too pissed off.'

'We want everyone there,' says James, squeezing Maya's leg under the table.

'So...?'

Maya puts her hand on top of James' on her thigh.

'Hazelworth Barns. Next Easter.'

'Easter! I love Easter!' shouts Nena. After the drama of the day, she's quickly tipsy. 'And Hazelworth – home – how lovely.'

Maya is relieved. The rustic tythe barn at Hazelworth doesn't have the glamour of the Royal Opera House or the hippie chic of Bali. But it's home. Home for Maya and James, in the town they hope to start a family.

'I'll need a sexy best woman of course.'

'Try stopping me,' Nena beams.

Which reminds Maya. This is Nena's day. Her official return as the star of children's television. Maya raises her champagne flute again. 'Here's to you, sweetie.' James and Tom follow suit. 'I'm so proud of you. Look at everything you've achieved.'

'*I'm* so proud of you,' Tom nuzzles into Nena's cheek.

Nena downs her fizz and looks like she's about to smash her glass on the floor in celebration. Fortunately she doesn't.

'We did OK, didn't we?' she says. 'I mean, we've *almost* survived the first year of parenthood. James has bloody rescued Manon Junot from the clutches of an evil psycho and is an actual real-life hero, and you, Maya... well, apart from wedding planning, what are you going to do?'

Maya pauses for a second, her glass poised at her lips, awash with a feeling of utter contentment.

'Me? I have no idea!'

Acknowledgements

I waited almost ten years to have my first book published, then (like buses) three seem to have come at once. So given this is my third novel in two years, my support network hasn't changed all that much: although it is about to. Sarah Ritherdon, my amazing editor, took a chance on me and made *The Note* a bestseller, and for that I will always be grateful. And I'll miss you terribly. But the axis of awesomeness will live on for ever. Rebecca Ritchie, my brilliant agent, you're the best. Thanks to Hannah Smith, Laura Palmer, Nikky Ward, Vicky Joss, Daniel Groenewald, Nicolas Cheetham and the whole team at Aria and Head of Zeus, I'm so excited about the road ahead. To Alice - thank you for the cover (is it weird to fancy a silhouette?!).

Huge thanks go to the people I have thanked before, the people I am grateful for every day. My parents, brothers and sisters. My friends, my cheerleaders. And to Mark, Felix and Max – I'm a lucky woman to live with and to love such fine men.

Finally, thank you to the kind people who message me from all over the world, telling me their love stories or asking me whether they should give a stranger a polite note asking them out (my answer: always). And to everyone who believes in love at first sight. Thank you for your kindness and support – it powers me on when I'm running and when I'm writing, and reminds me that love really does make the world go round.

About the Author

Zoë Folbigg is author of *The Note* and *The Distance*. Formerly a magazine journalist and digital editor, she started at *Cosmopolitan* in 2001, since freelancing for titles including *Fabulous, Glamour, Good House-keeping, Healthy, LOOK, Top Santé, Mother & Baby, ELLE, Sunday Times Style, ASOS* and Style.com. In 2008 Zoë wrote a weekly column in *Fabulous* magazine documenting her year-long round-the-world trip with Train Man – a man she had met on her daily commute. She has since married Train Man and lives in Hertfordshire with him and their two sons.